About the Author

A. Martin had a passion for stories for as long as she could remember. The moment she learned to read and write, she started to create her own and never really stopped since. So, when it came to writing her own fiction to publish, she blended it with her love of mythologies and histories from all over the world. There are so many fantastic myths out there from around the world that people don't hear about, and she hopes to shed some light on them.

Tales from the Archives

A. Martin

Tales from the Archives

Olympia Publishers
London

www.olympiapublishers.com
OLYMPIA PAPERBACK EDITION

A CIP catalogue record for this title is
available from the British Library.

ISBN: 978-1-83543-054-5

First Published in 2024

Olympia Publishers
Tallis House
2 Tallis Street
London
EC4Y 0AB

Printed in Great Britain

Dedication

I dedicate this book to my mum.

Acknowledgements

Thank you to my friend Jenna who had to put up with my constant babbling about these characters. I couldn't have done it without your support.

The Archives: 1

In hindsight, maybe playing a game of cards with one of the more dangerous gangs in the little port town of Kanaloa's Kingdom wasn't the greatest idea Aethalides had ever had. So sue him, he'd been bored and they were there and it was so easy to just count the cards. It wasn't his fault they couldn't play very well or that they were… not the brightest bunch.

Slowly, Aethalides lifted up his head, scanning the room and a grin spread across his face. Judging by the constant shifts of the many figures in said room, it had the desired effect. It unnerved them. Mission accomplished, now he just had to figure out how to get out of here by himself. Not an easy task for some, but Aethalides was confident in his escape abilities, just as he was with his card skills. Though, maybe he shouldn't be comparing the two since it was the cards that got him into this mess in the first place.

Judging by the smell in the air they were still in the little fishing town. Nothing screamed ocean quite like the smell of sea salt and the ever present cry of a seagull or two. Nothing else also screamed fishing town like the very obvious boat workshop he was trapped in.

Pieces of timber littered the room, the vague skeletons of different ship styles graced the shadows with ropes and tools placed haphazardly on benches or even laid on the floor. It was like looking at a place which had been frozen in time. Clearly, the workers had all upped and left, most likely when the gang that was currently holding him hostage showed up.

Ah yes, the Port Side Raiders. A well known gang led by a well known idiot. Said idiot was standing in front of him, flanked by two of his people, with two behemoths behind him.

Cillian Tealeaf, a fae who never used his magic and had an ego that did not match his success rate stood before him. He was dressed like a sailor, his pointed ears poked out of the side of the fishing cap he wore that matched the short coat that held the emblem of his gang on the shoulder. An anchor with P.S.R going across it, but the 'S' was made out of an intricately woven rope, like a Celtic pattern.

Cillian's red hair stood out against his pale skin, and a dusting of freckles went over his cheeks and nose. He was incredibly baby faced, with big round cheeks, a sweet little button nose and the pout on his face some might describe as just adorable. Cillian did not appreciate it when people did that, he especially didn't like it when old grandma's would pinch his cheeks, cooing over how adorable he was.

Sometimes, on the rare days that Aethalides's mind would drift to Cillian, probably in the two seconds of time he had to spare for the man, he wondered if his whole crime spree was based on too many people calling him cute. Maybe he wanted to be the ultimate rebel and prove them all wrong. It was a decent enough origin story, just too bad he was terrible at it.

Two flanking him included Satyr, who seemed more than a little drunk if the way he stumbled from side to side was anything to go by. His cloven feet would make a loud clip clop against the women's planks and he had a scraggy beard. The kind you could see getting bits of food stuck in it. He kept making eyeballs at the very uninterested sea nymph on the other side of Cillian. Her general appearance and look seemed to be like a Greek parrot fish, with bright reds and yellows, some silver added in here and there. Yellow surrounded her blue eyes and trailed down her face like tear tracks. Her skin seemed to sparkle like she'd been rolled in glitter before coming here.

Behind the three of them were two hulking giants, the norse kind from Jötunheim. Pale skinned, one with dark hair, the other with red, ice-like scales seemed to be covering their shoulders and a little bit on their arms. Both had pure blue eyes and they were fixed on Aethalides.

This should be the time when he... should get worried. Knowing Cillian he definitely had more security outside than he did inside. This little collective in this room, it was... it was honestly almost cute.

"So," Cillian spoke up, Irish accent thick and he got in Aethalide's face, having to bend down and lean on his knees to be somewhat comfortable. "You really thought you could steal from us? From the Port Side Raiders!"

"Is it really stealing when I won the game fair and square?" Aethalides returned, smiling up at him.

Cillian did not share his amusement and he blatantly backhanded him. Aethalides felt his lip split, blood trickling down his chin. It felt like his brain rattled in his skull for a moment, but it wasn't the first time. Besides, what could they honestly do? Kill him? Heh, wouldn't be the first time.

"I bet you think you're so smart don't you?" Cillian snarled, his lips pulling back to show the fangs at the corner of his mouth. "Aethalides, the immortal son of Hermes who keeps dying and every time he's gotta start right back at the beginning again," he stood up and pointed at Aethalides. "How'd you think it looked to those imbeciles that live here when my men are being schooled by a *ten-year-old?*"

13

Aethalides sniggered, breaking down into a fit of giggles and kicking his legs. "I'd say… it'd look a lot more embarrassing if they were getting schooled by a four-year-old," he broke out his manic grin, widening his eyes just a little and enjoyed the moment Cillian backed up at the sight. "Should I pencil you guys in?" Aethalides asked, still swinging his legs. "Next time I die and come back, I'll pay you lot a visit for a re-match as a four-year-old. Gods… could you imagine it? What would the people say!"

They'd probably say what they already said. People's opinions of the Port Side Raiders were definitely not what the Port Side Raiders wanted it to be.

Cillian was going red in the face and he suddenly grabbed Aethalides, pulling him up by the front of his shirt. Aethalides kept his grin on, it best not to let people like Cillian think they were getting to you. One because it gave people like this a bit of a kick and a power trip. And two. because it would simply be too hard to keep that act up. Aethalides was a good liar, even if he did say so himself, and even he would have issues.

"You're the most arrogant, pompous, self absorbed aristocrat I've ever had the displeasure of meeting!" Cillian yelled. "You're like the trust fund kid, but worse! Your daddy's a god!"

"Yes, yes he is," Aethalides nodded in agreement, still smiling. "And, Cillian, I really have got to ask… do you know what gods do to those who harm their children?" He tilted his head to the side, still smiling. "Because if this little slaughterhouse is anything to go by, I really don't think you do."

Cillian scrunched his face up. "We're in a shipyard."

"No, no we really are not. Especially if you insist on keeping me here and doing something unsavoury," Aethalides continued,

14

flashing the mega watt grin again. "So, why don't you do the smart thing for once and put me down? How about that? We like that idea."

"I'm not letting you go," he dumped him back on the chair again, reaching his hand up and backhanded Aethalides two more times. "Least not until you've learned your lesson. You don't steal from the Port Side Raiders!"

Aethalides mock pouted at him. "Aww… but you make it so easy, it's honestly hard to resist."

Cillian was going red in the face again, starting to growl and snarl, lip pulling up to show off his fangs once again. He was clenching and unclenching his hands by his side, so focused on Aethalides that he obviously didn't notice the face that appeared in the nearby window, but Aethalides did. He instantly felt himself relax even more when he saw who was peering in, squinting and then they widened at the sight of Aethalides who gave a subtle little wave.

The man on the other side of the window held a remarkably flat expression at the wave, shaking his head and turning away to shout to someone.

"You disrespectful little-," Cillian pulled him up again, his feet hung down and swung in the air as he grinned up at the fae. "You're not untouchable, Aethalides! I am going to kill you, I'm going to prove a point and then I'll display your corpse like a trophy!"

"Oh! Like I haven't had that done before," Aethalides rolled his eyes, sticking his tongue out and blowing a disappointed raspberry. "Are we using stakes or ropes? Maybe stakes with ropes?"

Cillian was visibly disturbed and the others around him didn't look much better. The Satyr had nearly clip clopped himself into a support beam in his desperate plea to get away from the ten-year-old tied up on a chair.

"You're out of your bleedin' mind," Cillian mumbled, staring at Aethalides like he was some kind of freak. He supposed he kind of was, there were no other people like him.

Aethalides nodded his head in agreement. "Yeah, I get that a lot..."

The fae snarled, tightening his grip on the front of his shirt, it nearly cut off his breathing supply, but Aethalides just grinned the whole time. Taking another quick glance at the window, seeing a much larger shadow appear in it, one that he knew all too well and his smile increased tenfold. Things were not going to go well for Cillian.

"Quick question," Aethalides said, watching almost eagerly as Cillian pulled his hand back to strike him again. "Do I seem worried to you? I mean, one might say that this smile on my face is ecstatic. Did you ever stop to wonder why?"

Cillian's hand lowered slightly and he stared at Aethalides with confusion for a mere second before the wall came down. Glass was shattered, and wooden planks and splitters shot off everywhere, smacking the unlucky Satyr in the face which sent him spiralling out of control. He ended up colliding with one of the unfinished boats horn first where he got himself stuck.

Everyone else was left coughing and trying to waft the dust out of the way. The sound of fighting could be heard loud and clear now, with screams of agony and cries of rage from a certain queen Aethalides was friends with. Followed by growls and the howling of a wolf. It sounded like utter carnage out there and he'd be lying if he said he wasn't a little excited.

The large shadow from the window now fell over both himself and Cillian as the owner of said shadow stepped through the hole they'd made. They blocked out the light coming from the hole and were almost unable to fit through it with their battle-axe and large visage, plus the extra height that the bull horns gave him. Everyone on the island knew who this was, the minotaur from Greek legend. Built like a walking wall, the body of a man with a bull's head. A ring went through his nose, dressed in cargo trousers and military boots with an Ancient Greek leather skirt wrapped around his middle. A wrestler's belt around the middle, with shoulder and arm armour going down his left side with a belt going across his chest, the buckle on full display that had a bull's head embossed on it.

He snorted, taking a few menacing steps towards Cillian, towering over him for a mere moment, resting his battle axe on his shoulder. He reached forward, picking Cillian up by the front of his sailor shirt, the fae's pointed ears had dropped at the sight of the minotaur and now they were nearly flat against his head. Cillian let out a yelp when he was lifted, dropping Aethalides in the process as he tried to uselessly claw at the big beefy arm that held him up with little issue.

Aethalides shuffled himself around so he was looking up at the minotaur and Cillian, smiling widely.

"Perfect timing, Asterion!" He addressed the minotaur with a grin. "You arrived just as I finished my monologue... couldn't have planned it better."

The minotaur, Asterion, raised an eyebrow at him, giving another snort before speaking. "You were monologuing again?"

"Don't I always?"

Through the hole in the wall, the man from before came running through. He was clearly from South America or Mexico way, dressed in a faded red leather jacket that was cut like a poncho, with a blue and yellow Mayan triangle pattern that wrapped around his chest and arms. A jaguar head formed the clasp that kept the jacket shut on the shoulder and he wore trainers with a jaguar fur print. His long hair was done up in a traditional Mayan style, with three big loops at the back, shaved at the sides and a fringe ending just above his eyebrows. A chunky blue nose piercing decorated his face along with matching mayan styled earrings.

He frowned at Aethalides. "You gotta stop doing that. We've talked about this," he said stepping through the hole and Aethalides noticed he had a small belt swung over his shoulder with multiple bottles and tubes filled with glowing liquid and a spear in hand.

"I was having fun, Xbalanque!" Aethalides protested.

The satyr from before had managed to yank himself out of the ship, spinning around on his hoofs a moment, before he balanced out. He shook his head, letting out a small bleat and then charged at Xbalanque, head down and horns at the ready.

Xbalanque sidestepped and stuck his foot out, easily tripping the already unsteady satyr, sending him flying into a piece of wall that wasn't broken. He flew into the wood, horns getting stuck in the wood, looking like some kind of bizarre dart. He bleated in a panic, hoofs scraping against the floor as he desperately tried to pull himself out.

"Besides the point. You could've died…" Xbalanque suddenly looked awkward as he trailed off. "Again."

Asterion snorted a laugh, casually tossing Cillian at the nymph, turning his attention to the two Jötun giants, widening his stance and readying his axe. The Jötuns had snapped out of their stupor and instead charged at Asterion who met them halfway. There was a loud clashing of metal against metal that made Aethalides wince slightly as he tried to sit up while still tied up.

Xbalanque reached him, pulled out a knife and quickly cut him loose. He helped Aethalides up, taking out a different set of knives and the belt, holding them out to him.

"Here," he said, handing the items to him. "Courtesy of Medea."

"Where is Medea?" Aethalides asked as he fastened the belt which was obviously filled with potions, holding his knives in his teeth.

"She didn't come because and I quote 'if the fool got himself into this mess, he can get himself out'," Xbalanque explained, rubbing the back of his head with an impressed look. "Honestly, her stubbornness is impressive."

"I resent being called a fool," Aethalides muttered, checking the belt was properly secured.

Xbalanque laughed. "She thought you might say that, so she also told me to say; 'I believe only a fool would be able to lose throwing knives that come back to him with a single thought', which, no offence Aethalides, I have to agree with her on that."

Aethalides grinned, taking said blades and spinning them around in his hands for a moment until he gripped them properly.

"Everyone has their talents, Xbalanque, mine is apparently losing objects that are meant to come back to you."

A bleat from the satyr alerted them to him freeing himself, not that his triumph lasted long, as with a simple flick of his wrist, Aethalides sent one of the knives into his stomach. He flexed his fingers and the blade immediately came back to his hand, the grin never left his face and he turned his attention to the rest of the fight. Cillian had managed to pull himself up to his feet and was fiddling with a crossbow, trying desperately to crank the bolt back. At the same time, Xbalanque had started a fight with the nymph who was hissing and baring her teeth at him. Asterion was still dealing with the giants, so Aethalides ran forward to give some backup, throwing both blades so they skimmed across the brow of the redhead. Blood immediately began to run into the giant's eyes, making him partially blind and giving Asterion an opening to swing his axe and take his head.

The giant fell with a loud bang, Aethalides turned to Cillian who was staring at the fallen giant in shock, then looking at him. Aethalides could only imagine what he looked like, the never ending feral grin plastered across his face. Cillian's attempts to crank the bolt increased tenfold and he never took his eyes off Aethalides. He teasingly span the blades around in his hand, pointing at Cillian in a challenging manner, making the fae scowl and hiss at him. He bared his sharpened fangs, still cranking the crossbow until there was a satisfying click and the scowl turned into an overconfident smirk.

Aethalides tossed one of the knives into the air and caught it, smirking right back at Cillian. "Easy peasy," he declared as he readied himself to smack the bolt out of the air with his knife.

Cillian took aim and fired, but Xbalanque was quick to dart across, scoop up Aethalides and run with him to Asterion, dodging the bolt in the process. He sent Aethalides an irritated look, scowling down at him.

"Who in the Xibalba do you think you are? This isn't a movie!" Xbalanque snarked at him. "You honestly thought you could've stopped that bolt!"

"I dunno, but it would've been fun to find out."

Xbalanque put him on the ground, backing up to Asterion as Cillian and the nymph began to close in, Cillian of course busy cranking the crossbow. He readied it, aiming directly at the two of them, a smirk plastered on his face when a howl came from the hole in the wall. Everyone looked to the hole in the wall, a growl coming from it and then a wolf bounded through. It dodged the nymph and instead leapt at Cillian, locking its jaws around his wrist. The fae screamed as the wolf shook his arm like some kind of over-loved chew toy, growling the entire time.

"Ha! Nice one, Vali!" Aethalides cried out, just as the door leading to the room burst open, with several injured gang members.

They were all dressed like sailors, all with the Port Side Raiders emblem on their shoulders. They were clutching various body parts of themselves, blood seeping through their clothes with expressions of pure panic.

"Sir, the Archives they're- uh…" the first goon stopped talking as they all took in the scene before them. Two of their colleagues died and their boss was being used as a squeaky toy by an overly enthusiastic wolf, while their prisoner stood with weapons at the rear and worst of all, back up.

The goon blinked before finishing lamely. "We have a problem."

"Oh, buddy you have no idea!" Aethalides cackled, chucking his knife and hitting the man dead centre in his forehead. With a snap of his fingers, the blade was back in his hand once the guy dropped to the ground.

There was a moment for silence, the goons staring at the dead guy on the floor, before nervously looking at the three of them. Aethalides with his feral grin, Xbalanque wrinkled up his nose at the dead body and Asterion as always wore an ever present stoic expression. It was hard to tell really, considering the man had a bull face.

They didn't wait a moment, easily taking out the other goons. Well, in truth it was mostly Asterion doing that, with Aethalides more there as moral support and Xbalanque constantly trying to convince them not to kill anyone. He was knocking people out as best he could, this was made easier due to most of them already being injured.

"Who's outside?" He asked as they sprinted away from the room where growling and screaming could still be heard. Slamming the next door open to reveal the carnage outside.

Several individuals lay either dead or dying on the floor, someone went running past them screaming while their hair was on fire. The next person to join the dead was a Jötun who got toppled, a spear in his head with the owner of said spear still holding onto it, standing on the dead giant's face.

Her wild tawny hair blew about her face, shield resting on her back, sword in hand, with blue paint smeared over any piece of visible skin. Dressed in a long dark blue coat with no sleeves and Celtic patterns running through it, a gold Claddagh ring around her neck and a bracelet made out of two different threads of hair that were woven together were wrapped around her right wrist. Tall brown boots and gold arm bands around her biceps almost emphasising them as she tensed her muscles.

"Hi Boudie!" Aethalides cried out, enthusiastically waving at her.

Boudicca, the once queen of the Britons, glared at him, slowly pointing her sword in his direction as she took heavy breaths. *"You."* She snarled. "What were you thinking? How do you turn a simple trip to buy fresh fish.." She extended her arms out, gesturing to the chaos around her. "Into this!"

Aethalides grinned. "Good to see you too!"

She yelled a curse at him before going back to fighting the other gang members, jabbing the spear through someone's chest and then going to stab someone else, almost creating an enemy spit. Asterion snorted in amusement, reaching down to ruffle

Aethalides's hair, much to his annoyance as he angrily battered away the hand. Then Asterion was off, kicking his foot as he readied a charge at an unsuspecting satyr.

They watched the minotaur charge, the satyr only just seeing and realising his doom a fraction too late, as Asterion ran directly into him, sending him flying across the open boatyard. He smashed through a skeleton of a ship that was still being built, taking out some of the support beams with the rest of the ship falling on top of him.

"So… where's Icarus?" Aethalides asked, Xbalanque who was busy blocking a blow from the nymph that had followed them. What could pass as a concerned expression crossed Aethalide's face. "He's not dead already is he?"

"We didn't think it would be a good idea to bring him," Xbalanque explained, gesturing to the utter carnage that was taking place on the docks, just as Boudicca cut through two Spartoi worriers with vengeance and Asterion took someone's head.

Aethalides idly watched one of the spartoi heads go rolling past him like a tumbleweed.

"Good point," Aethalides said, pointing at Xbalanque, before dodging a swing from a jötun axe, running up the handle and chucking his knife at his neck.

The jötun blocked the hits with his arm, growling at Aethalides who flipped over his hand just as he tried to squish him with it, still running up his other arm. He snapped his fingers and the knives were back in hand again, where he used them to help him swing across his back and climb up so he could rest on his shoulders.

Aethalides climbed up completely so he was sitting on the Jotun's head, fumbling with the potion bottles. He yanked one out of the belt, using his teeth to pull the cork, dodging the Jotun's waving arms as he tried to grab at him. Aethalides spat the cork out to the side, grinning.

"Let's see what this one does!" He shouted and poured the potion into the Jotun's mouth. Not a moment later the Jotun suddenly vanished beneath his feet in a puff of smoke and Aethalides fell to the ground, letting out a cry.

He sat himself up, sensing Xbalanque had come up next to him, probably to make sure he was all right, but his attention was quickly snatched by what sat in front of them.

Instead of a Jötun, there was now…

"Is… is that a chihuahua?" Xbalanque spluttered in disbelief.

Aethalides looked at the empty tube he had in hand. "Medea has a cruel sense of humour sometimes…" he mused and then yelped when the chihuahua launched itself at him. He grabbed it with his hands, desperately trying to keep the tiny snapping jaws away from his face.

Xbalanque gently slipped his spear handle under the dog and flipped it away from Aethalides. It landed in the dirt with a huff, quickly getting to his little feet and yapping at them.

"Oh thank the gods," Aethalides huffed as he sat up again. "I did not want to add 'Death by Chihuahua to my resume."

The chihuahua continued to bark and yap at them before Asterion ran over and drop kicked it into the building. It smashed through the window, barking the whole way and the minotaur huffed, nodding his head as a job well done, before turning to see the horror stricken faces of Xbalanque and Aethalides.

He screwed his face up. "What?"

"Asterion!" Aesthalides cried, getting to his feet. "You can't just kick a dog!"

"He wasn't a dog, he was a Jötun!" He protested, then waved them off. "He'll be fine."

Asterion turned on his heel, running back into the fight. Aethalides rubbed at his eyes, glancing back at the potions for a moment. He recognised some from Medea's excessive use of them, others... not so much. That chihuahua spell was definitely a new one. Sometimes her cruelty knew no bounds, he couldn't imagine condemning someone to the fate of being a walking handbag for the rest of their lives.

He jumped when he heard the sound of Xbalanque getting back into a fight, turning and letting his shoulders drop a bit when he found him fighting the same nymph from before. She was ferocious, swinging her arms left and right, trying to slash clean through Xbalanque. It didn't look like much of a fight, it felt more like an extreme game of keep away.

"You need me to get her?" he asked, gesturing with his knife.

"No, no!" Xbalanque assured, pushing the nymph away. "I got this!"

"You sure?" Aethalides steadily got himself in the right position, widening his stance and raising his arm to throw. "It honestly wouldn't take a moment. I could end it right now."

Xbalanque turned to him and raised his hand with a calm smile. "I'm fine, don't worry about it."

"Never said I was worried... but speaking of worriers..." he looked around the area again. "Where is Icarus? You didn't leave him alone with Medea did you?" Aethalides winced at the very idea. "Damn, Xbalanque, I thought you liked him."

"What?" Xbalanque threw him a bewildered look as he used his spear to keep the nymph at arm's length while she desperately tried to claw his face off. "Oh! No, we had him on the lookout, over there," he nodded in the direction of some stacked boxes outside of the shipyard.

Aethalides squinted and sure enough, he spotted a blond head poking up from behind the boxes of fish, watching quietly and at a safe distance.

"Good call," he mumbled and then turned to Xbalanque who was still dealing with the nymph. Aethalides frowned, rolling his eyes. "By the gods, Xbalanque, what are you doing?"

"I got this, don't worry!" Xbalanque assured, kicking the nymph away. She went a good distance but was quick to scramble to her feet, screeching at him. Her nails seemed to glow longer, like talons and her teeth got more pointed. Water started to run down her body, turning her nails into even bigger razor sharp ice claws as she screeched at them. The nymph quickly went charging at them, screaming bloody murder, razor claws at the ready.

Suddenly Boudicca charged her from the left, shield first and body slammed into the charging nymph, sending her flying straight into a pile of boxes. Only the nymph's feet were visible when another box landed on her, the legs pointing in odd directions.

Boudicca huffed a piece of hair out of her face, just as Asterion came over to join her, resting his battle axe on his shoulder.

He nodded in approval at the scene. "Nice move."

"Thank you," Boudicca turned to glare at Xbalanque who flinched back. "You finish it, permanently."

"I'm a policeman now!" He protested, eyes wide. "I can't finish anyone permanently!"

"Oh, so you're too good for the traditional ways?" Aethalides sassed, putting his hands on his hips, cocking his eyebrow up.

"That's not what I'm saying!"

Aethalides sniggered, grinning widely as Boudicca marched up to Xbalanque, using her sword like a pointer in a school room.

"You think your enemy would spare you the same sentiment!" She hissed, nearly shoving the blade right in Xbalanque's face. She looked like the world's most dangerous school teacher right now, all that was missing were some glasses resting on the tip of her nose. Aethalides could only imagine her grading system. She looked ready to grade Xbalanque a D for death.

Xbalanque frowned at her. "I'm a policeman," he reasoned, reaching up and pushing the blade out of his face. "That means I don't kill-."

"Okay, you're a policeman back topside, not here," Aethalides was quick to point out, ducking a satyr with a mace, swinging it widely at them. "So could you maybe, oh I don't know, quit knocking them out and actually- ah, thanks, Vali!" He gave a thumbs up as Vali took the satyr with the mace out, jumping right at his face. "My point is, when you knock 'em down, you make sure they can't get back up again!"

Xbalanque didn't look comfortable with the idea, he opened his mouth to protest or raise some other argument, when The sound of an alarm bell going off caught all their attention.

Far off in the centre of the small fishing town, the bell tower was going off, alerting the guards that something was wrong.

Apparently, their little brawl had gotten out of hand enough for someone to take notice.

"Right…" Aethalides started backing up as the others moved to regroup with him, spinning his knives in his hands he glanced up at Xbalanque, eyebrow raised. "Where'd you park the van?"

'Xbalanque stared with the look of someone 'whose soul had

just left them, before looking away and awkwardly rubbing the back of his neck. "We… left Icarus with it."

Aethalides's eyes widened. "You did what?" He cried out, face morphing to one of horror.

Horrible flashes of his beloved camper van coming back to him in pieces or not coming back at all played in his mind. He could easily see Icarus just coming over with the steering wheel and a nervous smile, acting like everything was fine because he at least had one piece of it. Sure, it was a camper van, but Aethalides had kept it clean, running and up to scratch from the sixties. He was proud of it and treated it like it was his child.

"Well, we couldn't bring it here…" Xbalanque tried to reason.

"You absolutely could've brought it here! Ah!" Aethalides pressed his palms to his face. "My poor baby! He's going to destroy the gearbox and wreck the paint job!"

"It's a camper van," Boudicca deadpanned.

"Wrong, it's *my* camper van!" He hissed, pointing at her. "Would you let Icarus near your chariot?"

Boudicca didn't answer him, too busy decapitating enemies to really care or notice. Then again, even if she wasn't doing that he doubted she'd be that invested in the fate of his precious van. It was his baby, he'd kept it safe, nurtured it from the sixties to the modern day.

The sound of tires screeching reached their ears and the group watched a slightly battered blue camper van charge into the open air, only just missing some of the injured, dead or unconscious. It finally came to a halt and the tires squealed when the brake was applied, making all parties wince and Vali let out a small wine.

Aethalides looked inside the front, Icarus was there, gripping the wheel tightly, looking every bit as terrified as he probably had when his wings broke all those years ago.

"Icarus?" Boudicca ran to him, opening the front door and helping him step out, as he gripped the side, barely able to stand up. "Are you all right?" She asked softly.

"Who cares about, Icarus!" Aethalides yelled, running to his van, he skidded across on his knees to be at the height of the bumper, checking it over. "What about my poor baby?"

Xbalanque pulled the door further open, turning back to the approaching men as Vali growled at them all. His hackles raised, teeth bared in warning. He was ready to pounce, his visage caused the men to slow down on their approach, watching the wolf anxiously.

"Vali!" Xbalanque shouted and the wolf turned to him. He gestured to the open door. "Come on! Get in, kid!"

The wolf ran over, using Aethalides as a stepladder to leap into the van, even though he didn't need to. Vali leapt onto the passenger side seat, with Xbalanque climbing in the driver's one. He slammed the door shut, turning the engine back on and getting the van into gear.

Aethalides was still on the floor until he was suddenly lifted up by Asterion, who flung him over his shoulder like he was a sack of potatoes, rushing to the back. Boudicca was already inside, strapping Icarus in as Asterion climbed in, dropping Aethalides like the aforementioned sack.

Xbalanque turned the van around, being careful to dodge anyone on the floor, just as Cillian came running out of the building, crossbow in hand. His wrist was a mess, hair all over the place and his lips were pulled back in a snarl. He even kicked one of the men who was still alive and trying to get up, screaming and yelling at them.

Aethalides saw him and a feral grin stretched across his face. He fumbled with the belt again, pulling out two potions he recognised and were undoubtedly his favourite ones. The liquid inside the tubes was a bright fiery orange that seemed to be constantly bubbling, the tubes were even vibrating slightly.

He kicked the back doors open, much to the irritation of the others as they yelled at him, saying something about closing the door, but Aethalides wasn't listening. Cillian was still yelling at his men, the ones who were left, desperately trying to crank the crossbow so he could fire a shot at them. His final last-ditch attempt that Aethalides wasn't going to grant him.

"Hey, Cillian!" Aethalides yelled and the fae turned to glare in his direction. "Heads up!"

Aethalides tossed the potions as far as he could, straight on the steps and the moment they smashed, a huge explosion blew up the steps and the front of the building itself. Cillian and his men were blown backwards, clothes blackened and torn, hair sticking up in odd directions and faces covered in soot. Cillian's baby face looked extremely funny with his big eyes and red hair shooting up skyward. He almost looked like a burnt matchstick.

Aethalides broke down into hysterics, hanging on the back door, swinging it back and forth until Asterion yanked him inside by the scruff of his jacket, slamming the door in the process. He dumped Aethalides on the floor of the van as he sat giggling, his knees pulled up to his chest.

"By the gods," Aethalides sniggered. "You should've seen the look on his face!" He abruptly poked his head up, pressing his face against the back window.

They drove out of the little fishing town and since it was Xbalanque driving it really was the world's slowest getaway. He really did drive like some kind of grandma. If Aethalides had his stilts on he'd be flooring the pedal by now.

Xbalanque navigated the narrow streets of the sea town that were decorated with palm trees, and wooden carvings of various Hawaiian deities were scattered here and there. Amongst them were other gods from different pantheons, a few elegant marble Greek statues of Poseidon and Triton, and boxy wooden-like figures of the Norse god Nyjord.

Kanaloa's Kingdom, the town they were in, was just one of two fishing ports on the island of Atlantis. Famous mostly for its beautiful blue seas, fantastic views and stunning beaches. It was mostly a place where people went if they wanted to spend a day at the beach or they treated it as a honeymoon destination due to the nice weather. Surfing competitions were a big staple of the place and the town was one of the biggest imports of fish apart from being a brilliant holiday destination.

If it wasn't obvious by the name of the town and the fact that there were various references to them that didn't include their statues, the Hawaiian gods were held in high regard in this town. Most of the occupants had been some of the native people of Hawaii, but gradually over time there came over races of beings from different lands, sea nymphs and satyrs liked it here, with many other land-dwelling races. Naiads and tritones mostly resided in the sea, helping with the fishing while also acting as guards and rescuers for anyone who fell in if the weather got a little stormy.

The streets were brightly coloured due to the jungle flowers that were used to decorate them in garlands stretching across the streets above, a few of the bigger homes had beautiful balconies that were equally as colourful and decorated. Some of the shops had seashells on the front, one shop was selling wind chimes made from seashells and sea glass. Most buildings were made out

31

of wood, but there were a few scattered here and there that were made out of stone or in very rare cases marble.

The sea town had a wooden and stone wall encircling it for protection from the jungle areas around its outer edge. Guards were patrolling it twenty-four-seven, always on the lookout and a few huntresses from Artemis's group would help patrol with them.

They drove under the large, wooden, archway to enter the slightly dense jungle that eventually opened up to hills, fields and wetlands once you got past it by following the dirt road.

Aethalides glanced up at the sign that swung above the entrance to the town and gave the small fishing town a wave.

"So long, Kanaloa's Kingdom! Until next time!" He yelled, breaking down into more giggles, the smile freezing on his face when he spotted the few glares sent his way. Namely from Xbalanque and Boudicca. "What? We'll be back, how else are we supposed to get our fish?"

Xbalanque pinched the bridge of his nose. "From the city that we live in?" He said as a suggestion. "Since we didn't even get the fish we originally came here to get."

"Okay, Heart's fish market is all right, but the ones by the docks are so much better!"

"And are you going to tell us just how you got in trouble with the Port Side Raiders?"

Aethalides paused, the smile finally fell off his face and he looked to the side, settling on giving an awkward grin.

Xbalanque stared at him for a moment in the mirror and then groaned in annoyance, rubbing at the frown lines appearing on the front of his forehead.

"You were gambling again!" He complained. "I thought you said you were going to stop?"

"No, I said I'd *think* about stopping and it's not my fault those imbeciles don't know how to play well," Aethalides huffed, leaning on the window, resting his head in the palm of his hand as a smirk graced his face. "Or that I can count cards."

"I think that's completely your fault," Xbalanque deadpanned. "What were you thinking?"

He shrugged. "Easy money."

"And do you have any of that money?" Boudicca quizzed him, sending a sceptical look his way.

Aethalides waved her off. "Details. Well," he sighed taking his seat and crossing his arms. "I would've had it, if those Port Side Raiders weren't complete sore losers. I played them fair and square."

"You were counting cards."

"There's nothing in the rules saying you can't."

"Maybe not," Xbalanque tried to reason, looking at him in the mirror again. "But maybe it's not a good idea to count the cards in a game when you're playing against a mob?"

"A mob?" Aethalides echoed before he cackled, gripping at his stomach and even wiping a tear from his eyes. "That's a good one. Please, Cillian and his Raiders are small potatoes in that world. Cillian definitely is no Rune."

Which was true. The general public of Kanaloa's Kingdom saw the Port Side Raiders more as annoyances or inconveniences than any kind of real trouble. They were small potatoes, tiny in comparison to someone like Rune and his lovely gang of Hel Raiders, people who could dodge the law. Cillian and his guys, on the other hand, were not the best. More often than not getting caught, being punished and Cillian definitely didn't help matters by not using his natural magic for some reason.

All fae like Cillian were gifted with magic, it practically

flowed through their veins, so the fact that he avoided using his or didn't use it at all was… strange. Aethalides wondered if he didn't use his magic because he was trying to prove a point. Make out he was some kind of dangerous figure without his. Aethalides didn't get that, if you had it, use it. Always take the easy option.

Still, he shouldn't complain too much, it meant he didn't have to deal with fae magic and that was always a welcome break. Fae magic was particularly nasty stuff and very difficult to deal with.

"What is wrong with you?" Icarus shouted. He'd been quiet for the most part and now he was looking at him with wide, panicked eyes. He was still shaking, wrapping his arms around his knees as he rocked back and forth. "Oh gods, we could've died! We could've died again! I don't wanna die again, why would you do that? Why would you get yourself into trouble like that!?"

Boudicca leaned over and gently rubbed the boy's shoulders. She bent down and picked up a blanket, wrapping it around his shoulders, still rubbing up and down his arms. Icarus weakly clutched the blanket with his fingers, still rocking back and forth on his seat.

Aethalides sighed. "It's not like I plan to make the good time better-."

"That was not better!" Icarus yelled. "That was worse! That was way, way, worse!"

"I don't know what you're so upset about, Icarus," Aethalides commented, pulling out a packet of cigarettes from his pocket, idly pulling one out and holding it between his teeth. "I mean, you didn't die. You didn't even get hit."

Icarus's eyes nearly bugged out of his head. "I had to drive the van! I can't drive!" He yelled out, pressing a hand to his chest.

34

"I could've died!"

Aethalides had mostly ignored him, patting his body, trying to find his lighter and he frowned in disappointment when he couldn't find it. Great, that's another lighter lost to the carnage of war. Well... street brawls that lead to unfortunate ends.

"Icarus, I assure you, if you ever do die again," Aethalides said, taking his cigarette out of his mouth and popping it back in the packet. "It's not gonna be my fault it happens."

"What's that supposed to mean?" Icarus cried.

Wordlessly Aethalides used his hands to perform a puppet show of Icarus's unfortunate flight. Smacking his flying hand into his other hand he was using as a stand-in for the sun, before dropping that hand into his lap and making an explosion sound.

He looked Icarus dead in the eye, raising a challenging eyebrow. The kid looked deeply unsettled by the crude retelling of his death, turning away from him and pulling the blanket closer.

Boudicca sent him a glare, staying by Icarus and continued to rub his shoulder in comfort. Asterion had closed his eyes, leaning back in his seat and looking like he was actually asleep. Either that or he was covertly avoiding conversation with anyone.

At the front Xbalanque had clocked out of the conversation, focusing on driving and he'd lowered the window at some point on the passenger's side and Vali had his head sticking out. His mouth was open, tongue lolling out and once the capital city came into view he let out a howl.

The rest of the drive through the open fields and farmlands to the city at the centre of the island was rather uneventful, getting inside the city and navigating the narrow streets was a little more difficult, but they managed it without hitting anyone.

Xbalanaque pulled up to the Archives's tall gold gates with

an insignia of a Greek temple on the backdrop of a large letter 'A'. Xbalanque fished in his pocket for a moment looking for the key. Vali pulled himself back inside the van, just as Xbalanque lifted up a key that looked like a coin, holding it up to the metal gates. The insignia on the coin glowed and the matching insignia on the gates glowed back before they slowly started to open.

Xbalanque drove through, packing up the van on the driveway, the gates closing behind them.

Everyone started to climb out, Aethalides pushed the backdoors open, climbing out and standing before the building.

The Archives were big. Three stories tall, the front looked like a Greek temple, complete with pillars, steps and a large door. Two different wings of the building extended out of the side of the temple looking part of the building, on their roofs at each corner were various statues of Greek gods. The outside walls themselves were even decorated with beautiful hand painted frescos. The building stretched up three stories and the two highest floors had balconies facing the front.

The front garden was just as impressive as the building itself, at least in his opinion. Decorated with symmetrical bushes, strawberry trees gave a splash of colour along with the crocus, hyacinths and daffodils. A Fontaine sat in the centre of the small courtyard-like entrance, decorated with the hippocampus, half fish, half horse creatures and the water flew out of their mouths.

Everything was white marble and gold, possibly a little flashy, but he was nothing if not old-fashioned.

"Aethalides!"

He paused mid step and turned to look, finding Brianna, the captain of the guard leaning on the small entrance gate for people. Next to her was the rookie in training. A rare satyr guard who looked far too innocent and young to be standing in that guard uniform.

Brianna on the other hand fit her armour like a second skin, her weathered face with a scar running up the side of her right eye, red hair pulled away from her face and steely eyes sharp as a knife. Her mouth was twisted up in a scowl as she focused on him.

"A word," she bit out, leaning away from the bars and crossing her arms. The 'no-nonsense pose' he knew all too well.

Aethalides sighed, turning to the others and flashed a smile. "Go inside, I'll handle this."

They did as he told with little complaint or protest. Probably another 'it's your fault you got us into this mess,' moment or maybe they'd taken one look at Brianna and decided that yep, Aethalides could deal with that himself.

He turned to the captain and grinned, skipping down the steps. "Brianna!" He called brightly. "What a *pleasant* surprise. To what do I owe the pleasure of one of your visits?"

Aethalides reached the gate and opened it, stepping through so he was on the outside of the Archives's walled off area, leaning against said wall with his hands in his pockets as he looked up at her.

Brianna narrowed her eyes. "Nice shiner."

He winced slightly, reaching for his eye which apparently was going to be black and blue by the end of today. Aethalides gave a nervous laugh. "Ha, yeah. you know how it is though. Dealing with those pesky renegade and wild creatures up top, when they decide to come knocking on mortal doors. The Archives is always here to help!" He declared proudly. "But given that you're still scowling like that, you're obviously not here for pleasantries."

"I'm going to take one guess as to how you got the eye,

Aethalides and I know for a fact I'm gonna be right," Brianna said, glaring down at him. "We got word from the guard in Kanaloa's Kingdom of a disturbance and wouldn't you know it, someone saw your van there."

"Oh please, that could've been *anyone's* van," Aethalides brushed her off.

"No one else owns a modern form of transport, you know that."

"Must of slipped my mind?"

Brianna narrowed her eyes at him and he sighed, rubbing the back of his neck.

"All right, so maybe, just suppose maybe, some stuff went down and things got a little wild," he said with a slight shrug. "No one got hurt…" Aethalides looked to the side, rubbing at his arm. "No one innocent anyway. you could almost say that what we did down at the docks was a public service! Don't worry, I won't charge you, consider this little pest extermination free of charge," he pressed a hand to his chest, eyes closed. "No need to thank me, I'd do it again out of the goodness of my heart."

She growled and pinched the bridge of her nose, looked like she had a headache coming on just from talking to him. Finally, after muttering a few choice words under her breath in Irish, she looked back at him, steely eyes now razor sharp.

"You're an idiot," she stated.

"I resent that," Aethalides replied, patting at his pockets, and finding his cigarettes, all the while Brianna continued to go babbling on about 'public relations this' and the duty of citizens and guards that', it wasn't anything he hadn't heard before and he was tired of hearing it. "You got a lighter?" He interrupted her, flashing a smile at her scowl. "I… seem to have lost mine."

Brianna didn't move but her rookie reached into one of his

many hip pouches, pulling out a lighter, leaning over to Aethalides and lighting his cigarette.

"Oh thank you, you're a lifesaver, kid," he said, breathing the smoke out the side of his mouth, smiling at him.

Brianna sent a glare at her rookie who flinched backwards, his ears dropping and he slinked away from her, a sheepish smile on his face.

"You are playing with fire, Aethalides," Brianna said slowly, turning to throw the glare his way. "Do you think that just because you're the son of a god it instantly gives you complete protection from any repercussions?"

"Do I think that because I'm the son of Hermes, the god of thieves, liars and the deity who built this place," Aethalides stated slowly, staring down at the burning cherry at the end of his cigarette. "That I'm well protected and won't have to worry about anyone? Hmmm… let me think about that for a second," he tapped a finger to his chin in mock thought and then flashed a grin her way. "Yes."

Brianna gritted her teeth at him and Aethalides pushes away from the wall with a shrug, opening the gate and slipping through.

"Do send me the bill for any damages," Aethalides said with a smile, pocketing his hands after he left the cigarette in his mouth. "I'm sure I can cover it."

The moment he was inside the Archives, he shoved the door shut, leaning against it and taking the cigarette out of his mouth as a great sigh left him. He heard footsteps, the oh-so-recognisable click, clack, of Medea's heels and immediately straightened up.

Medea came into view, with tanned skin, long black hair that went down to the small of her back, dressed in the latest expensive dress and like always wearing her crown from Colchis depicting ram horns. Honestly, if modern religions were anything to go by, the horns were fitting. She practically glided over to him, folding her hands in front of her. Everything about Medea was controlled and precise and unashamedly smug.

"We could've done with your help," Aethalides told her and the smug look intensified.

"Yes, I'm sure you could've done," Medea purred, checking her nails idly. "Sadly I was not willing to give it."

Aethalides smirked, pulling up the belt of potions. "Really? No help?"

Medea didn't look impressed, rolling her eyes before snatching the belt back. "That was so I could avoid the headache you'd give me with your *whining* if I hadn't helped at all," she said. "I'm going back to my potion room. Try not to get yourself captured again while I'm gone."

He watched her leave, listening to the click clack of her heels until they faded completely. Once he was certain she was gone, his posture changed and he slammed his back against the door again. Another tired sigh left him and Aethalides felt his shoulders drop as he closed his eyes, just taking a moment to gather himself. Collect his thoughts in some kind of orderly fashion. The voices were just at the edge of his hearing, whispering again, he could barely make out what they were saying…

He suddenly sensed a presence next to him, a shadow falling over his figure at the same time.

Glancing to the side, Aethalides couldn't help but smile at the many long, spindly, spider legs that greeted his immediate vision, before looking up at the woman they belonged to.

"People, Arachne," he said to the spider woman, who tilted

her head to the side, clicking the pincers in her mouth. "They're the worst." Arachne clicked softly, nodding her head in agreement, before she lowered the tray she was carrying to his height with a cup of coffee, the only one left on the tray. Circles were scattered across the tray where other cups had once rested but had now been taken away.

Aethalides's eyes lit up. "But not you, you're the *best*, thank you," he reached for his cup, taking a much needed sip and letting out a gasp in appreciation after gulping some of it down.

"So," Aethalides started, sounding much perkier than before, smiling brightly at the spider woman before him. "What's for dinner?"

Son of the Back biter: 2

Vali Lokison was slightly regretting agreeing to this little trip with Icarus to the magic section of the Heart of Atlantis. The capital was always busy, but this part of the city seemed to always be the busiest. He supposed it made sense, nearly every creature or being here had some kind of connection to magic. So if you wanted help of any kind, whether it be books, rune stones, magical material or even potion ingredients then the Heart of Alishr Alqadin, the magic section of the capital, was the place you went.

This part of the city was mostly focused on the Egyptian pantheon, as they had more than several gods or goddesses associated with magic. There were statues dedicated to Isis nearly everywhere, she even had an altar here, along with a few other gods and goddesses of magic. Sometimes even the gods themselves would wander these streets, Vali had a feeling they were trying to relieve the glory days, after all, in Atlantis all of them were still relevant. They hadn't been forgotten and turned into pop culture references.

The Heart of Alishr Alqadin had many protective seals and charms dotted around it. Huge tapestries hung from some of the buildings, mostly in dark colours if they were Greek to represent Hecate, the Greek goddess of magic. The streets were made up of stone slabs with shops scattered around in neat little rows. Most of them were family owned and he couldn't help but feel a stab of bitterness whenever he saw a mother or father interacting with their children. Then, like always, Vali would catch himself feeling those emotions and scold himself for feeling them at all.

He glanced into the shop window, looking for Icarus and finally spotted him at the counter. Thank the gods, he was getting antsy and just wanted to leave, people were starting to recognise him. One old man sent him a very horrid glare and Vali pulled his hood up around himself, shrinking into his overly large coat at the same time as a means to hide.

A procession of light elves suddenly started to walk down the streets, dressed in their long light green, silver and white robes, decorated with nature and wearing boar fur, some of them used the tusks as decoration and if they didn't have any that, they always had a charm with a boar embossed on it. The light elves from Alfheim, one of the nine worlds of the world tree, were huge worshippers of Freyr. It helped that he was also their king, despite being from Vanaheim, a completely different world to them, he ruled over the light elves. In response, the light elves treated him like he was the Allfather Odin. Though, if Vali was being honest with himself they'd probably worship Freyr even if he wasn't their king, they seemed to love him enough.

Vali scrambled to hide behind a barrel as the procession walked by, they thankfully didn't seem to notice him and he let out a sigh of relief. He could do without them reporting back to Freyr that they spotted the son of Loki in the magic section of the capital. They might get the idea he was here for himself and... that wouldn't do him any favours.

Once he was certain they'd passed by, he pulled himself out from behind the barrel and went back to standing around, looking awkward and not really fitting in with the environment around him. Actually in his effort to not stand out, he... probably stuck out like a sore thumb.

Finally the door to the store he was standing outside of opened up, Icarus coming out with a paper bag and his backpack hooked over his shoulder.

Icarus and Vali were like night and day. Direct opposites. Where Vali hid his feelings behind layers and layers of clothing and denial, Icarus wore his heart, not just on his sleeve but on his entire being. You just had to look at Icarus's face to know how he was feeling, he was terrible at hiding his emotions.

It wasn't just their personalities that were opposites but even their style of dress was opposite. Icarus mostly wore white and gold, usually with some form of Greek pattern decorating the item of clothing. This time he was in his favourite white hoody, with gold Greek patterns going down the sleeves and a gold zip. His skin was sun kissed and tanned, with sandy blonde hair and bright baby blue eyes. The only thing that marred his otherwise perfect normal teenager look was a burn on his left hand that stretched all the way up to his elbow.

Icarus looked like sunshine personified, which was ironic considering his tragic end. The only time he wouldn't be his bouncy, happy self, was any time his life was in danger or they happened to be very high up. Icarus couldn't stand heights, he'd freeze and start muttering to himself, eventually curling up in a ball and rocking. Vali didn't know what he said when he went through one of those episodes, mostly because he was speaking Greek at the time.

Meanwhile, Vali wore as many layers as he could, all of them far too big for himself. He looked like a little kid wearing his father's clothing, though in reality his father wouldn't be caught dead wearing the things Vali had settled on. He never went anywhere without his hood up casting a dark shadow over his face so all you could see was his chin and mouth, with a set of glowing amber wolf-like eyes. Occasionally the tip of his nose would be visible, but that was rare.

Any patch of skin that was visible, however, was marred with scars. Slices and cuts from various weapons that he'd collected over the years. Most were from the first ten years of his life as an enemy of the Norse Pantheon, the unfortunate prey of wild hunts that lasted from December to January.

Thankfully he was no longer hunted down for sport after some kind of agreement was set, but the scars still lingered. Most people in his culture were proud of their scars, it meant they survived the battle or whatever that had happened to produce such a scar. Vali though? He couldn't stand to look at them and he definitely didn't want anyone else to look at them, so he hid them. Wearing dark layers that made him look unhealthily pale, always dressed in his long oversized green and black coat that came down to his ankles. Norse patterns were printed on the leather and two huge brass buckles were situated on either side of his chest, sitting where his collarbone ended. A mimicry to the buckles people wore with their cloaks.

They had wolves embossed on them, curling around in a circle with their mouths open, chasing what looked like a ball. A gold band with various charms and runes carved into it stretched across between the two buckles, again more referencing traditional Norse clothing. The sleeves of his coat were tucked into brass and leather braces, ending over the back of his hand as some protection. These featured a wolf on one and a large snake on the other.

Finally, a belt with his sword was wrapped around his middle, the brass buckle for that featured an eight legged horse and on the hilt of his sword, Heltaka, was a depiction of a woman's head, that was half normal and the other half was a

45

horrifying skull.

He idly ran his fingers over the hilt as he looked Icarus over, watching him fiddle with the bag for a moment as he awkwardly reached behind him for his backpack.

"Did you get what you were looking for?" Vali whispered, his voice rough and horse. He tended not to speak often, preferring to listen. So whenever he did speak his voice sounded... awful.

Icarus gave him a concerned look, but he answered Vali's question instead of asking him if he was okay. Vali was grateful for that.

"Yep!" Icarus popped the 'p' at the end, grinning at him. "I got some Gryphon feathers and some Pegasus feathers. I'm hoping if I combine magic with my father's previous wing designs then..." he trailed off, wincing a little. "Well, maybe things will work out differently..."

"Wouldn't it be better..." Vali tried to word his sentence carefully, so he didn't upset Icarus. "If you. used Phoenix feathers? There um... ya' know.." He awkwardly looked away and gave a shrug. "Flameproof."

Icarus blinked, but then he smiled. "Great minds think alike!" He cried, opening up his bag and pulling out his notebook.

He stuffed the paper bag of feathers in his backpack, which was also white and gold, with a few key rings of godly symbols. Icarus eagerly flipped his notebook open, flicking numerous pages that were littered with calculations and scribbled notes. Some had been roughly crossed out, various different inks were used and there were even some smudges and fingerprints.

Finally, he stopped on a page that seemed to have a few rough pen sketches of wings and feathers, with more notes scribbled along the side. There was a slight problem, as Icarus enthusiastically showed Vali the book, everything was written in Greek and Vali… couldn't read it.

He stared, squinted, and tried to make out at least some words he might know, but in the end, he didn't have a clue.

"Umm… great minds?" He whispered, glancing at Icarus and giving an awkward smile. "I um… I can't read the writing, Icarus, it's in Greek…"

Icarus's eyes widened and he blushed a bright red. His mouth opened and closed, words seeming to fail him at that moment, before awkwardly coughing into his hand and laughing just as awkwardly.

"Sorry… sorry, I forgot that you can't read this… um, basically I'm trying out the feathers I have to make sure they work," Icarus explained. "And once I'm certain I have everything correct, I'm then going to move on to Phoenix feathers. I would've used them straight away but… they're so *expensive,*" he sighed, slipping the notebook back into his bag. "Like, seriously, Val', you have no idea the prices those feathers go up to."

Vali was still peering into Icarus's bag and it was like looking at a snapshot of Icarus's interests and habits. There were several sketchbooks and notebooks, a pencil case, a ruler, and some other things to help with technical drawing. A calculator was stuffed in there, the feathers were pressed against the books and a comic book for the latest issue was also in there. Then came the Hermes Energy Drinks and the El Tapozteco crisps.

"I thought you were banned from the energy drinks?" Vali croaked and Icarus was quick to shut his bag, swinging it onto his back.

"I need it to stay awake when I'm working," he explained. "I mean, you know what Boudicca is like, she wants us both to be in bed by ten, but I'm busy. So… the energy drinks help keep me awake and…" Icarus grinned. "I don't have to sneak out of my room. That way I won't get caught."

"Won't Boudicca just start checking on us if she suspects something though?" Vali asked, tilting his head. "She's only helping."

"I know…" Icarus sighed. "And it's nice to have a mum… but I gotta do my own thing."

Vali nodded slowly. "So… you're really going to try and rebuild your father's wings?"

Icarus screwed his face up, looking away for a moment and Vali feared he'd gone too far with his observations, but then Icarus turned back to him with a small smile. He shrugged a little, starting to walk off and Vali followed, bowing his head and keeping himself hunched in on himself, trying desperately to make himself as small as possible so he didn't draw too much attention.

"I guess… I just want to live up to him, ya' know?" Icarus mumbled, haphazardly kicking a small pebble, sending it skittering across the stones. "I mean, my dad is *Daedalus*, the great *inventor!*" As he spoke his voice was filled with reverence, the kind that Vali heard the light elves use when talking about Freyr, or an over-enthusiastic fan about a pop star. "And who am I?" Icarus pointed at himself, before dropping his hand and his face crumpled up, voice losing any hint of admiration. "The idiot who listened to a god over his father and ended up… paying for it."

The last part was mumbled so quietly that if it wasn't for his heightened senses he doubted he'd be able to hear him at all. He also didn't miss the bitterness and resentment in his tone, but he couldn't say who it was really directed at; the god or Icarus himself.

"So you're remembered as being a little gullible," Vali gave a small shrug. "There are worse things to be remembered for."

Icarus winced, looking away awkwardly. "Right. Yeah, sorry Val'."

"No worries. I've made my peace with it."

Big lie. *Horrendously* bad lie that any could see through and Icarus unfortunately fell into that category. Vali didn't look at him, even when he felt his eyes on him. He felt like Icarus was mulling over saying something, but thankfully he decided not to. There were some things. Vali wasn't open to talking about and that... topic was one of them.

In fact, it was a big part of why he was surprised that Aethalides had even allowed him to stay in the Archives to begin with.

He could remember it clear as day even now, the first time he was brought to the Archives, by Hermes of all gods, who'd stepped in and saved him from the Norse pantheon. Hermes was the one who saved him from the gods, and Aethalides was the one who gave him a home.

It had been raining, and Vali had been dressed in nothing but a pair of ragged trousers and a loose linen shirt that didn't do much to protect him from the weather, but he wouldn't accept the 'traveller's cloak that Hermes would constantly offer him the whole trip to the Archives.

Atlantis had been smaller back then, and the buildings had also been smaller than they were now, which was why the Archives stood out like a sore thumb. It was huge, clearly a sign of riches and wealth that the owner flaunted with little concern for how it might come across.

Vali had been intimidated at first, standing on those marble steps and staring at the door, until it was opened by Arachne and he felt at ease.

If they let someone like Arachne live here then... maybe they'd let Vali live here too?

Hermes took him through to the main room, the books had amazed Vali with the amount. He'd been wrapped up in a blanket, Arachne had cooked him a meal and got him a hot drink of tea all the way from China apparently. That was when Aethalides had walked in.

He was in his forties, a different body, left handed, with a beard that was neatly trimmed. Dark hair that was speckled with grey and wrinkles around the same violet eyes he had now. Apart from the eyes, the only other thing that hadn't changed was the manic grin that would spread across his face.

Hermes and Aethalides had spoken to each other in Greek, none of it was something that Vali understood, he'd just sat quietly and watched as his fate was in the hands of gods once again.

'So,' Aethalides had said, turning to Vali with a grin. 'A fellow child of a trickster god, huh? I know what that's like. Well, don't worry Vali, you have a home here.'

'I... I do?' He'd whispered, his voice was rough with disuse, he couldn't remember the last time he'd spoken to someone.

Aethalides had winced and turned to Arachne. 'Arachne, dear, do you think you could fetch our guest a warm drink with honey for his throat?'

Arachne had responded with a bizarre range of clicks, they seemed happy enough and then she'd left.

'Thank you, dear,' Aethalides called after her, before turning to Vali, a gentle smile on his face, kind... almost like Hermes. That was when Vali could see the familial resemblance between

50

the two of them. 'And in answer to your question, Vali, yes. You do have a home here, for as long as you want or need it.'

'Even after everything I've done?'

Aethalides snorted, rolling his eyes. 'Wait until you meet some of the other occupants of this house, trust me, you won't be doubting your place when you meet them.'

'R-really? You… you don't… hate me..?' He'd whispered under his breath, wanting to shrink into the carpet even more when Arachne came back with the hot drink.

Aethalides had screwed his face up. 'I don't hate unless I have a reason to. So, no, I don't hate you. You're as much of a victim as any of the people who live in this building. Consider this place a safe haven for those who have somehow managed to get on the wrong side of the gods one way or another,' he clapped his hands and grinned at Vali. 'So, without further ado! Welcome to the Archives! Drink up, drink up. I'll show you your room and you can decorate it however you like… oh and then we'll need to discuss food…'

And that was that. He was officially a member of the Archives and he met the others gradually. Vali had seen people come and go. Some left of their own accord, and others… were taken by Valkyrie or whatever death spirit or god they believed in.

He'd been one of the first people to greet Icarus when he'd joined them in the eighties. Culture shock had been big, but after getting over it, Icarus found that he quite liked what was considered modern life at the time.

Since then, the two of them had nearly been inseparable, which is probably why Vali let Icarus get away with convincing him to come out about town. If it was up to him, he'd never leave the Archives unless it was to do a job.

Vali glanced at Icarus and offered a tiny smile, holding his hand out to him. Icarus stared at the hand for a good moment, clearly confused, then looked to Vali 'whose smile grew.

"I won't tell Boudicca about your energy drink if you give me your packet of El Tapozteco pyramid crips," Vali said, his smile turning to a small grin.

Icarus gaped at him, before pouting. Then he reluctantly pulled his backpack off his back, unzipping it. "You sir, drive a very hard bargain and I'm not sure it's worth it," he grumbled, pulling out the crisps and slapping them in Vali's hand.

Vali let out a small happy bark against his will, opened the crisps and began to eat them. It was the orange packet too, his favourite.

"Oh, gods, ew, Vali! Ya' drooling!" Icarus complained as he chucked his bag back on. "Quit it, you're not in your wolf form right now."

"I know, but I can't help it," Vali spoke in a mouthful of crisps.

"Don't talk with your mouth full either."

"You're starting to sound like Boudicca."

"Oh ha, ha," Icarus stuck his tongue out at him, before smirking and lightly shoving him away. Vali gave a small laugh and shoved him back lightly, before offering him a crisps and Icarus took a handful. Against his will, Vali let out a small whine that had him flushed to the tips of his ears which were thankfully hidden beneath his hood, and Icarus burst out laughing.

Vali gave him a light shove in retaliation, still smiling and they fell into blissful quiet.

Unfortunately, the quiet gave Icarus time to see all the people who walked past Vali throwing insults, some even spat at him. The nicest thing they did was step out of his way, giving him a wide berth, but if anyone noticed and recognised Vali who was Norse... they would let their displeasure be known. Usually by shouting curses at him, some even shoved him, but spitting was the most common thing. Vali ignored them. If he reacted, he'd just give them what they wanted.

"Doesn't that bother you?" Icarus whispered, glancing around like he was scared they'd hear him. "I don't know what they're saying, but... they're obviously saying... mean things."

"*Mean* is a nice way of putting it," Vali whispered back, flashing a rare smile his way, hoping to lighten the mood, but Icarus continued to look at him concerned. "You get used to it," Vali settled on.

"Do you?"

He shrugged. "Hasn't changed in the last thousand years. Better to get used to it."

Icarus gave a slow nod, he didn't completely understand that much was obvious, he also didn't appear to believe Vali, but didn't comment further on it. Again, Vali was grateful that he didn't push it. As much as he was an advocate for talking about your feelings, he very much didn't talk about his own, especially if the topic of his brother came up. Better not to talk about that, there was little point anyway, it wasn't going to change anything. Narvi was still... gone.

As they continued walking, this time in more uncomfortable silence, people still continued to harass Vali. Icarus looked caught between saying something and being scared that would make the situation worse. Or staying completely silent and letting the abuse continue. Vali was still ignoring them, he hoped that would encourage Icarus to do the same thing, but when he grabbed his wrist in a tight grip he worried that Icarus was about to do something or say something. Vali hoped he wouldn't.

Whilst his heart would be in the right place, Icarus had a habit of saying or doing something that... well, made the situation worse than it already was. Another reason why he was constantly on lookout duty whenever they were doing a quest.

He looked to Icarus, finding him paler than usual, eyes wide and staring ahead of them in obvious fear.

"Hey um, do you think we can take the long way round?" He asked, grimacing and then awkwardly looking away from Vali, not meeting his eyes. "I just. I just don't want to walk through..."

Icarus trailed off and Vali slowly followed his gaze as he took another hesitant look forwards. He completely understood the moment he saw what was ahead of them.

His eyes flickered up to the signage that rested above the entranceway to the next part of the city. It was orderly and tidy, everything was kept pristine and clean. A light blue background with an elegant white script that read 'Centre of Noimosyni' and had white Greek-styled designs, similar to the one on Icarus's hoody, decorating the edge.

The Heart of Atlantis, the capital of the island they all found themselves living on, was a huge sprawling city, much like the ones they'd find in the mortal realm. The history behind Atlantis, no relation to the Atlantis of myth other than name, was a complicated one between various pantheons vowing for complete control until a small group from different pantheons got together and were able to convince their fellow gods that peace was always an option. In return for this peace, Atlantis was made. An island created by all pantheons, a sprawling heaven for creatures, races and gods alike, all of whom were being pushed out by mortals.

Dotted around the island were various small towns and villages which were taken care of by an individual pantheon. The capital though? That had been split into twelve sections, which were given out to individual pantheons to oversee.

Vali didn't know the full background, Aethalides would, he'd been one of the first to live here and hadn't left since. Also considering his father was Hermes, the god mainly responsible for this place being built, it stood to reason he'd get first pick.

Currently, Vali and Icarus stood outside the information, invention, learning and law section. Overseen by the Greek pantheon, this part was mostly dedicated to the very best schools, colleges, workshops, libraries and law schools. The whole place worked on a grid-like system, clean with beautiful white marble being used for most of the architecture, at least the many, many buildings owned by the Greek pantheon or races. Dotted through the sea of white were different architecture and materials inspired by Egyptian, Celtic, Norse, Japanese and so much more. Statues of gods and goddesses of knowledge were proudly placed amongst beautiful gardens. Essentially, this place was a student's paradise and also the area of the capital where Vali and Icarus lived, but on the other side.

They weren't students, far from it and some of the ones from the more *'prestigious'* colleges, schools and universities could be. difficult to deal with. That wasn't the reason Icarus wanted to dodge, the real reason was down to the University of Daedalus, something his father had apparently set up when he lived in Atlantis for a time. There was even a statue of the guy in the front and it was one of those more prestigious schools. Icarus hated walking past it because he always felt like his father was glaring at him, it didn't help that some of the students and even the teachers would whisper and snigger whenever he walked by. The son of one of the greatest inventors ever lived and he was an idiot, at least that's what they thought.

"Last time I walked through there by myself the students tarred me and chucked feathers over me…" Icarus whispered. "Then they threw me off the climbing frame telling me to try and fly again…"

He vaguely remembered that day. Vali hadn't been paying that much attention to what was going on, too busy reading, he just remembered Icarus coming in with feathers stuck to him and tar. He'd gone to ask, but Icarus had already sprinted upstairs. The next time he saw him he was without the feathers and tar, but his hair had to be cut short to the point that he almost looked bald. No one else seemed to know what had happened, except for him and possibly Boudicca, as for the rest of the evening at dinner she kept shooting Icarus worried glances that he blatantly ignored.

Vali glanced at Icarus now, who was gripping the straps of his bag tightly, looking five seconds away from passing out. His breathing was erratic and his eyes kept darting around in hypervigilance. Vali frowned, placing a gentle hand on his shoulder and Icarus nearly jumped out of his skin. He looked at Vali with big eyes as he offered a smile that he hoped was reassuring.

"We can go the long way around, it's fine," Vali assured him. "It'll be nice to stretch my legs."

"You sure?" Icarus asked cautiously. "I can understand if you. ya' know, wanna get off the streets as soon as possible. **considering how** people… are with you."

Vali pulled his hood closer around himself, still smiling. "Believe me, they'd be a lot worse if you weren't here."

Icarus looked like he wanted to ask, but ultimately decided against it, smiling at him instead. Vali offered another crisp and he excitedly took another handful.

"Hey, quit eating all of my bribe," he complained, taking another crisp out himself.

Icarus smirked. "Quit offering me them, then."

Vali opened his mouth to say something back, when a voice cut through their conversation, making his blood turn to ice and he froze up on the spot.

"Vali, is that you?" The voice crooned.

That voice… that voice, why was it here it shouldn't be here, *he* shouldn't be here.

Slowly, hoping against hope that it was just his imagination, he turned to find exactly who he didn't want to see standing there. Dressed in a light blue tunic with gold embroidery around the edges, fiery red hair falling around his face with a few braids woven through here and there. Pale skin that had scary and dark shadows around his orange eyes, and a slightly crooked nose from a break that had never been properly set.

Scarred lips pulled into a smile and the eyes of the man lit up the moment Vali turned around.

He excitedly clasped his hands together, face alight with pure delight as he cried out. "Oh, it *is* you!" He cried out, putting on a very big show and everyone gave him a wide berth, eyeing him wearily. "It is my bouncing baby boy, look at you! Come here and give your old man a hug," he extended his arms out to him, open as a clear invitation. It might have been welcoming, if it was coming from anyone but *him.*

Loki son of Laufey, once troublemaker and helper of Asgard, now public enemy number one. He had been popular with the gods once and in some cases maybe a little *too* popular. At least, those were Loki's claims and no one was ever going to admit to them, especially not after what he did.

Vali didn't miss the latest edition to his father's looks, the

57

way he had mistletoe decorating his hair, sometimes woven in, other times berries and leaves were done in the clasps that kept the hair tied. He really was so unashamed that now he wore the weapon he used to murder one of the most beloved gods in his hair like a damn *trophy*. He was just rubbing it in the other gods' faces now, probably enjoying every second he caused them pain and anguish.

'''Vali remembered a time long before now when his father hadn't been like this when his jokes had actually been funny instead of horrifying. When he didn't take vindictive delight in causing as many people pain as possible. When he *actually* tried to help. 'Sure, most of the time he had to be threatened into that help, but the Norse gods never did work out quite how to ask someone to do something for them without giving a reward they would inevitably refuse to give or threaten to murder whoever it was they wanted help from. The promise of death was a great motivator apparently.

Loki stood with his arms out, waiting, but Vali stood frozen, just staring. He didn't make a move to go towards his father, he wanted nothing to do with him. It made no sense... *why was he here?*

Slowly the arms dropped and the smile went with them. A dangerous look flashed in the orange fiery eyes of his father, as the dark shadows seemed to take over his features, making him look gaunt and undernourished.

"Ah. I see how it is..." he said, slowly making his way over to them. "You're *embarrassed* by me, aren't you?"

"What are you *doing* here?" Vali spluttered out, the only thing he had been able to say after unexpectedly seeing his father here at all. "You shouldn't be here, *why are you here?"*

"I came to stretch my legs, kiddo," Loki replied, standing in front of them, folding his hands behind his back and flashing another horrid grin. "Metaphorically speaking, of course. We both know where I really am," he reached forward and booped Vali on the nose, still grinning. "Don't we!"

"You shouldn't be here."

"You're probably right, but you see there's this little thing…" he lifted his hand, pressing his pointer finger and thumb together. "*I* don't *care. I* go where I please and when *I* want."

Vali looked to Icarus who just seemed stunned to have… who he did have, in front of him right now. Vali could share that sentiment, he wasn't expecting to ever see him again, not after… *everything.*

"You… need to leave, Father…" he whispered quietly. "I don't want. I don't want anything to do with you."

"Tough luck, kid, because I'm your father, which means I get to see you where I want, whenever I want and there's *nothing* you," he pointed at Vali and smiled. "Can do about it. You're my son. Get it? *My* son. That means… *you..*" He pointed to Vali again, before pointing at himself. "Belong to *me*. I did help make you after all. It wasn't *just* your mother," he raised two fingers, wiggling them around, that wicked grin curling up his face. "It takes two to tango."

Icarus, surprisingly, stepped forward, placing himself between Vali and his father, puffing his chest out and trying to stand a little taller than he actually was and all he achieved was reaching the man's chest in height. Loki raised an eyebrow at Icarus, looking amused and generally intrigued over what he'd do next.

"Hey, listen… you. you should leave him alone!" Icarus stuttered, pointing a finger at him. "Or I'll… I'll yell really loud and get the guard's attention!"

"Really?" Vali's father widened his eyes in mock shock and fear, pressing his hands to his face in an imitation of the scream. "Oh my goodness, whatever will I do?"

Lightning fast he reached out, grabbing Icarus's finger and bending it backwards easily until there was a sickening snap, followed by Icarus's shrieks.

Icarus stumbled back into Vali who easily caught him, looking at the broken finger and back to his father.

The smile slowly came back across his face. "Oops."

Vali felt himself snarl, the wolf starting to come to the fore, determined to protect Icarus. Tormenting him was one thing, but Icarus was another matter entirely.

Slowly he uncurled himself from his usual hunched-over position, standing to his full height, taller than even his father by a few inches. A growl rose at the back of his throat as he took a menacing step towards him. Loki looked up at Vali, placing his hands behind his back again as he looked at him with delight. Eyes sparking and the grin got wider.

"Go back to the pit you crawled out of, Loki," Vali snarled, his lip curling up to show longer canines coming out. "This is your only warning."

Loki smirked. "Ah… *there* you are my son, I was almost worried they'd tame you…" when Vali didn't budge or react, except for more snarling, Loki sighed. "Fine. I'll go. There's only so long I can openly present myself before I attract unwanted attention anyway… until next time," he wiggled his fingers at him as a goodbye. "T.T.F.N!"

There was a pop, like something just blinked out of reality and Loki was gone.

Vali waited a moment, amber eyes darting back and forth like he was expecting his father to pop up again, but no it seemed

Loki had taken his advice and gone away. At least for now.

He quickly turned back to Icarus, immediately wrapping his arm around his shoulders, and guided him towards the school district. He might now want to go this way, but his finger needed to be seen back at the Archives. The short way it was.

As they passed through the archway, someone tried to say something, but one look from Vali followed by a snarled growl, his eyes glowing a bright amber, people wisely didn't say anything. They moved out of his way, giving them ample space as they passed, not daring to comment. A few still tried and pushed their luck, but Vali just growled at them, even snapping a few times and they backed away.

When the Archives came into sight, Icarus was walking a little better, he'd stopped crying too, his tears now drying on his face. He sniffled and used his other hand to wipe any remaining tears out of the way, Icarus looked relieved once they walked through the gates, walking to the steps of the building.

"'Your dad's a jerk, Vali," Icarus finally muttered when they reached the door, still cradling his finger.

"Yeah."

"You're not though, you're nice," he looked up at him and flashed a smile. "I've never seen you stand up straight before, never realised you were that tall, dude."

"Guess I'm just full of surprises," Vali smirked. "Turning into a wolf notwithstanding."

Icarus gave a wet laugh, smiling despite the tear stains on his face. "You got any more surprises then?"

Vali laughed, flashing a toothy grin, an even rarer sight than his smile, as he winked at Icarus. "You'll just have to wait and see."

Happy Fathers Day: 3

Father's Day was… not a day the members of the Archives did much about. Mostly because the majority of them didn't have any parents left or they weren't close to their parents to begin with. Medea and Boudicca treated it like any other day, Aethalides was busy trying to come up with excuses not to attend his father's celebration of the day, not to avoid his father, but to avoid his siblings. Icarus and Vali would both actively avoid going outside, both to avoid their fathers. Icarus was busy avoiding a statue and Vali was busy avoiding a troublemaker. As for Arachne and Xbalanque, they never really put much into the day as both lost their father before they were born, so… it mattered very little. It was only Asterion himself who really had any plans.

This was why he was sneaking around the fields of Crete, on Father's Day, desperately cutting the tall grass down and bundling it up. A hood was over his face as he tried to hide his appearance. It was very early in the morning, there shouldn't be anyone around to see him, but just in case he had the hoodie on. Better to be safe than sorry.

Once he was satisfied he had enough grass, he bundled it up, then took off towards the old Minoan Palace, what had once been his home for a short time. It was… strange to see it as it now was, ruins. Just… foundations for the most part, but even now, people still searched for the labyrinth. Aethalides and the gods had sealed that place up years ago, they'd never find it and Asterion was in no mood to go back there.

Carefully he snuck around the historical sight, following the familiar pathway until he came to a part of the wall that was decorated with frescos. All around him were pictures and images depicting men leaping bulls as a form of entertainment. Some parts of it had been retouched in bright colours to give people a sense of what it would've looked like, instead of the sand-stained and faded walls that were left behind.

Asterion fished around in his pocket for a moment, pulling out a small coin that had the name 'Atlantis' written across it on the front and on the back were several printed symbols of different pantheons. He held it up to the wall, which glowed back in response to the now glowing coin. Slowly the wall faded away to reveal one of the busy streets of Atlantis and Asterion shuffled inside quickly, the moment he was through, the wall behind sealed up. They could really do with moving that gateway to a cave somewhere in Crete, instead of using a historical site, but the palace had been left to ruins for so long that people had thought it was safe to use.

Still, it wasn't like there was a lot of foot traffic going to the human realm, really only the Archives went up often and that was just to do their job of protecting humans from myths they'd forgotten. Or in Asterion's case, to collect grass for his dad.

. He made his way through the streets of Atlantis, gaining looks from people, and a few stares, but he ignored them. People didn't tend to bother him, the myth of the dreaded minotaur of Crete, the monster hiding under the palace, did wonders to keep away. Asterion wasn't complaining, he wasn't much of a people person anyway, so if his legend kept people away from him, that was fine by him.

Asterion was just walking by the edge of the marketplace when he heard the sound of screams and a whole group of people came running towards him. He carefully stood to the side to let them pass, watching them run away from the marketplace as fast as possible. Parents were busy carrying their children or pulling them along if they had more than one. Older siblings were helping younger ones, it was chaos.

"Asterion!"

He turned at the sound of his name being called, seeing the Archives running towards him, weapons in hand. So whatever this was… it was big enough to grab their attention too. Everyone seemed worried or concerned except for Aethalides and Medea. She just seemed aloof to the whole thing, while Aethalides looked… excited.

He was probably just happy to have an excuse to be away from his siblings.

"What's going on?" Asterion asked, watching more people go running past him.

"That's the thing…" Aethalides began sounding grave, and then the smile in his voice came back along with his megawatt grin. "We have no idea! Isn't it great?"

"Fighting something unknown isn't great!" Icarus spluttered. "We don't know what it is, it could kill us!"

Medea crossed her arms, looking down at Aethalides and raising an elegant eyebrow. The whole expression seemed to say 'Did we have to bring Icarus?' But like always Aethalides waved her away. He turned back to Asterion with his huge smile, practically bouncing on his toes at the idea of fighting something new.

"So, good job you're here! We could use our heavy hitter," he mimicked punching and dodging for a moment, like he was in a boxing ring, then jumped up and down in excitement. "Finally! A real excuse not to spend time with my family!"

"They can't be that bad…"

"Spoken like a man who gets on with his sibling."

Xbalanque sighed, pinching the bridge of his nose. "People could be dead or dying," he reminded them. "Can we have this conversation later?"

"Right, right," Aethalides waved him off again, then held his hand up in the air, holding his knife with a big grin. "Onwards to the unknown!"

Asterion watched the ten-year-old go charging off, everyone quickly following behind him, even Icarus, though he seemed reluctant.

The Archives were quick to reach the commotion, most of them didn't have fathers around any more or any way of celebrating them, or a need to, so they were free today. Asterion as always held up the back, given his size he made good cover from behind in case anyone tried to get a lucky shot in. Heading the charge was Aethalides, with Medea and Xbalanque flanking him, the rest following in the middle.

"Do we have *any* idea what it is?" Xbalanque asked, he had a day off from his job to the mortal world today, so instead of the neat suit he usually wore, he was dressed in what Asterion more associated him with. A dark red leather jacket, with blue and yellow diamond pattern that wrapped around the middle and the sleeves. His long hair was done up in a traditional Mayan style and he was even wearing his nose jewellery again. When he was in his police job, all of those things had to be taken away, since he had to dress a certain way.

"Um, no," Aethalides admitted, before giving a hundred megawatt smile in his direction. "But it's the mystery that keeps the brain intrigued!"

"Or dead," Medea added helpfully.

"Dead!" Icarus squeaked. "I don't want to end up dead!"

Aethalides sighed, pinching the bridge of his nose. "You won't, I promise, Boudicca will take care of you."

They skidded to a halt as a satyr went flying, smacking into the ground, but he was quickly helped up by other family members and rushed off. When they poked their head around the corner Asterion decided that he'd rather be in the labyrinth again than standing right here.

Oh, gods, this was *embarrassing.*

A beautiful white bull was charging around the streets, destroying anything in its path and trying to trample as many people as it could, or just flung them across the market courtyard. It was bigger than other bulls, broad and easily double their weight and height.

Aethalides narrowed his eyes at the creature, before pulling a face. "Is that the Creten Bull?"

"Yeah," Asterion sighed, pressing a finger between his eyes as he willed the embarrassment to leave him.

This was all because he was running late, wasn't it? Well, technically he wasn't running late, but his stupid bull of a father… couldn't tell the time. Plus he had really bad eyesight, an unfortunate issue he passed on to his son and the reason Asterion had a set of glasses for reading.

No doubt, due to his father's poor eyesight, he'd gotten confused by the time, broke out of his retirement field and come looking to cause trouble. The last time he'd been running around like this, due to the fact that Asterion had been locked away in the labyrinth, he ended up killing someone. The Creten Bull was no joke.

The Archives group flinched and winced at another loud clatter as the bull took out a market stall, scattering fish, crabs and eels across the floor. It was braying like crazy and when any of the guards dared to try and get close to it, the bull would see red and just take them out with one smack or they'd run away from the charging animal, climbing up out of its way.

"Asterion, buddy, your dad's really ticked off today…" Aethalides breathed and then gave another of his famous manic grins. "Did you forget to get him a Father's Day present?"

"I didn't forget I just haven't gotten to him yet! His field is far away and he," he gestured to the bull. "Is senile and doesn't know what time of day it is! So he thinks it's the evening and is now doing *this!*"

Silence greeted him and when he glanced around at the rest of them, everyone was staring at him like he was nuts. Aethalides for once actually looked stunned and unsure how to proceed or what to say. A first for him.

Finally, the son of Hermes found his voice, not that it ever really took him long to come up with something to say, but he still sounded a little unsure as he spoke.

"I- I was kidding…" he trailed off, looking to the bull again. "Seriously, that's the reason for all of this? Your dad… your dad…"

"Your dad is throwing a temper tantrum," Medea stated bluntly, elegant eyebrow raising. "Over not receiving a present?"

"I have the present!" Asterion grunted. "I had to sneak to Crete this morning, get the grass he likes and stay hidden… it was hard work," he huffed, looking over at his father who smashed into another store, sending beads flying. "Pater doesn't appreciate how long it can take sometimes and you know, he's the type of bull that'd complain if the grass wasn't fresh, so I couldn't even cut it yesterday and store it in the fridge, it had to be. ya' know… straight off the field."

"Huh... information I never thought I'd learn today..." Aethalides said slowly, looking back at the bull. "The Creten bull is a culinary snob."

The white bull shot across the marketplace, nearly slipping on the beads it had spilt across the floor, but it was able to right itself. Then the bull continued its trajectory of smashing into another market stall, sending hundreds of dolls flying through the air where they landed haphazardly across the floor. Then it continued to go through the other stores, taking down store after store, throwing streamers, coins, keys, and some small altar statues of gods cascading across the floor.

Asterion buried his head in his hands, while the rest stared on in amazement.

"Wow... your ah... dad seems really mad," Xbalanque mumbled, looking over to Asterion. "All over Father's Day?"

Yes, it was all over Father's Day, but if they thought this was bad they should've seen the rage his father went into when Asterion was put in the labyrinth in the first place. He only heard about it from his half sister Ariadne. She'd lean on the doors to the labyrinth, playing with some chalk and talking to him about the outside world. She told him all about how the bull had charged through the streets of Crete, breaking things, and attacking anyone who came near. His father was too big and strong to be kept at bay, no matter how many weights and chains they were able to get on him, it was never enough.

Ariadne had been his only connection to the outside world for a long time, until her father, the king, stopped her from coming down to the labyrinth. He wanted to keep his daughter as far away from her monster of a brother as possible. He'd never done anything wrong, the two of them used to play together as children, Ariadne would make flower crowns and hang them off his horns. It had been simple, their mother raising the two of them together, but Asterion had always been the great shame that the King had to live with. Old King Minos couldn't stand the sight of him, so in the end, he locked Asterion away in the labyrinth, where he never had to look at him ever again.

"Umm... so, how are we going to stop him?" Icarus asked softly, looking at Asterion almost awkwardly. "I remember when he went like this after Asterion was, um, locked away in the labyrinth. It... took them ages to calm him down."

"Also... isn't he supposed to be in the sky?" Vali whispered, practically curling into himself when anyone looked at him. "I mean... that's all I heard... he was put in the sky as the constellation Taurus...?"

"Pater is stubborn," Asterion huffed. "You think the stars and the sky are gonna keep him in place?"

"He was already dead, Asterion," Aethalides pointed out. "Theseus killed him."

"Like I said, he's stubborn."

"Are you implying your dad looked death, Lord Thanatos, death incarnate, in the face and went 'nah, don't feel like it' then stomped his way out of the constellation, underworld and came back to life?"

Asterion sighed, crossing his arms as he gazed at his father's carnage with a flat expression. Watching another store go flying and sending hundreds of coffee coasters through the air like miniature deadly shields. Some of them even embedded themselves into the wooden panelling of a house.

"Honestly?" Asterion deadpanned. "At this point, it wouldn't surprise me."

Aethalides nodded slowly. "I take it back, your dad is as stubborn as Great Uncle Poseidon."

"That's probably where he gets it from," Asterion muttered.

Everyone knew the tale. How the future king Minos asked Poseidon for something to impress everyone and gain rulership of Crete. So, the beautiful white bull was given to him, on the condition that he sacrifice it to Poseidon afterwards.

Minos agreed and after becoming king, did not do that. He thought the white bull was too beautiful to sacrifice, so instead he sacrificed a random bull in the hopes he'd trick a literal god.

Unsurprisingly that didn't work and Poseidon asked Aphrodite to curse Minos's wife, Parsiphaë, to fall in love with the bull... then one thing led to another and skipping the gory details, that's how Asterion came into being.

Minos hated him from the get-go, he was the black stain on his record, his shame that he eventually hid under his palace and used as a monster to keep the Athenians in line. It was all nonsense. Asterion had a bullhead, he didn't eat people. Plus, people were gross... you didn't know where someone had been.

It didn't matter though, a monster was a monster and apparently, in the eyes of humans, the only thing you needed to be to qualify as a monster was to be a little different.

"If this creature has some semblance of self-awareness..." Boudicca said, her eyes had never fully left the bull and even now she stood glaring daggers at it. "Can you not speak to your father and explain the situation?"

Asterion glanced at his father, then looked back at everyone else. It was worth a go, but honestly, the idea of it working was... slim. At best. His dad was, as stated, stubborn and it got worse when he got mad and right now he was very, very mad. Furious, Angry, right now his dad would be more pleased if he murdered someone in his tantrum than he would with his son coming over to him and explaining what had happened.

Really with parents like he'd had, it was a wonder Asterion had any semblance of empathy or... healthy mental state.

"I can try, but it'd be a good idea if you lot... covered the exits..." he grumbled, walking out into the marketplace, while he heard the rest of the archives making plans to cover said exits and get out of dangerous places. Like, say, the bull's line of sight.

He couldn't believe he was doing this, but they had to stop his dad from killing someone.

"Pater!" Asterion shouted and the bull turned on him, braying angrily. "Calm down, you senile old cow, it's the middle of the day! I was coming!"

That didn't seem to placate his father any and he stormed towards another market stall breaking it to pieces, but he kept going, sprinting towards the owner of said stall who'd dived out of the way. The old satyr shrieked before Xbalanque quickly gathered him into his arms and dived out of the way, rolling to safety. He helped the satyr up, directing him where to run away, while Medea used one of her spells to stop it from running down the streets.

"Hey, Asterion!" Aethalides shouted, standing on top of a stall that hadn't been broken yet, alongside Icarus who was using the other like a ten-year-old shield. "Maybe don't insult your dad while we're trying to calm him down?"

"It's how we speak to each other!" Asterion defended.

"Annnnd suddenly all the family issues are starting to make some sense..." Aethalides muttered and Icarus through him a look.

"Don't you insult your dad regularly?" He asked.

"But of course, only I don't do that to his face," Aethalides threw Icarus a look. "What do you think I am? Crazy?"

"Yes."

71

"That's very rude of you to say, Icarus," he flicked his nose in irritation. "You should respect your elders-."

"It's heading right for us!" Icarus shrieked, going to jump off the stall, just as the bull smacked into it, sending both Icarus and Aethalides tumbling to the ground, being buried under produce and wood. The produce happened to be a pile of different paints that landed on them.

Icarus and Aethalides looked like a Jackson Pollock painting, covered in multicoloured paints that staind everything it came into contact with. Aethalides spat paint out, while Icarus desperately wiped it away from his eyes and he was panicking, trying to scramble to his feet so he could run and put some distance between him and the bull.

Asterion watched as his father took a tight turn and charged right at Aethalides and Icarus. The younger blanched and quickly snatched up Aethalides, running as fast as he could out of the way of the bull. They only just moved out of the way in time, just as the bull came trampling over the paint, staining the white bull multiple colours across his hooves and under its belly. The Creten bull was slowly becoming the rainbow bull, leaving streaks of paint across its body like racing stripes.

Xbalanque quickly ran forward, grabbing the bulls horns and used all of his weight to push the bull's head down, but it barely touched the ground and the bull sent a glare at him. There was a split second where a look of dread crossed Xbalanque's face before he was flung up into the air and smashed through a market store on his back.

Vali was next, running at full speed, turning into his wolf form to jump on the bull's back, with Boudicca running forward to try and corner the beast, stopping it from bucking the wolf off. It was clear that none of them were actively trying to really hurt the bull, for Asterion's sake, but that wasn't really working very well.

"How did you stop this thing before?" Boudicca yelled as she dodged another charge attempt.

"Well, Theseus killed it," Aethalides yelled back, then took one look at Asterion and hastily added. "But we don't want to do that…"

He trailed off as Vali was bucked from the back, then took a hit to the face from the bull's back legs, sending him flying and rolling across the ground. He gave a yelp and when he eventually stopped moving he was back in his human form, looking very dazed and out of it.

"Vali!" Icarus shouted and made a run for him, sprinting past the bull and quickly gaining its attention. Thankfully Icarus wasn't so stupid to not notice the suddenly sprinting creature that ran at him, changing his direction so he didn't lead it towards Vali who still hadn't gotten up yet. It looked like the kid had been knocked unconscious after taking that blow to the head.

Xbalanque was being helped up and healed by Medea as they watched Icarus run, with Boudicca chasing behind to try and catch up. The Bull noticed, however, slowly to a stop to kick both back legs back at her and she only just got her shield up in time to protect herself. It cracked on impact and sent her flying backwards across the ground before the bull resumed its chase of Icarus.

Asterion watched as the kid ran himself into a corner, coming to a stop and turning to face the bull with a look of pure fear plastered across his face. Aethalides was already running to try and help, Boudicca was picking herself up off the floor, but her shield arm didn't look good, Vali was still out cold and Medea was playing medic to Xbalanque.

Icarus gulped watching as the bull built itself up to charge, classically kicking its front leg aggressively into the dirt, Asterion could almost picture smoke coming out of his father's nose. Icarus slowly reached for the paint, smearing it across his face like war paint and seemed to be building himself up. Asterion couldn't believe what he was seeing, was Icarus… really going to try… and leap the bull?

He charged forward, just as his father also charged at Icarus, who seemed to have glanced at Vali and a determined look crossed his face.

Icarus pushed away from the wall and started to sprint at the bull, Aethalides had slowed down to stop and watch, with Asterion doing the same because he had seen this kind of thing before. Way back in ancient Minoan Crete, where he was from, bulls were sacred to the people, they always had been. The bull was embedded into their culture, so it was only fitting that in the end, they ended up with a bull headed 'monster' to fit their aesthetic. Bulls weren't just sacred though, they also came as a form of entertainment, acrobatic entertainment and before Asterion had been placed under the palace in the labyrinth, he'd been able to watch those shows with his half-sister Ariadne. Youths would charge at the bulls, just like Icarus was doing now and they'd leap them, dive between their horns and use their backs as pummel horses.

Icarus had also grown up in Crete, he'd seen the shows too and now he was mimicking their very technique, running at the bull as fast as he could.

"Leap the bull, leap the bull, leap the bull!" Aethalides started to chant, shaking his fists up and down as his mega-watt smile grew across his face, that manic look glinting in his eye. "Leap the bull! Leap the bull! Leap the bull!"

Icarus ran, he jumped at the bull, extended his arms and dived between its horns, using the back to roll off of, it onto his feet and then sprint away.

"He leapt the bull!" Aethalides cried out, jumping up and down, fists raised to the sky. "Icarus! Thank the gods you didn't screw that up!"

Yeah, thank the gods he hadn't because if he had, there was a good chance he could've ended up dead. Icarus ignored Aethalides's comments and instead ran straight to Vali, crouching next to him and checking him over. There was still no movement from the kid, Icarus seemed to check if he was breathing and let out a breath, seeming relieved. After that he started to pull Vali out of the way of the bull, allowing more room for the others to get in a few hits.

Asterion and Aethalides turned back to the bull that had now turned itself around to face them. His father didn't look happy. Now steam was really coming out of his nose, as he kicked his front leg into the ground, shaking his head back and forth as he wound himself up to charge and attack again.

"We gotta slow him down," Asterion grunted. "Make him lose momentum. Like Xbalanque was trying."

Asterion could feel his throat getting sore. When was the last time he ever spoke this much? Usually, he didn't need to say anything much, but with this being his father... he felt like it was his responsibility to do something. Try and stop his father from ruining fathers Day for everyone else, just because the stupid idiot couldn't read the damn time.

"Agreed, but that's not gonna be me, is it?" Aethalides raised an eyebrow. "You wanna step up to the plate, big guy?"

"I can't. it's my father!"

"Asterion, buddy, I know, I get that," Aethalides gestured to

75

the rest of them. "But none of us are strong enough to do it."

Asterion huffed, looking away for a moment. "Fine."

"Great! I'll lead him past you, you then do what you do best…" Aethalides instructed him, running towards the bull. "Be that immovable object!"

Asterion watched as Aethalides caught his father's attention, sprinting as fast as he could while the bull chased after him, running as fast as he could, but the bull was gaining ground. There was no way Aethalides would be able to keep himself in front of the bull long enough, Asterion raced forward, but he wasn't quick enough to stop his father from smacking into Aethalides, tossing him across the market where he smacked the ground hard. Boudicca ran forward, using her shield to prop it against the floor as she crouched in front of Aethalides, the bull getting closer.

Asterion reached his father, grabbing the bull's horns and pushing them down. It was hard, both of them pushing against each other aggressively and the paint was making it difficult to hold onto him in any kind of way. Despite all of this, Asterion was able to get a good enough hold on him to slow him down.

"Knock it off!" Asterion snarled. "You wanna know why I was late? I was getting you ya' favourite grass, from Crete!" He bellowed, finally slamming his father's head into the ground where they continued to drag for a few more minutes, eventually coming to a stop.

Asterion stayed on top, resting his body weight over his father's shoulders while he kept both hands on his horns.

"You even listening to me! I said I got you a Father's Day present!"

The bull stopped struggling, giving a little grunt back and Asterion rolled his eyes.

"Yes, really," he moved to his pocket, pulling out a bunch of grass and holding it in front of his father. "See!"

The Creten bull slowly got to his feet after Asterion made sure he wasn't going to go running around in a rampage again, sniffing at the grass as his ears twitched. Then it seemed his eyes lit up and the white bull leaned forward, taking a bite from the grass, and chewing on it. He gave a pleased moo, looking up to Asterion who patted his back.

"Senile old man, I got more for you too!"

The bull mooed as Asterion led him away, rolling his eyes. "Yeah, yeah, Pater, you're big and scary. Come on, let's get you back to your retirement field."

Asterion glanced behind him to see the Archives had pulled themselves together again, Vali was being supported by Icarus gripping his head and all of them looked a complete mess.

Just as he rounded the corner, he spotted Brianna come marching through the carnage to the others, her rookie next to her. She looked absolutely livid.

Aethalides looked around the wrecked marketplace, offering up his winning smile that never worked on Brianna.

"The important thing is, nobody died!" He declared, chuckling slightly, that gradually died at her stern expression. Aethalides bowed his head in defeat, sighing. "Just forward me the bill…"

Just Another Day in the Office: 4

Xbalanque stifled a yawn, rubbing at his eyes tiredly and he silently scolded himself for going on that quest last night. Damn harpies, they always picked night to attack, less chance of being seen, he understood that, but at the same time they had no respect for sleeping in at decent hours. The only thing he could be grateful for was the police station he worked at wasn't overly busy.

The other members of the Archives had been surprised when he'd decided to start working, not just for them, but also with modern day people. He was human too, despite living for eternity now until he got killed, he wanted to reconnect with people. Xbalanque thought it would be bad if all of them lost contact with the mortal realm completely, they might forget the reason for doing what they did, protecting mortals from things they'd forgotten about. Now his second job was spent protecting mortals from… each other.

He should really stop referring to them as mortals, sticking a time limit on their existence wasn't helping him connect with them at all.

"Long night?" Jason Rose, his partner and fellow detective asked from across him, looking over his computer and smirking. "You look exhausted."

"Yeah, it was…" Xbalanque mumbled, rubbing at his eyes again, desperately hoping to wake himself up a little more. "We had some bird trouble to deal with."

"Bird trouble?"

"They were… roosting and kept us up all night," he awkwardly lied and wished that Aethalides was here with him. He was always better at lying to good people than Xbalanque was.

Sure, he could play trickster, as he had in his younger years, it was how he and his brother had overcome most of the obstacles they were put up against. Well, that and magic, but he… he hadn't used his natural magic in a very long time. Xbalanque didn't even think he could without his brother and… well, that wasn't happening any time soon. Hunahpu, his twin, actively refused to see him or even entertain the idea of patching things up. Xbalanque couldn't blame him, but it still hurt.

"Damn," Jason muttered, looking at him with concern. "Were they in the attic or something?"

"Something like that," Xbalanque said, looking around the office, filled with chairs, tables and computers. Officers and detectives bustled past each other, phone calls going off nearly every second, still, it was quieter than most police stations. That's why Xbalanque liked it.

He was currently working as a detective in the very small, but old city of Derby. It was a small city in comparison to others like London or Manchester, but he liked it like that. Major cities were almost too loud and too busy, Derby maybe didn't always have a lot going on, but for the most part, it was quiet. Easier to handle for someone who was used to ancient cities. Even Atlantis was mostly made up of open land and the various towns, cities and other settlements were small in comparison to the world above.

The city was easy to settle into, the people… not so much. Not that there was anything wrong with them, it was more that *he didn't fit in.* He was out of time, ancient compared to them and Xbalanque was finding it difficult to connect with the people of today. He imagined, from what he heard, it was how parents felt about their children, especially when they would go on about some kind of new dance for social media clout or a new anime series. Strangely, those Xbalanque understood, mostly because such things had also made their way into Atlantis and some of the shows he and Icarus enjoyed watching, with Vali occasionally pitching in, to watch the anime shows.

Xbalanque looked around awkwardly, Jason had gone back to looking over his classic car magazine. He collected them and they were the highlight of the man's day. Xbalanque doubted he had the money for one though, not unless he saved for a very long time... still...

"So..." he began and Jason's eyes flickered up at him, looking a bit surprised that Xbalanque was starting a conversation for once. "How is... umm..." Xbalanque fumbled with his words, quickly glancing at the magazine and awkwardly gesturing at the page. "Are you thinking of getting one of those?"

Jason blinked a few times, slowly looking down at the magazine and then back at Xbalanque.

"You know much about cars?" He asked, raising a sceptical eyebrow."

"I know they run...?"

Jason barked out a laugh. "Well, that's a good start... you can drive though, obviously? Since you're working here."

"Yeah, I can drive," Xbalanque admitted. "Don't really like doing it, but I can..."

"You don't like driving?"

Xbalanque's mind flickered back to Aethalides and what he classed as 'driving' which was more, take the corner as fast as you can and pray to whatever god you worship that you'll actually make it *around* the corner.

"It's more I'm not a fan of other people's driving, I can drive just fine…" he thought back to Aethalides and his stilts. "Other people… not so much."

Jason sniggered, nodding his head. "Yeah, most people think like that."

"So… are you getting one of the classic cars?"

"I wish…" he sighed, folding up the magazine and putting it on the side of his desk as he leaned his elbows forward. "I take this one and look at each and every one, but never do anything about it. My daughter, Leigh, she's threatening to turn all the magazines into a collage," Jason laughed. "I believe her too."

"Ah, so your daughter is an artist then?"

"She's still in school, but I think she wants to be.." Jason smiled. "Tell you the truth, I don't know what she wants to be, but that's only because she doesn't know either. She goes through phases. One week it's an artist, next week it's a vet and it just changes all the time. She's gotta make her mind up soon thought or at least that's what school's telling her."

Xbalanque tilted his head. It was a system he sort of understood. His people and many other ancient peoples were the same. There were set things you did or were introduced to at an early age and trained into. Children were often expected to carry on the family tradition or businesses and so were trained on how to do those certain things. At least that's what it was like in Greece, in Maya culture they worked on a barter system. Less businesses and more if you were good at something, you would trade those things for something else.

"And she doesn't know what she wants to do?" He asked.

Jason shook his head. "No, she hasn't got a clue. She's not

the only one, but schools pressure the kids into making up their minds so they can pick their subject in college and then fix themselves into it ready for uni," he rubbed at his forehead tiredly. "I mean, how is anyone supposed to know what they want their *lifelong* job to be at the age of fifteen or sixteen?"

Xbalanque... did not have the same experience. He'd wanted to be a warrior and so he'd trained to be a warrior, both he and his brother had decided early on what they wanted to do. A lot of people did, but that was more to do with the fact that people didn't live that long. All of the ancient Greek parties he lived with had helpfully discussed how you were an adult with responsibilities at the age of eighteen. Usually, you run a house or business and are expected to pull your own weight with little to no help.

"I... knew what I wanted to be at a very young age," he admitted quietly.

"Ah, so you always wanted to be a police detective then?" Jason teased. "I can picture it... did you have the whole you know, play set?"

Xbalanque awkwardly looked to the left. "...Of a sort..."

"Better than me, I had no idea..." Jason sighed, looking to the door and frowning as someone was brought in wearing cuffs, being forced to sit down on a seat and cuffed to the chair itself. "Oh come on..." he grumbled and Xbalanque looked over to the side, finding a man in a white leather jacket, with a dusting of black going from the shoulders and down the jacket. It looked like ash.

Silver hair fell down his back, some of it was braided around the side of his head and he wore sunglasses over his eyes. There were various Norse symbols and runes decorating the jacket itself in gold script. He was handcuffed to the chair and he made it look tiny with his height and size.

He was brought in by Cody and Suzanne, with her staying by the guy and Cody came over to them, holding what looked like a *sword* in an evidence bag above his head, waving it around.

Cody and Suzanne were two other detectives and partners that Jason was friends with and he'd introduced Xbalanque. They were nice, Cody was funny, even if he didn't always get his jokes and Suzanne had a rye sense of humour but preferred to get work done first, and joke around second.

Jason rubbed at his forehead. "Again? They're back?"

"Oh yeah," Cody grinned from ear to ear, then signalled for Suzanne to come over, dragging the guy they had in handcuffs in tow. Cody reached for a chair and placed it next to Jason's desk, grinning. "Think you can get this guy processed for me while I take this down to evidence?" He waved the sword around again and Jason's face went remarkably flat.

"Are you kidding?" He said, then put on a fake smile. "I just *love* paperwork, of course, I'll do extra!"

"Knew I could count on you, buddy," Cody slapped his back with a smile.

Suzanne shoved the man into the new chair, another one he barely fit in, handcuffing him to the seat. Jason eyed her a second and then looked at Cody with a raised eyebrow. He shrugged and flashed a dazzling grin.

"Suzanne's gotta take a hospital phone call and then make coffee."

"Ah, a perfect excuse for not doing your own paperwork."

"I'll make it up to you."

"Uh huh."

"Ram season tickets?"

Jason was quiet for a moment, then looked up at Cody to

show he wasn't joking. He had some in hand. Jason sighed and held his hand out for them and they were placed in his hand. Then he battered Cody away, muttering about bribery to which Cody just laughed and Suzanne left to take her phone call.

"The… Rams?" Xbalanque asked curiously as Jason slipped the tickets away in his desk.

Jason stared at him for a moment, looking like he was waiting for a moment that didn't come, so he finally said something.

"You know… the football team? Derby Rams?" He said slowly. "Home team?"

"Oh! The football!" Xbalanque's eyes lit up in realisation, then he blushed looking awkwardly away in embarrassment. "I thought you meant… watching a field of rams… never mind," he waved off Jason's smothered laughter as he watched him, then hooked a thumb at the guy in question at the desk. "Who's this guy?"

Immediately Jason's amusement left his face and he sent a small glare at the guy on the chair, who was curiously leaning over and looking at the classic cars magazine. Jason folded it shut and put that away too, giving the silver haired man a glare in the process.

With the guy being sat down to face away from him, Xbalanque could see the back of his jacket which featured what he recognised as the world tree from Norse mythology, followed by runes encircling it. They obviously spelt something out, but he couldn't read runes. Gods why couldn't Vali be here, he'd know what they said, that's if… the runes were being used correctly.

"This," Jason pointed to the man. "Is one of the *'Lords of Valhalla'*, they're a biker gang who see themselves as modern

Vikings," he looked to the man in the chair with a flat expression. "I thought we weren't due you lot for another month."

"Something came up," came the reply and Xbalanque was surprised to hear a Norwegian accent. He was expecting some kind of British one, but no… definitely Norwegian. Vali had a similar accent, though he was… verging more southern, this guy sounded very far up north.

Xbalanque glanced at the man in the chair, he focused on the imagery his jacket depicted, golden rams decorated each shoulder, nine waves on one arm and an interwoven rainbow went around the other arm. Well, it was easy to recognise who this guy was trying to imitate.

"He's impersonating Heimdallr…" Xbalanque said and almost flinched back when Jason was staring at him like he'd grown a second head. "I think… at least.." He mumbled lamely.

Another look at the guy in the chair and he was looking at him from over his shoulder, a small smirk almost slipped across his face, but he smothered it quite quickly. Then turned away from Xbalanque like it never happened.

"Are you good with myths?" Jason asked, pointing to the man again. "Because that's exactly who this guy is. Or, at least pretending to be."

Xbalanque blinked, giving a slow nod. "You could say I deal with them on a day to day basis…" he trailed off when he looked back to the man in the chair, finding Vali standing in the doorway with a backpack, he seemed to have frozen in place, staring at the individual on the chair.

Xbalanque glanced at the man and Jason, before getting up and hooking his thumb in the direction of Vali. Jason followed his direction, before nodding with a smile, gesturing for him to go over.

Vali still hadn't moved, gripping the backpack tightly as he continued to stare, he hardly seemed to register Xbalanque coming over to him. He didn't even say hello once Xbalanque had reached him, eyes firmly fixed on the man in the chair, watching him like he was expecting him to jump and grab him.

"Vali?" Xbalanque placed a hand on his shoulder and the moment he did, Vali flinched backwards, eyes wide with terror, then visibly calmed down once he recognised who it was. "You okay?"

Vali blinked, then slipped on his usual nervous disposition, with a slight smile. "Heill ok sæll, Xbalanque," he said.

Xbalanque blinked. "I don't know what that means…"

He watched Vali's eyes widen in mild horror, taking a quick glance at the guy on the chair, before focussing back on Xbalanque. His shoulders slumped slightly, but he looked more nervous than upset that Xbalanque didn't know what he said. His white-knuckled grip on the straps of the backpack was honestly starting to make Xbalanque feel nervous.

"Sorry!" Vali spluttered. "I just… old habits…" his eyes trailed to the chair again. "What… what is *he* doing here? I thought they didn't come around now, I thought… I had a month before *they* turned up…"

"Oh… yeah, apparently something came up so they… stopped off here early…" Xbalanque trailed off at the intense look Vali was giving him.

It felt like his wolf-like eyes were boring into his, then they darted around in clear hypervigilance and any type of loud noise or shout had Vali flinching, sometimes even jumping in the air a little. He was trying to make himself as small as possible again, eyes still flickering, lip pulling back in a minor snarl. Xbalanque had to do something before Vali turned into a wolf before everyone's eyes.

"Vali... do you know who that guy is?" Xbalanque asked, hooking a thumb at the man in question.

Vali's eyes fell on him again, big and imploring for Xbalanque to understand... something. "Yes..." he trailed off slowly. "Do you?"

There was a double meaning there and once again that sense of dread was creeping up his spine again. He had a good idea going on, but he didn't want it to be true because if it was... well, that would be an awkward thing to explain.

Slowly Xbalanque looked back over to where Jason was busy writing up notes, but his eyes focused on the man sitting next to him, handcuffed to a seat he was far too big to be sitting in. The man in the chair was looking dead at him and wordlessly reached up to lower his sunglasses. Xbalanque felt his stomach drop when swirling prism like eyes filled with rainbow colours met his own.

Yes, now he was *very* worried.

"Right..." he said slowly, turning back to Vali as what was obviously Heimdallr slipped his sunglasses back on. "I get why you're..."

"Why is he here? Why are they all here? It's supposed to be another month..." Vali continued to mutter, gripping the back straps and twisting them nervously with his hands as he looked to the floor. He was clearly getting lost in his own head, panicking over the fact there was a very obvious Norse god sitting not a few feet away from him. "They aren't supposed to be *here* yet!"

"Vali... what's going on? You knew they... wait... they?" Xbalanque blinked, closing his eyes and taking a moment to come to terms with what was most likely reality. "The *entire*

Norse pantheon are the Lords of Valhalla, aren't they? They're the biker gang."

"Obviously!" Vali hissed, then he abruptly stopped and panicked, eyes wide and he took a step back like he was expecting to get hit, cowering a little. "I'm sorry, that was rude... um, yes that's them, but they prefer the term 'clan' you know. makes it sound more. Vikingr."

"But, why are they here?"

"Oh!" At this Vali's eyes seemed to light up and he even showed a proper smile for once, standing a little straighter, almost proudly. "It's because Derby used to be a Viking settlement. They travel up and down the country visiting cities or places that used to have old settlements for our worshippers in them. It's like... re-living the glory days I guess, but that's why they're here."

"Derby... was once a Viking settlement?" Xbalanque said slowly. "And that's why they're here? They... what? Dip in, take a look around, say 'Oh look, we've been forgotten' and then continue on their way?"

Xbalanque flinched when he was met with a furious glare from Vali and when he looked to Heimdallr who was sitting on the chair... well if looks could kill he'd be dead ten times over, making his way down to the Mayan underworld of Xibalba. He... *might* have overstepped with his comments, but he didn't see the point in re-living the glory days.' Those days had happened, he'd been there for his own people and then their culture was eventually wiped out by the Spanish conquistadors, mostly at least. There were still small groups that spoke the two different languages that were slowly dying out. Not to mention the Mayan and Aztec towns in Atlantis.

He didn't see the point. You couldn't look back. You

couldn't change what had happened in the past, you could only alter what was in front of you, so Xbalanque made an effort to reconnect with both his people and people in general of the modern world. He hadn't been brave enough to go back to South America yet, baby steps, but baby steps were still steps.

"Sorry…" he mumbled, rubbing the back of his neck awkwardly. "I'm just saying… I don't see anything *Viking* when I'm here."

Vali's lip twitched up in amusement. "That's because you're used to it being plain and visible thanks to Atlantis. Derby's got its hidden gems here, trust me. You wanna know the biggest, most prominent Viking thing about Derby?" He smirked at him, another rare thing from Vali. "The name."

"The name?"

"Yeah! Derby is a Viking name. I mean, it's been changed and altered in spelling but it originated from us. We called it Djúra-by, which the old English wrote as Deoraby," Vali explained, pride slipping into his voice as he explained. "It means village of the deer," and with that, Vali took great delight in pointing at the Derbyshire constabulary crest which did in fact feature two deer on it.

It was odd to see Vali so smug, but it was a welcome change to the nervous disposition that he usually sported whenever he was out in public. This side of Vali was something you got behind closed doors when he was with the rest of the Archives group and felt comfortable. Sometimes you'd get glimpses of it outside of the Archives, but it would usually be very quiet, shown in small smirks or whispered jokes, never this loud and never this openly proud either.

Despite cutting himself off from his pantheon and by extension, his culture, it was clear that Vali still felt very proud of where he came from. It was just a shame he never seemed to think he fit in it any more, putting himself in the position of an outsider looking in, despite still knowing all of their traditions and practices. The fact that he knew where and when the Norse gods were supposed to be coming to Derby of all places, a tiny little city in comparison to many others, spoke volumes.

"All right, Vali, I get it, I'm an idiot," Xbalanque sighed, reaching forward to ruffle his head in the hood a little.

Vali smirked. "You said it, not me."

"Oh, you're cheeky now?" Xbalanque grinned. "You seem brighter."

Vali smiled. "I slept."

That meant more than just being able to sleep and Xbalanque noticed that despite Vali's obvious skittish nature, he did seem a bit more relaxed than usual. Good, the kid deserved a break, heck he didn't deserve any of the stuff or nightmares he had to go through on a regular basis.

The son of Loki looked over to Heimdallr with a grim expression. "They'll be moving through to Snottingham soon… once they get Heimdallr back."

"You mean *Nottingham?*"

"No he does not," Heimdallr spoke up, startling Jason who jumped a little at the sudden strong voice. "We called it Snottingham, the town of Snott."

"Hey, Heimdall, buddy, stay on task," Jason instructed, pointing to the screen. "I have to fill this form out, so what did you do that got you arrested?"

"I was protecting Havi."

"By doing?"

Heimdallr shrugged. "I drew my sword and threatened to eviscerate the man where he stood and hang his entrails from the walls."

Jason' facepalmed, muttering something into his hand and Xbalanque found himself raising a silent eyebrow, then he glanced to Vali who didn't look surprised in the slightest. In fact, he listened to the description of brutal harm with a mildly bored expression, like he was used to hearing such things. Probably was. Xbalanque didn't have many run-ins with Norse gods, but from what he'd heard… they were a *creative* bunch.

"You see that… that is why you got arrested," Jason mumbled, looking at Heimdallr who watched him with an unwavering expression. "You don't… you don't see what was wrong with that do you?"

"Not particularly."

"You drew a sword, which, one; who the hell carries a sword any more?" Jason ticked off. Xbalanque glanced at Vali, who subtly moved his coat tighter around himself, hiding his own sword. "Two, you threatened to use said sword and had it out with the intent to cause harm, death and body mutilation…"

Heimdallr didn't look impressed. Calmly he crossed his leg and rested the hand that wasn't handcuffed on it. It almost looked like he was giving a news interview, not giving a statement of events to a police detective. Even the way he sat was formal, with a straight back that never really bent or slumped over in a more relaxed position, unless he was trying to get a look at what was on Jason's desk that is.

"I had no intent to use the sword," Heimdallr stated and Jason threw him a dubious look.

"I find that hard to believe when you drew it and said what you said."

Heimdallr still continued to look at him unimpressed. "Detective Rose, if I was going to use the sword to inflict the

91

harm I threatened, I would not have given him the benefit of knowing beforehand. In other words, if I was serious... I would've just done it."

"Sooo..." Xbalanque turned to Vali. "Heimdallr's intense."

Vali shrugged. "He's the guardian of Asgard and protector of all its people and the world itself. It's an important job and he takes it seriously," he raised an eyebrow. "What? Were you expecting him to be mere words? Heimdallr is the first line of defence against any incoming attackers and as far as I can remember, no one

 got past him."

"In other words, don't mess with Heimdallr?"

Vali nodded. "Don't mess with Heimdallr."

"Right, noted. Anyway," Xbalanque continued. "Not that it isn't nice to see you and the history lesson has been fun, but why are you here, Vali?"

Vali smiled, swinging the backpack, opening it and searching through it. "Arachne had me bring you your dinner. In case you ended up working late."

"Oh..." Xbalanque blinked, watching Vali pull a tupperware box out and hand it to him. "Well, thanks for that, she really didn't have to."

"She also had me pack these homemade cookies to break the ice and share with coworkers," Vali went on taking out three boxes with different labels on them. "Honey, caramel and chocolate- *ah!*"

"Oh, chocolate!" Cody, who had magically materialised back from evidence, reached over and picked up the box from Vali grinning from ear to ear. "These might make the coffee we have taste good, Xbalanque."

"And they would definitely help break the ice," Suzann

laughed as she joined them.

"Look at that," Jason complained from his place at his desk. "They vanish for work, but back for food, every time."

Xbalanque was impressed Arachne even knew about... 'breaking the ice', which made him suspect...

He turned to Vali, who'd curled in on himself even more when Cody stood next to him, shrinking away from the man who was a lot broader and taller than him.

"Aethalides put her up to that, didn't he?" Xbalanque guessed.

Vali's lip twitched up in a smile. "Nice detective work, detective... is something Aethalides probably would've said if he was here."

"You should come over," Xbalanque said, gently placing a hand on Vali's back and ushering him towards the desk.

Vali went rigid, staring at Heimdallr and then, looking at Xbalanque with scared eyes, but he gave him a reassuring smile. It was unlikely that Heimdallr was going to do anything while he was in the presence of police and it would be good for Vali to talk to other people.

Slowly Vali started walking back with the group to the desk, noticeably keeping a good distance between himself and Heimdallr, but the watchman of Asgard kept his gaze locked on Vali. It didn't waver, didn't move or flinch away from him, just watching and not saying anything.

Xbalanque tried to send a warning glare at Heimdallr, but what could he honestly do against a god if things did go badly? Luckily he was correct and Heimdallr didn't seem interested in doing anything or causing a scene, he was just watching Vali like a hawk.

"So, Xbalanque," Suzann spoke up, standing on the other

side of Vali, smiling and gesturing to him. "You gonna introduce us?"

"Ah… yes, of course, sorry. Vali, this is Jason, my partner," he gestured to the man across from him, who was now standing up and helpfully instructing Vali to place the boxes down on the table. "Cody and this is Suzann."

"And who is Vali to you?" Cody asked, already cracking the chocolate cookie box open. "You're nephew or something?"

"No…?" He said and Vali threw him a minor annoyed look as the group now stared at him, because right… it would be weird for Xbalanque to randomly know a teenager. "I mean, we live in the same-."

"We live in the same building, it's group accommodation, he's friends with my mother," Vali butt in, speaking calmly and clearly. "Not Arachne though, she's a homemaker, sorta acts like a mother to all of us, even though some are older than her."

Xbalanque was impressed at how easily the slight lie rolled off Vali's tongue. It didn't sound staged or practised, it just sounded natural. It sounded like the truth even to Xbalanque though he knew it wasn't. At least not the whole truth. It seemed to satisfy his coworkers though and they all visibly relaxed.

"Ha, sounds like my Grandma," Cody sniggered, he offered one of the cookies out for the others to take, and Suzann shook her head, reaching for the honey cookies instead. "You should come round more often, Vali, especially if you bring more cookies that taste like this."

"Weren't you supposed to be on a diet?" Suzann raised an eyebrow and Cody waved her off.

"One cookie is not gonna kill me."

Jason leaned forward, resting his chin on his hands, looking up at Vali. It was like he was studying him, trying to work things out. Xbalanque knew the feeling, there were days when he was still trying to figure Vali out. Actually, Aethalides was the person he was *truly* trying to figure out, but he feared that if he understood the way his mind worked... he'd definitely lost his own sanity.

Suddenly Heimdall spoke, he said something to Vali in Norse and the boy awkwardly replied back in their native language. He looked surprised to have even been engaged by the god. Heimdallr hummed, nodding his head, then seemed to notice the glaring police officers.

"Don't talk to him," Cody hissed at Heimdallr.

"I knew Vali when he was a boy, I was merely asking how he's been," Heimdallr replied evenly but was quickly interrupted by Suzanne.

"Yeah? Does it seem like he wants to talk to you?" She questioned, gesturing to Vali and his obvious nervous state.

For the first time being there, Heimdallr's facial expression actually changed. He frowned in confusion, staring at Vali who was desperately trying to avoid his gaze. Eventually, Heimdallr let out a sigh, holding his hands up awkwardly.

"Apologies. Vali," he caught his attention again and Vali hesitantly looked to him. "Have you visited Jorvik recently?"

"Not in a long time.." Vali swallowed awkwardly, giving a little bow of his head. "Bifrost herra."

"We end our journey there," Heimdallr said with a smile. "I especially enjoy the food court with the longship."

"Hey!" Cody got in-between Heimdallr and Vali, glaring at the Norse god, who currently just looked like a member of a biker gang rather than a god. "What did we say? You don't talk to him, I don't care if you knew him before. Leave the kid alone."

"I meant no offence..." Heimdallr said slowly, trying to look at Vali again. "I… was merely…" he stopped talking abruptly, head snapping in the direction of the door. His lip ticked up slightly, it was like he heard something and then a smile broke across his face.

"Holy…" Cody muttered and everyone eyed the door as a new figure stepped through, after they bent down to crouch through the door itself.

It was a woman, she was huge, easily towering over everyone with a grim expression on her face and she looked down on the people like they were ants. Pale skin, long hair done up in braids, strands of silver, red and white were elegantly entwined with each other and her pale blue eyes looked right into your soul. She was also dressed in a biker jacket, pure white with blue and silver decoration, wearing a necklace, the only spot of gold on her and it seemed to be a Ram's head.

"She looks like a female wrestler mixed with a basketball player," Cody continued, staring at the woman whose face was harsh, grim expression ever present until her eyes landed on Heimdallr. Then they visibly softened.

"My Gullhrútr," she spoke to Heimdallr as she approached, reaching down to gently caress his cheek and he hummed, closing his eyes with that small smile. "Are you all right?"

"I'm fine, hríoar," he answered, reaching up to press his own hand to the one that caressed his cheek.

She nodded and turned to the room, straightening up to stand as tall as she could, with her shoulders squared. "We have paid his bail!" She growled out. "So whoever has the keys to these cuffs should come out and release him!"

Xbalanque had never seen anyone react so quickly as nearly everyone climbed over each other to release Heimdallr from the cuffs, undoing them and letting him get to his feet. He thanked them, walking to stand next to the woman. He was tall, easily standing at six foot five, but next to the woman... he looked... tiny.

"I'd like my sword too, please."

"You can't have that back," Cody said, marching forward, standing directly in front of Heimdallr, only seeming to be a little intimidated when Skadi went to take a step forward, but Heimdallr raised his hand to her, muttering something in Norse. She snorted, rolling her eyes and smirked a bit as she turned away, crossing her arms.

"Actually, I can have it back," Heimdallr spoke calmly. "As our lawyer has already discussed with you several times..."

Cody's eye visibly twitched but he sighed and marched off somewhere, muttering under his breath. Heimdallr stood straight and rigid back, Xbalanque could see some of the watchman's mannerisms clipping through this obvious human disguise.

As the commotion continued to go on, he leaned to Vali, whispering so only he could hear.

"You wanna get out of here?" He asked.

"Might be for the best..." Vali whispered, warily eyeing Skadi. "She wasn't a big fan of my father by the end... she's the reason there's the snake above his head..."

"The what?"

"Never mind. I'm just glad you like the food, I'll tell Arachne you said thanks..." Vali was then running out the door.

Xbalanque watched Skadi's eyes follow him and Heimdallr's too. They stood next to each other, speaking in old Norse that no one had a hope of understanding. Sure, Xbalanque could pick up on some words, but he had no idea what was being said, so he returned to his desk. It was only when a dark shadow fell over him that he jumped to find Heimdallr standing there.

"Vali is in trouble," he said and Xbalanque's eyes widened, standing up abruptly.

"What? Where? How do you-."

"Outside. The rest of the clan have spotted him and they're not letting him leave," Heimdallr explained, then gave a small shrug. "I have very good hearing."

Xbalanque didn't ask for further information, he just ran out of the room, down the steps and out of the building. He didn't have to look far. Just on the outside, in the car park, a group of bikers all of them towered over Vali. He was visibly shrinking in on himself, cowering and raising a hand in a placating manner, trying to get them to back off in a non-violent way. It was obviously not working.

Xbalanque ran forward, running to Vali and quickly pulling him behind himself once he got there. He stood in front of the Norse gods, protecting Vali as best he could while the gods themselves seemed stunned to have someone leaping to the boy's defence. It was like they expected him to be alone in this world.

"Back off!" Xbalanque hissed, sounding braver than he felt.

The Norse gods towered over him, both in height and weight. The biggest of the group, a man with red hair and a beard, arms the size of tree trunks. If the lightning bolts on his black jacket 'weren't any clue as to who this was, the hammer attached to his hip did.

Oh boy...

"Umm. Xbalanque... that's-."

"I know!"

Vali exhaled behind him, laughing nervously. "Oh. Good. It's been nice knowing you."

"You *dare* stand against me!" Thor, the god with the hammer rumbled and it felt like the sky above them thunder with him. The sun was suddenly gone, drowned out by storm clouds

98

as the rain picked up.

Xbalanque looked to the sky warily as lightning flashed across it, followed by thunder and then the rain came. It was pouring down on them, the gods hardly noticed the rain, but Xbalanque found himself nearly flinching at the abrupt drop in temperature. The cold water slipped down his neck and the lighting and thunder seemed to get brighter and louder with each passing second.

"I have fought *bigger* and *scarier* things than you," he snarled, glaring at Thor and squaring his shoulders. "You and your *tiny hammer* do not scare me."

The storm increased suddenly, getting worse. Lighting striking and dancing across the sky, the thunder rumbled over the head, loud and deafening. Xbalanque felt his ponytail being whipped around his face as he shielded Vali as best he could from the wrath of a god throwing a tantrum.

Thor raised his hand to strike, with Xbalanque bracing himself for impact, but the big beefy arm was stopped by a smaller hand.

Everyone was startled, a small gasp sounded and Thor turned an enraged gaze to Heimdallr, the one who'd grabbed his arm in the first place. Heimdallr stared back unbothered, never flinching, with Skadi standing at his back, towering over both him and Thor.

Thor snatched his arm away, getting into Heimdallr's face and he never moved, just calmly standing where he was as he watched him. Thor's eyes were sparking with blue lighting and the weather responded to his mood. Throughout all of this Heimdallr didn't move. He didn't even look *scared* or nervous.

"The boy is of little consequence to us," Heimdallr spoke up. "It is Loki we should be mad at."

"After what his father did!?" Thor yelled back, pointing at

Vali who flinched, curling up behind Xbalanque. "He should suffer along with him!"

"Yes, after what the boy's *father* did, not the *boy*. Vali was but a child when Loki murdered our brother," Heimdallr replied evenly, then looked to another god, this one seemed to be only in their twenties. "Forsetti, I ask for good council, Tyr," he turned to another older-looking god. "I ask for advice from the god of Justice himself, how would you two proceed?"

"Are you mad?" Thor bellowed, and the thunder rolled above them. "Do you not know who this is? Have you been enchanted?"

"My mind is clear and fine, brother, I am merely looking at this… from a logical standpoint," Heimdallr replied. "I *despised* his father, but not Vali. Forsetti, please. How do you view this situation?"

Thor scoffed, then seemed to get offended on Forsetti's behalf. "You dare to ask the son of the man who Loki killed! Forsetti-."

"Heimdall is correct," Forsetti's voice cut through the argument. The young god took a step forward, his blond hair stuck to his face, bright blue eyes like the colour of a clear sky met Vali's and he shrank further in on himself. "Vali was only nine years old. What damage could a child do at that age? When you all punished him you did without reason except for revenge."

"Revenge?" Thor scoffed angrily, shoving Xbalanque out of the way as he took a menacing step towards Vali. "It was justice-."

"There was no justice served that day," Tyr, a god who had a weathered face with his hair cut short, shaved around the back and sides, growing longer at the front almost like a backwards mullet. "Only vengeance. It is my counsel that Heimdallr is right, as is Forsetti."

"Perhaps, we should focus on honouring my father in the way he would've liked, through acts of peace and understanding," Forsetti said, placing a delicate hand on Thor's shoulder. "I know it is not in our nature, but it's what my father would've wanted."

There was silence amongst the group of gods, they looked at each other, finally turning to one who stood at the very back, An old man with one eye who looked over the state of affairs quietly. And just as quietly, he turned and walked away. That seemed to be answer enough, the other gods following him, even Thor, though he did look annoyed, walked away. Forsetti cast a look at Vali who wouldn't meet his gaze, the look the other god sent him was one of pity.

Eventually, all of the gods left, except for Heimdallr, who suddenly seemed to take Vali by the shoulders and move him to stand up straight, reaching his proper height, he was taller than Heimdallr himself.

"Stand straight and tall," Heimdallr instructed him, voice firm. "You are Vikingr, you're an Æsier. A warrior. Be proud."

"But I-."

"Vali, you are still Æsier. Head up. Be proud."

With that, Heimdallr turned on his heel, taking up his bike helmet that had ram horns on either side and got on his bike. The chrome was golden, in the shape of a horse, before driving away and joining up with the rest of the Norse gods.

Vali was silent. He didn't move, but he didn't curl up in on himself like Xbalanque was expecting him to do, instead, he seemed to straighten up a little further.

"Vali? Are you okay?"

"Yeah…" Vali whispered softly. "I think. I'm going back to the Archives."

Xbalanque wanted to say something, anything to get the kid

101

to stay, but 'Vali was already leaving. The rain had also stopped, but Xbalanque still felt cold, wet as he was. Then he heard the sound of people joining him, Jason, Suzanne and a very frazzled-looking Cody. Actually, Cody looked spooked, frightened, like he saw something he couldn't explain.

"Is he okay?" Jason asked, nodding to Vali.

"I... he will be," Xbalanque settled on.

Jason just stared at the place where Heimdallr had been, along with the other gods, had he seen them? Maybe, maybe that's why they were coming down, but Cody still looked freaked out.

"Are you okay?" Xbalanque asked and Cody jumped, looking startled for a moment.

"His... eyes..." Cody muttered. "They were... I've never seen..."

"They were probably just contacts," Suzanne shrugged. "No one has rainbow eyes."

Cody huffed, pocketing his hands and sending a glare her way. "They looked real to me," then he walked up the steps back inside with Suzanne following him. Jason didn't say anything for a long while, both he and Xbalanque had stayed to watch Vali vanish around a corner. Hopefully, the kid would get back to the Archives safe and sound, with no more run-ins with Norse gods.

"They *did* look real..." Jason muttered. "Heimdallr's eyes," he explained at Xbalanque's look. "The glasses he wears... they slipped down his face and... his eyes... they looked like they were moving and changing colour...

Xbalanque placed a hand on his shoulder. "You good?"

"Yeah, yeah, just.." Jason trailed off and shook his head, smiling. "Just another day at the office, right?"

Yeah, Xbalanque thought in mild panic that he didn't show on his face, just another day at the office.

Late night snack: 5

Icarus dragged his feet across the floor as he followed behind the others. He didn't really know how he was still walking, but food was calling him and he forced himself to take another step.

It was quiet at this time of night, the only people who were still awake were the guards. anyone that didn't appreciate a regular sleep pattern, like them. The entire Archives were walking through the deserted streets, heading in the direction to the only twenty four hour open fast food place.

It was a well known fact that some things from the mortal world had found their way down to Atlantis and one of those things was fast food restaurants. They were even copying the idea of delivering food. Of course, they went to places far more extreme than what the human delivery services had to go through.

For the Archives themselves, these fast food restaurants were a lifesaver, they pushed the door open to one of the few twenty four hour restaurants, their feet and weapons dragging across the floor. There was an ever present burning smell as they trudged across the floor, finally settling in their booth.

Demeter Eats, the restaurant they'd dragged themselves to, was one of their favourites, mostly for the quick service, tasty, if unhealthy, food and Aethalides liked it because he got a discount thanks to his father.

Icarus looked around at the group, no one made a move to get up and order, he wasn't too keen on getting up and ordering either. They looked awful, with hair sticking in every direction, some pieces of their clothes were torn and burned, and other pieces were blood stained. Ash and dust littered their features and they were covered in dragons black, sticky blood. In other words, they looked completely *done* with today.

Vali, wordlessly let his head smack into the table and the sound echoed around the mostly empty fast-food restaurant. He didn't even flinch or make a noise of complaint, he just stayed like that.

Icarus stared at him for a moment, expecting Vali to at least grumble and move his head, but no. Nothing.

Huh. He must be tired if he fell asleep that quickly and... that deeply. Sleep tended to elude Vali, Hades, what was Icarus talking about? Sleep eluded *all* of them in one form or another, but Vali seemed to skip it on a regular basis. He and Aethalides.

Icarus could sleep... he just... put it off for as long as he could. He had too much work to do, he'd been back since the eighties and he still hadn't made any inventions. He still hadn't made his father's wings to prove a point.

Icarus wasn't sure who he was trying to prove that point to any more, maybe to himself, but... he doubted that even if he succeeded in building them, he'd actually feel... like he was worth something.

Icarus knew he wasn't like the others. He wasn't some cool warrior queen, a master sorceress, a freaking god, or folk hero or even a terrifying monster. He was an idiot. A clumsy, useless, cowardly idiot who often made situations worse than better.

Medea had been the one to say that Icarus had more use the further away from the issue he got... he was inclined to agree.

"We are not taking on another dragon," Medea said to Aethalides, who was leaning his head back, eyes closed. "Not for at least another month."

Vali groaned.

"Another two months," she amended and next to Icarus, Vali wordlessly gave a thumbs up.

Aethalides opened his mouth to argue but seemed to think better of it, closing his mouth instead, and turning to Xbalanque. "Go and order something."

Icarus noticed that Aethalides was tapping his fingers against his hip flask in a rhythmic motion like he was trying to resist the temptation to grab it and start drinking. There was also the odd little twitching to his right eye and how he'd subtly shake his head. Muttering words that were too quiet for anyone to hear, but Icarus and everyone at the table knew they weren't words directed at *them.*

"Me?" Xbalanque huffed. "I got work in..." he squinted at the clock and grimaced. *"Four hours.* I'm not moving. Besides... you're the guy with the money."

"I'm also the guy with the hole in his leg!" Aethalides cried out, then seemed to whip his head around behind him and glare at something that wasn't there. "Shut it! You're more annoying in death than you were in life!" He hissed at the open air. "At least in life I could... ya know..." he vaguely gestured as he turned back to the table. "Run away. Not that I can do much of that at the moment anyway..."

Aethalides leaned his head back at his rant, rubbing at his eyes and continuing to mumble and mutter under his breath. Smacking away unseen hands. Having conversations and arguments with memories and people long since passed and gone, but for him... they were very frequently still around. As spectres at the edge of his memory and vision.

Depending how bad the day was, depended on what century

Aethalides would wake up in. Then it would be time for his medicine every morning to pull all his memories back together and in the correct order. Not that it always worked and as the day went on his grasp on history and time would start to slip and slide, that was when the ghosts of his memories would pop up.

In many ways, Aethalides had a haunted graveyard for a memory and sometimes those ghosts would come back whether he wanted them to or not.

Boudicca, who was sitting on the other side of Vali, looked on with a rather dull expression. "You should've moved."

Aethalides finally lifted his head to throw a small glare at her. "How was I supposed to move when I was being grabbed by a dragon!? Why did you throw the spear?"

"To kill the dragon."

"Didn't work, did it?"

"That's because your leg got in the way."

Aethalides slammed his hands on the table and opened his mouth to yell, when Medea waved her hand around in front of him, gesturing for him to go to the counter and order.

"Less arguing, more ordering," Medea drawled. "Xbalanque is right about one thing, you're the one with the money."

"Yes, *my* money that you are asking me to spend on you!" Aethalides snapped. "You all also live in *my* house... for free!" He slumped back in his chair, crossing his arms and pouting. "I should start charging you people rent."

"Aethalides," Asterion grunted, glaring at him. "Just order our usual..."

Asterion was so big he had to sit on his own chair that he dragged to be at the head of the booths' table.

Aethalides huffed, throwing his arms up and unceremoniously climbing over Xbalanque instead of letting the guy move. The hole in his leg was looking better and he could put his weight on it now at least.

Icarus nearly jumped out of his skin when he heard a loud snore next to him, startling to find Vali completely out cold and resting his head on the table. The others around the table were staring at him in a mixture of wonder and concern… because seriously how did anyone sleep like that? Sure, it wasn't that busy here, but they had been talking, well, arguing, right next to Vali. How was he asleep?

"Wish I could do that," Xbalanque complained. "I can't believe I've got work tomorrow."

"Sucks to be you," Asterion grunted and Xbalanque threw him an annoyed look which went ignored by the obviously tired minotaur.

Icarus could also feel drowsiness at the edge of his senses. The entire table seemed to be running on fumes by this point and it wasn't that surprising. Dragons were tough, norse dragons were a whole other level of toughness and they could wipe out an entire town in one blast of fire or ice, whatever element they could shoot out of their mouth. It didn't help that their back scales were like diamonds and attacking a dragon at the front was basically suicide. It had been a collective effort and some of that had gone into actually hiding away from the dragon to come up with another plan that might work.

Three hours later they'd left with one dead dragon and wanted some kind of food, but not the healthy kind. Aethalides had been the one to suggest the fast food and he was met with no arguments.

"How is he sleeping?" Xbalanque muttered, staring at Vali who was sound asleep, leaving him with just his forehead pressed against the table.

Medea raised an eyebrow at the boy in silent disbelief for a moment. "I doubt the halls of Asgard are particularly quiet..." she stated, looking back to the rest of them with a small shrug. "It's probably just... practice."

"I've seen Vali fall asleep standing up," Asterion grumbled, looking at him like he'd seen Vali perform some kind of magic trick. "It was freaky."

"Well," Aethalides said as he rejoined the table. "If the Minotaur thinks it's freaky then you know it's gotta be weird," he flinched when Asterion snorted at him in annoyance, fist raised. "Take it easy big guy, it was just a joke. What were you talking about anyway?"

"Vali's apparent ability to fall asleep standing up," Xbalanque answered for him.

Aethalides screwed his face up a moment and shook his head. "Oh yeah, that stuff is wild, don't know how he does it," he said, crawling across Xbalanque's lap to get back to his seat, much to the Mayan hero's annoyance.

"The sleeping part or the whole of it?" Medea smirked at him and Aethalides rolled his eyes back in response.

It wasn't much of a secret that Aethalides struggled to get to sleep. Sometimes plagued with... well, memories he didn't want to relive, but was forced to relive anyway. In the end, they'd stop him from sleeping because he'd be wide awake, reliving a memory, sometimes even performing the movements. From the outside looking in, it was always weird to watch because occasionally Aethalides would end up talking to people who were obviously not there. Like just now.

"Oh, ha, ha," Aethalides snarked. "Ya' know since you can crack jokes it makes me question how tired you really are!"

Medea smirked. "Never too tired to snark at you, Aethalides, it takes so little effort."

"And yet again," Aethalides replied, flatly, his face equally as flat. "You have me questioning our friendship."

"Never question it, darling," Medea cooed at him, resting her chin on the palm of her hand as she leaned on the table, looking straight at Aethalides with lidded eyes, teasing and slightly mean. "If I didn't like you, you'd be very dead by now."

Aethalides glanced at Icarus, silently pointed at him and raised an eyebrow.

"Hey!" Icarus cried in offence. "Medea likes me! Right?"

Medea raised an eyebrow. "Icarus, dear, I tolerate you and you should be glad Aethalides made me swear an oath not to poison anyone in the Archives."

"If I hadn't half the people who joined us would've died by *Medea* causes and not just left," he huffed.

Suddenly the doors opened, catching everyone's attention, since it was Cillian and his Port Side Raiders striding inside. They looked better than the last time they saw them. Not so burnt or sooty. Cillian still had a bandage around his arm from where Vali had swung him around like a chew toy and at their feet was... the chihuahua.

It was dressed in a miniature sailor uniform with its logo on its back, a studded collar with huge spikes and a tiny sailor's hat. So... the Jöt-huahua had survived the drop kick from a minotaur and the group had still kept him around, even getting him a uniform... which was... nice of them, Icarus supposed.

Icarus was really surprised the guy wasn't carrying the dog around in a handbag, but that might not work well for Cillian's image.

"What are they doing here?" Xbalanque mumbled, glaring at them and Aethalides's lip pulled back in a snarl.

"Oh no, they are *not* ruining my favourite fast food joint!"

Cillian leaned on the front desk, and the forest nymph, who looked like she was made out of silver birch, shrank in on herself as the fae towered over her. He grinned, showing his sharp teeth and from the floor, the little chihuahua growled. For some reason, the dog the size of a rat was more threatening than the tower fae.

"Hey sweetheart, we'd like to get an order to go," Cillian tapped the till with that smile. "If you know what I mean?"

"I um… I'll have to get my manager…" the nymph spluttered and then quickly ducked as a war cry came from behind her. Another forest nymph charged from the back, leaping the counter and tackling Cillian.

She was a rose species and when Cillian's group tried to drag her off him, she suddenly sprouted thorns up and down her arms and across her shoulders, making the others yelp in pain, backing away from her.

"Get off of me!" Cillian yelled, trying to shove her off, only succeeding in constantly stabbing his hands on the thorns on her shoulders. "Get off, do you know who I am?"

"Do you know who I am?" The nymph snarled, showing her own sharp teeth. "I'm the freaking *manager*!"

Petal, the aforementioned manager, was in a word, terrifying. No one messed with her in her store, there were so many videos uploaded to various social media platforms of her basically ruling the role of manager. No end of vids where individuals came to complain only to be met by the unmovable object that was Petal.

She picked him up and tossed him into his other men, thorns growing longer and sharper out of her arms. Her eyes were also beginning to glow ominously and some of the men wisely backed up, the only one who didn't was the tiny dog.

Cillian quickly pulled himself to his feet, brushing down his coat, only ending up smearing his blood across it and he growled in frustration. One of his men tried to clean it for him, but he battered their hands away in annoyance.

"You can't do this to me! I'm Cillian, the leader of the Port Side Raiders!" He yelled. "Now open the registers and the safe, give us the money!"

"Hey, port side idiots!" Aethalides shouted, spinning his blades in his hand as the others tiredly got to their feet, Icarus shook Vali awake who yelped and looked about in confusion. "You're a little inland don't you think?"

"Whus happenin'?" Vali slurred from tiredness, rubbing at his eyes as he climbed to his feet.

"A fight is going to be happening, Vali," Icarus mumbled and he heard him whine.

"I'm so tired..."

"You!" Cillian yelled, pointing at Aethalides who smirked.

"Me."

"Do you have any idea *how much* you cost me!? How long it took to get some of my men back in shape!?" Cillian continued, clenching his fists in irritation. "You cost me so much money!"

Aethalides threw him a funny look. "Honestly... it couldn't have been *that* much money," he pointed at Cillian with his blades. "You guys are very small potatoes... in a world of spuds."

Cillian growled, his ears perked up in irritation, gritting his pointed teeth. He let out a shriek of rage, pointing at the group, and baring his teeth at them.

"Kill them!" He yelled. "Kill them, kill every last one of them!"

"Hey, hey!" The manager of the place yelled, waving her

arms around. "No killing! That's a health violation!"

"Seriously? Aethalides lowered his hands slightly staring at her incredulously. "That's what you're worried about right now?"

She scowled at him, crossing her arms and tapping her foot in irritation. "Demeter Eats has the best health and hygiene score of the fast food restaurants and if you think I'm losing that, you're dead wrong!" She snapped, her shoulders lowering a moment. "Plus the paperwork is a nightmare!"

"All right, no killing," Aethalides sighed, then he flashed a grin. "But partial maiming is a-okay!"

"Okay, I seriously think you need to see a shrink of some kind," Xbalanque said, even though he took a fighting stance.

Then both sides charged, a few crossbow bolts were fired and the Archives either dodged out of the way or hid behind Boudicca and Medea, the only two of them with shields. Xbalanque pulled out his collapsible spear, spinning it around so he was fighting with the blunt end, dodging a few hits and blocking others. Icarus and Vali dived over the counter to take cover, along with the manager and the servers.

Icarus glanced at the manager. "So umm... Petal? What's the plan of attack?"

Petal glared at him, her long rose petal hair fluttered around her, thorns growing longer and sharper.

"Why'd you say my name like that? Is there something wrong with my name?"

"You just don't... really strike me as a 'Petal'," Icarus raised his hands up in defence. "Sorry!"

"Ugh, no, it's fine," Petal sighed, poking her head over the top before ducking at a crossbow bolt fired in her direction. "Ughhh! See, if I was a huntress of Artemis I wouldn't have this

problem! I'd have my own bow and arrows, but *nooooo!"* She rolled her eyes. "Mum and Dad said you had to get a 'real' job."

Icarus blinked a few times at her, pulling his own bow and quiver set off his back, wordlessly handing them to her.

Petal raised an eyebrow. "Don't you need those to fight?"

"Uhhh… I'm good. I can throw stuff…"

"I'll throw stuff," she huffed, pushing his quiver and bowing back to him, extending more thorns from her body as an example. " I can- is he *seriously* asleep right now?"

Icarus glanced behind him to see Vali had fallen asleep again, the two satyrs that were crouched down with him covering their heads were also staring at Vali like he was some kind of magician.

"Ah. it's been a long day," Icarus said, rubbing the back of his neck with a nervous smile. "Plus you know, he's Norse-."

"Ugh, say no more," Petal said, raising a hand to silence him. "All right, Demeter Eats, grab your weapons!"

"This isn't an armoury!" Icarus cried and Petal smirked.

"You're right. it's a kitchen," she turned to the back with that feral smile. "Stavros! Get up here!"

From the back came loud, plodding footsteps and Icarus felt pale at the sight of a cyclops crawling his way to the front of the store, a chef hat was placed on his head, his one eye swirled around in his socket, taking in all the fighting and he wiped a thumb down one of his tusks.

What the Hades was *that* doing here? Sure, cyclops were common, but only in a certain part of Atlantis, the rest of the time they weren't allowed anywhere else and for *very* good reason.

Whilst there were rules in place to stop them from eating people, it was pretty much a well known fact that if you happened to accidentally wander into the monster's side of Atlantis, you'd be greeted by human skulls and bones used as decoration. *Everywhere.* It was one of the places Asterion frequented and a reason that Icarus kept his distance from him.

Icarus had grown up in Crete, he knew the stories of the dreaded minotaur better than anyone. His dad had been the one to build its cage, so to now live in the same house as it was honestly surreal. He could imagine his father throwing a fit at the idea, Icarus personally threw a fit frequently in his head whenever he came across Asterion when he was alone.

One time he'd even been met with the image of the minotaur sitting by a lamp, reading a Jane Austin, glasses perched on its nose and a glass of whisky by its side.

How had his life become this… surreal that now, seeing the minotaur reading a classic, and drinking whisky while wearing glasses had become the norm for him?

Stavros looked put out, screwing his face up as he gazed out at the fighting and then turned his attention back to Petal. The nymph looked way too excited at the prospect of causing grievous bodily harm, she and Aethalides would probably get on like a house on fire.

"You know I'm a vegetarian…" Stavros mumbled and Petal smiled.

"Yeah, I know, but they don't. I just need you to scare them…" she gestured to his size. "Get up there!"

Stavros sighed, carefully taking his hat off and handing it to the silver birch nymph, then he delicately untied his apron, handing that to her too. He slapped at his face a bit, then crawled to the front, climbing over the counter. It was a bit of a tight squeeze and Icarus had to shuffle away.

Once he was near the front Stavros was able to sit up a bit better, watching Aethalides get tossed through the air towards him, but Stavros caught up, gently placing him on the floor. Aethalides looked a little surprised by the action, staring up at the Cyclops who lightly patted his head.

"Erm, excuse me!" Stavros called out, but everyone in the fight ignored him. "Hey! Excuse me!"

Oh, this was just typical, of course, Petal would have the world's most polite cyclops under her employ. Usually, they do little more than a go ahead to start smashing and squishing.

"Stavros, what are you doing?" Petal hissed. "Get in there!"

"Ah. I don't really wanna cause a scene..." Stavros said, rubbing the back of his neck nervously.

"Look out!" Aethalides shouted just as a chair flew through the air and smacked Stavros square in the face.

The room fell silent for a moment as everyone stared, only just seeming to realise there was a cyclops in the room.

The chair fell to the floor, and Stavros snapped his eye open, the pupil was a mere pin-prick. A low rumbling growl emitted from the cyclops until it became a full fledged roar and he got to his feet, ripping up one of the benches, swinging it like a club.

The Archives members ducked out of the way, Cillian pushed past his men, running for the exit, his men close behind him, followed by Stavros who launched another bench at them. He was trashing the entire place, smashing it to pieces, much to Petal's horror as she gripped at her hair, eye twitching and mouth agape. Pieces of the roof came down and windows were smashed as Stavros laughed, still swinging his makeshift club.

"Ha ha ha! I've missed this!" He roared, smashing through the front entrance still trying to smash in the Port Side Raiders with his makeshift club.

"Stavros!" Petal yelled, waving her fists around. "That's not what I meant!"

"Errmm… this might be a bad time.." Aethalides spoke up, showing a sheepish smile for once. "But… do you think we could have our food to go?"

The look Petal threw him was nothing short of murderous and Icarus worried for a brief moment that she was about to murder them where they stood right then and there.

"Order up!" One of the satyrs yelled, holding up a large paper bag with their number on it.

Asterion ran forward and snatched the bag up, before bolting to the door with the others close behind him. Icarus had to shake Vali awake again and drag him to the exit, while Aethalides gave a smile to Petal, running as fast as he could to join the others.

Outside, Stavros was making short work of the Port Side Raiders, scattering them whenever he slammed the bench he was using into the ground, laughing the whole time.

Cillian had curled himself up under a bench, desperately trying to hide from the irate Cyclops, he was even holding the Chihuahua close to his chest as the two hid. Icarus watched Aethalides give the fae a careless salute, which Cillian growled and started to yell curses at him, until his hiding spot was discovered when Stavros snatched up the bench, grinning widely.

"Ah! Don't eat me!" He screamed, holding out the dog in front of himself like it was going to protect him.

To the chihuahua's credit, it did start to bark and growl in the 'Cyclops's face.

"Heh. I don't do that any more, I'm vegetarian," Stavros rolled his eyes before a feral grin spread across his face. "Then again, I've never had fae before! Wonder if you'll be stringy."

"Stavros, if you eat him you're filling out the paperwork, not me!" Petal yelled, pointing at him in irritation. "And you!" She pointed to Cillian. "Are officially banned from Demeter Eats!"

Icarus turned back to Vali who yawned and looked halfway to falling asleep while they were running.

"Dude, seriously, how'd you sleep through all of that?"

"Compared to the halls of Asgard," Vali smothered another yawn, hooking a thumb in the direction of the carnage. "That was practically peaceful."

Eventually, they made it back to the Archives, pushing the large doors open and Aethalides made sure to double lock all the doors as they made their way through to the kitchen.

There was a light coming from it which was weird, it looked like the fridge light and after switching the lights on, Arachne froze as she was part way through looking in the fridge. A tube of yoghurt hung out of her mouth, her hair was up in rollers, with a pink dressing gown wrapped around her top half and pink fluffy rabbit slippers on each of her feet. She even had her special eye mask for her eight eyes pushed up to her forehead.

She stared back at them with her unblinking black eyes as they all stared back at her.

"It was *you* who's been eating all my tube yoghurts!" Icarus yelled pointing at her. "I thought it was Boudicca!"

Arachne stared at them, taking the yoghurt out of her mouth and clicking her teeth together, giving a little smile.

"You guys went out for Demeter Eats!" Came an indigent cry from the kitchen table as a large and colourful spider, about the size of a dinner plate, crawled across it. Somehow it was scowling at them. "And you didn't get anything for me!?"

"Anansi, feet off the table," Medea scolded.

"That joke doesn't get any funnier the more times you tell it," Anansi replied, transforming into his human form and hopping over the table, eight eyes still rested on his face and he had his own small fangs hidden amongst human teeth, dressed in west African tribal wear. "I still make my point that you. forgot to get me something!"

"Ughhh," Aethalides rubbed the part between his eyes in irritation. "I'm not going back there… the cyclops chef is having a blast trying to smash the Port Side Raiders into dust."

"Port Side Raiders?" Anansi screwed his face up. "What were they doing so far out of their territory?"

Aethalides tossed him some money. "You can find out if you go down and buy yourself your food."

"Nah," Anansi tossed it back to him, pulling out his phone, and waving the slim and sleek device made by Hephaestus and Hermes in front of them. "I'll just order with the app while I glare at you as you eat," he declared, taking a seat and doing exactly that.

"Whatever," Aethalides mumbled, most of the adults were throwing a very tired and flat look at Anansi, when a loud bang from the kitchen table had everyone jumping.

Icarus looked over with wide eyes, finding Vali's forehead against the table, arms hanging loosely by his side as he snored loudly.

"That can't be healthy," Xbalanque mumbled with a wince.

"I'll book a doctor's appointment tomorrow," Boudicca muttered, turning to Aethalides. "And your leg has healed up."

"No thanks to you," Aethalides scowled at her slightly.

"I told you to move."

"Again I had nowhere to move to!"

Asterion slammed the bag of food on the table, opening it up and started to hand it out, before he paused and frowned. The action effectively broke up the small argument that was brought up, all the while Vali… still slept somehow.

"Aww man," he looked up to the rest of them. "They forgot

the drinks!"

The group, still awake, looked at each other. The silent question of who was going back hung in the air and very slowly all eyes fell on Aethalides. He sent a look of betrayal at Medea who shrugged.

"You are the one with the money," she said as an explanation.

"And the order number," Xbalanque added helpfully with a little smirk.

Aethalides felt his eye twitch, snatching up his coin purse and attaching it to his belt.

"I really need to get you people to start paying rent," he growled out, turning to leave when Anansi stopped him, holding out a piece of paper and smiling at him. "What- what is- wait... is this your order?"

"Yeah, since you're going back, makes sense... ya know?" Anansi smiled at him. "And I am a god, so chop, chop!"

Aethalides scowled at him. "I hate you all, I just want you to know that."

Ancient History: 6

The Heart of Atlantis had another heart resting within it, in the form of the magic section of the city, overmatched by the Egyptian pantheon, the place practically oozed magic and was filled with all sorts of items. Spellbooks, potions, ingredients, rune stones and of course crystals were all located in this part of town and it was the one part of the city Medea spent her most time in.

Of course, whenever the powerful sorceress and priestess of Hecate, the Greek goddess of magic, happened to walk through the Heart of Alishr Alqadim, everyone else got out of the way very quickly. Medea was *almost*, almost as revered as Circe, well, maybe revered wasn't the right word, more she was feared by everyone.

Usually, she took these little trips by herself, but this time, she'd dragged an unwilling partner and Medea would smile every time she looked behind her at Boudicca trudging along.

"Come on," Medea called back cheerfully, unfolding her list that nearly reached the floor. "We haven't even gotten to the live supplies yet. For instance, we still need to go to Aquaria's Aquatic Animals Amalgamation!"

"Aquatic what?" Boudicca asked, raising an eyebrow at her and Medea laughed.

"She sells potion ingredients, she just wanted to use another word that began with an 'A'," Medea explained, looking down at her list. "And she is definitely somewhere I need to take a look

120

at. My frogspawn's out of date…since the last time I checked it there were tadpoles."

"What kind of spell would you even need frogspawn for?" Boudicca demanded as she caught up with Medea, following her through the crowds, not that it was hard, since people tended to part like the Red Sea the moment they laid eyes on Medea.

"A lot more than you'd think," Medea replied simply, looking back at her list. "Then we'll need to take a look at Crystal Clear. Vali wants to try out some amethyst to help him sleep or remain calm. I keep telling him that all I think it will do is make him immune to alcohol," she paused, tapping a finger to her lips. "Maybe I should get Aethalides some…"

"And another question," Boudicca interrupted her. "Why did you bring *me* with you?"

"We've known each other for at least a good few hundred years, Boudicca," Medea said with a sly smile. "And we hardly spend any time together. I thought us ladies could use a break from the boys and Minotaurs for a bit."

"Then how come you didn't invite Arachne if this is supposed to be a 'girl's day'," Boudicca did quotation marks.

Medea sighed, pushing one of the doors open to Sequet's Bane, Boudicca close behind her. The place had a weird smell to it and was littered with scorpion imagery, bottles lined the walls, each one with a gold, silver, bronze or cork cap in the form of a scorpion. The wall decorations were a deep blood red, one wall dedicated to tanks filled with all manner of poisonous or venomous creatures. Some of them were from the mortal realm, and others were clearly not supposed to be anywhere near mortals of any kind.

"I tried asking Arachne to come with us," Medea explained as she scanned the shelves pulling out one purple bottle with the word 'hemlock' written on the label and then she took another labelled 'Gorgon blood'.

"And?"

"And she didn't want to go," Medea huffed, turning to Boudicca with an irritated expression. "She likes to hide away from everyone except us, you know that. And there's always what happened the last time she went out."

"That wasn't her fault."

"That's obviously not how she sees it."

Boudicca crossed her arms, screwing her face up and then casting a look at the various ingredients that Medea was slipping into her basket. A lot of them were very poisonous, which then of course led to the question of why does this shop even *exist?*

"Why do you need two vials of 'Gorgon's blood?" She asked and Medea smirked, holding the different coloured vials up between her fingers.

"One's to slaughter your enemies, the other to heal any ailment that can afflict a mortal body. Honestly, considering what our job is, I'm surprised you didn't know what this stuff was," she said, making her way to the store clerk to pay for her items. "I mean, I have used it on you a few times."

Boudicca screwed her face up in disgust, only just managing to withhold her tongue. She glared at the blood like it personally insulted her, all the while Medea just smirked at her. She looked like she was having the time of her life, again, another thing Boudicca was baffled about.

It wasn't that she didn't like Medea, in truth she just hadn't made up her mind about her. She didn't trust her, that was for sure. Medea was a whole other level of scary and there was always that threat that she'd just dump them at the first sign of trouble they couldn't handle.

After paying for those ingredients, they left and the shop owner looked relieved the moment Medea left. That was a recurring theme around these shops, and Boudicca was starting to notice, the more she went into them. Everyone would become nervous when Medea entered them, the moment she left, it was like a great weight had been lifted off their shoulders.

"What did you do to these people?" Boudicca asked. "I've never seen a group of shop owners fear someone as much as you and I've been out shopping with *Asterion*."

"I did absolutely nothing," Medea replied, ticking off the items on her list she'd already gotten. "And that is real power. See, Jason, if you'd just stuck with me," she growled out through gritted teeth. "We could've had the whole world in the palm of our hands, but instead you couldn't be happy with what we had, you had to go looking for other things."

Boudicca raised an eyebrow at her and Medea seemed to abruptly collect herself.

"If you have to know, darling, the real reason I wanted you to come with me was so we could have some girl time," she explained. "Do some girly things."

"Girly things?"

"Yes, you know, shop for new clothes, shoes, nail polish and extremely dangerous poisons that can kill you in seconds. We can also go shopping for some new weapons if you want," Medea paused, tapping at her chin. "And I did promise Arachne I'd get her some silk."

'Medea continued to walk away, with Boudicca trudging behind her. Even after knowing her for as many years as she had, she still felt like she didn't know Medea very well at all. Boudicca supposed that was intentional. The only one who seemed to have any semblance of understanding of her was

Aethalides and even *then* there were moments where she could surprise him.

"Huh… weird…" Medea mumbled, looking at the end of her list, screwing her face up and Boudicca joined her, peering over the sorceress's shoulder, looking to the bottom of the page too.

"What is it?"

"Well, clearly Aethalides has written something on my list for me to get, but… I just don't understand why," Medea admitted, looking at the list with a screwed-up face. "Mesopotamian Oracles? No one's seen one of them in centuries."

"Mesopotamian oracles?" Boudicca frowned at her. "I thought Greece was the one who had the oracles?"

"Technically all cultures have a legend about some kind of oracle or individual who can foresee the future," she explained and frowned. "Hades, the ancient Hellenistic practices have several, not to mention way back when there were more than one oracle at any one time."

"And were they more highly revered than they are now?"

Medea gave a coy smile. "I don't know, Oracles are still very highly sorted out, especially with lottery numbers," the smile dropped as she looked back to her list. "But these ones? They're rare, so rare in fact that their entire lineage is… extinct."

"How come?" Boudicca asked.

"They didn't have anywhere safe to go."

"But there are Mesopotamian gods here," Boudicca cried, following Medea as she seemed to make a b-line to a bookshop kept out of the way, it seemed like one of the older stores, a Greek one. She looked up at the sign, 'Mnemosyne's Archive' and said. "Why wouldn't they save their oracles?"

Medea pressed her hand against the door and frowned.

"Because Atlantis didn't come quick enough for them. They were wiped out…" looking over to Boudicca with a shrug. "Which is why it's weird that he wants this book in the first place."

With that she pushed the door open, Boudicca following behind her.

The shop, from top to bottom, was nothing but bookshelves and ladders. It was a lot taller on the inside than the outside, probably more magic. She wasn't sure how she felt about all that.

When Boudicca had been alive the magic in the mortal world had mostly dwindled or hidden itself away in Atlantis by that point. To suddenly be thrown into this world where magic ran rampant and even had a special section in an entire city dedicated to it… well, it was still something that she needed to get her head wrapped around. Even after being here for hundreds of years, there was a lot to work out.

Medea weaved her way through the shelves and Boudicca struggled to keep up with her. More than once she felt like she'd lost her, until finally, Medea stopped at the final spot. The books on the shelves looked… old. They were obviously well taken care of, but the books themselves had seen better days. They were falling apart, some looked like they needed new spines, and the shelf they were on was also covered in dust. This whole part of the bookstore looked like it was very rarely, if it ever was, visited by anyone.

Medea ran her fingers over the spines for a few moments, before finally pulling one out, blowing the dust off the cover.

Boudicca peered over her shoulder as Medea idly flicked through it, seeming to be checking everything over and making sure this was the right book. She only caught glimpses, but the pictures that were being showcased throughout the book didn't seem to paint a very pretty picture.

It looked like the whole reason the oracles even existed was… some kind of curse.

Medea abruptly snapped the book shut, making dust explode in both hers and Boudicca's faces. They both fell into a coughing fit and wafted the dust out of the way, Medea scowled at her clothing that has now gotten dirty.

"Ugh. He owes me big for this," she grumbled.

"Or maybe you could just make him pay for your dry cleaning?"

"Or I could do that, but I prefer my idea better."

Boudicca raised an eyebrow. "And what was that?"

The sorceress chuckled, smirking at Boudicca mischievously, before she gave her a wink, walking to the counter to pay for the book. Obviously, that wasn't something she was going to let slip, knowing Medea she probably wanted to do it as a secret torture.

They left the shop after paying for the book and it seemed Medea wanted to get home after that. Either to give the book away to Aethalides straight away or to just get cleaned up, it was hard to tell.

Boudicca was half tempted to advise Vali to take Medea around with him wherever he went, it would certainly stop people from being needlessly cruel to the boy. People would take any chance they could to upset Vali, spitting at him, cursing or yelling, all for something his father did.

Speaking of fathers, when the two of them entered the main room of the Archives, the library, Aethalides was having an intense discussion with his own father.

Boudicca froze, staring at the Olympian god, Hermes, as he stood in his godly form. He looked like any other athletic human, except for the height. Tanned skin, white hair that fell around his face in waves, slightly pointed ears were visibly poking through his hair, decorated with earrings and dressed in a travellers cloak, classic chiton and a hat with his wings. As usual, there were also his famous sandals and he also had his staff resting by his side, but it was his face and eyes that really showcased that Hermes and Aethalides were father and son. They had similar sharp features, slightly smoothed over with youth and pale violet eyes that sparked with power.

Hermes, like all Olympians she'd noticed, was handsome, maybe even beautiful, his features were *sickeningly* perfect. Hermes, though, had the annoying ability to be charming. It wasn't surprising to think of him having a lot of kids.

"Ladies," Hermes greeted them, before pausing and bowing to the two. "Forgive me, I mean, *your majesties.* It's not often I find myself in the presence of one queen, let alone two. I feel honoured."

"Such a charmer, Lord Hermes," Medea smirked, looking down at herself. "You'll have to forgive my appearance, but your son requested a book," she pulled it out and slammed it into Aethalides's chest, causing more dust to blow up in his face. "It was very dusty."

Hermes's eyes twinkled with mischief. "Apparently," he leaned closer to her and snapped his fingers, immediately all the dust was gone from her form, making Medea sparkling clean.

"Hmm, I see your wife has taught you well," she purred.

"Would you quit flirting with my father," Aethalides snapped suddenly, looking over the book with a grin. "This is perfect."

Medea cocked her hip to the side, resting her hand against her hip. "Speaking of, why do you even need that?"

"Medea said that the Mesopotamian oracles are extinct,"

Boudicca said, joining in with the conversation and ignoring Hermes's charming smile.

"Oh can't be too careful these days," Aethalides shrugged. "I mean, the Mayan and Aztec pantheons are gone, but I still have books on those guys."

Hermes suddenly spoke up, sounding surprisingly stern as he spoke to Aethalides in Greek, a scowl on his face.

Aethalides shrank in on himself. "Sorry, Pater, I won't be so… careless when speaking about lost gods next time."

Like a switch had been flipped, Hermes instantly settled back into his relaxed and carefree nature that came more naturally to him. He smiled brightly at his son, reaching forward and ruffling his hair, much to Aethalides' obvious irritation.

"Well, I best be off. For a bunch of immortals who have *all* the time in the world, you have no idea how impatient they are when it comes to their letters," he huffed, waving his arms around. "I shouldn't complain, I'd be out of a job otherwise, but come on! We have modern technology, *phones* are a thing!"

With that, he picked up his staff, pointing it at Aethalides, who raised an eyebrow at him, clearly not that impressed by his father trying to be godly and imposing.

"Remember what we talked about?"

"Yes, pater," Aethalides rolled his eyes. "I'll contact you later if I find something."

Hermes grinned, patting him on the top of the head. "Good boy."

"I'm not a dog!" Aethalides snapped. "That's Vali."

"Whatever," Hermes rolled his eyes fondly. "I'll see you later!"

Then he… popped out of existence? Boudicca wasn't sure, screwing her face up as she looked to the absence of the god in the room, finally looking at Aethalides and his book. There was a map open behind him, several places marked out, but before she got to look at them properly, he was folding the map up and stuffing it in the book.

"If anyone needs me, I'll be in my office," Aethalides said brightly, picking up his apparent cup of coffee, and marching off. The eyes of the fluffy monster slippers he was wearing jiggled with each movement.

"He's up to something," Boudicca stated.

Medea laughed, flipping her hair over her shoulder. "He's a son of Hermes. They're *always* up to something."

Fitting in is harder than it used to be: 7

Xbalanque tapped away at the desk, occasionally looking over at the break room where Jason, Suzann and Cody were talking amongst themselves. Laughing, cracking jokes, just like it was back in the Archives and Xbalanque never felt like he was weird or out of time before, until joining the police in the mortal world. He couldn't help but stand out like a sore thumb, especially in a small English city.

Aethalides had suggested maybe trying Mexico or South America, but that was a *no-go*. It felt more alien to him there than it did in somewhere new, somewhere he'd never really been other than quick visits if they were dealing with a monster or creature.

England was a fresh start away from anything he knew or remembered, but... that came with the price of also completely ostracising himself.

Not for the first time that day he sighed and took his phone out, the phone case thankfully hid that it wasn't any sort of phone that people would recognise, these ones only being available in Atlantis.

The Archives had all gotten special discounts on them since it had been Hermes and Hephaestus who had made the phones and Hermes, being Aethalides's father, had practically shoved them into their hands excitedly telling them all about the brand new features and upgrades they had planned.

Xbalanque thought that Aethalides's excitement could

sometimes be a lot, but it was honestly nothing compared to the anthropomorphic incarnation of communication itself. Hermes's speech had reached speeds that no one could hear and Vali had started to whine at the climb of octaves that affected his altered wolf-like hearing.

In fact whenever the Olympians did stop by or any other god for that matter, if they did get excited about something… it would be a little intimidating, to put it lightly. Apollo as the god of light would make light bulbs pop, ironically plunging them into darkness. Set had caused a full on sand storm to sweep through the capitol and Aphrodite made several people fall in love on the spot. Gods were a lot, but people? Modern people at least, Xbalanque found them infinitely harder to deal with.

He'd take dealing with a war infused Ares or Enyo any day. At least those he knew how to handle.

Xbalanque glanced over at the break room with a small grimace.

He didn't know how to handle this.

As he was quietly scanning through the various news feeds, his phone suddenly started ringing loudly and he let out a yelp, juggling it a few moments before catching it. The screen was already cracked in one corner, he didn't need to add to it.

One glance over at his work colleagues he saw they were staring at him. Xbalanque smiled awkwardly, giving a little wave before answering.

He was greeted by Aethalides's over the top grin and wide eyes. It was a horrific visage to be greeted with and he'd probably have thrown his phone across the room if he wasn't used to this by now.

"Can I help you?" He drawled and Aethalides's ecstatic grin vanished.

"Wow. Vali was right, you do get grumpier at work," Aethalides said, face screwed up for one moment longer before he went back to the psycho grin. "But you better turn that frown upside down! Look at where we are!"

Xbalanque felt his face drain when the phone was flipped around to show the Derby station, the very station he worked at and he watched in more horror as they entered.

"What are you doing!?" He hissed at him.

Aethalides turned the phone back to face him with a smile. "We're seeing you, isn't that obvious? Figured you'd be bored, right? Plus, Arachne wanted to drop off your dinner. She had a feeling you'd be working late again," the smile left and he faced Xbalanque with a flat look. "Honestly, I wish you put as much work into your job in the Archives as you do with the one here."

Xbalanque gave him his own equally flat look. "Pay me and I'll consider it."

"Pay you? Why on earth would I pay you?"

"Don't bother, Xbalanque," Medea spoke as she leaned into view with her vaguely amused smile. "I tried to get him to pay for centuries. It's a losing battle."

Aethalides scowled at her, pointing at Medea, flicking it between her and Xbalanque. "Hey, hey! I give you a free place to live and I pay for most of the stuff myself!" He snapped. "So *no*, I'm not paying you!"

"You let us stay there because you like us, don't lie," Medea scoffed with a smirk.

"Exactly, I view you all as a friend and do you know what friends don't do" Aethalides smiled sweetly before it turned back into his scowl and he yelled. "Pay one another! Just like I don't charge you for rent... in fact, consider your work with the Archives your rent."

132

Xbalanque frowned, looking off to the side for a moment in thought. "Is that why my light is still faulty in my room?"

Aethalides turned to look at him again, exasperated and flat expression on clear display. "It might be."

"You could've told me that earlier?"

"Oh, so you can work hard down here to get your light fixed and then run off to the mortal realm again?"

Xbalanque rubbed the bridge of his nose, muttering in Mayan under his breath, as he took a cautionary glance at the door and the breakroom. He could see Jason, Suzann and Cody looking at him and whispering amongst each other. He couldn't tell if they were curious, gossiping or concerned and... oh boy he had been out of touch with people for a long time hadn't he?

"Look, we'll discuss that later, just.." He glanced at the door again in concern. "Don't make a scene when you get in here."

The smile and short chuckle Aethalides replied with should've been enough to let him know that he'd made a serious error. Especially when the call ended and he was left with the home screen of his phone.

Oh dear gods what had he done?

Slowly he lowered his phone and looked to the door in concern and of course, just as he looked at it, Aethalides poked his head around the corner. He scanned the room for a moment and when his eyes landed on Xbalanque, who desperately shook his head 'no', that devilish grin split across the archivist's face.

"Xbalanque!" Aethalides shouted loudly, marching into the room and of course catching everyone's attention. "There you are, buddy! Man, that was a lot of stairs! Yeah, that's right," he continued, looking around the room and pointing to Xbalanque ecstatically. "That's my buddy! My right hand man! Yeah, who wouldn't want a friend like this guy!"

Xbalanque just wanted to sink into the floor or drop kick Aethalides through a window. He was undecided.

Medea came gliding through, looking like a model and gaining attention from nearly everyone. Some of it is good, and some of it... not great. It only got worse when she elegantly sat on the edge of Xbalanque's desk and crossed her legs, looking like some kind of femme fatale from an old detective noir.

Thanks to Xbalanque being sat down he was virtually the same height as Aethalides and the guy took great delight in smiling like a megawatt, with his hands behind his back, rocking back and forth on his heels as Xbalanque scowled at him.

"Hey, best bud!" Aethalides practically sang, smiling big and getting bigger. "Ya' miss us?"

"You are so lucky there are witnesses right now."

"That's not a very nice thing to say."

Xbalanque nearly slammed his hands on the table, leaning into Aethalides's space to hiss at him. "You just marched in here and completely embarrassed me!"

"Xbalanque, darling, please," Medea said, looking at her nails and even taking out a nail file. "He's the ten-year-old," she pointed to Aethalides with her file. "Not you."

Aethalides scowled up at her. "Not ten," he grumbled.

"You sure?" Xbalanque raised an eyebrow, voice relatively calm. "Because you're as *annoying* as a ten year old!"

Aethalides scoffed, waving him off in a dismissive notion as he rolled his eyes. "Nah, that's just a Hermes brand family trait. *Everyone* finds us annoying!"

"I can imagine."

Seeming to ignore him, Aethalides looked around the room curiously, eyes falling on the trio that were still staring. Cody seemed particularly taken with Medea, who didn't help matters by flashing a smile and waving at him. Cody cautiously waved back, suddenly looking shy and Xbalanque had to resist rolling his eyes at the action.

"Medea, don't be cruel," he said.

"Just having fun, dear, don't be a spoilsport."

"People have feelings."

Medea looked at him, seeming amused. "And you say that like it should mean something to me?"

Sighing, he turned his attention to Aethalides. "Didn't you say Arachne was coming?"

"She is. She's taking the elevator."

"Shaft," Medea added on for good measure.

Xbalanque groaned, pressing his head against his hands as he tried to convince himself this was just a bad dream. Of course, it wasn't and not a moment later, Arachne came through the door. She had a huge dress on that fell to the floor, covering her eight legs, a head scarf wrapped around her head like some kind of 50s glamour model and huge shades to cover her eight eyes. She'd even managed to hide her fangs behind an even bigger scarf that she had wrapped around her neck.

Arachne waved once she reached the desk, pulling her bag around and handing him a box of what he guessed was his dinner.

He couldn't be mad at Arachne, she was just too sweet and Xbalanque smiled nodding in thanks.

Aethalides made a dramatic gasp, clutching at his heart. "Where was that greeting when we arrived?"

"You embarrassed me in front of everyone, you can go to the crows for all I care."

"Hey, don't say that kind of thing lightly," Aethalides hissed at him, suddenly looking very nervous. "We don't imply or use the one who receives many's name in vain."

"Are you kidding me right now? You curse Hades's name nearly every other day."

"That's the place, *not* the god! They aren't the same thing!"

He rolled his eyes, just as Cody and Suzann came over, of course Cody started up a conversation with Medea, while Suzann tried speaking to Arachne, but Aethalides was quick to jump in and translate, saying that Arachne was mute. Not a complete lie, but Xbalanque doubted that Suzann knew how to speak spider.

He watched the conversations for a brief moment, before getting up and making his way to the break room, coffee cup in hand. Jason was still there, looking slightly amused at the whole interaction and he grinned at Xbalanque when he reached the coffee machine.

"So... your other roommates?" He asked, pointing to the group and Xbalanque grumbled, muttering something along the lines of 'unfortunately' as he made his drink. Jason laughed, looking back to the group. "They seem nice though. Is the boy one of their kids?"

Xbalanque bit his lip to stop himself from telling the truth. "Aethalides thinks he's completely independent, doesn't really do the whole...listening to his parents thing."

Jason laughed. "Most kids don't when they start getting a little older," he glanced at him and Xbalanque could feel his eyes on him. "You okay?"

"I'm fine!" He spluttered and plastered a smile on his face. "I... just..."

"You're just very quiet," Jason said. "I hoped we hadn't done anything to upset you?"

"Huh?" Xbalanque blinked in confusion. "You've not done... *oh!* Um, no, listen," he rubbed his eyes and desperately thought how he was supposed to explain this. "I guess I'm just struggling to fit in around here. I'm a bit old fashioned and half the time I don't really know what in the Xibalba anyone is talking about..."

Jason raised an eyebrow. "Xibalba...?" He muttered before shaking his head and offering a small smile. "I know the feeling. My daughter goes talking about some kind of cartoon or anime. I don't know, new comics and...I have no idea what she's talking about."

Xibalanque supposed that was..quite accurate to his situation, given he was over several thousand years older than any of the people in this room, with the exception of the Greeks and Medea.

He glanced over at them to see both Medea and Aethalides were talking with Cody and Suzann easily. Even Arachne looked comfortable which was... more than a little bizarre given her spider form. They were far older than him and yet... they could talk to people just fine.

"So... did you see the game last night?"

Xbalanque blinked and slowly tilted his head. "The... football game?"

"Hmm. It was good, I thought at least. Cody disagreed with me," Jason laughed. "But he plays more attack, less defence."

Xbalanque stared for a moment before giving an incredulous look. "What is he nuts? That formation was perfect! Sure, maybe we could've done with a different upfront player, but with a more defensive minded upfront and midfield play, they actually came back to help the defence!"

"See that's what I said!"

Jason continued to talk about the game with Xbalanque adding in little bits and they gradually moved away from football, to talk about rugby, cricket, and rowing, Xbalanque ended up bringing out his phone to show Jason a few games of Pok-A-Tok, the mayan ball game he still played at the sports centres in the capital. He even showed Cody and Suzann when they came over, only just realising that Aethalides, Medea and Arachne had left. He hadn't even seen them leave, too engrossed in... making friends? Possibly. Well, at the very least, he had people to talk to about sports now, no one else in the Archives was that interested.

He looked back at the others who were now holding their phones watching a view more Pok-A-Tok games with rapped attention.

"Xbalanque?" Cody asked, pointing to the game. "Do you play this?"

"Oh yeah. I'm part of a little team," Xbalanque smiled, though it faltered slightly. "Um. it's just a private club, sorry. But it's fun."

"Must be killer on your hips though," Cody mumbled, looking back at the ball. "That ball looks heavy."

"Yeah, it can be, but you get used to it..."

"What are the rules?"

"The rules?"

"Yeah," Cody looked at him again. "I mean, I'm kinda following but... be good to know the rules..."

Slowly Xbalanque smiled and clapped his hands together. Oh boy. They did not know what they'd just gotten themselves in for.

"All right... but you'd probably want to sit down," he smirked. "It gets complicated..."

They took a seat, Cody muttering something about it not being that complicated, which only made Xbalanque smirk bigger. Ha, if only they knew. This was going to be a long break, he was certain by the end of it they'd be taking notes.

He joined them at the table, taking his phone back and folding his hands. "All right," Xbalanque said. "So, here are the rules... try to keep up..."

An Unexpected Visit: 8

Vali ran the toothbrush over his teeth, being careful to clean the canines that were always cursed to be slightly longer and more pointed than they had any right to be. Sometimes they'd even cut his lips if he wasn't careful, not that you'd notice considering how his face looked.

He leaned over the basin and spat into the sink. Like all bedrooms in the Archives, they came complete with their own bathroom. Save any trouble for a house of nine trying to use the bathroom at the same time, especially when they were all so different. Asterion was part bull after all and no matter how many air fresheners he put in his room it still smelled like a barn animal lived in there. On the opposite end of the spectrum was Medea, who was as Boudicca would sometimes mutter under her breath, high maintenance. Really, Medea was neat, and orderly, using her looks as a weapon and looking her best as a result. She had. expensive tastes.

Vali on the other hand was nowhere near as precious about such things. Sure he was clean and didn't smell, but… he hardly took care of himself beyond that. His long dark hair was cut in odd ways, hanging around his face and more often than not tangled in knots. Half the time, the reason it was in such a state was down to him not brushing it and instead just cutting the knots out, without making the rest of his hair equal. His pale features and dark shadows made him look gaunt, even to his own eyes he looked… unwell.

And where the dark shadows lost their impact, the multiple scars that criss crossed his face made up for it. The only ones that were visible for his friends to see usually were the ones going through his lips and a few on his chin, but the rest of his face and body looked like it'd been used as a training dummy for swordsmen. As well as a few holes for target practice, a few huge gashes on his side from a battle-axe or two and a round hole in his shoulder from a spear and those were just the few scars from weapons. The rest were from monsters, creatures, just the general life he'd lived.

His dishevelled appearance was… a stark contrast to his younger years and the culture he was from. Vikings took grooming very seriously, despite having the reputation of tearing chunks out of their enemies and their bloodthirsty nature, being clean, hygienic and well groomed was an important part of their culture. It was so important that when someone died, one of the things they were buried with was a reindeer antler comb, for them to take into the afterlife.

Vali's eyes slowly drifted to his own comb that sat in a pot by the sink, along with a few pieces of shaving equipment that he didn't use. He was surprised the items hadn't collected dust by now.

Sighing he wiped any residue from the toothpaste away with the back of his hand, taking a small glance at the mess in the sink. A mixture of white and red, with little chunks of meat. Not his blood, which was… worse. Oh sure, everyone thinks shapeshifting is great, being able to turn into a wolf to tear into your enemies? Fantastic! Until you turn back into a human and remember that your wolf mouth is exactly the same as your actual mouth.

Vali always carried a toothbrush and paste with him

whenever they went out. You never know when you'll need to deal with someone and then clean your teeth afterwards just to get the taste and debris out of your mouth. Toothpicks were also a must, to pick at the mystery meat.

In his haste last time, he'd forgotten to change his toothpaste and hadn't been able to clean them, forced to wait for the entire trip back to the Archives with the horrid, acidic-like taste of a tactful worm in his mouth. Gods, it was the worst, he'd never been more grateful for minty freshness in his life, even if the Greeks stared at him like he'd just decimated a corpse. They did the same thing whenever he had mint tea or treated himself to mint sauce with his lamb.

Vali stretched out his back, standing to his proper height, which made his face disappear from the mirror and only his torso be visible, feeling his back crack and click. Gods, it was hard to keep up the tiny bent over appearance, it was his poor attempt to not be visible, less noticeable, but his Jötun heritage was making that harder and harder every day. Especially since he was still growing, apparently. Vali didn't want to get any bigger or taller than he already was. He was stuck thin and the added height made him look like some kind of Norse lamppost wanna-be.

He curled back into himself, walking through the door back to his room, his coat haphazardly tossed over his bed. His room was the only place he ever took the coat off unless they weren't to someplace that required him to be wearing some more... weather appropriate gear. Other than that, the long coat and hood were on and up, hiding his thin body and scarred face from everyone.

Despite the rest of the Archives being undeniably Greek inspired, with marble and mosaic, Vali's room was Norse in every way. Made with wooden walls and floors, all the furniture was dark wood that had intricate Nordic carvings on it. A bookshelf filled with books of sagas and poems sat near his bed with a wardrobe next to it. A desk in the far corner with a bench that had fur on it, along with a lovely fur rug on the floor. Viking shields decorated above his bed, along with two axes that crossed each other. A painting of Asgard was on the other side of the wall and next to that was a beautiful map of the world tree itself.

Everything in his room was neat and orderly, except for his desk which had papers scattered around it and a few missed attempts to throw scrunched up pieces of paper into a bin. As if the paper was bad enough, there were also ink stains scattered all over it, along with pens and ink quills haphazardly left.

Vali liked writing poems, some of the books on the shelves had actually been sketchbooks he'd bought himself and wrote poems in them. He never shared this passion with anyone else, even the other Archives members didn't know. Mostly because Vali was… embarrassed. Here he was, a Viking god and yet he enjoyed writing poetry… it wasn't exactly the impression people got from the Vikings. It was almost like they were unaware of Bragi, an actual Viking god of poetry, music and song. Among other things.

Vali ran his fingers over the papers with a small scowl. "More like the god of boastful bragging and little to show for it," he mumbled under his breath.

A sudden knock at the door had Vali yelping and nearly shooting into the air. He stared at the door, catching his breath, half expecting Bragi himself to come bursting through the door to give him a piece of his mind. Probably in some form of a poem or overindulgent song piece, he'd written up. Bragging Bragi, bragged about his attributes in song and poetry without the very good use of metaphors or innuendo.

"Vali? Are you in there?" Came Aethalides's voice through the door and he let out a breath he didn't know he was holding.

"Yes… yes!" Vali cried through the door, darting towards his coat and picking it up. "I'm here!"

"Ah, good, listen um… there's someone at the door for you," Aethalides explained and Vali froze up. "Don't know why," the Greek continued. "You'd have thought they'd done enough to you…"

The wolf-like whine, which was honestly pitiful even to his own ears, came out of his mouth before he could stop it and Vali shrank in on himself. He could feel the anxiety creeping up his back and he desperately wanted to hide somewhere. Under his bed or in his wardrobe, he was weighing up his options.

"W-who is it?" He called through the door.

There was a long pause which didn't help one bit. Vali could feel his anxiety and fear creeping up higher and higher. His hand was beginning to shake and he felt his breathing going off pace.

"It's Heimdallr," Aethalides said and Vali let out a breath.

Heimdallr. It's only Heimdallr. The least likely to mindlessly try and bludgeon him to death and definitely not Bragi. Thank the gods for small mercies.

"Oh. Coming!" Vali pulled his hood up and ran to the door.

When Vali opened the door he found Aethalides leaning against the wall, a notebook in hand with a detailed map drawn on the page. Various Xs were drawn on them and some seemed to be scribbled out. Vali looked at Aethalides's general appearance, noting all the bits of twigs and leaves sticking out of his hair and the various grass stains. Not to mention the various bug bites.

Vali frowned. "Did you go to the fields of Xipe Totec?"

Aethalides froze, quickly snapping his book shut and he

turned to look at Vali, clearly alarmed by the question.

"Huh?"

"Did you go to the Fields of Xipe Totec?" Vali asked again, raising an eyebrow.

"Oh! Uh, yeah, I did," he rubbed the back of his neck nervously.

Vali furrowed his eyebrows and looked over all of Aethalides's injuries. He looked like he'd had a very inexperienced trip into a jungle, which... considering what the fields of Xipe Totec had turned into, wasn't too far away from the truth.

"What were you doing there? No one goes there since the Aztec Pantheon... well, ya know.." He rubbed at his arm awkwardly, looking away from Aethalides.

It wasn't nice talking about lost pantheons. Gods tended to think they were immortal, which they were, but the loss of the Aztec and Mayan pantheons had proven otherwise. It had hit everyone hard, none more so than the worshippers of both pantheons. Even now, no one really knew what had happened to them, other than they vanished and were assumed dead, because what else could they be?

"That place is an overgrown mess and not even the nature spirits go there any more," Vali continued. "It's filled with dangerous plants, who knows what else, Hel, they had to fence the place off, it's guarded!"

"Believe me I am aware and remember every one of those things," Aethalides said and then he shrugged, flashing that grin of his. "But it's nothing to worry about! I was just looking for something. Wasn't there though."

"What were you looking for?"

"Look, I could talk for hours about that, but there's a Norse god at the door," Aethalides said, placing a hand on his back and slowly guiding him towards the stairs. "And while I don't fear anyone, I really don't want to keep a god waiting. There are worse things than death after all."

Didn't Vali know it?

He followed Aethalides down the stairs and to the door, it was still closed, he could only imagine how irritated Heimdallr would be. Whilst the god didn't show it, always a stoic figure on guard duty and barely ever letting a single emotion break through that visage, occasionally there would be. tiny cracks. Enough for Vali to know, without a doubt, that Heimdallr would not appreciate having a door slammed in his face.

He reached for the door handle, but Aethalides grabbed his wrist with a surprisingly strong grip. Vali looked down at Aethalides somewhat startled and even more surprised to find him giving Vali a serious look.

"I didn't invite him in because one that's your choice and two, this is my home and by Hellas hospitality rules. I can't do anything bad to him once I let him into my home," Aethalides looked to the side awkwardly. "The moment I welcome him in here officially he's a guest and then I have to follow the rules..." he trailed off and scowled. "The really stupid rules."

"Should you be saying that out loud?" Vali asked, worriedly.

He knew how... touchy and temperamental Greek gods could be. Out of all the pantheons they were the ones who could generally find offence in anything you did. Aphrodite, the goddess of love and beauty, once took offence to the mere existence of a pretty mortal.

Aethalides just snorted, shrugging. "What are they gonna do?" He gestured to himself and raised an eyebrow. "Kill me?"

Finally, Aethalides stopped out of the way to allow Vali to

open the door and let Heimdallr in if he wanted to. He didn't leave, staying by the door and watching Heimdallr with a scowl.

It was odd to see the god again but comforting to actually see someone dressed in Æsier clothes, even if Heimdallr always had a little flare with his things. Gold. *So* much gold and precious metals were interwoven with the watchman's clothes, giving it a quality that had rainbows appearing on the cloth whenever the clothing hit odd pockets of light. A short blue cloak hung down his back along with his shield and he had a ram fleece, complete with its head, around his shoulders for warmth, the golden claps also had ram heads depicted on them. Not to mention his sword hilt was designed as a ram's head too, the horns coming around to stop any blood from running down the handle.

Now he wasn't among mortals he could show his rainbow eyes off perfectly, silver hair done in braids, trailing down his back and even for a god from the Norse pantheon, Heimdallr was pale. Vali would almost be worried he was sick if he didn't know that was just how Heimdallr always looked.

Along with his look, the other ever present thing about Heimdallr was his lack of smile.

"Lord Heimdallr?" Vali bowed, remembering his manners and also not wishing to get on the bad side of any other Æsier gods. "What brings you to the Archives, my Lord?"

"Vali Lokison," Heimdallr replied evenly, with barely any inflection in his voice. Vali noticed Aethalides twitching slightly next to him, narrowed eyes scanning Heimdallr's person as the god continued, gesturing to a large chest at his feet. "Might we have this conversation inside and… in private?"

"I. Um, of course… my Lord," Vali stepped to the side, letting Heimdallr in, the god carried the chest on his shoulder with one hand easily. Aethalides was still glaring at him but begrudgingly left the two alone.

Vali knew that wouldn't be enough for Heimdallr. It was a little known fact that the watchman of Asgard had heightened sense and this… unfortunately meant that he found it very hard to get any moments of peace or silence. Vali couldn't imagine what it would've been like walking through the Heart of Atlantis just to get to him.

He led Heimdallr through the halls, walking back to his bedroom and he kept noticing that the watchman was constantly looking around. His expression never changed, not once and Vali could vaguely recall when he was a child how much Heimdallr's lack of visible emotional response to anything going on used to really irritate his father. Loki liked watching people get annoyed or laugh at his jokes, Heimdallr did neither. He would just stare back at Loki with his stoic expression, not once cracking a smile or even a slightly irritated scowl. Nothing.

"So…this is where you live now?" Heimdallr suddenly broke the silence once they reached Vali's door. "It's very Greek."

"Not in my room it isn't," Vali responded as he opened the door and held it open for Heimdallr. "My Lord, can I ask what this is about? I haven't done anything to offend the gods, have I?"

Other than surviving this long of course, but…it wasn't like the Æsier and Vanir actively went out of their way to try and kill him… any more at least.

Those first few wild hunts had been… *not fun.*

"No," Heimdallr replied and placed the chest down on the floor, pushing it towards Vali. "This is yours. Everything in it is yours."

"Mine?"

"When…" Heimdallr paused and for the first time in Vali's lifetime, he saw the other god looking almost awkward. "When you and your family were taken away for Loki's punishment," he worded carefully and Vali felt himself starting to scowl. "You left your things behind."

"Funnily enough you don't get to pick up your stuff when you've been grabbed by guards," Vali bit out, crossing his arms and rolling his eyes, finally settling a glare at Heimdallr. *"My lord."*

Heimdallr was frozen for a moment, looking a little bit like he was seeing a ghost and then shook his head. "Yes. Of course. Afterwards… your room was cleared out and I… I took it upon myself to save your things."

Vali let his arms drop to his side, staring somewhat dumbfounded at Heimdallr. He almost wanted to ask him again if he'd heard him correctly, but Heimdallr wasn't the only one gifted with heightened senses now and yes, he had heard him clearly. Heimdallr had brought his stuff.

Slowly he cast his eyes to the chest that Heimdallr had been hulking around with him, now that he really looked at it, he could recognise it as one that had been in his room. Vali was almost scared to open it.

"I thought it was about time I… finally gave it back to you," Heimdallr explained.

Vali didn't know what to make of it, but soon he was kneeling in front of the chest, opening it up and it felt like all the air left his lungs. He stared at it quietly, feeling almost detached when he looked at the items inside. His old clothes were neatly folded inside, a pair of extra boots, even a pin with his father's symbol or the symbol he'd claimed was inside. It was the toys though, they were the things that struck Vali harder than the clothes.

Most were giants or trolls with a few heroes he remembered from his mother's stories, there was even a Greek soldier, a little gift Hermes had brought him. He'd gotten his brother one too and they'd played for hours with them.

Vali reached into the box, shifted things aside and pulled out another doll, it was barely finished, clearly over and he held it in his hand easily.

"Is that-." Heimdallr started, but he abruptly stopped talking when Vali tightened his grip on the doll.

"Yes, Heimdallr, it's you. My mother made it for me. I was always scared when my father left for his travels because there was no one there to protect us," Vali got to his feet, straightening out his back so he stood tall, easily standing taller than Heimdallr now. "I wouldn't sleep, so my mother told me stories about you, the defender of Asgard and the Æsier. She made me this," he held the doll up for Heimdallr to see, even the little doll had a permanent scowl on its face. "So I would feel safe whenever my father was away. She told me that no matter what I would always be safe because you always would be there. *You,* the unmoving, unwavering protector of Asgard." '

"Vali-," Heimdallr tried but Vali shook his head, scowling, feeling his canines grow as his lips pulled back in a snarl, face starting to elongate slightly.

"You know the really stupid thing? I *believed* her," Vali bit out, his fingernails grew into claws, piercing the doll as he held it out in front of him, directly in Heimdallr's face. "But on *that* day *neither* of you kept me safe! Instead, my father was held back and you stood idly by... as I tore my brother *apart!"*

Vali took the Heimdallr doll in both hands and ripped it to

pieces right in front of the god himself. His speech was starting to devolve into growls and barks, canines were poking out, cutting his lips as he continued, closing the distance between him and the watchman. Heimdallr didn't move, staring up at him, face twitching into what could almost be described as horror.

"So how *dare* you come in here, *lording* the fact you saved my things over me! Do you think just because I was polite when I saw you at the police station that I had gotten over what you did to my *family?*" Vali snarled, drool ran down his chin, and he was starting to froth at the mouth, almost looking like a rabid dog, a human hybrid. "You said it yourself… It was *Loki's* punishment! Why did you have to punish me with him? I didn't do *anything!* None of us did, but him!"

"I wasn't lording your things over you, Vali, they're your things," Heimdallr explained calmly, reaching out a hand to place it on his shoulder, but Vali stepped back. "Listen, I just came here to give them back to you. The others. destroyed everything else, but you were still alive and-."

"Get out."

"Vali-."

"Get out!" Vali roared, gripping his head with his claws digging into his scalp as he shook back and forth, desperately trying to control the wolf that just wanted to claw itself out of him and sink his teeth and claws into the watchman. "Aethalides might be bound by laws of hospitality, but I am not! If you want to not end up like my brother, my lord, get out!"

Heimdallr bowed his head, face grim and gave a slow nod. He walked to the door, pausing a moment to look back at Vali who was still changing into his wolf form violently. He even kicked the chest and sent it flying across the room, smashing on impact with the wall.

That was when he let out a howl and Icarus suddenly appeared at the door, pushing past Heimdallr to grab at Vali in his full wolf form, trying to dodge the teeth as he held him back from launching at the god.

"Dude!" Icarus yelled, scowling at him. "What did you do!?"

"I was just… returning his things…" Heimdallr said slowly, the horror now visible on his face as he stared at Vali.

"Oh gee," Aethalides said sarcastically as he also appeared at the door, shoving the god away as best he could, standing with one of his knives drawn and his herald staff in the other hand, blocking the way to Vali's room. "Nothing like shoving a guy's trauma right in his face and expecting him not to react violently!"

"I didn't think-."

"That much is obvious," Aethalides snapped back, pointing his staff at Heimdallr when the god reached for his sword. "Get out. You're only making it worse."

Vali wasn't sure when Heimdallr left, but by the time he'd calmed down and settled, the watchman was long gone.

He sat in Icarus's room with his legs curled up against himself, the room was littered with various tools and failed inventions, drawings and diagrams of other ideas. Hundreds of sketchbooks and notebooks were spread about the room, some in a vague attempt at an order, but most were open with half finished equations or drawings. Icarus himself was on the floor, eating from a bag of El Tapozteco, square pyramid shaped crisps complete with a dip. They'd been watching some comedy shows to try and cheer Vali up, but the chest kept coming up in his mind.

He couldn't ignore it forever.

"I think. I'm just going to go and lie down for a bit," Vali said quietly, getting to his feet.

Icarus cast him a worried look. "Are you sure?"

"Yeah. I'm just tired."

"Okay… well, you know where I am if you need me?"

Vali smiled and nodded, walking back to his room quietly. He hoped that Boudicca hadn't been told about what had happened. She cared and treated Vali like a son, there wasn't a doubt in his mind that she'd come to make sure he was okay if she knew, but right now… he just wanted to be by himself.

It was too much trying to force himself to be happy by watching comedy when he didn't feel happy on the inside… it was… it wasn't fair. To anyone, to him, to other people trying to make him feel better… to Heimdallr…

Vali paused as he finally found himself standing in front of the broken chest. His once well kept and neat things were now strewn across in a crumpled heap. The others had tried to pack it away when he'd been in his wolf form, but he'd growled at them the moment they'd tried to touch his stuff. His… stuff.

Heimdallr had only been holding onto his stuff for thousands of years and he'd been trying to find the right time to give them back to Vali. Perhaps… because Vali had spoken to him, Heimdallr had thought that the items wouldn't hurt him as much to see. maybe he'd made the mistake of thinking Vali was okay.

He'd looked after his stuff, kept it safe and neat, all for Vali to yell and fling it across the room… his stuff…

Vali felt his lip wobble, a soft whine escaped him and he tried desperately to keep the tears in until the weight became too much and streamed down his face. He hadn't cried about what had happened to him in years, always burying it under the surface, letting it come out in a rage as the wolf. It was one of the few times he felt close to his father again.

Eventually, he cried himself to sleep, still on the floor of his room and missing out on dinner. By the time he woke up, it was the next day and breakfast was being served. No one, thankfully, asked any questions. Even Anansi didn't ask, though Vali knew that the spider god was filled with curiosity.

Weeks went by, things went back to normal, Vali tidied away his old things and put them neatly on his shelves, his clothes he slipped under his bed and the pin he hid under a floorboard. He didn't want to look at that, not now and probably not ever, but he couldn't bring himself to destroy it either.

Vali had gone out that day by himself, trying to build up the confidence to buy some rune stones. Medea had gently tried to encourage him to try out his magic a bit more. He was still unsure of it, but... well, runes would be the first step.

What he wasn't expecting was being stopped by Skadi. She had a large chest in hand, glaring at him, the grip on his shoulder was painful. Vali wanted to back away but she was stopping him.

It was safe to say, he was nervous. If there was a god or goddess who hated Loki more than Heimdallr, it was most likely Skadi. She'd once found him funny, all the Norse pantheon, bar Heimdallr, had. Then he killed Baldur and insulted all of them, Skadi included, insinuating that... they had shared a night in her bed together. Vali was very surprised that Skadi hadn't put an arrow through his father's head the moment those words left his mouth, she had more restraint than he gave her credit for.

Now that he was alone in the streets of Atlantis, where very little would care if she suddenly murdered him, Vali desperately wanted to run away and get as far as possible from the goddess. What did she even want with him?

"Did you get your things?" Skadi asked.

That... had not been what he was expecting.

"I did..." he said slowly. "Heimdallr brought them for me."

"Good. He didn't know if he'd be able to get time away to give them to you," she let him go and shifted the box under her hand.

Vali sniffed the air and paused, staring at the box a moment in confusion. "Is that… *chocolate?"*

"Fudge," Skadi explained. "My- I *mean,* Heimdallr requested it, along with the other few hundred things he requested," She shuffled around for a moment before showing a list to Vali.

He squinted at it, reading between the lines that were crossing out various objects and the longer he stood there the more the frown increased. What in the world was he looking at? A shopping list? It was bizarre.

"These are all things from Midgard," he stated and Skadi nodded.

"I'm aware."

"Why does…?"

"Heimdallr enjoys collecting things from Midgard due to them being his descendants and because he doesn't tend to move from one place often," Skadi huffed. "He's a bit of a hoarder."

"Okay… and the fudge?"

"He requested the sweetest thing I could find," Skadi pulled the list back with a scowl. "And that stuff was so sickeningly sweet I nearly threw up in my mouth and could feel my teeth rotting at a mere bite. It's perfect," she folded the list up as best as she could, sticking it in her pocket as she muttered. "The god sweetens his *mead* for Norn's sake, it makes me wonder about the gold teeth being natural or not."

Vali blinked. He'd forgotten about that particular aspect of Heimdallr's… *unusual* character. The many times he'd peeked a glance at the watchman when he'd been at the watch, taking the horn that was ever present on his hip and worked as an alarm bell, instead using it as a drinking horn of honey-sweetened mead. Honestly, Vali couldn't work out how he got the mead to not leak out of the horn.

"Right… and umm… the Giraffe?" Vali asked, only to be met with a scowl from Skadi.

"He is not getting one of those. He keeps asking for one because he thinks it would make a good mount. I keep telling him no," she huffed. "They aren't meant for cold temperatures."

Vali rubbed the back of his neck. "Well… maybe you could get him a cuddly one?"

Skadi gave him a scathing look. "Please do not add or encourage this madness…" then she paused and seemed to think it over. "Though, it may work to stop him asking for a real one."

"Yeah um, Lady Skadi… do you think you could… ask Heimdallr to come down here… and see me?" Vali said awkwardly. "I'd like to talk to him."

Skadi narrowed her eyes at him a moment and he panicked that she was going to smack him or kill him. He wouldn't put it past her, Skadi had no qualms about killing anyone that vaguely irritated her. They called her grim Skadi, Vali idly wondered if it was really due to her dower expression or because she was giving the Grim Reaper a run for his money in his job. Skadi had a hit list a mile long.

"I'll ask him but it might take a while," she eventually said, turning on her heel and leaving.

Vali let out a breath he didn't realise he'd been holding. All things considered that could've gone worse.

The weeks passed and finally, Heimdallr returned. This time he was sporting an ice pick with a chain that was attached to his belt. It was new and Vali had questions, but he didn't ask. Right now wasn't the time. Also… Heimdallr had clearly stopped off at a sweetshop in Atlantis because he was also helping himself to a packet of sugary gummy world serpents.

Vali took a step towards him, holding a box in hand and then held it out to Heimdallr.

"I wanted to say… thanks for looking after my stuff and apologies for… um… snapping like I did and-."

He trailed off as Heimdallr held his hand up and shook his head.

"I should apologise to you. You're right. I was supposed to protect you and I failed. For that, I'm sorry."

"It… look just take this, will you," Vali held the box out again. "I'm not gonna tell you it's okay because it isn't, but… I know you weren't the one completely responsible for what happened."

Heimdallr nodded and took the box from him, opening and pulling out the object from Midgard. The moment Vali had seen it, he knew he had to get it for Heimdallr.

Heimdallr pulled out the Rubik's cube, tilting it from side to side, seeming to be fascinated by the multi colours.

"It's… the Bifrost as a cube?"

"It's called a Rubik's cube and it reminded me of you," Vali explained. "It's complicated and confusing and ya' know…" he gestured to it. "Rainbows…"

"I see…" Heimdallr slowly lowered it and tilted his head to Vali. "Do people of Midgard enjoy the Bifrost that much? I know the rainbow has become quite popular recently."

Vali frowned slightly. "Not for the reasons you're thinking of, but this is a puzzle, look," he gently took the cube and moved the colours around watching Heimdallr's own rainbow eyes light up in fascination. "And then you have to put them back. into place to complete all the sides."

"Fascinating…" Heimdallr reached for it and turned it over in his hands. "I'll put it with the rest of my rainbow items…"

Vali blinked rapidly. "You have *more?*"

"Of course..." Heimdallr trailed off, looking to the side and almost smiled. "Skadi recently came back with a *rainbow giraffe. I* wanted a real one, but I couldn't say no to the cuddly rainbow one... I now have a petting zoo of soft cuddly toys. They may not be the real creatures themselves, but it's close enough. I can proudly say I'm the *only* Norse god to have a *jaguar* in his hall."

Vali didn't know what to say to that, so he just gave a slow nod, acting like he did understand, but really... Vali was starting to learn a lot more about Heimdallr than he had. He'd always been this... constant figure, guarding the entrance to Asgard, but that was about it. Heimdallr had been nice to him and his brother, but it always felt like there was this cold distance between Heimdallr and... well *everyone.*

Now Vali was learning that Heimdallr was a collector of things from Midgard, had a sense of humour and enjoyed more than just sweetened mead... he liked, sweetened everything.

Heimdallr looked up at the sky with a small scowl. "I have to return to my post. Thor is losing his patience."

"You let... *Thor* take your place?" Vali said slowly.

"Not by choice. He was all that was available. Actually, I tell a lie, Bragi was there... anyway." Heimdallr reached to the back of his belt and pulled out a phone. "What is your number? I shall stay in contact and if you need anything you can contact me."

"Oh!" Vali felt his eyes widen in surprise. "You really don't need-."

"Vali," Heimdallr interrupted him sternly, giving him a hard look. "I *need* to do this. You are still three quarters Æsier... my job is to protect the Æsier and. I already failed once. *So please,* your number."

Vali blinked and hesitantly reached for his broken and cracked phone, sharing his number with Heimdallr and when he sent a text back to Vali he saved it into his phone. This still felt weird, even more so for Aethalides, Icarus and anyone else who had once been mortal, because nowadays they had a few gods on their phones that they could text or speed dial. It was very surreal.

"Good," Heimdallr put his phone away after that, the phone case, Vali noticed, featured nine waves all a different colour. Rainbow waves.

"I… feel like I should teach you what the rainbow means in some circles…" Vali mumbled and Heimdallr raised an eyebrow at him.

"I know what it means. I know what they *all* mean," Heimdallr explained, raising a finger to make a point. "I have a poster. I am what the children of Midgard would say; *with* it."

Vali stared. "No one says that…"

"They do not?"

"No…"

Heimdallr looked dumbfounded like his entire world suddenly got flipped upside down. "Huh…" he mumbled to himself. "Interesting."

Thunder and lightning suddenly shot across the sky, Vali flinched away, but Heimdallr only watched the display with an unimpressed flat look. So his normal face. He wasn't affected by it at all.

"I really do need to go now. Thor's throwing a tantrum," he placed a hand on his chest and bowed to Vali. "Until next time, Vali Sigynson."

Vali gave an awkward wave as Heimdallr left, he was caught off guard by the name change. Sigynson… as in Sigyn, his mother…

He smiled, pocketing his phone and turning to head back to the Archives.

Sigynson… he liked that better.

It's a Secret: 9

Aethalides leaned back in his seat, hidden away in his office as he nursed a small drink. He was taking a break from searching today, why his father had him do this... ugh, it was starting to become a pain, especially when he was instructed to keep it as undercover as possible. It was almost like his father forgot that Aethalides was related to him, the literal god of thieves.

Still, peace and quiet were in short supply these days and Aethalides took it when he could, right now he was just enjoying a little moment to himself, away from everyone else. Some might say he was anti-social, he would just say he needed some me time so he didn't get put in prison for a lifetime.

Of course, his small moments of peace never lasted long, not when you lived in a three-story building with several different individuals from different cultures and time periods who got along for the most part but not always.

The knock at the door, hesitant and nervous in nature, had Aethalides peeling his eyes open and scowling at it. He'd gotten very good over the years of telling the difference between knocks and knew instantly who this was.

"Icarus, I swear if you've to tell me that Asterion has used you to make *another* wall extension.." He growled out, but the door opened and Icarus poked his head in.

He wasn't covered in brick or plaster debris so he had to assume he hadn't been used as a human battering ram.

"Umm... hi... Aethalides... *really* hate to bother you..."

Icarus looked behind him and then back at Aethalides. He was clearly terrified, not uncommon for Icarus, but uncommon for it to be happening in the Archives.

"What is it?"

"Rune is... here."

Aethalides grimaced slightly, pinching the bridge of his nose and muttering some choice words under his breath in Greek.

"I swear... I have had it up to *here,*" he lifted his hand and vaguely gestured in the air. "With the Norse pantheon or *anyone* Norse pantheon adjacent..."

"Tell me about it, I ran into Loki and he broke my finger," Icarus muttered and Aethalides suddenly sat up straighter, staring at him.

"You... met Loki?"

"Yeah."

"And you only got your finger broken?"

"Yeah, he- wait. What do you mean *'only'?*" Icarus gaped at him. "It felt freaking painful and very significant! I couldn't draw or invent for weeks! Not properly at least."

"It's *Loki,*" Aethalides replied, picking up his drink and swirling it around in the glass. "The god doesn't know the difference between *slapstick* and *death*. He finds both equally as funny, so I'm just saying, you're very lucky."

That sentence was almost funny in itself. Icarus? Lucky? Never did Aethalides think he'd ever use that to describe the boy who was too stupid and flew to the sun.

Sure, they all had their shortcomings and they'd all been messed up by gods in some way or another, but Icarus? He was really the architect of his own demise... or maybe his father was? Daedalus was not always known as the sanest individual in the block... Aethalides could relate.

160

"Well, you might as well let Rune up…" Aethalides paused and looked up at Icarus warily. "Does he have the gorilla with him?"

"The big dude?"

"Yes, Icarus, the 'big dude'."

"Yep."

He growled and pressed the heels of his hands into his eyes, muttering under his breath again, kicking his legs. He looked like a toddler having a temper tantrum. He felt like a toddler having a temper tantrum but he didn't care. Not right now.

He hated it when Rune brought that walking wall with him.

"Fine," he spat. "Get them both."

Icarus nodded and quickly vanished, giving Aethalides time to get his office ready. He wasn't scared of dying, though his quick movements of slipping his knives in easy reach under his desk in the holders, before laying his herald's staff, a gift from his father, by his desk in reach, would say differently. It was more that death was just an inconvenience for him and he was too busy to die at the age of ten… this time around. Starting from scratch was always a pain too and he was rather enjoying this go around.

Aethalides downed the rest of his drink, waiting patiently for the knock at the door to come again and then Icarus poked his head in.

"You ready?"

"Yeah…if I must."

Icarus sniggered quietly and then opened the door properly letting Rune and his walking wall inside.

Rune was the leader of the Hel Raiders, a light elf from Alfheim, who got tired of living the stereotypical 'pure and good lives' that the rest of his kind lived. Even ditching their traditional dress for a steampunk-inspired suit, decorated with Nordic

161

patterns around the sleeves and on the shoulder was a crest of a golden boar and the rune nauthiz going through the middle of it. It looked like someone had drawn a lowercase'' with the line that went across going down diagonally.

Like all light elves, Rune was exceptionally pale, near pure white, like his skin was glowing. Silver hair fell around his shoulders and down his back, with piercing silver eyes that had white glowing pupils. Right in the centre of his chest was a glow that faded and increased to a beat.

He looked like a steampunk gentleman and horse rider, with his boots, waistcoat and long overcoat with tales. A gentleman, however, Rune was certainly not, at least not the real Rune that he kept safely under wraps until the time was right.

Behind him, dressed equally as smart, but except for the overcoat and he had his sleeves rolled up, came Viggo. The Jötun was Rune's right hand man and he barely fit in Aethalides's office. Glaring irritably at Aethalides, like it was his personal fault that the room was too small for the giant. Aethalides wished he could say he cared, but he didn't.

Viggo had a huge scar going down the side of his face, his pale skin looked tanned compared to Rune and his dark hair was braided off to the side.

"Aethalides, it's good to see you," Rune said with a smile, taking a seat at the one on the opposite side of Aethalides's desk. Mostly it would be Medea sitting in that one, the only other person who was allowed into Aethalides's office without his permission. "But do you really have to have your office on the third floor?"

"I like the quiet," Aethalides replied simply, looking to Icarus and nodding.

Icarus nodded back, leaving the room and closing the door.

Aethalides knew it was probably a bad idea to lock himself away with Rune of all people, especially with Viggo, but he was taking his chance by doing this. He wouldn't be threatened in his own home.

"What do you want, Rune?" He asked.

Rune smiled. "Direct and to the point. That's what I always like about you, Aethalides, you don't mess around with pleasantries. Though I'll admit I didn't come here for my own needs, I came here about yours."

"How unlike you," Aethalides drawled.

"I know, but I feel like our relationship has moved past simple business at this point," he folded his hands on Aethalides's desk and smiled pleasantly. "Why, it's a friendship, wouldn't you say."

"You are not my friend."

"How hurtful. Especially when I came all this way because I was worried you'd lost something," Rune mock pouted at him and Aethalides felt his blood run cold. "I mean, you *have* lost something, haven't you Aethalides? That's why you've been going from cost to cost, near enough, looking for it."

Aethalides grit his teeth, glancing up at Viggo who has that smug smirk on his face. Gods he really wanted to smack it off his ugly face, Rune was at least pretty to look at, even if he couldn't stand the man. At least, that's what he kept telling himself. Deep down, Aethalides knew that he would actually be friends with Rune in his past lives, Hades, maybe even now, if it wasn't for the glaring obvious fact that Rune would never lower himself to have friends.

"I think... you need better sources," Aethalides replied carefully, folding his hands on his desk, and smiling pleasantly at him, just mimicking Rune's movements that made the light elf's eyebrow twitch ever so slightly. "I've not lost anything."

"But someone has lost something and it would need to be very important to get the Archives involved and not the guard," Rune examined his nails a moment with a smirk. "We all know that the guard can be bought after all. How much do you even have saved away to cover all your costs in damages and so on?"

"Well, you of all people should know, you can never have *too much* money."

"Start talking, brat!" Viggo snarled, slamming his hands on the desk, not as hard as he could because Aethalides's desk was left standing. "We aren't here to play games! You're looking for something and we want to know, what it is!"

"Viggo, the adults are talking," Aethalides replied, pointing at him. "And be very careful with my things, young man."

Viggo looked like he wanted to smash Aethalides into the floor with one hit, but Rune held his hand up and the Jötun immediately settled down. That was a scary amount of power that Aethalides had to respect, albeit begrudgingly.

"Why don't you wait outside, hmm?" Rune spoke, pulling out a cigarette case from his inside coat pocket. "This is merely a conversation between friends," his silver eyes fell on Aethalides again and he smiled all teeth at him.

Viggo grumbled but did as he was told, getting up and leaving. Aethalides would love to know what kind of power Rune held over Viggo to have such loyalty in the Jötun. It was impressive, especially when he could get the guy to calm down with his anger at a mere hand raise.

"Aethalides, I really am just here out of concern," Rune went on, pulling out a cigarette and offering it to him. "It's odd to see you so… unsettled."

"I'd believe you if I didn't know you," Aethalides replied,

taking the cigarette and lighting it instantly. He needed this right now.

Curse the prohibition for getting him hooked on these things, he really wished he could stop, but no one said quitting was easy. It wasn't and Aethalides, when it came to his vices, was not the strongest of wills.

"Hm. Clearly, you don't know me *too* well," Rune smiled ruefully, placing his case away. "Now, what are you really doing?"

Aethalides blinked and then felt a constricting force around his neck, his tongue felt like it didn't belong to him any more and as much as he tried to keep his mouth closed, it was like someone was yanking his jaw open.

"I... my father has requested I look for a Mesopotamian oracle..." he found himself saying against his will, eyes wide and panicked, mouth still moving without his consent. "Lord Apollo foresaw one coming back into existence."

"A Mesopotamian oracle?" Rune looked very intrigued, leaning forward on the desk, eyes sparking with light. "There hasn't been one of those in centuries. I thought they were extinct?"

"They are," Aethalides growled out, his hand clenching and unclenching on the desk, finally taking a glance at the cigaret he still had in hand. There it was, shouldn't have been that surprising, but drawn neatly on the underside of the cigaret was the rune Ansuz, looking like the love child of a capital 'F' and a stick fur tree. Ansuz the rune of truth.

He'd briefly forgotten Rune's skill in... well, runic magic. Probably all those cigarettes were secretly laced with drawn-on runes. More reliable than potions and poisons some would say.

"Interesting," Rune hummed, getting to his feet, and slowly

pacing the floor, hands clasped behind his back. "And if I recall from what I've heard... Mesopotamian oracles are quite powerful, yes? Not just gifted in the art of seeing the future but also gifted healers. Now that is an individual I could have a use for."

"Except Mesopotamian oracles are peaceful," Aethalides bit out, allowing himself a small crooked smile. "They'd never join you."

"Yes, which is probably why they all got killed. Oracles, they get such bad wraps," Rune sighed. "It's not their fault though, they're just the messenger, they don't control fate itself, but... they could prove to be an early warning system," he smirked at Aethalides. "Oh, the things I could prepare for and get done with a little bit of knowledge ahead of time."

Aethalides glanced at his staff. If he could just get his arms to move and reach it, Rune's hold over him would vanish. It didn't seem that far away until now.

"Fate isn't kind to those who try to avoid it," he snarled at him and Rune raised an eyebrow in question. "You've surely heard the stories."

"Well, you should also know that we Norse are always trying to avoid our ill fates."

Aethalides did know and despite all his best efforts, Odin was still getting eaten by Loki's monstrous son, Fenrir, the giant wolf. You couldn't avoid your fate, no matter how hard you tried to prepare for it, it would always have its way.

"So, where is this oracle?" Rune asked, still pacing back and forth, while Aethalides desperately tried reaching for his staff.

"I don't know."

"But you have some idea."

"My father... gave me a few places they could be,"

Aethalides groaned out between clenched teeth. "I've been searching."

Rune smiled at him. "And where are those places?"

"Various… locations in Atlantis. Skadi's Rest… Forest of Stories… Land of Apothis, Sea of Nine Mothers…" his fingertips brushed his staff and ground his teeth together so tightly he thought he might actually break them. "Mixcoatls' Edge- *ah!*"

Aethalides snatched his staff up finally, the spell breaking instantly as a golden glow encompassed him. He instantly climbed onto his desk, taking one of his blades with him, taking a fighting stance as he towered over Rune.

Annoyingly the light elf didn't look phased, he just looked amused.

"Oh dear. Whatever will I do against an *old man?*" He teased with a smirk. "Still, I do forget how powerful Olympian magic is…oh well. It was fun while it lasted. So nice to have you speaking truthfully to me for once."

"Get out before I take your head!" Aethalides snarled.

"Ah, ah, ah," Rune wagged his finger at him with a smirk. "You welcomed us in, *remember?* You are bound by the rules of hospitality, Aethalides," he gave him a pitying look. "Don't you know your own culture?"

Aethalides cursed at him in Greek, not something that Rune would understand, but the message was clear.

Still, the light elf didn't react irritated, he just laughed, pocketing his hands with a shrug.

"Don't be like that. You and I both know you get bored easily, now it's a race to the finish," he smirked, leaning towards Aethalides and beckoning him with a finger. "And don't you worry," Rune whispered to him. "I won't let anyone else know what it is we're both looking for. It'll be our *little secret."*

"Get out."

"But of course!" Rune bowed, turning on his heel and leaving the room, the steps of Viggo coming up behind the elf reached Aethalides's ears and he walked to his door to watch them start walking down the steps.

Icarus was just coming up and he looked over at Aethalides worried, he could probably see the sweat running down his face and the fact he was panting like he'd just run a mile probably wasn't helping convey a look of 'I am *completely* fine, don't worry!'.

"Aethalides?" He asked hesitantly.

He glanced at Icarus, walking past him to stand on the third floor balcony at the front of the Archives, watching Rune leave. It was like the elf just knew how to get under his skin because he turned to look at Aethalides and waved with a smile.

Aethalides's grip tightened on his knife and staff. He was *very* tempted to embed the knife into Rune's chest, but was able to,Icarus joined him, watching Rune leave and gave a shudder.

"Ugh, I hate that guy," the kid grumbled.

"He's not exactly my favourite person either," Aethalides mumbled.

Icarus looked at him expectantly. "What did he want?"

"What Rune always wants, power and trouble," he muttered, looking at Icarus. "But do you want to know what *I* want? A *vacation!"* Aethalides broke out his thousand watt grin that had Icarus shuffling back nervously. "What do you think of a winter break at Skadi's Rest? I think it's a great idea, go and tell everyone Icarus! Make like a herald and run!"

He shoved Icarus back inside and the kid darted off, looking a little startled, but still, it seemed the idea of a ski trip was enough to curve his curiosity over Rune. At least for now.

Slowly he cast a look down at his staff that was in hand, feeling the power flowing through it that gently brushed against his fingertips. His father's power, a gift that he'd bestowed on him, despite the two never meeting. He remembered it clear as day, of course, he remembered everything.

He remembered how when Hermes appeared before him for the first time he looked like a god, dressed in royalty, a golden glow surrounding him. His very presence lit up the entire room that Aethalides had been in, conveniently while no one else was around.

"You've done very well for yourself, my son," Hermes had spoke and Aethalides had stared at him in wonder. It was the first time he'd seen his father and if his mother's stories were anything to go by, he hadn't aged at all.

Aethalides had been dressed in fine clothes himself, as a Lord, but compared to his father he looked like a peasant.

Quickly he'd fallen to his knees, head bowed arms raised up in respect as he greeted him. So different to how he greeted his father these days. Sometimes he didn't even bother to stop working, letting him take the seat opposite him and proceed to rest his feet on his desk.

His father had just laughed when he performed the act of great respect and it sounded so carefree. Like no human or mortal laugh, he'd heard. Spoke of someone who didn't know hardship, not like mortals did.

"None of that," Hermes had said, pulling him to his feet. "You and I are family. You're my son, I do not expect you to grovel."

"I- I er, sorry my lord- father- my lord father?"

Hermes rolled his eyes, ruffling his hair. "Just father will do. Only people I don't care about refer to me as lord."

"Okay lor- I mean, father!" Aethalides cursed himself in his head for making such a fool of himself. In front of his father no less. "I... might I be so bold and ask why you're here?"

"Ah!" Hermes beamed, placing a hand on his shoulder. "I heard someone was going on a trip! A dangerous one too, you'll be the messenger is what I've also heard. Don't worry about it," he waved away his son's questioning gaze. "I find these things out all the time, but I figured you'd need a little something to help you get by..."

With a snap of his fingers, a caduceus like his father's appeared in his hand, except instead of snakes it was ribbons wrapped around the staff.

"That shall protect you from any harm, should you carry it with you of course," his father twirled his own staff around. "No snakes I'm afraid, they're a divine exclusive!"

"T-thank you, father!" Aethalides had stared at his gift in wonder. It was beautiful, it looked hand-crafted and it hummed with power. It seemed to have its own glow to it, much like his father's glow that seemed to follow him wherever he went.

Hermes smiled, pulling his son close to him and laying a gentle kiss on his forehead. "May you be safe and good fortune find you, my son. May the fates be kind."

He looked back at the window and sighed before the huge smile fell across his face again. He clapped his hands together and grinned at him, he almost looked like he was planning something. Considering his father's reputation... it wouldn't surprise him.

"Well, I must be off! Immortals are the most impatient lot you'll ever find, ironic when you consider that they live forever," he turned on his heel, the wings at his heels fluttering in anticipation of flying. "No, they want it now, now, now! Ugh, they are a bunch of impatient- ah! Can't say that word in front of the child!"

"Wait, father, please I have so many questions!"

"Of course you do, I'd call you a liar if you didn't."

"Will you answer them for me? Please, I... I've never been able to speak with you!"

Hermes placed a hand on his shoulder and squeezed it gently. "Another time, my son. I'm afraid I must be off! Got places to go, people to see... you know how it is."

"But-."

"I'm sure you will enjoy your adventure!"

"I will, but-."

"Must go!" Hermes grinned running to the window. "Goodnight!"

Then he was gone. Just like that.

The staff was the only thing left behind that gave any sort of indication that he'd been there at all.

Aethalides of course had taken it with him, determined to protect himself and it never hurt to have his father's power close at hand. There were, of course, occasions where he wondered if not being related to Hermes would make his life simpler; he'd probably be free of this life if he'd been simply a son of a mortal or a different god.

There were moments, and occasions where he resented his father for his life, for being the reason he was still here and why he would never find peace, at least not in the near future. Who knew what the fates had in store for him, surely they wouldn't be too cruel? He could only pray.

So yes, there were moments when he resented his father, when he hated him, when he wished he had nothing to do with him, but... well, even he couldn't deny that his father helped him more times than hindered him. This time was no different. If it hadn't been for the staff, who knew what else Rune could've squeezed out of him with the use of runic magic. Damn, cheater. No wonder his father favoured him.

Aethalides took one last look at Rune who was meeting with the rest of his gang of miscreants.

The Hel Raiders were notorious and people feared them, even the guards didn't tend to mess with them, giving Rune and his cronies a wide berth. It meant they got away with murder and he unfortunately meant that quite literally.

Modern-day gangsters had nothing on Rune and his near-perfect planning, trying to beat him to the oracle wasn't going to be easy, but what kind of child of Hermes would Aethalides be if he didn't enjoy a challenge?

"A race huh?" He muttered under his breath, spinning the blade around in his hand until he saw his face reflected in the blade and smirked. *"Game on,* Rune."

Skadi's Rest: 10

"Skadi's Rest! A place to relax and enjoy the ever-present slopes perfect for skiing and snowboarding. A land filled with hidden hot springs!" Aethalides slid the door to the camper van open and jumped into the snow, placing his hands on his hips, the grin plastered on his face. "It's a *perfect* vacation spot!"

Medea climbed out of the van, tightening her fur-lined coat around herself; it wasn't a coat designed for any quests, not nearly for the cut but for the fact that it was black with red manticore fur lining around the edges, complete with a matching hat.

She looked around the mostly cobble streets, Jötuns were the most common race in this place since Skadi had it built for any who were more peaceful to find a home, far away from the constant warring between the Æsier and other Jötuns respectfully. They'd been here for thousands of years, gradually other races began to live here too, not to mention there was a daughter of Artemis stationed here.

Skadi herself even had a vacation home off in the woods away from everyone but close enough she could make it to town easily. Funnily enough, there were rumours amongst the gods that Heimdallr would also frequent the place, but her grandfather, Helios the titan god of the sun, said that it was probably just idle gossip.

Skadi's Rest wasn't all snowy resorts and hot chocolate, there was the dreaded plane at the very tip of this part of Atlantis that was nothing but a barren wasteland with no cover from the weather. It had been graciously named Itztlacoliuhqui's Plane, named after the long-dead Aztec god. Of all the spirits or gods of winter, he in particular was a nasty piece of work who would purposely turn people into ice sculptures. Plenty of people, Jötuns too, would venture up there and come hastily back. It wasn't a place for the faint of heart, nothing but a barren wasteland as far as the eye could see.

As for Itztlacoliuhqui, Medea knew she probably shouldn't think it, but from her point of view, she happily thought good riddance to that particular god. They were already mighty and powerful beings, they didn't need to mindlessly kill just to keep proving a point, or in his case, to settle that never-ending bitterness.

"Yes, darling, it's lovely…" Medea mumbled, biting her lip when another cold gust of air blew past. "But we had better not be camping."

"We're not!" Aethalides grinned, then pointed in the direction of the biggest building in the place, looking like a cross between a cabin and a Greek temple. "We're staying in Khion's Resort."

Icarus poked his head out of the van as Boudicca and Vali climbed out. Asterion was already at the back grabbing their bags and Xbalanque was peeking out of the van, staring at the snow like it was personally going to bite him.

Icarus looked over at the resort with a slight frown, scratching at his head. "I never get the names of some of the things around this place… or like Atlantis in general. I mean," he gestured to the resort, tilting his head. "Does the Greek goddess of snow actually own a ski resort or is it named after her?"

"Ah, well, my dad said it was a bit of both," Aethalides

explained. "It's more that they get power or worship whenever people use these things and they're kinda attached to it in a way. Though usually in the old days, as I remember, the gods themselves actually ran the places until they became popular and they got workers. You know, like corporate companies tend to do once their brand gets big?"

Icarus blinked several times, rubbing at his eyes and then gestured wildly at Aethalides. "You knew that the *whole* time!?"

"Yeah…?"

"I've asked that question before! Why didn't you say anything?"

Aethalides stared at him and then shrugged. "I just couldn't be bothered before."

"Couldn't be bothered-?"

"Icarus," Vali laughed, taking his hand and pulling him out of the van. "Ignore him. You know what he's like."

Icarus shivered, pulling at the, quite frankly, *tacky* white and gold winter coat. Looking Vali up and down for a moment. The child hadn't changed his coat from the usual one he wore; he just had a polar neck underneath and snow boots for grip. Everything else about his clothing hadn't changed.

"How are you not freezing?" Icarus growled out, throwing a hand at Boudicca. "The other Nordic person here isn't wearing an autumn coat!"

"I'm from England," Boudicca frowned at him. "It gets cold, but not this cold."

"And to be fair to Vali, he is a quarter Jötun," Aethalides piped up, coming round to take his bag from Asterion.

Vali shrugged, a twitch of a smile coming to his lips. "Cold never bothered me anyway."

"All right Elsa, please don't break out into song now,"

Medea rolled her eyes, then looked to Xbalanque who was still staring at the snow-covered ground like it was going to swallow him. "Xbalanque, Cipactli isn't here. The ground won't eat you."

Xbalanque threw her an irritated look, then hesitantly placed his foot on the ground, still gripping the side of the van like a lifeline. Very slowly he began to put weight on it and climbed out of the van, standing to his full height, still with a knuckled grip on the van. He waited a few moments, getting his bearings and let go of the van slowly.

The group watched as he stood up straight, raising his hands in the air as to say, 'hey mum, look at me, no hands!' And a grin started to form across his face as he nodded to himself.

"Yep, fine, I'm fine," he said and it was unclear if he was saying it to himself or to them. "Completely fine."

"Hey, completely fine," Asterion grunted, holding out Xbalanque's bag. "You want to take this?"

"Yes, because I am completely *fiiiine!*" The way Xbalanque's voice shot up an octave as he slipped and grabbed hold of the van again, his feet still sliding out from under him before coming to a stop. Setting him at a slight ninety-degree angle.

He stayed quiet for a moment, eyes wide and the only part of him that moved and looked around rapidly. It even looked like he'd stopped breathing.

"No longer completely fine!" He squeaked.

Aethalides rubbed at his eyes, while Medea openly laughed at him and the rest looked a mixture of confused and bewildered.

"Vali, help him, would you?" Aethalides asked as the boy shrugged his bag onto his back, walking to Xbalanque. "Let's get the police officer off the ice. Man, how are you going to cope when it gets cold in England?"

"Well, like Boudicca said," Xbalanque grumbled as Vali helped him to stand up straight and took his arm to help with his balance. "It doesn't get cold like this in that country."

Boudicca stared at him with an openly flat look. "We still get ice," she stated before turning and marching away.

Xbalanque stared after her for a moment with an expectant look, but she didn't say anything further than that, making her way to the front of the resort.

The Mayan hero looked to Vali who offered a little smile of encouragement. "I may have made a grave mistake."

"You'll get the hang of it," Vali encouraged. "It's just one foot in front of the other."

"Easy for you to say, it's like walking on glass!"

"Jötunheim is worse."

Medea rolled her eyes, turning to follow Aethalides up to the resort, the rest following behind them.

Inside the resort was beautiful, somehow mixing rustic wood cabin with ancient Greek design, giving that feeling of a winter get away with a Hellenistic touch. Fur carpets, frescos painted the walls showing off Khion, Oreithyia and Boreas, a beautiful marble fireplace and a few dark blue draperies were added for decoration. And of course, no monument to Boreas would be complete without a few depictions of horses.

The staff were dressed in clothes that looked a cross between Ancient Greek and modern resort uniforms. The colours were a pale blue with white accents, with the managers being decorated in purple with gold accents.

Aethalides was already checking them into their rooms, the front desk was run by a winter nymph. Her pale white hair was pulled in pretty braids away from her equally as bale features, eyes a shining, sparkling blue, with a delicate layer of frost over her features. She smiled at them, the classic superficial front desk smile that didn't quite reach her eyes.

"Good morning, welcome to the Khion resort, how may I help you," the nymph spoke up and Aethalides flashed his charming smile. A gift that all children of Hermes had apparently. She'd believe it. She'd seen Hermes use the exact same smile that had gotten him all sorts and the majority of his children got that smile too.

She looked behind herself to see the Mayan hero and banished Norse god making their way through the front door. Xbalanque finally let go of Vali, resting his hands on his knees and letting out a breath. He looked exceedingly grateful to be back on solid ground. She doubted he'd be leaving the resort at all.

Vali on the other hand looked exceptionally happy, he was nearly bouncing on his tip toes. She was pretty certain that if he was in his wolf form, he'd be wagging his tail.

"All right, gather round children," Aethalides spoke up which earned multiple scowls from the adults as he handed out their keys. "Medea and Boudicca you're together, Vali, Icarus you're also sharing a room across from the ladies, per Boudicca's request. Which means... Asterion, Xbalanque and I are bunking together," he flashed his megawatt grin. "So, this is going to be great! Still, shame Arachne didn't want to come."

Xbalanque glanced out at the window. "I can understand. I struggle enough with *two* legs, she's got *eight.*"

"And bare feet," Medea added, taking her bag from Asterion.

"That too."

"Still, it's a shame. Think how cool her weaving would look," Aethalides muttered, then he flashed a smile at Vali who

178

seemed to be bursting with a need to ask a question. "And yes, Vali, you can rent skis."

"Yes!" Vali whooped and even jumped around, letting out an excited bark. "I want to ski!" He suddenly remembered he had company and abruptly stopped, curling in on himself again, offering a shy smile. "Sorry... got a little... carried away there..."

Medea was honestly surprised, it was the most animated she'd ever seen the boy, ever. In the hundreds to thousands of years she'd known him, Vali had never been this... *expressive.* Maybe the cold mountain air was good for him.

They made their way to their respective rooms, Aethalides was muttering something about going exploring, Vali had spoken to Icarus about teaching him skiing and Xbalanque seemed to be making an exit strategy that would allow him to get to the van without slipping. Boudicca and Asterion seemed to be making plans to visit the town and have a look around. They hadn't ever visited Skadi's Rest, at least not with the mind to actually enjoy it.

Medea found herself on the balcony of her room after unpacking, sipping at a hot chocolate. She poked her head over the railing occasionally whenever she heard something interesting going on, and found it very strange to see Aethalides leaving by himself. Yes, he said he was going out to explore, but completely by himself and this early on? Well, she knew him well enough to know something was going on, but for now she would enjoy her hot chocolate.

Xbalanque came to take a seat with her, his own cup of hot chocolate in hand, wrapped up in furs and blankets looking very irritated by the cold temperature.

"Weather not to your liking?" Medea asked with an amused

smile.

He glared at her, then looked about Skadi's Rest. "Who in their right mind would like to live here?"

"I believe the Jotuns might find that offensive."

"I just mean..." he pinched the bridge of his nose. "It's honestly freezing cold here, you can see my breath!"

"It's not that bad."

"She's right," Vali suddenly appeared, smiling at them his cheeks were a little rosy but other than that he seemed fine and that's when she realised, she could actually *see* his cheeks.

Vali didn't have his hood up, he was wearing a ski jacket and a hat, showing his face off for the first time in... well, ever. He never left his room without that hood hiding his face. A pair of snow goggles rested above his head and a scarf was around his neck, ready to be pulled up at any moment when he needed to start skiing.

"Although," Vali continued. "I've heard the storms up here are wild."

They were both staring at him and Medea knew she shouldn't be, but it was just a shock to actually see Vali. Then there were the scars. There were so many and they were criss crossed over his face. The second noticeable thing was the deep eye bags and dark circles under his eyes. He was young, incredibly young and at the same time he looked like a weathered old man who wasn't getting enough rest.

She'd never seen him, no one had except for Aethalides. It was probably best not to say anything about it otherwise Vali might shrink back into his shell again. He'd been different since that Norse god had come around. A little more confident.

"Okay..." Icarus said as he slowly came onto the balcony. "I think I'm dressed right... Are you sure skiing is a good...

idea…?" He trailed off and openly stared at Vali, eyes wide, mouth falling slightly agape and a blush appeared on his face, though it would be easy to wave that off due to the cold. "Vali…?"

"You look great!" Vali beamed, smiling and that only seemed to make things worse for poor Icarus.

"You… I can see your face…" Icarus stated dumbly.

"Well, I can't go skiing in a hood easily," Vali explained, but quickly raised his hands in a reassuring manner. "Don't worry though, I can still hide my face!" He reached up and pulled his goggles down and then lifted the scarf up around his face. Pointing to his face. "See!"

Icarus blinked, laughing a little nervously and high pitched, the end going squeaky. "No, no, no… you don't need to hide your face at all…" he said, reaching forward and lifting up the goggles and pulling down the scarf. "Like, you don't need to hide it ever again! You look like a… a real Norse warrior!"

Vali frowned, tilting his head to the side looking like a lost puppy. "But I need to put them on when we ski?"

"Yeah, that's fine, but you don't need to do that now!" Icarus cried out, then he took his hand excitedly. "Skiing right? You can teach me to ski! Let's go skiing!"

He darted off, dragging a very confused Vali behind him, leaving Medea and Xbalanque to watch them go. Whilst she wasn't usually one for finding such… adorable awkwardness… *cute*, she would admit that it was sweet. Nice to see, even if Vali wasn't completely aware of what was going on.

"Does… Icarus know you have to go up a ski lift?" Xbalanque asked slowly and Medea shrugged.

"Probably not," Medea smirked. "Still, it would give him ample time to grip those strong Æsier, Jotun biceps."

Xbalanque threw her a completely blank look. "What are you talking about?"

Medea stared back at him for a very long time, taking a sip of her hot chocolate. She waited for several more moments but he still didn't seem to get it.

"Forget it," she sighed, leaning back and waving him away. "Now can you leave me? Mama wants some peace and quiet so she doesn't accidentally murder anyone. I'm going to enjoy this vacation."

Xbalanque didn't move. He continued to sit there, fingers pressed to his lips, thinking. It looked like he had his 'detective head' on. *Thinking* when he was on vacation so shouldn't be doing anything other than just *relaxing*. He looked unsure, a frown across his face and taking a hesitant glance at Medea.

"Don't you think it's weird," he started slowly, sitting back and resting his chin on his hand, "that Aethalides… *workaholic* Aethalides suggested this in the first place?"

Medea sighed, taking out her sunglasses and sliding them over her eyes. "The man is insane, Xbalanque, you do remember that, don't you? I've given up trying to work out how his mind works. Now shoo."

She heard him sigh and eventually leave her in peace. Medea stayed out on the balcony enjoying the peace and quiet for the entire day, ordering herself some room service and it was only in the afternoon when everyone started to come back and disturb her.

Apparently, they'd decided that it should be her and Boudicca's balcony where all the meetings would happen at the end of the day before they went out for a meal.

Lucky her.

The first to arrive back were Boudicca and Asterion, with

the minotaur looking very put out, slumping in a seat and letting out a snort.

"I hate this place." He grumbled and Boudicca sympathetically patted him on the shoulder.

"What happened?" Medea asked, taking off her sunglasses to observe the two properly.

They looked okay... was that blood splattered across Asterion's coat? Should probably get that cleaned before Xbalanque came back.

"Someone tried to ask Asterion if he could have his horns," Boudicca explained. "To put them on a helmet."

"As a *legitimate* 'Viking helmet'," Asterion did quotation marks with his fingers. "I *live* with a Viking god, I *know* they don't have horns on their helmets!"

"It was just a cheap tourist attraction," Boudicca agreed. "But they wouldn't leave us alone."

"Not even when I punched him in the face!"

"And broke his jaw."

"And his nose!"

"And I think an eye socket."

Asterion threw his hands up in annoyance. "Still didn't get the message!"

Medea sighed, pinching the bridge of her nose. "Some people are too dense," she looked over at the door when there was the sound of more feet, this time it was a bit of a commotion and she nearly dropped her sunglasses when Vali appeared in the doorway carrying Icarus.

The boy looked a mess, his hat and goggles askew with snow and ice melting off his coat and onto the floor. That and he looked very shell shocked, which didn't get better after Vali tried to fit him in through the door and only succeeded in smacking his head.

"Ow!"

"Sorry!"

"What on earth happened to you?" Boudicca cried out, worry etched on her face as she practically engulfed the two boys.

"We went skiing," Vali explained, looking at Icarus worriedly.

Medea could already feel a headache coming on. "Let me guess, Icarus crashed?" She returned her gaze to her magazine. "How unlike him."

"Ah no," Vali walked past Boudicca gently placing Icarus on a chair while Asterion moved another chair for Vali. "He got hit by a snowball thrown by a tall Jotun... and then he crashed into a snow drift," he explained, moving the chair to Icarus instead and gently setting his right leg down on it. "I think he broke his ankle."

"By the gods..." Medea complained. "You were away from adult supervision for *a single day!*"

Just then Xbalanque came crashing through the door with a big grin on his face. He looked immensely proud of himself, not reading the room either as he pressed a hand to his front, puffing his chest out.

"I managed to walk from the front door to the van without slipping once!" He declared loudly. "Sure, it took me the whole day to get there and back again, but I did it! Vali, you were right! It's as easy as one foot in front of the other."

"So long as you move as slow as a snail, apparently," Medea mumbled under her breath. She looked at the time and frowned, before looking about the room, even poking her head over the bannister, to look at the floor below... but no. There was no sign of Aethalides. Where was he?

"Whoa, what happened to you, Icarus?" Xbalanque asked, finally taking notice of the boy, while Vali moved inside to make him a hot chocolate.

"I got taken out by a Jotun," Icarus mumbled.

Xbalanque winced. "Ouch. Medea?" He turned to her with a smile. "Do you think you can heal him?"

"No, I don't think I could."

"What?"

Medea flicked her sunglasses out again, sliding them over her face with a smile. "It's my vacation. Meaning it's my time off. Meaning I'm not working, so no healer today."

Icarus gaped at her. "Are you serious? My ankle is broken!"

"Not my fault, not my problem," she waved him away. "Get someone to carry you downstairs. I'm sure the front desk will have a first aid kit."

She heard a few mutterings, but then there was the sound of Icarus being picked up and once again leaving her in peace.

Eventually it became too cold to be comfortably outside so Medea retired from the balcony and went looking for the others. She didn't have to look far, at least not for Icarus, he was sitting in the main lobby, his foot now bandaged and resting on the table. He was looking at the notice board with a noticeable frown on his face.

"Something the matter?" She asked in way of greeting, taking a seat next to him.

Icarus gestured to the board. "Look at all the missing posters. There were a bunch on the ski lifts too."

"We saw a lot of them in town as well," Boudicca confirmed as she and Asterion came over. "We managed to get a table, Vali and Xbalanque are there now."

Medea frowned. "Just Vali and Xbalanque?"

"Yes," Boudicca frowned at her, while Asterion picked Icarus up. "Has Aethalides not come back yet?"

"No… at least… I thought he might be down here…" Medea trailed off, rising to her feet. "I'm sure he'll be fine."

The minutes ticked by agonisingly slowly as they sat at their table. Everyone looked uncomfortable, glancing around, constantly looking to the door, Xbalanque would ask the staff if anyone had seen Aethalides with a 'no' always being the answer.

Those missing posters kept plaguing Medea's mind, tapping her fingers against the table, another look at the clock had her standing up abruptly.

Aethalides had been missing for seven hours now, that wasn't like him, not in the slightest. Something was wrong, something was very very wrong.

People do not realise how close she actually was with Aethalides. She'd known him the longest, she'd known him in his first life, when he'd been the herald of the argo.

After that trip they'd parted ways, of course, Aethalides returning to his home in Larissa, while she went with Jason and… everyone knew how that marriage ended.

It was a few years after her life with Jason ended and had started again in Athens with Aegeus.

Medea could remember clear as day the moment she met Aethalides again. It had been while she'd comfortably been living in Athens and he'd appeared. Older, but she recognised him and of course, he recognised her immediately, even bowed.

"Lady Medea," he'd looked up at her and flashed a smile that was quite charming. "Or is it Queen now?"

"Queen," she replied, smiling herself looking the now young man up and down.

He'd grown taller, his skin was tanned quite dark for a lord, but given that he was a herald that was also to be expected. It was to reason that he spent a lot of time outside. Despite clearly wearing a 'traveller's cloak, the rich blue material screamed expensively, and so did the sleeves. As always there was his staff clutched tightly in hand, the ribbons fluttering in the slight breeze.

"Ah, I see, King Aegeus has good taste," he winked and she stifled a laugh, rolling her eyes instead.

"Should you really be speaking to me like that?"

"Certainly not, but rudeness runs in the family," he'd shrugged, still smiling, violet eyes sparkling with joy. She imagined he looked a lot like his father. "I shan't ask about Jason, I heard about his end."

"His end...?"

Aethalides blinked. "He... died?" He frowned. "I'm sorry, have you not heard, I'd just assumed that's why you were here..."

Medea had held her hand up to silence him, remembering that sometimes Aethalides had a habit of his words running away from him.

"How did he die?" She finally asked.

"Crushed... under the broken bow of his ship," he said slowly, gauging her reaction.

She would admit that at the time she had been shocked. Of course, she knew he'd die at some point, she prophesied it, she just didn't realise until now how right she'd been.

"Crushed under the weight of your greatest achievement," she whispered, recounting the last words she ever said to Jason and then after a brief moment of silence, she laughed.

Aethalides, for his part, had looked startled at her laughter, but then he relaxed a little, offering a smile and a small laugh of his own.

"Yes, I thought it was rather ironic too," he looked around briefly before leaning in close to her, whispering like they were co-conspirators. "Couldn't have happened to a nicer man if you ask me."

Medea snorted, hiding more laughter behind her hand. "You are rotten, Aethalides, but I approve of the humour. Athens can be… rather dull."

"For a lady as ingenious as yourself I can imagine it is," 'he leaned away, resting his chin against his fist as he leaned on his staff. "Why Athens? Sure, being married to King Aegeus, I can see the perks…" he looked around the beautiful city, filled with white marble and decorative pieces of art. "But it's not so keen on smart women," Aethalides hooked a thumb up at the statue of Athena, goddess of wisdom. "Ironically."

She'd raised an eyebrow, offering a coy smile. "Aethalides, are you complimenting me?" Medea leaned closer. "Should my husband be worried?"

"Nothing wrong with complimenting you," he'd replied, his own coy smile on his face. "And in regards to your husband, only you can answer that. I could make all the advances in the world, you'd have to choose if you wish to reciprocate," he winked and then looked around again. "But my question still stands…" he extended his arms, gesturing to Athens as a whole. "Why here?"

"The men of Athens are scared of powerful, intelligent women," she replied, her smile turning a little bit sharp. "Where else would I be?"

He'd smiled back at her at that statement, before joining her around the city, explaining that he was working on bringing up trade routes between Athens and Larissa. He knew it was a bit of a stretch considering how far away the two locations were, not only that, but Athens tended to do more sea trade than on land.

Though, at the time that hadn't been going well either, down to King Minos and his dreaded pet under the palace. Medea herself had offered to deal with the creature, but the king had denied her, insisting that he wanted to keep her safe. Really, King Aegeus was sweet and caring, far too good for a woman like her, but she appreciated him all the same. It was a shame that things ended badly between them… she heard that he hadn't met a very kind end, all for the fault of his supposed long lost son Theseus.

Medea had clocked Theseus as bad news the moment she saw him and had opted to get rid of him the same way she got rid of all her problems… unfortunately he found out and she was forced to flee with her own son in tow.

Her life hadn't been too bad after that and the next thing she knew she was with Aethalides once more, but more permanently than any other passing greeting.

Medea would deny it, but she cared for him. He was her only friend in this world and she had a feeling that Aethalides knew that. Unlike other people she'd met, they didn't squander it, Aethalides kept her close and held her in high regard. So, the idea of him missing now and no one knowing where he was or what had become of him, well, she was past the stage of nervousness.

Vali abruptly stood up, pressing his palms against the table as he eyed the clock on the wall. "I'm going out to look for him," he declared.

Medea could have kissed him. Thank goddess she didn't have to jeopardise her own reputation to save the little miscreant who was the only friend she had in this world.

"I'll come too!" Xbalanque went to get up but she shook her head.

"You can barely walk on snow and ice; you won't be of any

help. Medea said as she got to her feet, and turned to Vali, grateful that the boy had made the first move so she didn't need to. *"I'll* go with him."

Vali nodded. "Let's go."

"Boudicca, Asterion, try searching the town," Medea instructed. "Xbalanque and Icarus, you two stay here, just in case he comes back."

With that, Medea left to get herself ready in her coat, boots, hat and gloves. Pinning her long hair up to give herself some more visibility, Vali took his wolf form. After smelling a small bit of Aethalides's packed clothing, he wandered around outside for a bit, before picking up his scent and barking.

Medea followed him as Vali continued to follow his nose, she had to take a torch with her, lighting the way for Vali as they continued up the path.

It seemed to be going up into the mountains, which was dangerous at night, gods... she was going to kill him. It wasn't that she cared... far from it. Medea didn't care about anyone but herself, it was just... Aethalides was the only person she could have a decent conversation with and she wasn't losing that just yet. He was only ten... again, after all, they had a whole lifetime to get through before he inevitably bit the dust once more and she'd have to wait for his new life to begin.

This little trip was all about her mental health, it was nothing to do with being concerned for Aethalides's safety and she'd personally murder anyone who said otherwise.

They continued to walk up, following the path until it quickly went off to the left and down a steep climb towards a lake and a small hut.

Vali whined and the two of them looked at each other. There was no other way, they just had to go down the embankment.

Vali had no problem with the hill, having extra feet and better grip made it easy for him, Medea had to be a little bit more careful, sliding the last part down the hill.

She checked over the lake which was completely frozen, but there didn't seem to be any holes in it and Vali was going off to the right and past the small hut. So Aethalides had come down here, but he hadn't stopped to do any lake fishing. No, instead he'd gone past the hut and continued into the trees behind, which... led to the one place of Skadi's Rest you didn't go.

They wandered through the trees, the only sounds the call of owls and other nighttime beasts, Vali had to growl and bark at a few of them, but they didn't seem that interested in following the two of them. That was... worrying.

Finally, they reached an open stretch of nothing but ice and darkness, with whistling winds that seemed to have a constant snow storm blowing through.

Medea knew what this place was, Itztlacoliuhqui's Plane. The place where even the local residents feared to walk.

Vali turned back into his human form, staring out across the plane as his dark hair whipped around his face.

"He... he went.."

"He went onto the plane, didn't he?" Medea stated more than asked, Vali giving a small nod. She sighed, pinching the bridge of her nose, and biting back a growl. "I'm going to kill him."

They ventured out onto the plane, Vali turning back into his wolf form as they continued to walk. The wind and snow seemed to get worse and she could barely make anything out through the blizzard, even Vali was having a hard time making it through. Thanks to the snow, nothing quite seemed dark so it at least made seeing slightly easier, but at the same time with rapid winds and ever-present snow was getting worse and worse the further they went.

Medea took another step and tripped over, hitting the ground hard, and covering her coat in snow and ice. Not that you'd really notice much.

Vali came over to help her get up and she pointed her torch at the ground to see what she hit, freezing when she spotted something that looked like a foot.

Medea and Vali looked at each other, following the foot up to a leg and finally to a fully frozen Jötun who had their hand raised in a defensive position, expression one of pure terror.

"We need to find Aethalides," Medea said. "Fast."

Vali was quick to pick up the scent again, but as they continued more and more of these frozen ice structures appeared in the ice. All of them were Jotun's of various sizes and they were frozen in various looks of terror. Bodies encased in ice, shielding themselves from an unseen attacker or trying to run away from them and failing.

Vali whined a little as the sea of ice statues got worse and worse the further, they went, then his ears perked up and he barked once.

Medea chased after him as he took off, finally coming to find Aethalides, frozen like the Jotun's, his face a look of surprise. He wasn't frozen solid, just an icy outer shell.

Thinking fast, Medea conjured up a spell and hit Aethalides's icy prison with a small amount of heat from the sun itself. There were perks to being a granddaughter of Helios. One such perk was having a connection to the sun in more ways than one.

The moment the ice was gone, Aethalides collapsed on himself, clutching at his sides and shivering, teeth chattering against each other.

Vali turned back into his human form, slipping off his coat and wrapping it around Aethalides quickly, before turning back into a wolf. Aethalides weakly gripped at the coat, looking up at Medea and offering a shaky smile.

"Medea... y- you have no i-i- idea how happy I am to-o see you..." he said between chatting teeth.

Medea reached down to help him up and help him into the coat. "Who did this to you?"

Aethalides looked past her and his eyes widened in fear. *"Him!"* He cried out, pointing up into the swirling snow storm.

Medea and Vali whipped around to look up at what he was talking about, seeing a figure hovering above them in the middle of the snow storm. She quickly shone her light on him and felt her blood turn to ice just by looking at him, like she'd been hit and turned into an ice sculpture herself.

She hadn't seen Itztlacoliuhqui in hundreds of years, but she would never forget that face. The Aztec god of frost hovered above them. His skin was white with patches of frostbite littering his features, mostly at the tips of his fingers and toes. Black face paint came down the front of his face in three long stripes, dressed in a pointed hat decorated with the same black stripes and spikes coming out of it. A nose ring decorated his face too and in the middle of his forehead, a broken and bent arrow pierced it. She shouldn't see his eyes or mouth and the only piece of real colour on him was his large blue, red and gold necklace and bracelets. The rest of him was pure white and he carried a straw broom in hand that was littered with specks of frost and ice.

Itztlacoliuhqui's long black hair billowed in the wind as the snow encircled him like a tornado.

"How *dare* you take away my ice sculpture!" He roared, lifting up his broom and the snow seemed to collect and swirl around it faster and faster. "And *don't* look at me like that! I'm only doing my *job!* Sweep away the old life… to make way for the new!"

He swung his broom and a huge gust of wind sent Medea, Vali and Aethalides flying across the barren land, her torch slipped out of her hand and went shooting off somewhere. They only came to a halt when they smacked into a few of the other ice sculptures.

"And all of you… you're so very *old,"* Itztlacoliuhqui continued, letting himself land on the ground as he weaved his way through his ice sculptures. "You're taking up too much space and you *have* to go! That's the way the world works, you get rid of the *old* to make way for the *new!"*

Medea pushed herself up on her hands and knees, looking over to Vali and Aethalides as they stared over at Itztlacoliuhqui who was still making his way to them.

"We got to run!" Aethalides cried out, getting to his feet.

"How is he alive?" Medea yelled, getting to her feet and following the other two as they started to run. "The Aztec gods are dead!"

"Ask questions later!" Aethalides shouted. "Preferably when we're all wrapped up warm with a cup of hot chocolate!"

They ran past a small group of statues when Itztlacoliuhqui suddenly slid in front of them, reaching his hand out to grab them while he raised up his broom.

"I'm not the bad guy here!" He snarled out, as they backed away, watching the way the snow and wind swirled around the broom. "I'm just doing my job!"

"You're job!?" Vali spluttered as he turned back to his human form. "What about all those Jotun's? Was that you just doing your job!"

"Yes!" Itztlacoliuhqui screeched. "Things die. Frost wipes out the weak to make way for the strong and new life! If there's too much of anything in the world, it becomes too *packed!* There *has* to be *balance!"* The storms and snow picked up; frost started to spread out from under Itztlacoliuhqui's feet as he screamed into the sky. *"I* am that balance!"

"You're turning them into ice sculptures!"

Itztlacoliuhqui scoffed and waved them off, sending the group backwards across the ice. "Blame the other gods for that. They kept going on and on about how my ways were a waste of life," he gestured to the sculptures. "So, I decided to find a use for them! Not so much of a waste now, huh?"

Aethalides pulled himself up using one of the sculptures as he gave the god an incredulous look. "Oh, I see, you're one of those insane gods, got it? I haven't seen one of you in centuries."

"I'm not crazy…" he snarled between gritted teeth. "I'm just tired of being the bad guy because I do a job… no… one… likes!"

Itztlacoliuhqui swung his broom around violently, sending a whirlwind of snow, ice and frost in their direction. The three dived behind a large frozen Jötun, taking cover from the ice blast, with ice crystals and snow flying past them.

"I think this is a job for someone a lot more qualified than us," Aethalides said between his chattering teeth, pointing to another set of ice sculptures they could hide behind. "We have to get out of here! We can't take on a god."

"What about the Jötuns?" Vali asked as they hid again.

"What about them?" Medea snarled.

"Well, we can't just leave them!"

"Vali," Aethalides tried to reason with him. "They've been frozen here for gods knows how long-."

195

"They're still alive!" Vali cried out. "Jötuns can withstand cold temperatures, remember? They're just stuck in place, not dead."

Medea sighed, pressing a finger to her forehead. "I can maybe cook up a spell that's big enough to clear this whole place of snow and ice, but I'll need time to build it up."

Another icy wind shot past them, Itztlacoliuhqui screaming behind it.

Aethalides still looked uncertain, gritting his teeth as he debated arguing with Vali, but the kid looked at him with big eyes. For a small moment they shone with so much childhood innocence that they almost reminded Medea of her own sons' eyes before…

Before she brutally slaughtered him and his brother to get back at a man who didn't care about. She wasn't one for regrets but there were some things that she wished she could take back.

"Aethalides, Medea…" Vali begged, eyes imploring. *"Please."*

It looked like Aethalides was having a war with himself over what was the right thing to do and what he wanted to do. He wanted to run away, he wanted to leave this god to… well, the gods, for them to deal with and not him.

Unfortunately for him, Aethalides was a good person at heart, as much as he liked to pretend like he didn't care, he did. It was the whole reason he started the Archives in the first place, because he cared too much about people who didn't give a damn about him.

He was and would always be the forgotten unsung hero of the Argo, the bravest of the lot, the one who had to go ashore before anyone else to speak to the kings of foreign lands, as it was his job as a herald. He'd been the first person to enter her

196

father's court, the first of these travellers Medea had ever seen.

She remembered how he stood tall and proud, herald staff in hand, cloak wrapped around his body, smelling like the sea and like he hadn't had a bath in months. Despite all that, he carried himself like a lord would, walked how a man of wealth and little hardships did, like he owned the place.

The words he'd spoken that day had been laced with silver and sly tongue, a charming smile on his face despite the tiredness in his violet eyes. He'd spoken of their travels and won over the court very quickly with his tales, gaining them at least safety for now and for Jason to have an audience with the king.

Aethalides, the first time she'd seen him, had been ready for adventure, but she could see the good soul underneath it all. How he was here not just for the epic journey and fame, but for Jason, a man who had been robbed of his kingdom. As much as it was clear that Aethalides couldn't stand that man, he did believe in things being fair and had a sense of justice, right and wrong.

She hadn't seen that man who had stood in her court in a very long time, but right now, looking at Aethalides, he suddenly held a strong resemblance to who he had once been.

"All right," Aethalides sighed, pinching the bridge of his nose, but he nodded to Vali. "We can keep him distracted so Medea can get the spell ready."

"Try not to die," Medea said helpfully, gripping his arm when he turned to leave. "And when we get out of this, you and I are having a talk. Starting with what we are *really* doing here."

Aethalides grimaced, looking very put out, but he nodded and then disappeared around the corner.

She could hear the sounds of yelling and shouting, the ice and snow god was putting up a huge fight, getting frustrated with Vali and Aethalides by the sounds of it. Medea knew she wouldn't have long so she concentrated, muttering the spell under her breath and building up a ball of light, letting it get bigger and bigger.

She ignored the sounds of fighting going on in the background, or the occasional yelps from Vali, she just focussed all her energy on the small ball of sunlight she was gradually building up in her arms, finally reaching the size of a spacehopper, Medea raised it above her head. Her eyes glowed, she felt the heat baking down on her and then she curled her fingers and violently extended her arms outwards like she was pulling the sun apart.

The light and warmth shot across the open plain, the sound of breaking ice and gasped breaths hit her ears as well as the scream of pain.

"Medea?"

She opened her eyes and looked down at Aethalides who gently touched her arm. Glancing around she found the Jotun's moving and actual ground under feet, not ice or snow. The Jotuns took one look to where Vali stood in front of a kneeling Itztlacoliuhqui and booked it away from him. They didn't even stop to say thank you.

It was very rude in Medea's opinion.

Slowly they made their way over to where Vali was standing, staring at the god that was only put on pause, not beaten. His head was bowed and his broom lay next to him, the arrow sticking out of his forehead had a constant drip of liquid sunlight hitting the ground in front of him, melting away the ice.

"I wasn't always this…" Itztlacoliuhqui mumbled, finally looking up at them. "I was Tlahuizcalpantecuhtli, the god of *dawn*. I was the morning star, but when one of our sun gods, Tonatiuh, wanted the rest of us to obey and give sacrifices to *him*, I lost my temper. He was vain and arrogant… I… I wanted to *teach* him a lesson, so I threw an arrow at him," he reached up for the arrow sticking out of his head. *"This* arrow."

"What happened?" Vali asked softly.

The god bowed his head again, clenching his fists and a distinct chill filled the air.

"I *missed!"* He spat, bitter resentment and hatred dripping off his words. *"He didn't."*

Aethalides opened his mouth, probably to say some kind of snarky comment, so Medea carefully wrapped her hand around his mouth, giving a warning glare. Sometimes Aethalides's nature as the son of Hermes got them into more trouble than actually getting them out of it.

Itztlacoliuhqui looked back at them, it felt like he was glaring right into their souls. The chill was getting up again, the type of cold that burned instead of numbed. It hurt her face, the wind whipping around them sent bitting chills and flakes of snow against them.

It was a *fraction* of what this god could do and he seemed to prefer his solitude over beating them. Plus, Itztlacoliuhqui wasn't stupid. He'd know that the Olympian gods would do anything for their children. If Aethalides was lost out on the plane, Hermes would come looking for him and that would not suit the ice-cold god one bit.

"Leave," he bit out, rising to his feet. "Before I change my mind."

Vali picked up Aethalides and went sprinting away, with Medea not far behind the two of them. They didn't stop running until they reached the forest and when they looked back, Medea was certainly surprised to see Itztlacoliuhqui had followed them. Maybe he was making sure they actually left.

Then the blizzard picked up again and he completely vanished into the snow.

They all stood watching the snow silently, waiting, almost like they expected him to just… pop out again and freeze them anyway. Like some kind of messed up joke, but he didn't and the silence was broken when Aethalides let out a huge sneeze.

Right. Back to the others.

So, with Aethalides wrapped up in multiple blankets and coats, feet in a tub of hot water and several tissues, the others gathered around to sit and listen. Though not too close, they didn't want to get sick too. He could probably do with the rest, but you don't get rests when you keep things from your friends or at least that's how Boudicca had worded it.

"Didn't know you cared Boudi'," Aethalides laughed, before he broke down into sniffles and sneezed into his tissue again. "Ugh. Getting ill doesn't get easier no matter how long you live. Okay…" he looked at them all and sighed. "So there was an alteria motive for coming here… the thing is… my father has requested that I locate a *Mesopotamian* oracle."

Vali's eyes widened. "Those are extinct. There… hasn't been another one since-."

"Yeah, yeah, I know. Big wipe out and all that," Aethalides sighed. "See, thing is, my uncle Apollo had a prophecy and there is one *right now*, alive out there and probably not understanding their powers or abilities very well at all. Anyway, father requested I find them and now. 'Rune is also looking for them."

"Rune?" Icarus squeaked. "How did Rune find out?"

"He… used a runic spell on me and forced me to tell the truth," Aethalides muttered, a dark look crossing his face. "Not my finest moment. So… it's a race now and one of the places was Skadi's Rest, but they're not here."

"And there's also the fact that an Aztec god is somehow still alive," Medea added and everyone who hadn't seen him looked startled. Xbalanque nearly shot out of his seat.

"An Aztec god!" He cried out."Which one!?"

"Itztlacoliuhqui,," Vali whispered. "He froze Aethalides… and the other Jotuns."

"There was a great celebration earlier, the Jötuns made it back to Skadi's Rest and people were throwing parties," Boudicca confirmed. "I did wonder if you had anything to do with it."

"Yeah, well, the mystery of how Itztlacoliuhqui is alive will *stay* a mystery for another day, but I'll make my father aware," Aethalides said, brushing away the issue of the Aztec god of frost. "The more pressing matter is finding that Oracle. I don't need to tell you how bad it would be if an oracle like them fell into the hands of Rune."

"So, it's a race then?" Asterion snorted and Aethalides gave a nod.

"Rune thinks if he gets his hands on the oracle he'll be able to change his fate. See what is coming and protect himself.," he sighed leaning his head back against the chair. "That's *not* how oracles work, but that's never stopped anyone before. We have to get that oracle first, whatever it takes…"

"And so, they're not turned into a slave for Rune," Icarus added.

"That too."

"But if we do this," Medea stepped forward, standing over Aethalides and glaring at him. "We do it *together*. No more secrets."

Aethalides barked a small laugh, smiling up at her. "A little ironic coming from you…" he said, but sighed and nodded his head. "Still… yes… no more secrets."

Medea raised an eyebrow. "You swear it?"

He looked up at her and nodded his head. "I swear it."

Scavenger Hunt: 11

"So, you want to go looking for scraps in a scrapyard for your inventions..." Vali began, glancing over to Icarus who was dragging a cart behind him as they pillaged their way through the Atlantis junkyard. "Instead of buying the raw materials themselves?"

Icarus sighed, his shoulders dropped a moment and he looked over to Vali. "I mean, sure, I wish I could use the raw materials, but we don't have a forge and I don't have moulds," he leaned down and picked up an old spring that looked like it came out of a mattress. "At least this way the materials are already made for me. I just gotta put them together."

Vali tilted his head, squinting at the rusty spring that looked like one hell of a tennis shot inducer. Some of it was flaking away, it was a wonder the spring was in one piece.

He slowly looked around the rest of the junkyard, filled with all manner of things. Pieces of broken furniture that hadn't been used for firewood yet, cloth, hunks of metal, a few broken chairs and tables. There was so much... junk.

He couldn't really see the value of any of it, this was all stuff someone threw away, but Icarus was treating it like it was pure gold.

"Right and... probably clean it too... right?" Vali called over to him, with a small, hopeful smile.

Icarus paused and looked back at him. "Um. .Yeah? You gotta clean it and spruce it up so I can use it. It's funny though," he flashed a smile. "I didn't think you'd be such a clean freak."

"I'm not that much of a clean freak."

"Val'," Icarus laughed, picking up a bucket and sticking it in his cart. "You carry a toothbrush and paste with you everywhere we go."

Vali felt his eye twitch slightly. "Okay, you know when I'm a wolf, it's still *my* mouth," he pointed to said mouth as it twisted up in annoyance. "And some of the people I bite taste awful! Not to mention I get all the blood and stuff in my mouth, it's so *gross!*" He shuddered at the mere thought of it. "So yeah, I carry a toothbrush with me."

Icarus climbed up a trash pile, starting to tug on a chair leg, it was made of metal and it wasn't budging. Buried under a heap of trash, but Icarus didn't move the trash on top of it. Instead, he kept pulling and tugging, not getting anywhere. He eventually lost his grip and tumbled backwards, rolling down the small hill of trash until he smashed into his cart.

''Vali rushed over, helping him up and checking him over. "You all right? You didn't cut yourself did you?"

Icarus had wide eyes and bright red cheeks. Probably just embarrassed from falling off the mountain of trash.

"I'm *fine!*" He laughed awkwardly, rubbing at the back of his head with more nervous laughter. "Honest! Just... whoop! Tripping over, as usual! Just clumsy old Icarus!"

"Right," Vali smiled, looking around a moment, and then he climbed up the trash pile himself. Reaching for the chair leg and easily pulling it out. It was a lot bigger than he was expecting, probably a chair for a giant of Cyclops. He hoisted it on his shoulder and made his way down the pile, before carefully placing it in the cart so he didn't accidentally tip it over.

Vali dusted himself down, wiping his hands on his coat a

moment and looked to Icarus with a bright smile, which gradually dimmed at the wide-eyed and open-mouth expression he was wearing.

"You're strong," Icarus stated dumbly.

"Oh! Right, yeah…" Vali laughed, now feeling it was his turn to be embarrassed. "It's um… you know, the whole… Æsier and Jotun genes… They help a lot."

"Huh…" Icarus looked in the cart for a moment at all the stuff, then turned back to Vali. "Could you pick that up?"

"The whole thing?"

"Yeah."

Vali shrugged. "Probably. I don't really work out though and I'm not the strongest around…"

"Wait…" Icarus held his hand up as he mulled something over in his mind. "So gods need to work out too? You can't just snap your fingers and suddenly.." He made a body builder pose and pouted his lips. "You're buff, body builders."

Vali stared at him for a long, very confused moment, as his eyes flickered up and down Icarus's figure. He'd even flinched away slightly the moment Icarus struck the pose.

"Ah… no… and what are you doing?"

Icarus frowned, raising an eyebrow. "This is a bodybuilder pose."

"Ummm…"

"This is what they did in Greece! Have you not seen our statues?"

Vali looked away a moment, his lips twisting up slightly uncomfortably. He had seen the statues, they were hard to miss in all honesty. Usually, they were tall and anatomically correct in too many ways. There were some things he didn't need to see of his dad's old friends or other people he was supposed to respect.

Besides, some of the gods went walking around wearing little to nothing anyway, he didn't need the statues constantly reminding him of their fashion choices or lack thereof. He wasn't much of a prude, you couldn't be in the old days, especially when you were adjacent to the viking gods. Sailing took a long time on those long boats, where everyone was neatly packed together and there were no places to disappear into for privacy... you just... did everything in front of everyone.

Times had changed though and he'd grown accustomed to things like baths and showers, going to the bathroom alone was also a nice upgrade. Houses being more than one room so you could have a little bit of privacy, that was also nice. Not that he'd had much issue with that back on Asgard. Loki had quite a big home and Vali had shared a room with his brother before... everything.

"The really naked statues?" Vali spluttered out. "Kinda hard to miss."

"Okay, before you go judging," Icarus sassed, as he started to pull his cart along again, Vali walking next to him. "There was a reason for the statues looking like that and a reason why we... used to dress like that in ancient Greece. The weather was hot for one and two-."

"The peoples of ancient Greece were like rabbits?"

"What? *No!*" Icarus's face had flared up an impressive shade of red. "I mean, sure there was Pygmalion that one time...but my personal opinion is that if anyone is starting to get the hots for a statue... they need to get out more."

"Pygmalion fell in love with a statue?"

"He... made it himself and thought she was so beautiful. Gave her a name and dressed her up in fancy clothes, even bought her jewellery," Icarus reeled off the list casually. "In the end

Aphrodite gave her life and the two got married. I'm not really sure how it all worked out because he never really liked… people that much in the first place. Or, at least he wasn't attracted to anyone, that could talk or… kiss or anything…" he slowly trailed off and frowned in thought. "Come to think of it, I think they've got a word for that now."

"Huh… interesting story… wait…" Vali thought about it a moment, the name Pygmalion had rang a bell. Where had he heard it before…? Oh. "Wait a minute isn't-?"

"Yeah."

"So that means-?"

"Yep!" Icarus grinned at him. "The Pygmalion and his wife, Galatea in the capital? The same as the story."

"So… she was…"

"A statue."

Vali blinked a few times, rubbing the back of his neck. "Huh."

It was honestly shocking just how powerful the Olympian gods were. They could bring to life a living statue, literally change their forms on the regular, make kids out of anything and literally stitch themselves back together like it was no issue. Æsier gods couldn't do that. Neither could the Vanir.

Actually now that he thought about it, there weren't a lot of gods or pantheons he could actually think of that were anywhere near on the same power level as the Olympian gods. Perhaps the Egyptian pantheon, but it was hard to say. They could still die, the Olympians though? Nope. They were deathless. You could literally do anything to them and they'd just put themselves back together and be fine. A little miffed at being torn apart in the first place, but over all they'd be okay.

"I… really can't get over… as a race, how insanely powerful

and different your Olympian gods are," Vali mumbled. "I mean, they can literally bring statues to life."

"Dude, you have a half brother that's an eight legged horse," Icarus deadpanned. "And that's before we get to your other half siblings."

He grimaced at the mention of them, but he guessed that Icarus did have a point.

They fell into comfortable silence, Vali even rolled his sleeves up so he could help carry a few of the heavier pieces. Picking up more stuff and filling up the cart, in the end, Vali had to be the one who dragged the cart around as it got too heavy for Icarus to pull, but he still managed to find a bucket he could fill with small scraps that he started to carry around.

"So..." Icarus began. "Are we going to talk about it?"

"Talk about what?"

"Ya know..." he trailed off, looking around nervously. "The *Oracle?*"

Vali went wide-eyed and glanced around himself, just on the off chance anyone was listening. "Yeah... I... I guess it's a big thing, huh?"

"Yeah!" Icarus cried out. "And that whole... deal with that Aztec god also being alive? That's crazy!"

That was one way of putting it. Vali didn't know the full ins and outs, but what he did know was that the Aztec pantheon, along with the rest of the Mesoamerica pantheons had just vanished sometime after the invasion of the conquistador. It was about half way through the invasion and enslavement of their people that the gods seemed to just poof out of existence.

The other gods wrote them off as dead, which caused a whole existential crisis amongst the remaining pantheons. A bunch of immortal beings suddenly looking down the barrel at death on the other side? The norse pantheon were at least somewhat familiar with the concept of gods dying, the greek pantheon, not so much. In fact, they even referred to themselves as the deathless gods, so confident in their immortality, but after the Mesoamerica pantheons ceased to be they suddenly got really scared.

Still, the Aztecs, the Mayans and the Inca were gone. They'd been gone for a long time and even when a few gods actually went looking for them, they didn't find a trace of them. Not a magical one or even a physical one. It was like they'd just ceased to exist.

So yeah, to see an old Aztec god like Itztlacoliuhqui, who had apparently been living there for a long time without anyone knowing? It was crazy.

"Yeah…" Vali whispered, gazing off into the distance, not really seeing. "Really crazy."

"Was he scary?"

"Well.." Vali thought about it and how Itztlacoliuhqui had appeared out of the snow, how he'd nearly frozen all of them and turned them into ice sculptures. "Yes…" he settled on. "Yes, he was scary."

"How scary?" Icarus asked.

"Let's just say…" Vali started slowly. "I'm in no rush to see him again."

Icarus laughed and went to say something, but Vali heard the sound of voices, someone was speaking, it was faint like they wanted to stay hidden. He gripped Icarus's wrist and raised a finger to his lips, ignoring the way Icarus's face flared up red. More embarrassment maybe? He couldn't think why, he hadn't tripped over anything.

Vali tilted his head, pulling his hood to the side and cupped his hand around his ear as he listened.

There were voices and they were just coming over the top of the hill, on the other side of the giant pile of trash.

"Why did you pick here to meet?"

"Fewer people around. What? I thought a fae who spent his time by the docks surrounded by fish guts would be used to an area like this."

"I- that's not what Kanakoa's Kingdom is like!"

"Calm, Cillian, it was a joke."

Vali went wide eyed, standing up straight. "Cillian?" He mumbled and looked to Icarus. "I think something's going on on the other side of-," he paused and sniffed at the air a few times. "Rune... Rune and Cillian are meeting up."

Icarus blinked and looked up at the top of the trash hill. "On the other side of that? Well, they haven't seen us, so... why don't we leave-?"

"No, come on... we can find out what they're up to," Vali hissed, quickly running to the bottom of the trash hill. "Remember what Aethalides said? Rune was trying to find the oracle too."

Vali started to climb up the trash, dodging some of the more mucky or dirty parts. He heard Icarus sigh, but the sound of him following was distinct against Vali's quiet footsteps. He scaled the trash hill easily, poking his head over the top and peering down into the clearing that had trash towering around it. Rune was standing there with his right hand a bunch of his gang and Cillian was there too with a few of the Port Side Raiders.

It was weird. Rune was a big-time criminal, but Cillian? Small potatoes, like Aethalides, always said.

"So, what do you want me to do again?" Cillian asked, crossing his arms.

"I am… in the process of procuring something," Rune explained, stepping forward with his hands firmly pressed together. "It's vital that I have some way of getting it out of Atlantis. When the time is right, of course."

Cillian seemed to nearly beam with pride. "And you went with me? Well, I don't blame you," he placed a hand on his chest, puffing it out as he said. "The Port Side Raiders will more than happily lend their services. We'll be partners in this, right?"

Rune smiled calmly. "Of course. I just need you to be ready at your earliest convenience. We are still in the process of procuring the item and…" he placed a finger to his lips in thought. "It's vital that we have that exit to the mortal realm planned."

"So, what is it?"

"Oh, something very important," Rune chuckled. "So important that I'm currently having to dance around the Archives to procure it."

At the mention of them Cillian scowled, he snarled, pulling his lip back and showing his pointed teeth.

"The Archives? You know, if this messes with them I'll do this one for free."

Rune raised an eyebrow and let out an amused chuckle. "Are you not a fan of them?"

Cillian snorted. "Of course not! Why? Are you?"

"I… find them amusing," Rune settled on. "Useful too."

"Useful," Cillian rolled his eyes. "Yeah, sure, they're as useful as a shoe with a hole in them."

A loud noise startled Vali and he looked down to see Icarus was virtually next to him, but had accidentally tipped some pieces of scrap down to the floor. He watched the pieces of metal and wood tumble to the ground, making a noise as they smacked into every service.

Vali winced, Icarus was staring with wide eyes and then looked up at Vali worriedly.

He paused and waited for a moment, but didn't hear anything from the other side that hinted to them knowing they were there. He held his hand down and pulled Icarus the rest of the way up, then cautiously poked his head up to see if anyone had taken notice of them.

Cillian and Rune were still there, no one had moved, but they were all looking directly at him. Cillian snarled and let out a hiss, getting his crossbow ready, but Rune stepped forward with that cold smile.

"Well, hello," he said politely, stepping to the side and gesturing towards the clearing. "Would you like to come and join us?"

"What?" Cillian shrieked.

Vali gulped and pushed up from the trash and desperately pushed Icarus down the hill of trash. He took a glance to make sure he got down safely, before looking back at the two gangs.

Rune still looked amused. "So that's a no to the invitation? A shame," he smiled, showing off his teeth as his eyes glowed brightly. "You seemed so eager to listen in earlier, I only assumed that you were interested in having a conversation."

Vali shrank back before he jumped down, off the pile and grabbed the cart and Icarus, tugging it along as he ran. He knew he was probably dragging both the cart and Icarus along but he knew they needed to get out of here.

His ear twitched and Vali could hear the tell-tale sound of people chasing after them. He was quick to empty some of the things from Icarus's cart and handed him the handle so he could pull it.

"Huh? Wait, what are you-?" Icarus began, but Vali cut him off, placing his hand on his shoulders.

"We don't have a lot of time!" Vali hissed at him. "You go back and get the others. I can distract these jerks."

"What?" Icarus cried, shaking his head. "Nu-uh, no way. I'm not just going to leave you-."

"I'll be fine," Vali cracked a grin and gave a wink. "Trust me."

Icarus was staring up at him with wide eyes, a light blush to his cheeks and nodded wordlessly.

Vali patted him on the shoulder, then ran quickly back towards the rest sound of running feet. He easily jumped to halfway up a trash mountain, looking over to make sure Icarus was getting away and he spotted him disappearing around the corner.

Good. At least he would be safe now.

"I think he went this way!" Came the voice of Cillian and Vali felt a deep growl emit from himself. "I owe the little backbiter one," the fae continued. "The brat really bit into my arm!"

Vali picked up the heaviest thing he could find, just as the small group rounded the corner, led by Cillian himself. Too bad they hadn't brought any Jotun's with them, then he might actually have a problem.

He hefted up the piece of metal that happened to be a filing cabinet, raising it above his head and then tossing it as hard as he could.

Cillian only just saw it in time to dodge, but the cabinet smacked into two of his five men sending them hurtling backwards.

"Up there!" Cillian shouted, aiming his crossbow and firing

it at Vali, who slid down the pile to dodge the bolt. "I'm not finished with you, you mutt!"

Vali scooted around the corner, picking up an old shovel with a bent handle. It was a little cliche, but eh, it would work.

He could hear Cillian's footsteps as they got close, his men too, the ones that were left, that is, not far behind him.

Not wasting a moment, the second he smelt Cillian's scent literally right next to him, Vali swung the shovel. He was able to crack the fae right across the face, not hitting him as hard as he could've done, but hard enough to snap off the spade end of the shovel. It was little surprise that Cillian was out cold.

With inhuman speed, Vali cleared the small distance to reach Cillian's men, jumping in the air and swinging the makeshift staff he had. He cracked one of them right in the temple, knocking him out cold, and then he dodged the swings of the other, blocking one of his bunches with the staff for a moment. The thug took another swing at him, which he caught with his other hand and then the big idiot thought it would be a great idea to headbutt a three-quarter Æsier right in the face. It wasn't.

He ended up knocking himself out and falling to the ground unconscious.

Vali stood silent for a moment, staring at the guy and poking him with the shovel handle. He was still breathing, wasn't he? He hadn't given himself blunt force trauma or at least... not too much... right?

Vali squinted, looking closer and yep... still breathing. Right, well, that was one less thing to worry about.

Slow clapping alerted him to another presence and he lifted his makeshift weapon up to attack, freezing when he found Rune standing by himself, clapping with a small smirk plastered on his face.

"Nicely handled," Rune said, clasping his hands behind his back. "It makes me wonder why you've been holding back for so long. Are you worried about what the Archives would think when they realise how much of a god you *actually* are?"

Vali raised his staff up, spreading his stance to one of battle, glaring at Rune as he let out a warning growl.

Rune raised an eyebrow and chuckled. "You are scared. You're terrified or maybe the issue is more personal," he started to circle Vali and he countered him by moving too, always keeping his eye on Rune. "Maybe, you want to forget how much of a god you are, so you... don't have a connection to the people who murdered your family?" He suggested airily. Rune smirked when Vali growled louder at him. "Ah. So it *is* that. Good to know. Still, you of all people should know, Vali, that no matter what you do, blood is blood," he flashed his fangs at him, glowing silver eyes practically piercing. "And you'll *always* be the son of the backbiter and the same people who destroyed your family. Certainly, though, I see the family resemblance between you and Loki even more now. I mean," he looked to Vali, grinning. "He was a coward too."

Vali let out a roar of anger, rushing at Rune, stick raised. He leapt at the elf who was taking his time in getting away.

Rune took a step backwards, dragging his foot along the ground and drawing a mark for just a moment, then he jumped back completely just as Vali landed on the spot he had been.

He stood up, finding Rune only an arm's length away and he went to move, but his feet stayed firmly to the ground. Vali looked down, he couldn't see anything stopping him from moving, nothing was holding him or was caught around his leg, but he couldn't move his feet an inch.

He continued to try, tugging uselessly against an invisible

force, Rune standing only just out of his reach. Vali tried swiping at him with his clawed hands, slashing nothing but air that occasionally wafted Rune's hair.

Rune chuckled deeply, reaching into his pocket and pulling out his bag of runes.

"It really is shocking your lack of knowledge regarding runic magic, Vali," Rune said as he pulled out one stone, it looked like it had a capital 'I' drawn on it. "Did you forget about Isa?"

Slowly Vali looked down at the line Rune had drawn in the dirt with his boot. Except it wasn't a line, it was a rune, Isa, the rune that meant stillness, ice, block or challenge. Like all light elves, Rune's skill with runic magic was undoubtedly good, especially since he didn't even need to use rune stones to complete his magic.

Vali looked up at Rune in silent terror as the light elf smiled at him.

"It really is embarrassing on your part. You can't do a single piece of magic can you? Not even runic magic?" He laughed, holding the stone between his fingers as he examined it. "Truly, a loss and ironic. Considering it was Loki who taught me."

Vali felt all the breath leave his lungs. "What..?"

"Yes, which is why I'm surprised he *never* taught you," Rune went on, carefully slipping his bag away. "But, it's not too late of course. I can always take his place, given that he's... *indisposed* at the moment? You know, I could teach you runic magic better than anyone," he held his hand out to him and smiled. "What do you say?"

"I..." Vali looked at the hand and then looked back up at Rune's smirking face. "I... say that I don't trust you..." he snarled. "Especially if my **father** thought it was a good idea to teach you runic magic!"

Vali took on his wolf form, slowly morphing and changing, feeling his bones change shape and fur cover his body, until he was on all fours, snarling and snapping at Rune.

"Hm. Well, that's disappointing," he slipped another rune out of his pocket and held up with a smirk. "I hope you can swim."

Vali watched him slam the stone into the ground and the moment it was removed a sprout of water shot out of the ground, before it was followed by a massive tidal wave that completely wiped him out.

He went hurtling through the junkyard, turning back into his human form and grabbing onto the nearest object until the water vanished completely and he smacked the ground hard. The mud was almost welcoming, with puddles dotted around him and a completely wiped-out area of scrap.

Vali lifted his head up slightly, catching sight of Rune's men grabbing the port side raiders, dragging them off. Rune himself was the only one completely dry and clean. He tossed his rune stone in the air and caught it, looking over at Vali and smiling, before leaving his sight.

Vali groaned and smacked his head down into the mud. It had been a very long tiring week. He just wanted to curl up in a ball and sleep for a bit, maybe not in the mud though.

After a moment he slowly pulled himself up to his feet, walking towards the exit of the scrap yard just as the others came running through it. They slowed to a stop at the sight of him and he could only imagine what he looked like in his went and bedraggled form with mud stains littering his person.

"Vali?" Aethalides tilted his head. "What happened to you?"

"I don't want to talk about it," Vali mumbled, walking past them. "Thanks for coming through. I appreciate it, but I'm fine."

He *really* didn't want to talk about it. The last thing he needed was for any of what happened here to reach the ears of the Æsier. By the gods, Heimdallr would never live it down, insisting that he train Vali how to fight. He knew how to fight, Rune had just... caught him off guard, that was all.

Icarus caught his arm as he went past. "Are you sure you're, okay?"

"I've been worse," Vali said and gently pulled his arm away from him. "But I'd like to go home now. Please."

"What about Rune?" Asterion asked.

"He's gone."

Aethalides took a step forward, raising his hand to everyone else. "Home, we can go home. Icarus can tell us what happened and what was said while Vali was cleaned up," he looked up at him and nodded. "Okay?"

Vali looked down at Aethalides and nodded back, offering a small but grateful smile. "Okay."

The Great Seal Adventure: 12

"All right people, we got a job to do. So," Aethalides cried out and gestured to his right as he looked at the rest of the group. "Everyone on the boat!"

Very slowly Icarus looked to the boat quietly, it 'wasn't... *great*. It looked like it had several holes in it and the sail had seen better days. It was probably the cheapest boat out there and Aethalides, with all his money, had bought it.

"I'll pass," Medea said as she looked up at the boat. "One boat trip was enough."

"You've been on more than one boat trip."

She smiled sweetly and looked back at him. "Aethalides, I am not going on that thing."

He threw his hands up in the air. "What? It's not bad! Look it's got everything you need, a sail, no holes and a wheel."

Icarus watched a seagull land on a piece of the ship where very suddenly the wooden perch it was using broke under it and the seagull let out a squark of surprise as the wood fell into the sea. It would've been funny if that wasn't the ship he was about to get on.

"It doesn't have holes for now," Boudicca mumbled, crossing her arms. "It's too dangerous. The children are not getting on that thing."

"Oh, come on, the Argo was far worse," Aethalides argued.

"No, it wasn't," Medea said simply and he scowled at her.

"Quit contradicting me! It's fine, it's safe and ship ready!"

He assured them all, gesturing to it. "Come on, we have a job to do, you know that."

Icarus shivered when a gust of wind blew through the harbour. Coasts were never the warmest of places at times, but Njord's Harbour was taking the cake for being a literal freezer.

Besides the cold it was impressive that Aethalides found such an unkept ship here, since Njord's Harbour specialised in ship making, from long boats to barges to triremes. The fact that Aethalides found this thing as badly kept as it was, honestly… he was slightly impressed and a bit disturbed at the same time.

"I'm not going on that thing," Asterion grunted.

"With all that money you have, how can you be such a cheap skate on safety?" Medea asked, raising an eyebrow at him.

Aethalides flashed his megawatt grin. "Because it makes it more *exciting* this way!"

"Does it… at least have life jackets?" Icarus asked, shuffling from foot to foot.

"Bah!" Aethalides scoffed, rolling his eyes and crossing his arms. "We didn't have life jackets in the old days. It was swim and hope someone spots you if you fall overboard or die."

Anansi, surprisingly, was with them this time and he eyed the ship a moment, then threw his hands up in an 'I'm out' gesture, turning on his heel and marching away.

"Whoa, hey, where are you going!?" Aethalides cried out, jumping off the box he was standing on to try and catch up with Anansi. "You can't leave! I need you; we need at least some godly assistance on this!"

"I'm not going on that thing!"

"You're literally a god, you can't die!"

"Aethalides," Anansi scowled. "It's not happening. I don't like ships anyway," he looked over at the rickety old thing that swayed in the wind. "And I definitely don't like ships like that. I'm not going on it."

Aethalides awkwardly tapped his fingers together and flashed a little smile. "Would it help if I got a better boat?"

Anansi's reply was as flat as his expression. "No."

"But-!"

"Just come back in one piece," Anansi said, leaning down and poking his chest. "The last people I saw get on a ship like that," one of his other hands pointed at it. "They didn't come back."

"I... right. Okay," Aethalides nodded. "We'll come back. I promise."

"Good!" Anansi brightened, standing up to his proper height. "Well, good luck with all that sailing, try not to die while I'm not around and come back with some interesting stories for me, okay? Okay!" He flashed a grin at them before excitedly waving with his two right hands. "Byyyyyyeeee!"

Icarus watched the spider god sprint off and he really wished he could sprint off with him. Or pay Xbalanque a visit. He was missing this madness because he was at work in the mortal realm. Lucky guy. Maybe Icarus could get a part time job in the mortal realm instead of risking his life day after day for a lunatic that couldn't die.

Sometimes Icarus would question his decisions, joining the Archives was a decision that he often found himself questioning, but it would always lead to the same conclusion; where else was he going to go?

Part of the reason that many of them were even living with Aethalides in the first place was all down to having nowhere else to go. Working day to day, saving people and stopping monsters... it was almost like paying rent. For Icarus though, as much as he questioned his choices, it was also a chance for him to prove himself, to show that he wasn't a waste, that he was more than just 'the boy who flew too close to the sun'.

"Okay," Aethalides span around on his heel and grinned. "Okay, so it's just us, but that's okay! We can do this. Now, who's ready to go on a sailing adventure?"

A large crash sounded behind them and Aethalides's shoulders dropped completely. Everyone spun around, startled to find the mast had completely collapsed and a seagull was busily flapping its wings in surprise, hovering above where the mast had been.

"Oh, come on!" Aethalides complained. "The guy said that would only happen *after* the trip!"

"What?"

"Nothing!"

Medea pressed a finger to the bridge of her nose and took a few deep, calming breaths. Icarus could imagine her counting to ten in her head, thinking happy thoughts so she didn't think murderous ones.

"Okay, you and me," she gestured between herself and Aethalides. "Are going to find a more ocean ready ship, the rest of you find something to do... this might take a while."

"I can find a ship myself," Aethalides protested as he followed Medea anyway, the high priestess of Hecate glared at him.

"You have more money than sense, darling," she bit out and interrupted him when he opened his mouth to protest. "Do not even try to defend yourself."

Icarus, Vali, Boudicca and Asterion watched them leave Awkwardly standing on the dock for a moment as they looked around. What was there to even do in Njord's Harbour? The place was… well… shipbuilding and fishing. There wasn't much else to do around here. It wasn't a tourist seaside attraction harbour or holiday destination like the southern port of Konola's Kingdom.

"Let's find a tavern or something," Asterion muttered. "Beats being in this cold."

"Will you be allowed in?" Boudicca asked worriedly and the minotaur snorted.

"What? You think they're going to say no to me?" He jabbed a thumb in his sternum. "Like to see 'em try."

Yeah, Icarus would not be the one to get in-between Asterion and a tavern. The last guy who did got thrown through a wall.

They started to walk off, but he paused when he noticed that Vali was on his phone, texting someone. It was weird, because Icarus wasn't sure who Vali would have to text. Everyone was basically here and it wasn't like he was chummy with people like Xbalanque and Arachne. Vali mostly kept to himself, only spending a lot of time with Icarus and sometimes Aethalides. Everyone else he tended to keep his distance, not out of finding them irritating or that he didn't even like them, but more like he didn't think he deserved to be close with anyone. Or that he was scared something was going to happen.

Vali tended to look after Icarus, be the one there for him when everyone else would criticise him or get angry whenever he screwed up. Still, as much as Vali liked to keep an eye on him, the whole thing worked the other way too and Icarus paid close attention to make sure he wouldn't go too far into himself.

"Val'? You coming?" Icarus asked and Vali looked up alarmed, like he'd been caught doing something he shouldn't be.

"Huh? Oh, right yeah!" Vali slipped his phone away and quickly caught up.

They eventually found themselves in a tavern called 'the Selkie and the Sailor' which led to a short debate over whether or not selkies were even real, to begin with, and when they entered they got the classic dead eyed glare and stares. Honestly, the looks the locals were giving them, it was like they'd been accused of killing their mothers.

They found a place to sit and hey, at least the owner was nice, coming over with a welcoming smile. He was tall and human, but one closer look and Icarus would see that he was half human, half Jötun. The guy's ears were slightly pointed and he had the same unnaturally blue eyes that most Jötun had, with silvery hair. Apparently, he took more after the human side in height and he didn't have the same pale skin as Jötuns tended to have.

He was also awesome because he brought over their drinks.

"We don't get a lot of city people come up here," he said with a deep and thick Norwegian accent. Icarus had to really concentrate to understand him, but Vali seemed to get it completely. "What brings you up here?"

"We're looking for something," Vali answered and the owner sighed, getting a slightly irritated look on his face.

"You're not here looking for the sea ram, are you?"

They shared a look amongst themselves for a moment, then turned back to him.

"The... sea ram?" Vali asked.

The owner huffed, slipping his tray under his arm after putting their drinks down. He pointed over to a corner where a group of different beings stood, all dressed for sailing and carrying nets and other fishing tools that Icarus couldn't name.

"We keep getting these lunatics up here looking for the sea ram. I've never seen it myself," he shrugged. "But I doubt I've

223

seen every creature or being whoe lives on this island. They want to catch it. I say leave it be."

"What is the sea ram?"

"Umm... a ram..." the owner said slowly. "That... comes out of the sea. Apparently. Personally, I think it's a bunch of drunk fools mistaking the foam for wool," he then brighten up and smiled. "Still! Can't be too upset, I mean it brings in plenty of customers!"

The owner patted Vali's shoulder, saying something in Norwegian to him that had Vali sniggering and nodding his head. It was weird to see someone treating Vali nicely outside of the Archives. Either the guy didn't know who he was or he just didn't care.

The owner left them alone and they turned to their drinks, Vali still had his little smile on his face as he took a sip of his drink.

"What did he say?" Icarus asked and Vali waved him off.

"You wouldn't get it."

They didn't have to wait long for Boudicca to get a text from Aethalides saying they've managed to get a boat. Vali checked his phone and let out a sigh of relief when he read whatever was on it, as they made their way back to the front of the docks.

Icarus could kiss Medea if he wasn't certain she'd kill him on sight. The ship was so much better than what it had been. A big trireme and it was immaculate. Beautifully crafted with a depiction of Triton at the front of the ship, his trident raised and ready to face incoming objects, with the colour scheme of the boat being blue and green.

The real test came with a seagull landed on the ship and nothing broke off it.

"That's better," Asterion mumbled. "Why didn't you get this

before?"

"Well, we're renting this one," Aethalides muttered, casting a glare at Medea. "Which I still think is a bad idea."

"Why on earth do you think that?" She asked, climbing onto the boat, shortly followed by Asterion and Boudicca.

"Because," Aethalides began, climbing up himself. "It's *us.* Do you think we'll be able to get this thing back in one piece?"

"Well, that's where your money comes in," Medea replied simply with a smile.

Aethalides scowled. "Woman, stop spending my money!"

"Darling, we'll be fine. Stop worrying."

Icarus and Vali got on the ship, looking around and Aethalides seemed to be mulling everything over in his head. Icarus saw Vali stand at the edge of the ship, looking on the dock, glancing left and right. It was like he was looking out for someone.

"You're right!" Aethalides snapped his fingers and flashed his grin. "I mean, with me, the herald of the Argo and Vali," he gestured to a startled Vali. "A Viking deity, we'll be fine!"

"I... I don't know how to sail," Vali spluttered. "At least not well."

"But you're a Viking god!"

"Just because I'm a Viking god, doesn't mean I know how to sail," he scowled at Aethalides slightly, then checked his phone and grinned. "Don't worry though, I got us some help!"

Vali excitedly waved someone over and Icarus was not expecting Heimdallr of all people to step onto the ship. His silver hair was braided intricately and neatly against his head, dressed in a slightly longer cloak that still had ram wool around the top for warmth and his hand rested on his sword, shield slung over his back.

225

Aethalides rubbed at his eyes. "You... you asked Heimdallr to come with us to help with sailing?"

"Yeah?"

"You just said that being a Viking god doesn't mean you know how to sail and you picked the god that *doesn't move* from one place to help us... sail!" He blinked a few times, seeming to be bewildered and yeah, Icarus would give this one to Aethalides. He was also questioning Vali's logic on this.

"I know how to sail, Hermesson," Heimdallr said evenly, his voice as flat as his expression and Icarus got the feeling it wasn't going to change much. "I did go travelling in my younger years."

"Oh right, yeah..." Aethalides muttered. "I forgot how you went out to find yourself and like anyone who goes out to find themselves, they end up finding other people."

Heimdallr narrowed his eyes slightly. Who knew a rainbow could look so intimidating. Then again it might have more to do with the giant sword at his hip than the glaring eyes. "What's that supposed to mean?" Heimdallr said with an edge to his tone.

"Oh nothing, nothing," Aethalides brushed it off. "I just mean... it's funny... considering you kicked off the whole human race, at least in the Scandinavian countries."

"That's pretty ironic coming from a Greek," Heimdallr replied evenly.

For a brief moment, Aethalides looked offended, opening his mouth to protest, before snapping it shut and mulling it over a moment. He shrugged his shoulders as if to say 'eh, the man has a point' then turned to start ordering a few of the others around.

Of course, it was them so nothing was easy and as Heimdallr seemed to be getting himself acquainted with the ship another person stepped on and Icarus felt all the air leave his lungs. Oh gods, no, not *him*.

226

Loki stepped on board and Vali instantly shrank away as his father extended his arms and grinned widely.

"Have no fear, Loki's here!" He shouted and not a moment did the last word leave his lips was Heimdallr directly in front of him with his sword to his throat. Loki smiled. "Heh, was it something I said?"

"What are *you* doing here?" Heimdallr snarled.

"I came here to help, is that so hard to believe?"

Did the guy really need to ask that?

"Plus," Loki gestured to Vali and grinned. "My darling boy is going on his first sailing trip, I wanted to be here for the occasion. It's a parent thing, Heimdallr," he said, gently pushing the sword away from his neck with a finger. "You wouldn't understand."

That line actually seemed to cut Heimdallr deeply, the watchman visibly flinched back, but he soon schooled his features into the impassive expression as before.

"Besides," Loki went on, casually strolling across the deck of the ship, a hand to his chin as he subtly judged it. "Aethalides is the only one who knows how to sail here, so I figured you could use all the help you can get and here I am," he bowed before them all. "You're welcome."

"We already have someone to help us," Vali whispered, awkwardly pointing to Heimdallr. "I asked Heimdallr to come with us, to help."

Loki looked between his son and the watchman a moment, pointing to Heimdallr and his expression morphed into one of disbelief.

"*Heimdallr!*? You asked the guy who *never moves* his feet from one place to help you... with sailing!?"

"Never thought I'd say this, but for once I actually agree

227

with Loki," Aethalides mumbled under his breath.

Heimdallr's head whipped around with a scowl on his face in Aethalides's direction and the son of Hermes went wide eyed.

"Oh, did I say that out loud?" He muttered and then flashed his big grin. "I mean, *yay!* Two Viking gods!"

Heimdallr and Loki both went wide eyed, looking to each other for a moment and then, childishly pointing at the other person, crying out.

"I'm not sailing with him!"

"Looks like you are," Medea smirked.

Icarus subtly shuffled his way over to Vali who looked like he wanted the sea to swallow him whole while his father and Heimdallr seemed to annoy each other. Loki with being... Loki and Heimdallr with... just his presence alone.

They did eventually leave the docks and started sailing off into the Sea of Nine, Aethalides at the helm, Loki and Heimdallr on either side of him. It was the Norse equivalent of having the devil on one shoulder and an angel on the other.

Vali was looking up worriedly, his grip tight around his arms as he watched Loki and Heimdallr alternate between annoying each other and annoying Aethalides with their annoying each other antics.

"Quick question," Icarus whispered to him. "Why did you ask Heimdallr to come?"

"Because he comes from the sea!" Vali hissed at him. "He was born of nine mothers; this is the Sea of Nine Mothers!"

"His... what now?"

"His mothers... the nine daughters of Aeger and Ran?" Vali explained with a raised eyebrow. "Did you not know that?"

"Ummm... no."

"Oh, well, Heimdallr has nine mothers, he was born in the

sea and then came to land."

"Nine mothers… how does that even work?"

Vali shrugged. Right. He probably didn't know and besides, like most things with gods, it was better to just nod your head and say 'okay'. Trying to work out the logistics of any of their births could be a headache sometimes.

He knew for a fact one of the Aztec goddesses got pregnant from a ball of feathers, Perseus's mum by a shower of gold that was Zeus and Anubis had two dads and one mum. Yep, it was sometimes just best to nod your head and smile, because if you thought about it for too long it would drive you crazy.

"Vali!"

They both jumped at the yell, turning to look at Aethalides who seemed one bad word away from committing murder of some kind.

"Get your dads away from me right now!"

"Excuse me!" Loki hissed, pointing at himself. "I'm the only dad here!"

Aethalides ignored him, glaring intensely at Vali as his eye twitched. Huh. Apparently, he did have a limit on how much he could handle. Who knew.

Vali slowly walked over to the two gods and guided them away from Aethalides, Medea was looking on in amusement, while Boudicca and Asterion seemed to be mostly keeping to themselves. Though the Celtic queen did cast concerned looks their way, Vali shook his head. They would be fine, apparently.

Icarus glanced at Heimdallr and Loki who were glaring daggers at each other.

Boy, he hoped Vali was right about that.

"Fudge?"

Icarus jolted backwards at the packet of fudge that was

shoved in his face by... Heimdallr Loki seemed to be silently judging the god and Heimdallr as always was impossible to read.

"I er... thanks...?" He reached into the bag and took a small piece out, Heimdallr nodded and offered the same to Vali.

Icarus took a bite of the fudge and had to stop himself from spitting it out. What was this? Did Heimdallr add... extra sugar? To fudge!? Next to him, Vali sniffed the bag and whined pitifully.

"How much sugar did you put on that stuff, Heimdallr?" He asked and the god shrugged.

Loki pressed a finger to his forehead, closing his eyes and muttering under his breath. Icarus didn't catch it, but Heimdallr did and he span around to glare at the trickster.

"Don't you dare talk about my mother's like that!" He snarled.

"Why?" Loki smirked. "What ya' going to do about it?"

"Guys..." Vali sighed. "Please stop."

Loki and Heimdallr looked offended, pointing at each other in outrage. "He started it!" They both shouted at the same time.

Oh boy... this was going to be a long journey.

Icarus didn't know how long they'd been sailing for, but it felt like days, even though it was probably only hours. Loki and Heimdallr continued to irritate each other and throw casual death threats that Vali seemed to ignore for the most part. When Boudicca asked if everything was okay, Vali waved her off and said yeah, it was fine. They were always like this.

Well, wasn't that just great to hear.

If they didn't die at sea due to it being... the sea, they were more likely going to die to a godly tantrum or a battle, it was hard to say.

In the end, Vali reluctantly took his father away from

Heimdallr on the other side of the boat, leaving Icarus with a scowling watchman. Not for the first time, Icarus wished he was anywhere but here.

"Why did *he* have to come," Heimdallr grumbled. "The backbiter isn't welcome."

"I guess… he just wanted to spend time with Vali…?" Icarus tried, flinching at the murderous look Heimdallr shot him. "I don't think he should like, but his intentions seem pure…"

"Loki's intentions are never pure," Heimdallr scoffed. "I told everyone that. I said to them 'we can't trust him' and they all brushed it off with excuses; 'oh that's just Loki' or 'he wouldn't do anything to hurt us' and my favourite 'that's just his sense of humour, Heimdallr, maybe you should get one too'."

"Oh… so… no one guessed that he was…"

"The most untrustworthy, cowardly and bitter individual that ever graced the halls of Asgard?" Heimdallr rose an eyebrow. "Ha! No. All except me. I saw him for what he was, pure chaos… just like that insufferable squirrel."

"Insufferable what now?"

The god waved him off. "Never mind," he crossed his arms and continue to glare daggers at Loki. "I just wish they'd listen to me, but no, I'm too serious to take anything lightly. I can be funny," the god continued and Icarus stared at him worriedly. It seemed Heimdallr was having a bit of an emotional crisis, even if it was… subtle. "Skadi thinks I'm funny, but no one seems to get my jokes!"

"No offence dude, but your face and voice… barely change," Icarus said slowly, trying to word himself carefully. "You… kind of speak in a flat monotone the entire time. It's hard to tell when you're joking or not."

Heimdallr regarded him a moment. "I have not been joking

the entire time I've been on this ship, Icarus."

"Soo… all those threats you said to Loki? About ripping out his innards and making him eat your sword," Icarus ticked them off and then shuddered. "And some I don't dare repeat… you were being completely honest?"

Heimdallr gave a single nod.

Icarus turned away slightly stunned. "Wow. You're creative."

"Thank you."

"Yeah that… that wasn't a compliment…"

"Hey we're here!" Aethalides shouted, coming down from his place at the top of the ship.

Icarus looked out around them to see nothing but sea. They weren't even near any kind of land as far as he could see.

"Umm… we're where?" Icarus called over to him.

"Did you get lost?" Boudicca scowled at Aethalides and the other scowled right back.

"Hello, the guy with immortal memory here," he tapped at the side of his temple. "Believe me, I wish I could forget and say I got lost, but no… we're in the right spot."

Vali peered out across the sea, squinting at it. "Is… is the land invisible?"

"In a sense," Aethalides carefully climbed up to peer over the edge into the water. "It's in the underground caves of the sea bed. 'There are places to breathe once you get there. So," he clapped his hands excitedly, turning to everyone. "Who wants to go in first?"

Unsurprisingly there were no volunteers to head into the cold ocean.

That was until Loki slipped his shirt off and proudly stepped forward. Placing a hand on his tattooed chest with a grin. Icarus

232

grimaced at the tattoo on Loki's back, done in careful orange ink, it depicted the world tree on fire.

"I shall go bravely into the depths for you," he declared. "I just… what is it I'm looking for?"

"Trust me, you'll know it when you see it," Aethalides replied and Loki shrugged, climbing up so he was on the other side of the railing.

Unsurprisingly, Heimdallr was quick to stop him, grabbing his arm and glaring at the half giant.

"You're not going alone," he bit out. "I'm going with you."

Icarus watched as Heimdallr began slipping his cloak and shirt off, with Loki scoffing and rolling his eyes.

"And what are you going to do exactly?" Loki scoffed.

"I'm going to shapeshift into a seal," Heimdallr stated, climbing the railing and throwing the tiniest smirk at Loki. "Or did you forget I could do that?"

"You got lucky that day," Loki promised darkly, his eyes sparking with power for a brief moment. "And know that I will never forget an insult. I can't wait for the day of Ragnarok," he stood up, getting into Heimdallr's face. "Words can't describe how much fun it's going to be to run you through with my sword and watch the light fade from your eyes. I'll cherish every second of it."

"I wouldn't get your hopes up," Heimdallr replied evenly, then shoved Loki into the water and the other god let out a yelp. Then Heimdallr jumped into the sea too.

The Archives poked their heads over to stare into the sea, watching as the two gods got consumed by light and then a pair of seals were in their place. One silver, the other a reddish seal who barked at the other, which splashed him making the Loki seal snort and spit out water.

The two dived under the waves, leaving the others to wait quietly on the deck. Icarus wasn't too sure how good it would be to let them go alone, considering how much they hated each other, he wouldn't be surprised to see blood coming to the service at any moment. Or, if only one of them resurfaced. His money was on Heimdallr, the guy seemed intense and not in a good way.

"I thought… male gods didn't use magic in your culture?" Boudicca asked Vali who flinched away for a moment.

"My father has always used magic, but yes… it's… frowned upon." Vali said quietly. "Men are supposed to fight with weapons, women are supposed to use magic, because it's a woman's art."

Aethalides chuckled as he leaned against the railing casually tossing one of his knives into the air and catching it. "Yeah, that's the rule… unless you're Odin. Then it's a-okay."

Vali scowled. "The Alfather… is a perfect example of do as I say, not as I do. Besides, he craves 'knowledge'," he did quotation marks with his fingers and scoffed. "He uses it as an excuse to practise magic. He's a better liar than my father."

Medea casually leaned against the edge of the ship with a smirk. "You have to tell us, Vali, have Loki and Heimdallr always hated each other so much?"

"For as long as I can remember."

So now all they had to do was wait. Waiting was the worst part of the whole thing. At least for now everything was quiet, the open ocean meant they didn't have to deal with any surprise attacks or gangs that thought way too highly of themselves. It was just them and the open ocean, which was… made up of Heimdallr's mothers apparently, but they also walked on Gaia the literal personification of the earth so… weirder things existed out there.

Icarus sat down on the boat next to Vali who seemed content to just pull his hood up and bury himself in his clothing. He seemed more embarrassed by his dads' behaviour and sure, Loki and Heimdallr despised each other but there was no denying that they were both trying to fill the role of father for Vali. It was... kind of funny to watch. Another thing those two were going to have a falling out about.

"Hey...?" Icarus nudged him with his shoulder. "Odin... isn't that bad, is he?"

"Even the people who worshipped us didn't trust Odin, Icarus," Vali replied with a scowl. "I'm not sure any of the Æsier truly trust him."

"I mean, sure... gods are tricky, but like Zeus isn't the most honest person in the world.."

"Icarus, believe me, Odin is no Zeus. Odin is worse," Vali looked to him with a serious expression. "Once he came back to Asgard after hanging himself on the world tree he found out that... in his absence his wife had slept with his two brothers. Apparently all parties thought Odin was dead... but they didn't mourn for long."

"Okay...?" Icarus frowned. "Still failing to see-."

"Odin found out. Long story short... his brothers 'disappeared'," Vali did quotation marks again with his fingers. "After that. It doesn't take a genius to work out what happened..."

"Isn't... killing family, a big deal in your culture?"

Vali smirked and looked to him with a smile that didn't reach his eyes. "It is. But... the rules don't apply to Odin. Sometimes I wonder if he made my dad the father of lies and deceit just to distract everyone from his own."

Icarus shuddered slightly. Yep, Norse gods were... intense

no doubt about that. I mean, sure the Greek pantheon had its moments, but they were more dramatic than intense, for the most part at least.

A dark shadow fell over the group and when they looked up a huge fishing ship greeted them. It was massive and the crew glared at them, jumping down onto their ship, causing it to rock violently.

Man, the fates must really hate them.

The other crew were a mixture of half humans, Jötuns and Cyclops that all glared at them. The weapons on their person did not bode well and instantly everyone was reaching for their own weapons just in case.

"This ere is our turf," one Jötun growled out, standing in front of them. He was obviously the captain and had a large scar running down the side of his face, making one of his eyes a blind milky white.

"I didn't know fishermen had turfs?" Aethalides responded evenly. "Well, not to worry, we're not here for fish."

"Yeah, I know what you're 'ere for," the one eye growled, pulling out his sword, pointing it right at Aethalides's neck. "You're here looking for selkies."

Icarus exchanged a worried look with Vali. Heimdallr and Loki had both turned into seals when they'd dived and selkies were famously water-based people who turned into seals when they were in the sea. They couldn't have gotten mixed up? Surely not? No one could be *that* dumb.

Aethalides narrowed his eyes. "There are no selkies here and even if there were, I wouldn't be hunting them. They're people."

One eye huffed a laugh. "Sure, they are. You know what else they are, money. An' it's just swimming in that ocean out there," he vaguely gestured to the sea, grinning horribly at them. "You know it and I know it. So why don't you quit lying."

"We're not lying," Medea bit out with a scowl of her own. "And I'm not one for morals, but hunting a race of people for their coats... is barbaric and inhuman beyond imagination."

"I know you're lying," one eye turned to one of his men and nodded. "Lookie what we got!"

They looked over to the other ship as a large net was lifted out of the water and held above it, showing Heimdallr and Loki, still in seal form, crumpled onto each other. Loki even seemed to have a seal pelt in his mouth and one eye walked over, reaching to try and stanch the pelt from Loki, who snarled and barked at him.

"Heh, feisty little selkie aren't ya'?"

Aethalides raised a hand with a vaguely worried expression. "That's ah... not actually-."

"Quiet! See I told you, you were lying," one eye smirked at them. "So, we're going to tie weights to your feet and drop you over the edge and keep these two for ourselves," he turned back to Loki and Heimdallr and practically leered at them. "I've never seen a silver or red one before... oh, you two are going to fetch a pretty penny."

"Dude!" Icarus shouted angrily. "They're not-."

"No, no, hold on, darling," Medea said, raising her hand to silence him. "Let this play out, it could be fun."

"What are you talking about?" One eye thundered, causing the ship to rock dangerously back and forth. "I got the selkies!"

"No dumb, dumb," Aethalides scoffed. "You didn't. They're not selkies."

One eye looked confused, standing up straight and a bright light appeared behind him. When he turned around, he looked dumbfounded to see both Loki and Heimdallr, scrunched up in the net. Heimdallr looks ready to murder and Loki looks the same with a hint of amusement.

Loki raised his hand and waved. "Hiya!"

"Ah. Um... Lord Heimdallr and Loki... I..." one eye spluttered as the two gods looked on. "I didn't mean, I'm not really hunting down selkies honest! I'm not... I just... I'm just looking for them to help them! Yeah!"

Neither God looked impressed. Loki looked visibly insulted that one eye had even attempted to lie to his face and Heimdallr just looked bored and mildly irritated. Still, the expression didn't change much.

Loki turned to Heimdallr. "Please, can I kill him?"

Surprisingly, Heimdallr gestured to the Jötun. "Be my guest."

That was all Loki needed before he cut the next open and leapt out, unfortunately sending Heimdallr into the sea again with a lot of yelled curses directed at the trickster.

The Archives took this as the 'okay' to start fighting themselves. Nothing like getting a seal of approval from a god to encourage less than okay behaviour.

The fishermen weren't hard to deal with, the hardest part was not trashing the boat too much, they did have to return it after all.

Heimdallr climbed over the railing looking irritated and sopping wet, leaping at the first enemy he saw with a feral cry.

Vali was using his sword for once and covering Icarus who shot at the few fishermen on the boat still. They were obviously trying to get away, but he wasn't having it. Running and jumping at the netting and using it like a rope ladder to get up to the top. Usually he wasn't nearly this brave, but Icarus had been a prisoner too once, so on the off chance there were selkies on this boat, he wanted to help them.

238

Boudicca wasn't far behind him, climbing onto the ship and giving him protecting from behind as a half human, half fae charged at them. Boudicca ducked his swing and slammed her shield straight into his face, knocking him out cold.

Soon, Loki and Heimdallr were joining them on the boat, running through it and taking out anyone they came across, until the few remaining fishermen surrounded, dropping their weapons and holding their hands up.

"Cowards," Heimdallr growled, getting his sword ready, but Vali intervened.

"We hand them over to the proper authorities," he insisted, stopping the watchman in his tracks from decapitating anyone.

"Yeah!" Aethalides shouted up. "I can use it to get in on good books with Brianna! Wouldn't hurt."

"Oh, you lot are no fun," Loki scowled. "I was looking forward to watching Heimdallr start lopping heads."

Heimdallr sheathed his sword, shaking his head. "There would be no honour in killing unarmed opponents."

They searched the ship, but there were no selkies there, plenty of their pelts though. It made Icarus sick to his stomach and Loki added the one he'd apparently brought up to the service after venturing into the caves.

They tried the crew up and shoved them into the cells in their own ship, tying the other ship to the one they were using and putting the few bodies they had on the other ship, while Icarus was forced to clean the deck of the one they'd leant. After all, they had to return it in one piece.

Aethalides was busy texting Brianna, while also asking Loki and Heimdallr about the caves below as they sailed back.

"There was nothing there," Heimdallr reported. "But.."

"There definitely had been!" Loki filled in with a smirk.

"You aren't going to believe it, but there was a whole settlement down there and that's where we found the selkie pelt!"

"So, they had been living there?" Icarus asked from his part on the deck, mop in hand. Vali was on the other ship, gently staring at it so the ship didn't sail too far away or end up smacking into the other.

"Sure did, but the place down there has been abandoned for years."

"Selkies..?" Medea whispered, turning to Aethalides who looked equally confused and worried. "I thought... Well, there's Selkie cove but I don't think anyone has actually seen a selkie. I thought they were just a myth."

Heimdallr shook his head. "Not a myth. But... selkies are in danger. Their coats are different to seal pelts, and highly sorted out. As you've seen."

Icarus screwed his face up in disgust. "I can't believe people steal selkie pelts to sell them!"

"Oh, dear me boy," Loki sniggered. "They don't just do that. Selkie poachers will literally cut the selkie coat away from the body. They'll kill them to get their hands on their pelts," he said with a grin. "Do you have any idea what they're worth?"

"But... but Selkies are... they're people!"

"Well sure," Loki leaned back on the boat, sitting on the railing, while pointing at Icarus. "But people lose their humanity the moment money is involved. Oh Heimdallr," he simpered as the god busily ate his fudge, throwing a glare Loki's way. "You must be so proud of your descendants."

Heimdallr's consumption of fudge increased tenfold. Icarus guessed the god was using it as a way to distract himself from murdering Loki on the spot right now.

The trip back was nice and easy, Brianna and her men were

there to arrest someone else that wasn't them. She looked like she was going to chew them out for killing a few of the guys again, but at the sight of the two gods she, somewhat begrudgingly, snapped her mouth shut and marched off.

One less thing to worry about. Loki made himself scarce pretty quickly too. Probably didn't want to stay around Heimdallr much longer, but not before speaking to Vali.

Icarus couldn't read the expression on his face, but he seemed to be looking at Heimdallr a bit more warily this time. Whatever Loki had said, hadn't been a good thing, but it wasn't like Vali was going to talk about it. He didn't tend to talk about himself at all really.

"So..." Medea stood next to Aethalides who was busily scribbling another place out on the map with a grim expression. "Still no luck. Are we sure this... individual is coming back?"

"Positive," the son of Hermes mumbled. "We still have other places to look, like the desert and such."

"Oh, I can't wait for those trips," she rolled her eyes at him. "I might be away when you decide to go there."

"Convenient."

"Isn't it just?"

Heimdallr came over to them, still looking as stern as before, shoulders straight and back even straighter. It was like the guy never did relax.

"I must return to my watch, but... I did enjoy this trip," he turned to Vali. "Be sure to contact me should you need my help."

"Sure, thanks Heimdallr," Aethalides smiled up at him and the god nodded, pressing his fist to his chest and actually bowing to them. Icarus was more than a little bewildered by the action. Him? Being bowed to by a god? Surreal.

"By the gods, you live!"

Everyone except for Heimdallr was startled when Anansi appeared out of nowhere. Extending his multiple arms out.

"Honestly I can't believe it! Oh, hi Heimdallr!" He waved at the other god and Heimdallr offered one of his rare smiles in return.

"Anansi," he nodded to him. "Been to the desert I see."

Anansi grinned standing with his arms out. "Went for a visit in Inanna's Haven. The people there love my stories and the sun whoo! Reminds me of home."

Heimdallr nodded in understanding and said, "Feel free to drop by with some new stories. Bragi wishes to turn more of them into songs."

"Sure, sure, I'm working on one at the moment," Anansi grinned widely. "It's called the Tale of the Sea Ram!" He dramatically moved his arms like he was reading the title of a novel. "All the locals around here have been talking non-stop about the thing, and figured I could take a shot at it."

"The… sea ram?" Heimdallr frowned.

"Oh yeah, these knuckleheads are insisting they keep seeing a ram enter and leave the sea late at night or something like that. Every so often it just pops up," Anansi sniggered. "They want to capture the thing apparently. Crazy, right?"

Heimdallr blinked and then nodded his head. "Yes. Crazy. I must take my leave now."

Anansi walked over as the other god vanished in a blur of rainbows and Bifrost magic, leaving the Archives alone.

"I take it from those dower expressions you didn't find them?" The spider god stated.

"No," Aethalides sighed. "But at least that's one more place ticked off our list. So, we're one step closer to finding that Oracle."

One step closer and it still didn't feel like they'd gotten any closer, no matter what Aethalides said.

Icarus subtly moved around the group to stand with Vali, who still seemed to be a little lost.

"Are you okay?"

"Huh? Oh, yeah…" Vali waved him off. "Just something my father said, it's nothing."

"Are you sure?"

"Yeah. Promise."

"Okay.." Icarus nudged his shoulder playfully and smiled at him. "But you know you can tell me, right?"

Vali laughed and nodded his head. "Yeah, I know."

Dreams are just pretty nightmares: 13

Aethalides wandered down the steps of the Archives, dressing gown on, monster slippers on full display as he wandered down the steps towards the kitchen. He needed a coffee, no one else was up yet, it was just him. Not something that was unusual, he did get up early, just to have a little bit of time to himself where the building was quiet. It felt like even The Heart of Atlantis itself was asleep, but he knew for a fact that by now people would be setting up their various shops.

He reached the kitchen and instantly set about making a cup of coffee and putting some toast on. Glancing up at the clock he knew he'd have at least fifteen minutes of silence and then on the hour, all hades would break loose. The Archives would suddenly come alive, filled with noise and voices.

Toast and coffee made, he sat at the table, taking a bite as he grabbed the newspaper and started to read... except... he couldn't read. The paper was... nonsense. His chewing slowed and he stared at the paper in confusion.

Was Eris in control of the gossip column again and she'd just outstretched her magic to the rest of the paper? He wouldn't be surprised, she tended to do things like that. Either way, she completely ruined his morning paper.

Aethalides sighed and slammed the paper down on the table, continuing to eat his toast and drink his coffee. Another glance at the clock and it was only ten minutes to go. He hurriedly finished his toast and drank his coffee in silence, closing his eyes and enjoying the moment of peace.

With five minutes to go, Aethalides made himself another coffee, sitting and waiting, glancing back to the clock that only had one minute left.

He took a breath and closed his eyes, counting down in his head for the final moment his peace would be broken, but nothing happened.

He snapped his eyes open and looked up at the clock. It was past the hour. Maybe... maybe they were just late getting up. Yeah, that would be surprising, the whole mess with the trip a few days ago had taken a lot out of some of them.

Aethalides shrugged and went back to his coffee, but as the minutes ticked by he became more and more anxious. He kept looking at the clock, poking his head round to look into the library, anxiously waiting for someone to step through and walk to the kitchen but nothing happened.

They were just late getting up, that's all it was.

He awkwardly tapped away at his coffee cup, looking up at the clock again, then the door and then took an anxious sip. Soon, he couldn't even concentrate on drinking the coffee, what was left of his drink went cold and his anxiety spiked when the clock struck half past.

This wasn't right. They were supposed to be up. They were supposed to be here with him right now, arguing and bickering. Xbalanque was supposed to be up at least half an hour ago without a doubt to get his breakfast so he could go to work. This wasn't right, where was everyone!?

Aethalides pushed away from the table and got up, walking to the stairs and taking them two at a time. He didn't want to rush too much, just in case he was being silly and they really had just slept in. It would certainly be a first, but… well, stranger things had happened in his life then his entire household having a lie in.

He went to Xbalanque's room first, knocking on the door because if the guy really had just slept in, then someone needed to get him up for his job. He might make fun of the fact it felt like Xbalanque was leaving the group, but he was in fact, quite proud of him. It took a lot for any of them to try and reconnect with the modern world, to get back with people after so long. Sure, sometimes Aethalides would go up and see Xbalanque and seem to make talking to modern people easy, but it wasn't. He'd been scanning the internet before he got to the police station to build some sort of knowledge about the modern world and modern interests of kids, since he was physically ten again. Besides, Xbalanque was… well, he was being brave. Reconnecting with the world they'd all left behind because they no longer fit in it and then Xbalanque decided to get back to the modern world, make friends.

Aethalides wasn't brave enough to do that. He wouldn't be able to deal with… saying goodbye at the end of it.

He rocked back and forth on his heels for a moment, but still nothing happened. The door didn't open, he didn't even hear someone shout.

Aethalides bit his lip and knocked a little harder, but still nothing. Soon he was slamming his fists against the door but there was absolutely nothing, not a single sound came from the other side of the door.

"Xbalanque!?" He shouted. "Hey this isn't funny! Are you all right!?"

Nothing.

"I'm coming in!" Aethalides yelled reaching for the handle. "You better be there and unconscious or something…"

He opened the door and there was no one there. There was nothing there. No bed, no furniture at all. Not a single thing that hinted to anyone having ever lived there in the first place.

Aethalides stumbled inside and looked around. Nothing. Not Xbalanque's jacket, none of his Mayan artwork or his weapons that were always proudly displayed above his bed as one of the first things you saw. The room was empty and plain.

"Xbalanque!?" He shouted, even though he knew it was fruitless. He wasn't here. Nothing was here.

For a moment, he almost worried he'd gone into the wrong room, but Aethalides knew he hadn't. He had an immortal memory, he knew exactly where everyone was.

"This is wrong..." he mumbled. "This is wrong, this is wrong... Xbalanque! Medea!" Aethalides ran out into the hall, running to the end of the hall and slamming it open. "Arachne!"

Nothing. Just another empty room. None of Arachne's weaving supplies or piles and piles of thread, wool or any other material she would weave with. No pitch black room to help cope with the brightness, it was just like Xbalanque's room. Blank. Empty and like no one had ever been there.

Aethalides ran through the rest of the Archives, slamming all of the bedroom doors open and every single one of them were empty. Devoid of any personal effects and no matter how loud he shouted or screamed, no one answered him. The only room that had anything in it was his room, but the room was wrong. It was completely wrong.

Aethalides almost stumbled out of his room when he found his old room, not the one he currently had in the Archives, but the one he used to have in ancient Greece. Back when he'd been a Lord of Larissa, everything was exactly as he remembered it. Drapes, furniture and fur. Even the air smelt like home, something he missed but knew he could never have again.

He backed out of the room, smacking into the wall behind him and staring at it. He could hear the sound of birds chirping, the horses they kept in the nearby field that his room would overlook and even the distinct sound of servants walking back and forth in the corridors outside his room.

"Aethalides?" Came a sweet, sweet voice he hadn't heard in centuries but would recognise anywhere. It made his legs shake and he stared at the room in wide eyed horror as he heard his mother calling to him again. "Aethalides? Aethalides, where are you?"

He shook his head rapidly, running to the door and slamming it shut, pressing his forehead against it as he took a few breaths.

"Okay… okay, this… this was a good trick, Medea, honest, one of your best ones!" He called out, straightening and looking around the corridor. "But it isn't funny any more! This has gone too far! Cut it out!"

Silence.

He licked his lips, feeling his mouth go dry and sweat start to trickle down the side of his head.

"Y… you can come out now!" Aethalides yelled, spinning around on the spot. "You all can! Haha, very funny! Let's all make fun of the guy with the mental issues, I get it, it's hilarious!" He shouted as anger started to creep into his voice, desperately trying to battle the fear. Vying for control. "But it isn't funny any more!"

His voice echoed down the corridors but still no one answered him.

"Hey!" He screamed, running down the corridors and sprinting downstairs again. "Come out! Quit messing with me, this isn't funny!"

Aethalides ran, he ran around the entire archives, opening door after door, but there was nothing. He searched the bookshelves for Anansi, but the little spider god was nowhere to be seen. In desperation he even started to yank all of the books off the shelves, searching for the spider, but there was no trace of him. He wasn't here.

Aethalides sprinted out of the library and began to search every single room downstairs, throwing doors open to find them the same as he left them, except for the fact there was a layer of dust and elements of decay in them. Whichever room was used more by his friends, that room would always be worse than the rooms he would use and that meant only the kitchen and library were in any good kind of condition.

He slammed the door open to the dining room and froze at the sight. The table was set for all nine of them, but a layer of dust lay across all the furnishings and table set. Cobwebs hung from the chandeliers and candle holders, some were even on the chairs.

Suddenly a loud creaking sounded behind him and he nearly jumped out of his skin at another noise other than his own shouting, footsteps and ragged breath.

Aethalides slowly turned around, looking down the corridor to find the door opened to the one room he hadn't checked.

It was a room he didn't like to go into, not even at the best of times because it hurt too much.

The memorial room was small, sort of shoved into the corner when it really should be centre stage, but Aethalides couldn't do that. He couldn't have his own failures, see the many members of the Archives they had lost over time from various quests shoved in his face. Each life lost was a life he could've lost for himself and saved the other, only for him to bounce back a few years later. He wanted to commemorate them, they deserved to be remembered, but he didn't go in, at least, he only went in to add another photo to the wall and leave.

Some people he'd lost so long ago he didn't even have a photo, just a detailed sketch.

Aethalides stared at the ajar door, feeling his hands shake and he swallowed uneasily. Walking towards the door, it felt like the short distance across the hall got longer and longer, like each step he took got him nowhere.

He reached it and hesitantly placed his hand to the door, pushing it open. Inside was pitch black. He slowly stepped in, even the light from the corridor didn't light the way, the room stayed completely dark.

Aethalides shakily reached for the light switch and flicked it. All the air left his lungs as he looked at the photos before him, shaking his head rapidly. There were new ones. Icarus, Vali, Xbalanque, Boudicca, Asterion, Anansi, Medea and Arachne's photos were all facing him, surrounded by a myriad of other photos and sketches. They ran up the walls, reaching the ceiling and seemed to be steadily increasing with every moment.

"No, no, no, no... NO! No that's not... that didn't happen, they're alive- they're.." Aethalides choked on his words, letting out a scream when the door behind him abruptly slammed shut. "No, no, no, no... no, no!" He scrambled for the door, yanking on the handle but it didn't budge, no matter how hard he tugged at it, screamed and beat his fist against it.

Looking back at the photos they'd all changed to be glaring right at him. Each image and sketch, altered and charged so the pictures were glaring with accusing eyes right at him, just by looking at them he knew they were blaming him.

"No!" Aethalides yelled and slammed his hands against the

door. "Let me out, let me out! Let me out!"

The light above him flickered, once, twice and then went out completely, plunging him in darkness.

"No, no, no! No, put it back on, put it back! Don't leave me in here!" He scrambled for the light switch on the wall, flicking it back on, the light amazingly turned on too.

Aethalides glanced behind him in fear and when he did, he wished he hadn't. The images had all changed, they were still the people but they'd morphed to stretch their features, blacked out eyes with screaming faces of pain. The words 'All your fault' and 'it should've been you' were painted in big red letters across the warped photos.

Aethalides screamed, tears finally spilling down his cheeks and he let out a pathetic whine as he tugged and tugged at the door handle desperately, sobs wracking his frame.

"Let me out, let me out!" He whimpered tugging at the door, shoving himself against it. "Let me out! I... I'm sorry, I'm sorry!" Aethalides turned to the warped images, watching in horror as blood started to bubble up from the images themselves. "I'm sorry!" He shouted again. "I tried! I would've tried... I would've..." Words failed him as the blood on the walls began to alter and change, turning into another sentence that read 'you should've tried harder'.

All at once the images began animated, still with their distorted features as the faces contorted and changed, finding their voices.

"Now we're all dead because of you!" The photos screamed, the noise was deafening and Aethalides curled in on himself, covering his ears as he shook and cried out.

"Let me out... let me out!" He whimpered, reaching for the door handle again, but now... there was no door handle. "No...

no, no, no… let me out! I didn't mean… for this to happen! I didn't mean… I'm sorry!"

The noise and the yelling got louder, he wasn't sure if he was trying to drown out the voices with his own yelling or if he was trying to get them to believe he really had tried. Each time he got louder, each time he screamed or yelled, the voices seemed to scream and yell louder, blocking and deafening his own excuses.

Then, just when he thought he wouldn't be able to stand it any more, everything went silent. He'd squeezed his eyes shut over time, but now he slowly opened them. He was scared to turn around and look at whatever it was that would greet him. He didn't want to see. He didn't want to look at whatever the pictures had turned into now.

Aethalides sucked in a breath, trying to calm his breathing, slowly turning back towards the wall and he felt sick to his stomach. There was no one. Not a single photo or sketch littered the wall.

This was almost worse than before.

"Oh gods… no, no don't go… don't leave me here!" Aethalides cried and pressed his back against the door, screaming when it abruptly opened behind him and sent him tumbling backwards.

Aethalides looked up and let out a broken cry as photos and sketches of all that had died now littered the entire walls and ceilings of the archives around him.

He needed to get out, he needed to leave, he couldn't be here any more. He had to get out.

Scrambling to his feet he ran down the corridor, finding the images now littering the floor as well, almost causing him to trip up or slip over several times, but eventually, he made it to the front door.

Aethalides threw it open without a second thought, dashed down the steps and skidded to a halt, eyes wide and disbelieving.

The Heart of Atlantis was in ruins. The city was nothing but crumbled pieces of debris and fallen statues littered the streets.

Slowly he walked towards the gates on feet that didn't quite feel like his own. Reaching the gate and pushing it open, looking up and down the empty streets, filled with wreckage and broken down homes or pieces of timber blocking the way. He didn't even need to walk the streets to know they'd be devoid of anyone.

A dark chuckle echoed around the streets and he watched all the shadows move, pulling across the floor and suddenly shooting up into the air, forming a rough shape made of jagged edges. Slowly they took shape, forming a long thin, shapeless body with broad shoulders, eight sharp black legs ripped out of its back, forming some kind of halo backed by huge bat-like wings with dark purple insides protruding out of its shoulders. Then the head of the thing formed, with a pointed, sharp edged crown, a pointed smile of jagged teeth and finally glowing purple, sharp eyes, snapped open. No arms, no legs, just a long thin body that could bend and curve in inhuman ways as the being stretched up to the sky, blocking out the light and leaning over Aethalides, purple smoke left its mouth as it started to chuckle and laugh at him.

"Poor, poor Aethalides…" the thing spoke, breaking down into more laughter, each time it spoke, smoke would filter out of its mouth and it looked like its teeth would move. Almost like a demonic version of an old-timey cartoon. "It sure sucks when you outlast everyone." The thing leaned down so it was in his face and Aethalides felt himself choking on the smoke. "Even the gods…"

Aethalides coughed and tried to scramble out of the smoke,

staring up at this… this thing in utter terror. "W-what? No, I can't… I can't outlast the gods!"

The black mass rose up again, laughing the entire time, shoulders shaking. "Look around you," it crooned, finally growing long arms that were a mixture of insect and tentacle-like. "Does it look like there's any gods around here? Does it look like there's anyone here?"

"I can't outlive… I can't outlive anyone…" Aethalides whispered. "I can't outlive the gods…"

The thing chuckled, the laughter echoed around him, bouncing off the walls and nearly blowing out his eardrums. Aethalides covered his ears desperately and tried to back away from the thing. Smoke and shadows slowly reached across the floor, wrapping around his legs and arms like grotesque tentacles, pulling him up and towards the monster.

Aethalides yelled and shouted, tugging uselessly against the makeshift restraints as they lifted him up towards the thing's chest.

The insect and tentacle-like claws suddenly plunged into the monster's own chest, still laughing and billowing out of its mouth. It ripped its chest apart, opening up to reveal a purple glow and Aethalides could feel the glow burning him already. The ribs were still there and he let out a scream and jolted backwards as far as he could when spiders, dead people, scorpions and tentacles reached out between the ribs like they were prison bars.

"Let me go! Let me go! Help! Medea! *Father!*" Aethalides tried to grab at something, anything, but there was nothing to hold and the city started to fall down into broken ruins around him. Mocking laughter filled his ears as he was dragged closer and closer towards the ribs and the outreaching nightmares within. They grabbed at his shoulders and arms, pulling him closer as he tried to pull back, feeling the heat of the purple glow as it started to sizzle and burn his skin.

He let out a shriek as he felt the skin on his face starting to boil and blister up, the digging in claws of the skeleton like hands and a few more of the tentacles wrapped around his body and face, muffling his screaming.

Aethalides tugged and yanked, squeezing his eyes shut and finally yanked himself away, shooting upwards with a scream that hurt his throat and he was greeted with... the concerned faces of his friends and his father who were all surrounding him.

"Aethalides?" Hermes, his father, placed his hand on his shoulder to comfort and ground him.

"Whu- what? What happened... I don't..." Aethalides panted, looking around in alarm and disbelief. Sweat was dripping down his face, his hair was plastered to his forehead and he could feel the shirt on his back was much the same thing. He looked up to his father in confusion. "Is this real?"

His voice was quiet, too quiet for him and in a rare moment of humanity his father pulled him into a hug. Aethalides felt frozen for a moment and then shakily wrapped his arms around his father, burying his head into his chest and started to sob.

"It's okay," Hermes whispered, running his hands up and down his back. "It's okay, you're okay. You're safe."

Aethalides didn't say anything, he just held on tighter as his whole body shook from his crying. He felt like a little kid. Like a scared, frightened child and he couldn't help but feel a little bit pathetic.

"Look at what you did!" A new voice sounded up, their tone was sharp, but there was a tired edge to it, which only got more obvious when the owner yawned. "I told you, scare a little, but not to that extent… what were you thinking?"

"B- but daaaaaad!"

Aethalides snapped his eyes open and shoved away from Hermes staring in terror at the shadowy figure in the doorway, the same one from before.

He shook his head. "No, no, no…" he muttered like a mantra. "No, I'm still here… I'm still-."

"Whoa, whoa, no," Hermes placed his hands on his shoulders, turning Aethalides to look at him. "You're awake. You're here and you're awake."

Aethalides blinked owlishly at him. "Awake?" He echoed in confusion and Hermes nodded, smiling softly.

"Yes, Aethalides," Hermes soothed, brushing his sweat soaked hair back from his face. "You were trapped in a nightmare…" the last part growled out as his father turned a glare at the shadowy figure in the doorway. "Because Phobator doesn't know when to *quit!*"

The shadowy figure in the doorway shrank back a bit, looking to the other being next to him. Clearly the other was a god, with ashen grey skin, fluffy white hair that looked like a cloud, wearing an equally fluffy dressing gown and blanket, that was wrapped around his shoulders and decorated with poppies. A sleep mask with the words 'sweet dreams' written across it was pushing his fluffy fringe away from his eyes, big fluffy slippers that were miraculously staying on his feet as he hovered in the air. A cup of hot chocolate was in his hands and he looked worn out. Lidded eyes with huge eye bags that stood out against his pale ashen skin. His silvery purple eyes were glaring up at the Smokey figure of Phobator. It honestly looked like the god had just rolled out of bed.

"Do you have any idea…" the god continued, then yawned,

rubbing at his eye with his fist. "What time is it? Hermes had to come and get me because you never know when you got to stop."

"But... but dad, I was just-," Phobator began, but the other god held a finger up to silence him, taking a sip of his hot chocolate for a moment. Surprisingly, Phobator waited diligently for his father to finish.

He pulled the drink away, smacking his lips. "Phobator, we have talked about this on numerous occasions. You do your job, give them a nightmare or two," he ticked off and then hit him with an irritated look. "But you let them wake up. No trapping people in nightmares, you'll drive someone insane if you do that."

"But-."

Suddenly large wings expanded out of the god in the dressing gown's head and Aethalides's slow brain eventually caught up. This was Hypnos the god of sleep, the very incarnation of sleep itself. His son, or one of his sons, was Phobator, the incarnation of nightmares.

Nightmares... like what had just happened to him, that had been nothing but a nightmare, some twisted dream created by Phobator to torment him.

"The hades is wrong with you!" Aethaldies screamed trying to charge the god, but Hermes caught his arm and held him back. "Do you have any idea what you did to me? What did you put me through?"

Phobator, somehow, managed to hit him with a look that screamed 'well yeah, duh!' And it both irritated and angered him. How could anyone be so careless with their ability?

Hypnos flapped his wings angrily, sparkling, silver dust, like stars, fluttered from his fluffy wings.

"Phobator... it is... currently eleven a.m. eleven in the

morning!" Hypnos cried out, rising a little further in the air as his wings flared out, almost acting like Hypnos's arms while he nursed his cup of hot chocolate. "That is so late! I should be in bed, I should be asleep.." He yawned again, as if to emphasise his point. "Instead," he continued to speak while yawning. "I'm here... fixing this..." Hypnos loosely gestured towards Aethalides, flopping his hand by his side, like he didn't have the strength to hold it up any more. "Mess you made. And to an *Olympian* son as well! Are you *asking* for a punishment? I raised you to be smarter than that."

"Clearly, ya' didn't," Hermes chimed in, glaring daggers at the other. "What were you even hoping to accomplish?"

Phobator looked to the floor, swinging his body back and forth. He didn't have so much of a form in the real world, like this... smoky self was as much of himself as he could pull into the actual world and not the dream one. He mumbled something under his breath.

"I didn't catch that," Hypnos mumbled sleepily, rubbing at his eyes desperately. "What did you say?"

"I said I was prayed to. Someone wanted me to... to mess with him," he gestured to Aethalides. "So I did. I did what I was prayed to do, dad, what do you want me to do? Ignore my prayers?"

"In most cases no, in the case that the one in question is the son of an Olympian... yes!" Hypnos pinched the bridge of his nose. "I thought I taught you better... I told you... what was the one thing I told you?"

"Never get mixed up in Olympian business.." Phobator droned, sounding like a moody teenager who was forced to repeat what their parent had said many times over.

"And?" Hypnos prompted causing Phobator to let out the

longest sigh he could.

"And never get mixed up in Olympian adjacent business."

"There we go."

Seeing him being scolded by Hypnos made Phobator a lot less terrifying and Aethalides made his way up to the god of nightmares. He stood in front of him and the other tried his best to still look menacing, but after seeing the goth child of the god of sleep be told off and scolded like an immature toddler while their father, Hypnos, was wearing fluffy bunny slippers... Well. He lost his fear factor pretty quickly.

"Who was it?" Aethalides demanded. "Who was it that ordered you to do that?"

Phobator scowled. "I don't need to answer to you, half a mortal!"

"Phobator," Hypnos warned.

The god of nightmares swayed his body around irritably. "But daaaaad! It's my job!"

"Tell him or you are grounded for a month and with no hot chocolate."

He gaped at Hypnos for a moment, then he started to shake and fizzle, his body loosing it's shape, bubbling up as he pulled himself into an ominous floating ball of black goop, smoke and dust. Letting out a shriek of rage, spikes expanding out of his body and a shockwave was sent through the whole Archives, almost sending the semi mortals in the room tumbling to the floor. The two gods were fine. Hypnos didn't even look bothered, just casually took a sip of his drink as he watched his son a moment longer before he took his drink away, smacking his lips.

"Are you done?" Hypnos asked with a raised eyebrow.

Phobator quickly regained the form that at least gave him a head, arms crossed in front of himself as he tapped his finger against his elbow angrily.

"Fine," he spat, turning to Aethalides. "It was Rune! Rune was the one who prayed to me! There! You happy? You got your answer? Great, good!" He threw his hands up in the air. "Can I go now?"

Hypnos sighed. "We'll talk about your attitude later, young man," he placed a hand on his shoulder, pushing him out the room. "See you next time, Hermes!"

"Bye Hypnos," Hermes replied getting to his feet. He looked down at Aethlalides, placing his hand on his shoulder. "Are you sure you're okay?"

Aethalides nodded, smiling at his father and he hoped it was convincing. He didn't know why he was trying to lie to the literal god of liars, but hey he could hope.

"I'm fine dad, honest," he looked to everyone else. "Can someone please tell me what happened though?"

"You weren't downstairs," Xbalanque explained. "We knew something was wrong the moment you weren't there and when we all confirmed that no one had seen you at all… well, you get the picture."

"So, we went upstairs to check on you," Medea went on. "You were trapped in a nightmare and no matter what we did, we couldn't get you to wake up. So I contacted your father."

"And I," Hermes said. "Went to Hypnos. We would've gotten you up sooner but… It took me two hours just to get Hypnos up and even longer to get him to actually put some clothes on," he frowned a moment. "Dude sleeps in the *nude* under that expensive duvet. I did not need to know that and now the image is forever burned in my brain," Hermes clapped his hands together and smiled a very familiar megawatt smile. "Well that's something I'm going to have to live for eternity! *Fun times!*"

Aethalides nodded slowly, taking it all in. That seemed... right. Not the part about Hypnos, but everything else that made sense and checked out with his nightmare.

"Wait... what are you doing here?" Aethalides asked, pointing to Xbalanque. "Shouldn't you be at work?"

Xbalanque shrugged and offered a little smile of his own. "I called in and told them I had a family emergency."

"A... family... emergency."

"Well, yeah," Xbalanque threw him a bewildered look. "What else was I going to say?"

"Umm... no, you're right..." Aethalides said slowly. "You're right. Makes sense. Anyway, that means we have a problem," he pressed his finger tips together in thought. "Rune is obviously not above playing dirty, I just never expected him to go to these lengths. He's trying to slow us down... stop us from finding that oracle by distracting us."

"I'll inform the other gods not to answer any of his prayers," Hermes said. "I can't guarantee any results on that matter, but... I can at least ask."

"That would be... helpful," Aethalides nodded. "And... thank you, father... for... for saving me."

Hermes laughed, ruffling his hair, much to Aethalides's annoyance.

"No need to thank me, kiddo, it's what parents do. Anyway, I really need to get going now," Hermes sighed. "immortals... they have no patience!"

He blinked out of existence and Aethalides turned back to the others. They were looking at him expectantly, probably waiting for him to give a new plan of attack and oh boy he had one.

"What do we do now?" Icarus asked. "And are you sure you're okay?"

"I'm fine."

"Aethalides," Vali whispered. "You were crying."

Was he? Well, now he was definitely going to get even with Rune.

"Rune wants to try sabotaging us? Fine. We'll just double our efforts, which means splitting up," Aethalides said, a grin forming on his face. "Oh, but we're not just going to stop there. Thanks to Vali and Icarus we know that Rune, for some reason, is making a deal with the Port Side Raiders to get something out of Atlantis. We can only assume he aims to go to the mortal realm," he looked to Xbalanque and smirked. "Hey Xbalanque, you want to use your new job to help us crack down on their little operation back mortal side?"

Xbalanque grinned. "Sounds like fun."

"Oh it will be fun," Aethalides confirmed with a little laugh and the feral smile was back. "Rune's going to get a little lesson on what it means to cross a son of Hermes."

Port Side Raiders: 14

Xbalanque pulled his coat closer around himself as he got out of the car to view the docks, along with Jason. Well, he said docks, it was more a dock for canal boats and a few sailboats built for lakes, not the sea. Still, canals used to be good routes for trade and it wasn't uncommon for people to still use them for it, just... not so legal trade. Despite it being nearer the middle of spring, it was cold with the wind biting against his skin. Then again, this was England and it wasn't uncommon to see freezing cold temperatures in the middle of summer. Or at least they were freezing cold temperatures for him, Jason didn't seem to mind that much.

Jason shivered slightly, but he just shrugged it off, wandering over to the crime scene that was still being processed. At least this time, no one had been murdered, there was only someone that had been injured. He was already being seen by paramedics, but Xbalanque was starting to feel nervous.

He didn't catch much of it, but as they walked past the guy that was being seen to, clearly in shock, was bawling about monsters and demons. It wasn't demons, Xbalanque was certain of that, but he had a feeling he knew who it might be.

It was common knowledge that the Port Side Raiders used docks and canals in the mortal world to continue with their trade. Though there weren't many, there were a few humans that didn't live in Atlantis, but knew about 'its existence and to that extent, the existence of magic as a whole. They weren't supposed to have anything from Atlantis, those kinds of things and trade routes had been closed off and made illegal around the thirteen hundreds, but it didn't stop guys like Cillian from taking advantage of the situation.

Didn't stop gods like Hermes from openly encouraging it either.

Who'd have thought that there'd be a black market for magical items often procured by witches, warlocks, mages and any other individual that still lived in the mortal world but were gifted with magic. Not to mention all the monsters that would happily invade various places to cause trouble.

Most of the cryptids that people went on about were actually monsters from various mythologies that were just on a holiday, hence their usual appearance. By Xilbaba, sometimes those 'cryptids' were even *gods*.

With that in mind, he was also reminded of what Aethalides had said and he had to smother a grin.

Dealing with the Port Side Raiders was never a hard task, so to have the chance to really hammer it home to Cillian that he wasn't as good as he liked to think he was... well, Xbalanque wouldn't call himself petty, but it would be nice to rub that smug look off his face. 'Runes too.

Sure, stopping Cillian's operation here wouldn't be that detrimental to Rune, but it might set him back a little bit.

"Sir," one of the other officers came over to them, hooking a thumb towards the warehouse. "The dock hand said that whoever hit him was trying to load things into that warehouse. We're in the process of trying to find out who owns it and get the keys."

Xbalanque knew that there'd be... all sorts in there. Both human stuff and things from Atlantis. The mortal things were fine, but the Atlantis stuff? How could he get rid of it, especially with Jason around? Guy was like a hawk for certain things, anything suspicious he would catch in an instance, he already had done with Vali and some of the others who'd come to visit Xbalanque at work. Asking questions that Xbalanque had to think on the fly for an answer and he wasn't always great at that, not like Vali, not like he had been... but those were the good old days and that had been when he'd had his brother...

Xbalanque shook his head, turning his attention to the warehouse instead. If they could just get inside and if he could figure out a way to get Jason away for a bit... Well, getting rid of or hiding the various smuggled-out goods from Atlantis would be easy.

"Come on," he directed Jason towards the warehouse, finding it locked. Eh, easy enough.

"I told you it's locked," Jason sighed, pocketing his hands. "Wonder what they got in the-."

"Shh," Xbalanque raised a hand and pressed his head against the door, listening and could hear the sound of feet and... hooves. Oh. *great.* "There's people still in there," he explained to Jason who instantly reached for his phone.

"I'll get people down- X' what you *doing?*"

Xbalanque was busy dealing with the lock. He could handle this, by himself and make the Port Side Raiders pay and maybe cut off one of their connections to the human realm. On top of everything... it would inconvenience Rune a little. It was the little things.

In hindsight it made sense that Cillian would use Derby as a trade spot. It had been a Viking settlement, the Romans had also once settled here, there'd be old magic running through this place, along with descendants of various gods. And where there were descendants of gods there were bound to also be people who still had links to their ancestor's abilities and powers.

"Stay outside, I've got this," Xbalanque insisted as he muttered a little bit of a spell under his breath, easily breaking the lock. He hadn't used his magic like that in a long time. It was a good job it had actually worked and not... blown up in his face, which could've happened.

Those times as a kid when he and his brother were practising their magic had some interesting results . Not all of them were good either.

"What?" Jason hissed the phone still in hand. "I'm not just going to leave you here to deal with this! That's not how this works... we're partners."

Xbalanque slowly stood up straight and bit his lip. He didn't want to think about it, but he was unable to get the memories of his brother from his mind.

Many of the Archives did not know about his brother, the only ones who did were Aethalides and Boudicca. He didn't feel comfortable telling anyone about him, since what happened to his brother... hadn't been good. Hunahpu and himself had been... inseparable when they were children, which was expected for twins. Unfortunately, because of this, it meant that Xbalanque, as brash as he always was, would get them both into trouble. He'd been overconfident then, overconfident and over-ambitious, convinced that with their magic and semi-divine origin the pair of them would be fine no matter what faced them. That confidence had only grown after they defeated the vain bird god Seven Macaw and his two mountain-destroying sons, Zipacna and Cabrakan. With the final challenge is to defeat the Lords of Xilbalba, the heart of the underworld.

Xbalanque and Hunahpu had been at the top of their game by that point, confident and self-assured. Nothing was stopping them from getting what they wanted and defeating the gods. They felt unstoppable.

Unfortunately you have to learn the hard way that arrogance is the fall of many great men and after what happened to Hunahpu... well, Xbalanque dropped his ego pretty quickly.

Xbalanque shook his head and turned to Jason. Over the past few weeks of the pair of them working together and after the initial awkwardness they'd become close. They were friends.

In many ways though, Jason slightly reminded him of his twin brother. He was calm, understanding, tried his best to see the good in everyone and was to a degree quite humble. Just like Hunahpu... too much like him and he wasn't about to lose a second brother.

"Jason..." Xbalanque started and then flashed a smile. "I'll be fine. Just trust me."

"I *do* trust you, but we're a team on this!" Jason snapped and shoved past him, pushing the door open as he did. "We do this together. I have your back, you... have... mine..."

The last part was squeaked out as he came face to face with a centaur who stood proud. The centaur was wearing a sailors outfit, at least on his human part, with the Port Side Raiders crest on the arm.

Jason stumbled backwards, eyes wide and visibly shaking. Xbalanque's gaze flickered between the centaur and Jason, watching the centaur smirk, take his battle axe from his back, before he charged forward.

Jason was frozen, eyes wide and unable to move. Just as he brought the axe down, but Xbalanque shoved his spear in the way. The two weapons *clanged* against each other as Jason flinched back, stumbling over his feet and falling to the ground, which probably made the situation a whole lot more terrifying.

Xbalanque shoved the centaur away and span the spear in his hand as he glared at the centaur and heard the sound of more feet. Glancing around he found fae, a few Jötuns and even a fire giant... which was *odd*. Never thought he'd see a fire giant with a *port* based gang.

"Wait a minute..." the centaur chuckled. "Xbalanque is that really *you?* Ha! Didn't think we'd have a member of the Archives up here!" The centaur got his axe ready, kicking his front leg, building up to charge. "Cillian really wants to kill all of you. Especially that backbiter's little brat. He hates all of you, but... he *really* hates that brat."

"I'd probably hate a teenager that could plant me on my backside on the regular," Xbalanque quipped and smirked. "And his men 'aren't much better."

The centaur snarled and reared up on his back legs, charging at Xbalanque with his axe, swinging it. Clearly, the centaur was the one in charge, the others hung back until that moment, charging with him.

Xbalanque dropped to the ground and tripped the centaur up, sending him skidding across the floor and past Jason. The detective looked stunned and couldn't move, staring in shock at the madness going on around him.

Xbalanque rushed to him, pulling him to his feet and only just managed to block a Jötun's strike, then ducked the other swing before kicking the Jötun in the knee and dropping him to the ground.

"Jason, you need to get out of here," Xbalanque instructed, pushing him towards the door. "It's too dangerous, go."

Jason looked like a dear caught in headlights, staring at him and then the chaos around them, before crying out and pointing a finger at something behind Xbalanque.

The fire giant was charging and swinging his flaming sword at them. Xbalanque shoved Jason out of the way, ducking the blade, and jumping to the side until he came to a support beam. Then he ducked under the blade again which went straight to the support beam. It cut through the metal like a knife through butter, leaving hot molten metal dripping down the post.

"You're a weak little thing, huh?" The fire giant laughed, eyes blazing, its skin was black with a crack of fire poking through. It looked like it was made of volcanic rock, almost like the creature was made of a walking volcano. "All flesh beings are weak against the might of the fire giants!"

Xbalanque ducked the hand that reached out to grab him. Jason suddenly screamed and Xbalanque span around in worry.

Jason was being grabbed by the Jötun and lifted off the floor, with a face on the giant's shoulder, knives out and a smirk on their face.

"Are you going to tell me your name, human?" The fae purred, smiling to show their sharp teeth and pressing the blade against Jason's throat. "Just tell me your name and we'll let you go."

"*Don't!*" Xbalanque shouted and tossed his spear straight at the fae's hand, causing the fae to flinch back and snarl at him. "Don't give them your full name!"

"Shut it!" They screeched at him, crawling up the arm to grab at Jason's face, their claws starting to stab into his skin. "Tell me your name... that's all it takes, it's just a small thing..." they cooed, brushing Jason's hair from his face. "Speak your name, mortal and all of this..." they gestured around them. "Ends."

"Listen to me!" Xbalanque yelled as he ran forward, preparing to climb up the Jotun and dodge the fire giant. "It's fae magic! If you give them your name they'll have control of you!"

The fae growled. "I said-!"

Xbalanque held his hand out as the spear came out the wall, the handle nearly smacking the fae across the face. The spear landed in his hand and he used it to propel himself up the Jötun and grabbed the fae, pulling them off the Jötun. Then he climbed up onto his arm and stabbed the Jötun in the wrist, causing him to yell and let Jason go.

He jumped to the ground and grabbed Jason, yanking him up to his feet and encouraging him to run, but then the fae tried to attack him.

Xbalanque snatched his hand and stamped on the fae's foot before elbowing him in the face. There was a satisfying crunch and the fae let out a shriek, clutching at their nose and crumpling to the floor.

"X...Xbalanque," Jason stuttered, backing away from the remaining gang members who were surrounding them. The ones that were left standing at least. "What... what do we do?"

"*We* don't do anything," Xbalanque hissed at him. "*You* need to get out of here! *I'll* deal with this!"

"I'm... I'm not just going to leave you to deal with this!" Jason protested. "I'm not going to leave you to deal with these things!"

"Whoa!"

"Hey now!"

"Yeah, come on dude!"

It was almost hilarious how the incoming groups of people stopped and raised their hands up, taking a few steps away.

"I mean sure," the Jötun said. "We're going to kill you, but there's no need to be rude."

"Yeah!" The fire giant snapped. "We're giants, not things!"

Xbalanque pinched the bridge of his nose and looked to Jason who stared at the two giants, then looked back to Xbalanque, back at the giants. He opened and closed his mouth a few times, snapped it shut and seemed to mull everything over it for a moment.

"I… I'm sorry…" he stuttered, raising his own hands up in a placating gesture. "I just… I didn't know, I've never seen…"

The two giants looked at each other and nodded their heads in understanding, waving him off.

"Hey it's okay man, don't worry, totally get it," the Jötun spoke up. "We're the first giants you've ever seen… ya probably a bit confused right now."

"Yeah and we just thought that because you were friends with Xbalanque," the fire giant agreed, nodding his head. "That you already knew about all of this and our species… obviously not. Just… ya' know…" he shrugged. "Now ya know."

"Please," Xbalanque cut in. "Can we go back to fighting? It would honestly be less painful."

"Heh," The Jötun smirked. "Sure."

In hindsight he should've expected the kick to the sternum that sent him flying through the back of the warehouse. He felt his ribs break under the impact and Xbalanque clutched at his side, desperately trying to push himself up to his feet, only to be kicked again, this time it sent him to the edge of the docks. The fire giant came towards him, his blazing sword burning in the early morning light, and he wore a horrid grin.

"I'm going to enjoy doing this. The other one is going to take care of your little friend back there," he went on, swinging his sword above his head, getting ready to bring it down. "Maybe

271

Cillian will give me a promotion after this!"

He brought the sword down and Xbalanque squeezed his eyes shut expecting to feel a burning pain of some kind.

Suddenly, out of nowhere, Jason let out a battle cry and charged the back of the fire giant, holding a pallet to protect himself from the heat the giant gave off, shoving as hard as he could. Thanks to the sword, the fire giant was completely out of balance and he toppled over, falling into the canal where a large puff of steam shot up into the air after his descent.

The Jotun came stumbling out of the warehouse looking completely shocked by the transgression, running as fast as he could to the docks, reaching a hand in and pulling the fire giant out.

He growled and glared at the two of them, swinging the fire giant on his back and pointing threateningly at them.

"This isn't over! We'll get you for this! Just you wait!"

He turned on his heel and ran, meeting with the centaur and the fae who had both pulled themselves up to their feet at his point, making their getaway.

Jason turned to Xbalanque and helped him up. He still looked terrified. Terrified and confused, looking in the direction that the group had run off to.

Xbalanque held out his hand and his spear immediately came to him, making Jason flinch and he stumbled backwards, staring at Xbalanque and the spear. He could only imagine the kind of things that were going through Jason's head.

"Are… are there dangerous things in the warehouse?" He asked, his voice was barely a whisper.

Xbalanque nodded. "A lot of it shouldn't be anywhere near mortals."

"Mortals…" Jason echoed, then shook his head. "Can you

get rid of it?"

"Yeah, I can."

He nodded his head. "Okay…" he mumbled. "Get rid of it, I'll… stall and… get you a paramedic."

"Jason…?" Xbalanque frowned, reaching a hand out to grab his shoulder. "Are you all right?"

Jason was quiet for a long time. His back was turned to him and he only just glanced over his shoulder to look at him, then he turned away again.

"Get rid of the stuff," he mumbled, pocketing his hands and walking away from him. "I'm gonna take some leave for a bit…"

Xbalanque was quiet and watched him leave, clutching at his ribs as he sat up a bit more.

"Idiot," he muttered under his breath to himself. "Stupid, why are so *stupid*…? Why don't you wait?"

He'd messed up again. Just like he always did. His brother lost his head and now Jason would probably lose his job.

Xbalanque punched the ground, pushing himself up to his feet as he got ready to destroy any of the stuff from Atlantis or take it away. Why was he always impatient? Why didn't he just wait?

Praise be: 15

The problem with having parents who were also gods was the fact that they were busy all of the time. Sometimes they weren't even doing their jobs, but that didn't negate how little free time they got.

Aethalides had tried to call his father to give an update on their progress, but he hadn't been able to get through to him. He tried his mobile, because yes gods had those now, but nope, nothing. Not a single thing. If it had been anyone else this might have been a cause for concern, but in the case of his father? Nope, not worrying, just irritating and it also meant that he'd have to get in contact with him the old fashioned way.

Aethalides was loathed to do it. Not nearly because of where his father's temple was located, but also down to the fact that he really, really didn't want to go anywhere near the high priest of his father's temple who was... a little bit of a fanatic.

He snorted to himself. A little? Nah, his father's high priest was full blown crazy. Talking to anyone who'd listen about how fantastic Hermes was. Aethalides had known his father for a very long time and could tell you that while he loved his father he really wasn't that great. At least not all the time.

Aethalides was having a nice day and he'd actually woken up in a good mood and that mood was steadily getting ruined as he got closer and closer to the hills of devotion.

The closer he got, the more a feeling of dread would fester in his stomach, getting worse and worse. It almost made him feel sick. It was akin to the feeling he got when he'd been on the Argo, resting just off the shores of Mysia.

A pounding began in his head and he grimaced, reaching up to press a hand against his temple and squeeze his eyes shut. Oh god, not now… not in *public.*

"Aethalides… Aethalides… *Aethalides*!"

He snapped his head up, staring up at a ghost.

Hylas, one of the sailors of the Argo, who had been only two years older than Aethalides at the time of their voyage. He wasn't from the richest of families, but he wanted to strive for some adventure, so joined the quest.

He was holding a bag that seemed to be filled with skin bottles, holding his hand out to him.

"You want me to refill yours?" He asked. "We won't be making another stop for a while, I'm just going ashore to refill."

"Oh, of course," Aethalides handed his bottle to him. "Thank you. Um… where are we?"

Hylas hooked a thumb in the direction of the island and Aethalides poked his head up to see it.

Rolling green hills, nice sandy beaches, with a few mountains and forests for as for as the eye could see. It looked beautiful against the blue sky and the deep ocean, a little piece of paradise in the middle of the unrelenting ocean. It all looked very idyllic and it made Aethalides feel uneasy as he continued to stare at it.

It was too perfect.

"Mysia," Hylas answered. "Heracles, Jason and the two sons of Boreas are going ashore with me to get some supplies."

Aethalides frowned, looking at Orpheus who also seemed mildly concerned. Next to him, Atalanta, the only female member of the crew, who had been silent for the most part and sharpened her arrows finally spoke up.

"I hear Mysia is treacherous for young men," she commented idly, holding the arrow she'd been working on up to the light, squinting as she made sure the point was sharp enough. "The rivers and forests are riddled with nymphs who like to snatch unsuspecting men away who take their fancy."

Hylas looked vaguely uncomfortable, glancing at the island again. "I... should be okay, right?" He turned back to Atalanta. "If I don't go too deep into the forest?"

"I would stay in the eye sight of your companions," Atalanta offered instead as advice. "Just to be on the safe side."

Hylas gave a slow nod, looking back at the three of them and then making his leave. He passed the bag to the sons of Boreas before jumping off the ship with Jason and Heracles. The ship was close enough that it would be such a hard swim and Aethalides watched them reach the beach. The sons of Boreas, the god of the north wind, flew down to hand Hylas the drink bottles again. Then he marched up the hill and vanished from sight.

Hylas never made it back to the ship.

Suddenly someone bumped into him from behind and Aethalides was back in the present, no longer sitting on a rocking boat in the middle of the Aegean sea.

He rubbed at his temples, mumbling under his breath about asking his father for a stronger dose of his medicine. The only thing that kept these memories in some kind of check, but sometimes it took a while for the medicine to fully kick in, because of course it did. Nothing was ever simple or easy.

Aethalides took a breath and continued his walk up to the hills of devotion.

They were huge grassy hills, set in the centre of the capital,

276

which had been kept natural. Some had gardens and water features decorating them and scattered throughout the hills were temples for many, many gods and goddesses of different pantheons and beliefs. Some were just statues, others had huge monuments and gardens dedicated to the gods.

It was mostly just the major deities, but around the bottom of the hills were many little statues dedicated to smaller ones, that would constantly get new ones added on a daily basis. Even right now there were a few new statues and temples being put in place and built for the many worshipers and followers.

People would travel from all across Atlantis to reach this place, especially if you had a god you needed to pray to and your little town didn't have a temple or statue dedicated to them.

The temple of Hermes, like all of the temples or statues for the gods that had first initiated peace between pantheons, was on the largest hill and their structures were beautiful. That's not to say that any of the others weren't, but these were made as a way for the many different peoples and races in Atlantis to give their thanks for this safe haven.

Unfortunately for him, the temple of Hermes was at *the very top* of the freaking hill. It was the only time Aethalides wished they had some sort of…he didn't know, tram system, that'd be nice. Apparently though, walking to a destination of worship was a way to show your immense devotion. Aethalides had seen the documents from the council, he knew the real reason. The real reason being, they didn't want to waste money on a modern transport system, when they could use it to buy a modern jacuzzi or gods knows what else.

Aethalides climbed the many steps, carefully dodging out of the way of other gods and goddesses, worshippers and so much more. Priests and priestesses were darting back and forth, taking care of their charges and temples.

By the time he reached the temple of Hermes, he was exhausted. Leaning on his knees and sucking in breaths. Stairs. Stairs were not his strong point.

Aethalides looked up at his father's temple, the beautiful marble building decorated in frescos depicting many of his father's stories; Hermes stealing Apollo's cattle, Hermes killing the hundred eyed giant Argus, Hermes helping in the defeat of Typhon and of course the most recent of events, Hermes helping in the creation of Atlantis.

The gardens surrounding the temple were filled with crocus flowers and strawberry trees lined the way. A few tortoises were walking back and forth between the grassy patches between the pathways.

Aethalides noticed the priests and priestesses walk around, busily keeping the temple tidy and up to scratch, as well as the outside. He walked up the rest of the steps and inside, more frescos, a huge statue of his father, holding his herald staff, the caduceus, winged helmet and shoes on full display. At the foot of the statue was one of many, many offering tables with various items. Sheep wool, hand carved cows, gold, traveler's cloak and so much more.

Thankfully there was no one else other than a few priests and priestesses in the temple. He looked around worriedly, but no, he couldn't see any sign of the high priest.

Aethalides let out a breath he didn't know he'd been holding, proudly marching up to the statue and placing a bag of gold on the offering table. He raised his arms up towards the statue, every action was more muscle memory than anything else.

"My Lord Father, I would ask for your presence, please! I

have news I wish to share with you," he declared loudly, glancing around to see the priests and priestess had paused in their duties to look at him. Recognising him for who he was and quickly leaving the temple. "I would greatly appreciate it if you could come down here and speak to me," Aethalides continued smiling up at the statue.

Nothing. Radio silence.

Aethalide's face dropped and he scowled at the statue instead.

Freaking typical.

"Lord father!" He called out again. "It is greatly important that I speak with you!"

Still nothing. Oh, so he was purposely ignoring him? Was the offering not enough?

He looked down at the bag of coins, then looked up at the statue of his father again, scowling at it.

"Oh come on, how much gold do you need? Realistically?" Aethalides shouted indignantly at the statue. "You literally. *Do not*. Have. To. Pay. For *anything!*"

"Lord Aethalides!"

He nearly shot out of his skin at the sudden cry, flinching and falling to the floor. When he looked up he wasn't surprised at all to see the high priest with a smile that rivalled his own when he was in a good mood.

Atticus, the high priest of the temple of Hermes, was a nut job. Plain and simple. Verging on zealot behaviour and practically worshipped the ground Aethalides walked on since he was the son of Hermes.

Atticus had manic eyes and a manic smile, weathered face and dressed in his royal robes, decorated in gold and his white hair was brushed off his face.

"You have graced our sacred halls and myself with your presence today! Blessed, I am! I am blessed!" Atticus cried, reaching his hands to the sky while Aethalides quickly scrambled to his feet, desperately putting distance between the two of them. "What can I do for you this day?"

You can take a five-mile hike is what he desperately wanted to say, but he couldn't do insulting his father's priests. No matter how much he wanted Atticus to stay away from him.

All the other priests and priestesses were fine, but Atticus? He was a whole other level of nutter.

"I'm just here… to get in touch with my father…" Aethalides said slowly, walking up to the statue again, raising his hands up to the sky. "Lord Father! Please can you… hurry up?" He hissed at the statue in annoyance, glancing behind him at Atticus briefly and then looking back to the statue. "Any time now!"

"My lord Aethalides," Atticus suddenly took his hand, suddenly going to his knees and staring up at him like he was a god. "Is there any way I can help you?"

Aethalides stared at him a moment before awkwardly looking back to the statue, gritting his teeth. "Seriously! Any time now!"

"Aethalides?"

He jumped again and span around to see his father who was staring at the whole scene a little bewildered. Aethalides really wished people would stop making him jump any moment they got. He was ten, he did not want to die of a heart attack at the age of ten.

Atticus's eyes widened more… somehow and he suddenly let go of Aethalides's hand and pressed his hands to the floor, bowing completely, kneeling to Hermes.

"My lord! Truly this is the most blessed day! You and your son have graced me with your presence today! I have never been so blessed as to have both of you here at the same time!"

Aethalides frowned at the back of Atticus's head in confusion and then looked to his father who looked equally as confused by the whole situation. Father and son shared a look with each other while Atticus continued to babble on.

Hermes nodded over to his left, indicating that they should leave and Aethalides nodded his head in agreement. He carefully and quietly side stepped Atticus and wandered outside along with Hermes. There were pleasant advantages to being the son of the god of thieves. Part of those advantages came with the ability to sneak without being heard.

They started walking the gardens once they made it outside, Hermes was noticeably staring down at the crocus with a quiet longing. A melancholy suddenly flitted across his face, but he looked to Aethalides with a bright smile.

Right. He was a god and they never talked about their feelings, they just wiped out cities and towns. Get other people to deal with their problems whether they know it or not. His father was no better and was probably the worst when it came to confronting his problems properly and dealing with them.

"So? What was it that you needed to speak to me about?" Hermes asked.

"Well, looking for this oracle has been more challenging than I was expecting and now Rune is involved," Aethalides sighed, pinching the bridge of his nose. "Oh and we have a mortal that's seen a bunch of Port Side Raiders."

"Port Side Raiders?" Hermes asked, thinking about it for a moment, snapping his fingers as he remembered. "Oh! You mean that small potato gang run by Cillian?"

"Yes. Those guys," Aethalides sighed. "They've... ya' know, revealed themselves to a human, Xbalanque's partner in his detective job."

"Oh boy," Hermes rested his hands on his hips. "Wow. Okay, that's worrying. Well, we can come up with something," he tapped his chin. "I could always get some water from the river Lethe..."

Aethalides was barely able to keep his expression in check at the mention of the Lethe. Both the river and the goddess, he had an interesting relationship with the goddess of forgetfulness and oblivion. No one who drank from her waters remembered her, except for Aethalides, who wanted nothing more than to forget.

So, maybe... it was out of some selfish need to have someone else go through a fraction of what he did every day that had him quickly objecting to the idea.

"*No!*" Aethalides quickly interjected. "We are not doing that!"

Hermes seemed surprised, looking him over, Aethalides felt like he was looking right through him. Not looking at him as a father, but as a god, judging him for it.

"Xbalanque... has a hard time making friends," Aethalides went on, wording himself carefully. He was just as gifted with his words as his father was after all. "And we don't know how much water we'd need to keep the balance even. Plus, there's no guarantee that it would be *right* bit of information Jason would forget..."

After a moment, the hard lines on his father's face eased off, returning to the expression he was used to; easy, carefree, relaxed. The kind that only came with someone who... didn't know hard labour. At least not how mortals did.

Hermes shrugged, "Then I got nothing."

"Right, well... on a different matter," Aethalides hooked a thumb towards the temple. "Can you please get a different high priest? Atticus is a maniac!"

Hermes grimaced, rubbing the back of his neck nervously. He obviously knew just how fanatical Atticus actually was and it didn't just end with Aethalides, he believed for some reason that Hermes was the best and greatest god out there and that everyone should be worshipping him and only him.

In fact, it was a little-known fact that some of the temples got a little damaged or vandalised. No one could really prove it was Atticus, but everyone had a fair idea. It had caused some problems, but when did fanatical believers in any cause not raise issues?

"Yeah..." Hermes trailed off. "You're not the first person to suggest that, but... I... you know how this all works. He has to actually be shown to disregard his faith or whatever," he suddenly slammed his hand into his palm as he said. "And he is not doing that."

"Well yeah, but he's trying to get people to only join your cult. That's not-."

"Yes, yes, I know!" Hermes threw his hands up. "I'm aware! By the gods, all I did was bless him when he was born for his mother and now the man is a complete zealot! I've tried talking to him, but... it's not worked. Anyway," he continued, waving away the issue. "Atticus is so far down my list of priorities right now. Anything else happens?"

"No.." Aethalides admitted. "But I'll be taking a small group of us into the desert to check there."

"Right, good, you do that."

"Father?"

"Yes?"

Aethalides chewed his lip, looking down at the ground for a moment. He wasn't sure how to completely phrase this question, given that it was his dad and a god, but... well he had to know.

"How come," he started slowly, carefully choosing his words. *"You* didn't look for the oracle? You could've gotten this done a lot faster..."

Instead of trusting this issue in the fate of a chronic alcoholic, heavy smoker and all-around mentally unstable guy. Son or not, there were plenty of better options than Aethalides that his father could've trusted this with.

At the start, he'd even only trusted Aethalides with the information and no one else had told him not to inform the others and work the case alone, but fate had other ideas. Or, maybe he'd realised that this was too big for him to handle by himself and got help from the others.

He wasn't someone who didn't trust his own capabilities, he was just also highly aware of his shortcomings. For the most part at least. He didn't think he was egotistical at all and had no idea where people got that idea from. Aethalides believed he was the perfect picture of humility.

Hermes grimaced, looking around again, then knelt down so he was Aethalides's height, beckoning him to come closer with a finger. Oh boy, it was that serious.

Aethalides stepped closer and Hermes raised his hand to cup his ear so he could whisper.

"It's because the only people who know about it are me and Apollo' I love my father, but I'm not idiotic enough to tell him about a rare oracle coming back randomly. He'd take that as a threat to his power in some way or another and after years of carefully crafted peace..." Hermes pulled his lip back in disgust.

"I really would rather not destroy all that hard work."

"Do you think an oracle coming back could really create a war between pantheons?" Aethalides asked.

His father laughed, a little high-pitched and very strained. The look on his face was somewhere between panic and a grimace.

"It's **us**. I wouldn't put it past us," he mumbled. "Sometimes… it's too much effort not to have a war. But as a god of diplomacy. I tend to think that most issues can be solved by talking."

"Even the issue with Rune?"

"Oh gods *no*, he definitely needs to get his shiny arse kicked to the curb," Hermes laughed, standing back to his proper height, resting a hand on his son's shoulder. He offered a small smile. "I have faith in you. Now, my son, you just have to have faith in yourself."

The Bane of Jason: 16

The Underworld was a place filled with mystery but also a place that many feared, for obvious reasons. It was the final resting place of many and the concept of death or even the idea of it was enough to make the strongest of individual quiver.

Medea, however, could care less. She carefully thumbed the coins in her hand as she waited for the boat driven by Charon to arrive. The other souls around her looked nervous, shuffling from side to side, scared of what was to come next. Medea on the other hand was calm, collected and tired of waiting.

Thankfully, she didn't need to wait too long, the boat came into view and eventually docked against the edge. She waited for the souls to get on the boat out of respect, and then she walked on herself, passing a coin to the boatman.

He was a thin, spindly, almost skeleton-like figure with hard lines and sharp angles. Cheekbones that looked like they could and would cut anyone that touched them, with pale violet eyes set in dark sockets. He looked like he'd been starving, but despite his frail and fragile appearance, the boatman was a force to be reckoned with. People didn't mess with Charon, this was his boat, his river, he was the one who shipped you to your final resting place so it was best to stay polite.

Dressed in long black flowing clothes, a hood up to cover his head and cast more dark shadows over his sunken, pale face. He was almost a perfect picture of the Grim Reaper.

"To Hecate's please, Charon, thank you," she spoke up with

a charming smile that did nothing at all to the boatman. He just stared at her flatly, clearly unmoved by her display.

Medea got on the boat, shuffling slightly next to a few of the souls, trying to avoid being touched by them.

The boat journey down the river Styx was quiet, save for the occasional bout of weeping from the surrounding souls. People from all walks of life were situated on the boat, of various ages too. Some were old and had lived a long life, and others had been taken from the world far too early.

It might seem cruel, but if there was one god from the Greek pantheon that Medea could say without a shadow of a doubt, who did not have a cruel bone in his immortal body, it was Thanatos. The incarnation of death only did his job, there was nothing malicious out of it, he was simply there to end one journey and start you on the final one.

Finally, the boat came to a stop for her to get off the boat. She was grateful, despite being calm the dead really did have a habit of bringing down her good mood.

Medea stood and watched the boat continue up the river towards the rest of the underworld, instead of her stop, which was just on the edge of Hades's domain. She wandered the same track she had before whenever she needed extra advice from her goddess.

Medea had an idea. A location spell of some kind to help shorten this little trip to find the oracle. It also worked double as she could avoid visiting the desert area like a few of the other members of the Archives were going.

Sand got everywhere and never left once it found 'its new home. She was determined not to get covered head to toe in sand and so came up with the idea to visit Hecate and ask for advice or even the spell itself. It would cost a great sacrifice, not something Medea was unused to paying, so she was more than willing to sacrifice whatever her mistress asked of her.

Medea stood at the edge of the entrance, waiting patiently for someone to answer her and she didn't need to wait long. One of Hecate's servants, an Empusa came up to the entrance.

Empusa were... unique creatures. Beautiful women with flaming hair, one bronze leg and one donkey leg, with a thirst for blood. Vampires of the Ancient Greek world and servants to Hecate.

"Medea, High priestess of Colchis," the Empusa purred, looking her up and down. "What do you want with our mistress?"

"My mistress too, if you haven't forgotten who I was the high priestess of," Medea replied with a smile. "Is our lady Hecate free to speak?"

The Empusa looked her up and down, then quickly scuttled back into the dark. She waited for her to return and when she did, the Empusa had a twisted expression on her face. It was enough for Medea to know that she had been welcomed inside, they tended to not like letting her enter Hecate's domain, almost like it made Medea at the same level as them. Empusa believed they were higher than any kind of mortal or human, due to their immortal status as well as them being the direct servants of Hecate.

Really, her Lady Hecate did keep some interesting company.

"She will see you. But make it quick," the Empusa hissed. "Our Lady is very busy."

"Thank you," she walked past the hissing Empusa, taking the steps down to Hecate's cave. Torches lit the way for her, the closer she got the more she heard the sound of a bubbling cauldron, bottles being gently clinked together, like someone was searching through them.

Medea entered the cave, finding the goddess hunched over a bubbling cauldron, torches burning by her side, and rows and rows of shelves filled with bottles decorating the cave walls.

Hecate herself was… an *interesting* goddess, at least in comparison to most Greek gods. She was dressed in ceremonial garb, with a crown of spikes and a single candle in the middle of it. A set of keys hung from her belt, along with a knife and a bag of divination stones. Wearing purple, black and grey, dark makeup decorated her faces of which she had three. The one on the right was young and almost like a late teen or early twenty-year-old, her middle face was middle-aged and had an air of calm about her, while the one on the left was old and wise, with a twinkle in her eye that was a little mischievous.

"Well, well, well, look at who it is," the youngest face spoke up, grinning maniacally at Medea. "If it isn't our lovely Medea. Killed anyone recently?"

"Oh yes," the middle face looked to her with a calmer smile. "Do tell, have you been up to anything bad? You know how much I *adore* bad girls."

"Always, my Lady Hecate," Medea bowed. "In truth, I have come here for some. help."

"Help?" The middle face echoed. "By the gods, it must be… bad if you need my help."

"Yes," the oldest head crooned. "You're always so selfslethicient."

"So, like me," the younger head cried out with the other two echoing her, bursting its cackling laughter which set off the pack of dogs in the corner, sitting up and howling into the cave. The noise echoed around them, bouncing off the walls and Hecate cooed to her dogs, throwing some meat to them as well as other treats.

When Medea looked over to the dogs she noticed that the animals almost had shrines themselves, their area was done up as a dog palace with blankets and toys for days. One dog was busily chewing on what looked to be a Zeus squeaky toy.

"I need a locating spell," Medea explained as she stepped closer. "But everyone I know isn't working."

"Well, to locate anything you first need to know what it is you're looking for," Hecate explained. "For instance, I need to locate my gorgon blood."

"This pot of healing and invigorating life potion won't make itself ya' know," the first head sniggered.

"Oh, and this will be the first of its kind! Doesn't just heal, but also increases speed and stamina!"

"Hermes suggested it."

All three of the faces sighed wistfully, sounding like a schoolgirl with a crush for a mere moment and then they burst out laughing.

"I never would," the middle face stated, smirking at Medea.

"I mean, I never would *again*," the younger face giggled, then the older one butted in, smirking and offering a wink to Medea, somewhat awkwardly from the angle she was facing.

"But by the gods, that is a fine figure of a god... mama like," the crone's face wolf-whistled. "So occasionally... we'll do a little favour for him."

"And this potion is a little favour."

"He wanted to know if we could make it."

"Got the idea from a video game," she waved her hand around airily. "Or something like that."

"Wait, what were you here for again, dear?" The crone's head spoke up. "Sorry... I got a little... side tracked..."

Medea smirked, bowing her head. "A little side tracked in

the realms of Olympian bodies apparently… but it was the location spell."

"Well, do you know what you're looking for?"

"Yes, my lady."

"Ah!" Hecate clapped her hands. "Should be easy then! But you say that… none of the spells you know are working?"

Medea watched as the goddess suddenly formed two more sets of arms, reaching for a few of the many books her goddess owned and some reached for bottles that they poured haphazardly into the cauldron.

"Umm.." Medea frowned slightly as she watched Hecate pour potions in willy nilly into the cauldron, never measuring them out, never checking if they should go together. The liquid changed colour several times as she stirred and read books and poured in potions all at the same time.

"Yes, dear?" The old face spoke up.

"I don't wish to question your talents, my lady, but… do you not need to… measure those out?"

"Well… yes, it is advised…"

"But!" The middle face spoke up as she threw an empty bottle behind her where it smashed on the wall, quickly reforming into a usable bottle afterwards. "Where's the fun in that!"

"And I only ever blew myself up once," the youngest face said as she continued to look over the books.

"Yes, that was a bad day, wasn't it?" The crone said and all three faces nodded, echoing the words 'bad day' in agreement.

"Ah, here you go!" The youngest held out the book towards Medea. "Will this help?"

Medea squinted at the page. "Find my friend?" She said reading the title, thinking it over a moment and then turning her squinted gaze at the goddess. "Is that like the find my phone app?"

"Oh no, that's this one!"

The page was flipped to show another page that read 'find my herald'.

"Are you sure? That looks more like a find Hermes spell?"

"Huh?" The faces blinked and then looked to the page. "Oh yes, so it is! I forgot I made that one. It's just, well, everyone loses him."

"He goes by so fast."

"Half the time no one knows where he is."

"Sometimes I wonder if he even does."

"Right…" Medea trailed off, thinking about the previous spell she was shown. She didn't think that one would work because she didn't know who the oracle was and they certainly weren't friends. Spells were tricky like that, they had to be precise otherwise you could want one thing and get something completely different. Dyslexic witches were known to have an absolute time with their potion-making and spell-casting.

"I'm not too sure that one would work, my lady, I don't know the person I'm trying to find."

"Okay!" Hecate haphazardly chucked the book behind her, it landed with the dogs who began sniffing at it. The goddess had turned her attention to the bookcase again, snatching up books, and quickly scanning over the pages.

Medea watched in quiet fascination as a snake slowly slithered across Hecate's arm and along her back, before using her other arm to take itself back to the bookshelf. Hecate didn't even flinch or move, she hardly seemed to notice the snake at all.

With each book she opened her brows creased more and more. Medea watched the goddess grab several bottles of gorgon's blood, pouring it into the cauldron and turning the liquid blood red before she tossed the bottles and grabbed a box made out of a skull where she... had some healing herbs it would seem. There was a certain irony to that choice of container.

"Do you have anything that belongs to this individual you're looking for?" The goddess asked, picking up a pester and mortar, grinding up the healing herbs as she placed the skull box back.

"Unfortunately not," Medea frowned. "There are no spells that will work are there?"

"Doesn't look like it, dear," the older face said.

"But that does give me a new idea for a spell!" The youngest cried out. "Ohhh, no one has ever thought of a location spell that requires no items that belong to the individual in question!"

"The possibilities," the middle one hummed, spreading their hands out as a look of excitement crossed her face. "Oh, how much trouble we could get certain gods in."

"Perhaps, we can make a new spell of 'find my god'," the younger said, taking up a notepad and pen, and scribbling down a note. "Or find my husband. Oh, Hera is going to *love* that one!"

Medea had a fair idea that Hecate wasn't even paying attention to her now. She bowed respectfully and left the goddess as she went back to making her potions and goodness knows what else.

The Empusa glared at her as she left, Medea ignored her, walking to the dock to wait for Charon to come back up and catch the boat so she could leave the underworld. She thumbed her coin out of her purse to pay him, minding her own business. A few shades were dotted around here and there. Medea payed little mind to them, shades were just curious, they'd stare, but that was about it.

A chill suddenly went up her spine and her hand moved to

her curved blade. Slowly, very slowly, she turned to face the edge of the shores and she was surprised by who she saw.

It had been thousands of years, but she'd know Jason of the Argo anywhere. The man who had ruined her life, along with the gods, who used her and broke his oaths.

Looking at him now… gods, she never realised how *pathetic* he truly was.

There had once been a time where… he had been the light of her life, her everything. Against her own will of course, it was only after her grandfather told her what had happened years later that she knew the full extent of Hera's manipulation.

Oh yes, Hera, she favoured Jason, she helped him whenever she could, she encouraged Eros, the little infuriating god of love to take the shot with his magic arrows and make Medea fall in love with Jason.

After that, she betrayed her family, her people, her kingdom, for this… *nothing*. He wasn't a demigod, he wasn't even heroic, he couldn't even complete his own quest by himself, he needed an entire crew.

Of course, that was where she also first met Aethalides, though the two didn't speak to each other much. She'd been so infatuated with Jason, but the brief conversations she did have with Aethalides had confirmed to her that she liked him. He was smart, witty, sarcastic and hardly seemed to care what other people thought was proper behaviour for royalty and lordships.

Still, he was one of the few she actually parted on good terms with, Jason was less than that. They'd stayed together, and travelled to Korinth… everything went wrong after that.

Medea looked Jason up and down, then huffed a laugh, turning away from him and facing the river once more.

"Don't you dare turn your back on me, Medea!" Jason

hissed. "Not after *what* you did!"

"I made my peace with what I did," Medea replied evenly, still not turning to face him. "The only one who seems consumed with guilt, Jason, is you."

Explained why he's here. Hecate did look after the souls who were not ready to move on, often sitting and talking with them, encouraging them to find peace. She was probably dealing with a lost cause if she'd been doing that with Jason. He saw himself as a victim, he saw himself as the hero who should've gotten all the glory and all he got was a disappointing end, crushed under a boat.

Couldn't have happened to a nicer person.

"I felt guilt for not being able to save my children from the treacherous witch that you are!" Jason snarled out.

Medea pulled out her small compact mirror, checking herself over, gently pushing some strands of hair back in place. She could see him reflected behind her. He didn't look much different to the last time she saw him, except maybe there were a few more lines around his eyes. His blonde hair was the same, kept in the nice ringlets at the back, wearing rags with dark circles under his eyes and a tanned complexion from hours of being out in the sun.

So… someone fell on harder times in the last days of his life than she originally thought… funny.

"You murdered my children!"

She snapped the compact closed, slipping it away. "It's funny," Medea mused. "How suddenly when there was a tragedy they became 'your' children," she finally graced him with her face looking at him. "Since for their entire lives they were always *my* children," she smirked at him. "Your brokenhearted tragedy is convenient at best and I heard you didn't meet a very glorious end… I suppose that's what happens when you lose the favour of the gods."

Ah yes, the man who once carried Hera over a river and gained her favour, the man who had the queen of the gods and the goddess of marriage, family and rulership on his side, the world 'should've been his oyster. For a brief time, it was and then he betrayed Medea, betrayed his wife and broke his oaths to the gods. It was clear that the fool thought he was untouchable until life came round to remind him that even the gods couldn't escape consequences. What made him so certain that he'd escape them too?

Jason's face contorted to one of rage, his hands were clenched in fists as he glared at her. Teeth bared and... oh that was such an ugly look on such a pretty face.

"You dare-."

"Oh, I do," Medea finally turned around completely to look him in the eye, marching up to Jason who looked on at her with a sneer. "I do dare, because after everything I did for you, after you swore an oath to me and to the gods, you betrayed all of that... for status..." she laughed, smiling at him. "And yet... you got nothing. Tell me, how long did you cry out for fury to avenge you and do your bidding before you realised that the gods don't always give us what we want?"

She looked up the river spotting Charon paddling his way back, to take her back to the surface where her chariot was parked outside. She had to hope that her sun dragons hadn't burnt anything down while they waited for her to return. The poor dears did have a habit of getting antsy when left to their own devices for too long.

Medea smiled, eyes flicking to Jason as he seethed in place, unable to do anything.

"It was lovely catching up, darling," she simpered, pouting

at him. "A pity you didn't even have a single kind word for your dear ex-wife. For shame."

"One day, Medea, one day you're going to get what's coming to you," Jason hissed.

"And you'll have to live with the fact that it won't be you delivering that fate," Medea bit back, smiling until it fell off her face, expression going impressively emotionless. "If you thought I made your life a curse, just think what I could do to you with an *eternity.*"

Jason looked deeply unnerved, his eyes widened and he held an expression of disgust on his face, but there was fear woven through it. And gods... wasn't it *delicious.*

Medea suddenly went back to smiling, walking back to the dock and stepping on the boat after paying the ferryman. She turned back to Jason and waved at him.

"Toodles! It's been fun catching up, Jason," Medea's smile got a little sharper and her eyes sparked with a dangerous glint. "I can't wait to see you again."

Desert Fangs: 17

Aethalides looked over the map, screwing his face up as he scanned over the many scribbled out dots, then he looked to the sky and threw a glare at the sun. Why did the desert have to be so hot? He almost... almost would take Skadi's rest and the little surprise in the form of an Aztec god over this. Speaking of, he really should look into that once he was done with this oracle mess.

His dad didn't seem to have any knowledge or clue that the Aztec god was still alive and around, not only that, but it seemed like no one knew he was there. No one except the Archives.

Again another mystery for another time.

Glancing to his left he found Boudicca and Vali looking like they would rather be anywhere else but here, with Icarus glaring at the sun like it personally insulted him. Well, it did kill him, so he guessed that was a bit of an insult.

The desert was the last place they hadn't looked. If the oracle wasn't here... well, he would be at a loss.

"Okay, so I know things are a little warm..." Aethalides tried to reason, receiving glares in response. He pointed warningly at them, glaring. "Listen, I survived a boat trip with Jason of the Argonauts, you can survive a little bit of sun. Shut up, Icarus!"

Icarus screwed his face up. "I didn't even say *anything!*"

"You didn't need to," Aethalides answered back, turning to his map again. "Your face said everything."

"My face? What the *hades*-?"

"Do you have a clue where we're going?" Boudicca asked, standing over Aethalides and giving him some well-deserved shade if only for a brief moment.

He peered up at her, flashing his trademark grin, which did nothing to dissuade the glare being sent his way.

Honestly, you would think after living together for hundreds upon thousands of years that she'd have a little more faith in him. No, Boudicca thought he was a maniac and wasn't too shy to say it at times and there was always that... level of doubt in her gaze whenever he made a plan. It got on his nerves.

"I have a vague idea where we're going," Aethalides answered, pointing to his map. "As for where the oracle is, I have no freaking clue, because if I did, I'd have been there *ages* ago, but instead I'm *here!*" He yelled, waving his hands around. "Running around all of creation like some kind of headless chicken with my dad breathing down my neck and on top of all of that, I had to deal with Atticus! *Atticus!*" He pointed aggressively at her, teeth grit in a small snarl. "Do you have *any* idea the kind of stress that puts me under?"

Boudicca stared back at him impassively, not even flinching from his outburst while Icarus wisely hid behind her and Vali stepped a little closer, looking like he wished to comfort Aethalides, but not knowing how to.

"And you don't care!" Aethalides burst out, throwing his hands up in the air again. "You *do not* care that I am up to *here,*" he vaguely waved his hand up in the air. "With stress and I just... I need... I need a smoke.." He patted his pockets, then his hand landed on his flask, not containing water. "Scratch that, I need a *drink.*"

"Aethalides," Boudicca warned. "You know the rules."

"Yes..." he hissed at her, removing his hands from the hip

flask, scowling at her with a manic smile. "I know the rules. No drinking while we're on a quest... I know..." Aethalides roughly crossed his arms, turning away from them and sticking his nose in the air. "That doesn't mean I need to be *happy* about it."

"Also," Vali whispered. "Alcohol dehydrates you, which... in a desert..."

"Oh, why do you have to spring logic on me!"

"Map, now!" Boudicca hissed. "It's too hot in this place to stand still."

She was right and Aethalides let out a defeated sigh, nodding his head, before he looked to his map again. Scanning over it, he took a few steps forward, then turned to the left, looking up at the small mountain range in the distance with a small scowl.

"We got to head that way," he said, pointing to it. "They might be in a cave in the mountains. They'd be cool under this heat, and provide good shelter."

And so, the treck began. Walking through the sand, climbing up desert dunes and across miles and miles of sand, the sun baking down on them. Aethalides was pretty certain if he cracked an egg the heat and sun alone would cook it.

Vali had taken his long coat off, pulling his hair back in a loose ponytail and already, Aethalides could see his neck was starting to burn. They had put on sun cream, but this heat was a killer.

He was getting sand in his shoes, silently he cursed Medea and her clever idea to visit Hecate and avoid this whole mess. Aethalides, though, didn't want to come with her. He got to see enough of the underworld on a daily basis to last him all of his lifetimes and yet, he knew he had so much more to see of it. Wasn't that a happy thought?

A yelp made him startle and he only got to see a cloud of

sand as Icarus went tumbling down a dune, landing in a sandy pile at the bottom of it.

The group made their way carefully down the dune, Vali helping Icarus up, with Boudicca checking him over to make sure he was okay.

"Couldn't we of taken the van!" Icarus complained. "Why do we have to walk?"

"Have you ever seen a camper van try to drive in sand like this?" Aethalides scowled at him. "It's not happening and besides, the sand would rain havoc on the paint job. My poor baby has gone through enough trauma after you drove her."

Icarus scowled. "I was saving you guys!"

"Besides the point!" Aethalides snapped back. "You almost chewed up the gearbox! You absolute madman. I've had that car for years and it's never gotten a scratch on it. You drive it once and suddenly it's almost ready for the scrap heap!"

"You're overreacting, it was not that bad."

Aethalides childishly kicked some sand in his general direction, before continuing with the walk to the mountains.

He wasn't ahead by himself for long, Vali was quickly joining him, still quiet and hunched over. Aethalides had an idea that Icarus was probably sulking with Boudicca at the back.

"You seem to be in a bad mood today," Vali whispered, tilting his head. "Bad night?"

"Ugh, I think it's this sun," Aethalides complained, looking up at the big glowing orb in the sky, raising his hand a little to shield his eyes. "It's just making me more… irritable than usual. Sorry. I don't mean to be."

"It's all right," Vali shrugged. "I think we're all a little on edge," he flashed a cheeky grin. "And you got to see Atticus again, I bet that was fun."

Aethalides rolled his eyes. "Oh yeah, *so fun*, having to deal with my crazy stalker. I keep thinking he's going to pop up behind one of those dunes."

Vali let out a short laugh before his expression changed to serious. "What are we going to do when we find the oracle?"

"You think we will?"

"I'm confident in our abilities, even if we're missing our heavy hitters," Vali screwed his face up, raising an eyebrow at Aethalides. "Why didn't Asterion come?"

"Because the heat makes him more antsy than me," Aethalides explained flippantly. "And I'd rather not deal with a minotaur suffering from heat stroke."

"That's fair."

They continued their walk, Aethalides hating the desert every second. Sure, he came from a hot country, but not like this. He didn't live in a desert, Larissa was open fields and farm lands, and he used to sell horses. It was almost funny, how once he'd been a lord and now he was running around at the beck and call of the gods trying to do anything he could to protect people.

Finally, they reached the mountains and the group paused, staring up at them, he could see the heat rising, all that was missing were the circling vultures. Despite Atlantis being made for everyone there were still places that were dangerous. The desert was one of them and there were two. Currently, they were walking through Set's Rage, the smaller of the two, but it made up for that in heat and intensity alone. Some would say the best thing about the desert was the isolation and that's why Inanna's Haven was so popular for pilgrims and trainee healers. Inanna's Haven was filled with schools for healers and one of the main places the light elves of Alfheim took up residence.

Inanna's Haven was to the right of them, set amongst the

mountains and shielded from the desert, animals and any other unsightly things by a huge wall that was built around the settlement.

Now they were standing at the foot of Manticore Mountain, which… was aptly named.

Maybe he should've brought Asterion and just watered him a lot.

"Okay, stay sharp," Aethalides said, pulling out his knives and spinning them around his fingers. "I've died by manticore… it's not fun. Not from the Mesopotamian ones or the Greek ones."

"There are different ones?" Icarus spluttered, carefully taking out his bow and notching an arrow.

"Yes and they hurt," Aethalides smiled brightly. "On the bright side at least we're close to healer central!" He idly gestured to Inanna's Haven. The others did not share his enthusiasm. "All right gang, let's go!"

The desert was hard, the mountain was worse.

Climbing up a mountain in the burning heat, it should be getting colder the higher you went, but it didn't seem to help at all. There were caves dotted all up the mountain and at each one, they carefully searched them, often finding a few bones and evidence of a manticore, but… thankfully no manticore. At least for now. Aethalides knew their luck would run out eventually, unless his father was really smiling down on them, but Hermes tended to get distracted easily by anything shiny.

"Okay, just remember that Mesopotamian manticores can mimic voices, so keep each other in eyesight. We can't be too careful," Aethalides spanned his knives around again out of habit. "Not to mention it isn't just manticores that are the danger around here."

"Are you referring to the terrain?" Boudicca asked, screwing

303

her face up. "Because this weather... I feel like I'm walking through a forge."

"I grew up in Greece and even I think it's too hot!" Icarus mumbled. "Are we sure this oracle is here or that Apollo is certain it's this desert?"

Aethalides raised an eyebrow and smirked. "Are you doubting lord Apollo, Icarus?"

Icarus flushed red and this wasn't due to the heat. "N-no! No! Of course, I'm not!"

He sniggered until Boudicca smacked him on the back of the head. Aethalides grumbled and rubbed the back of his head in annoyance, throwing a small glare at her.

They climbed another set of rocks, finding yet another cave. This one... was lacking bones. The group shared a look at each other, entering the cave, and finding that someone had definitely lived there.

There were burnt-down candles, and a few blankets had been left behind, with some blankets too. The place was covered in a small layer of dust, whoever had lived here... they hadn't been here in a long time.

Vali sniffed the air, screwing his face up a moment in slight confusion. "It was just a kid... well, teenager, living here. There's no adult scent at all."

"Seriously dude?" Icarus stared at him. "You can tell the difference."

"Icarus, all animals give off different scents depending on their age."

"Wait what?"

Aethalides rubbed at the middle of his forehead, mumbling under his breath. "Can we please focus? Vali, you think you could track them?"

Vali sniffed the air again, turning into his wolf form, pressing his nose to the floor as he seemingly followed a trail, reaching outside. He continued to follow, until it got to the edge of a cliff and stopped. He peered over the edge, giving a small whine and turned back to his human form.

"I'm confused," he admitted. "There was a scent here... but it just stops," he looked down over the edge. "But they didn't fall, it was like they were here one minute and the next... they were gone. But.." He sniffed again, frowning in confusion. "There's a second scent now, it's faint, I... I think I know it... but it's hard to say."

"Why is it hard?" Boudicca asked.

Vali shrugged. "I don't know... it's like... it changes...?

"Wonderful!" Aethalides threw his hands up, pacing back and forth. "So we have no idea who this other is, but what we do know is-."

"Viggo," Vali suddenly muttered, a growl entering his tone, lips pulling back in a snarl.

Aethalides peered over the edge of the cliff with everyone else and sure enough, there was Viggo with a small collection of Rune's gang. That wasn't the worst of it, they were speaking to the small gang of desert dwellers. Bandits that lived out in the deserts and usually dealt with thievery or illegal animal trafficking. Looking at the big fluffy red fur manes they had decorating their backs, it was clear these guys dealt in hunting manticores, which meant... there was only one gang it could be.

"Oh, wonderful..." Aethalides mumbled, wiping away the sweat from his forehead. "Desert Fangs... bunch of hunting obsessed maniacs, they believe that all animals should be hunted for sport," he screwed his face up. "Compared to the hunters of Artemis who do it for protection, animal control or food."

305

"Looks like they've been hunting manticores.." Boudicca mumbled, narrowing her eyes at them.

"They don't just work in trading animal fur or claws, they'll trade the whole animals," he rolled his eyes in irritation. "You wouldn't believe how many of the rich folk in Atlantis would just love a manticore as a pet."

Icarus screwed his face up, looking a little disturbed. "Are they stupid?"

"Yes. Very. Which is why we can only pray that the manticore will escape its cage and eat them," Aethalides said casually, smirking. "Ya know... natural selection is a wonderful thing."

"What's Viggo doing here?" Vali mumbled. "Why would Rune, of all people, be branching out to other gangs like this? He doesn't need to, he has the heart literally in the palm of his hand," he gestured towards the scene of a deal going down. "These guys are known criminals and are constantly being hunted."

"If Rune is involved it's not good," Aethalides said simply and then a smile curled up his face. "So why don't we put a spanner in the works and give him a *reason* to want us dead."

Icarus, as predicted, looked at him like he was nuts. "Why in the hades would we want to give him a *reason?* He's kicked our butts *twice* just this week and he's done it several more times before."

Aethalides threw him a look. "That's exactly the reason."

"I for one would gladly like to release the animals the Desert Fangs have captured," Vali snarled, standing up to his full height for once, easily towering over all of them. "No animal should be captured and sold off for cheap entertainment or a wealth flex."

Boudicca nodded in agreement, already making her way carefully down the mountain with Vali not far behind.

"And we're all going to ignore the fact that Medea literally has a winter coat decorated with manticore fur?" Icarus mumbled as he also started to climb down, Aethalides close behind him.

"Actually," Aethalides stated. "Medea got that coat before hunting manticores became illegal in the Victorian ages."

"Yeah, but still?"

"Eh, you know Medea, she likes the finer things."

They made their way down, Icarus stopped at a higher point so he could snipe away with his arrows and give cover, while the others scrambled down to the camp. Sure enough there were cages and cages of animals, a few of them were manticores, there were other animals here too, a few Aethalides was pretty certain had been declared extinct years ago. Nope, just the Desert Fangs keeping them captured.

Vali was making short work of the cages, smashing the locks while Boudicca made short work of the guards.

They seemed to have everything handled so Aethalides snuck up, hiding behind the curtains to listen in on the conversation between Viggo and the leader of the Desert Fangs, Gulltanni.

Named for his gold teeth that had been filed down to points, like fangs, Gulltanni was a tall man with broad shoulders. Dark hair fell about his face, done up in braids but he was oddly pale for a guy that spent his time in the sun. A Norse bow and quiver were strapped to his back, wearing clothes that were dirtied by the desert. Everything about his clothes was practical, a whetstone at his belt, a sword and knife too, wearing oranges and browns to hide amongst the dunes.

The rest of his people were dressed very similarly, except their weapons ranged from Greek to Persian and a few Mesopotamians here and there. Most had bows and quivers or a hunting weapon of some kind.

The only other thing shared between the group was the large manticore manes they had around their neck and shoulders. It had to be uncomfortably warm, but it was all part of their big initiation ritual. Whoever wanted to join them, which thankfully wasn't many, had to hunt down and successfully kill a manticore. Then they would wear their skins with pride, proclaiming themselves to be a royal douche.

It seemed that Rune's men were uploading a manticore to a desert sledge while Viggo talked with Gulltanni.

"You promise it's been well trained?" The giant grunted, glaring down at the desert dweller. "Rune doesn't like his time being wasted."

"It's trained, it'll track down anyone you're looking for," Gulltanni assured, the startling thing was the very out-of-place Norwegian accent.

Viggo narrowed his eyes. "And it won't kill on sight."

"Yes, yes, I followed Rune's directions to the letter!" Gulltanni insisted. "I mean... I don't know why he wanted a manticore, especially a Mesopotamian one! Do you have any idea how hard those are to beat into submission? I suggested several other creatures better suited to what-."

"Rune wants this one," Viggo said, crossing his arms and a smirk slipped across his face. "He likes the irony of it."

"Irony?"

Viggo narrowed his eyes. "If you know what's good for you, you won't ask. Now," he pulled out of his pocket a bag of what was definitely money. "Here's your pay. You didn't see us and you didn't speak to us if you get caught. Got it?"

Gulltanni waved him off. "Yeah, yeah, I know! This isn't my first time!"

"I got to wonder," Viggo continued, looking about himself. "What your father would think if he knew you were the one doing all this…"

Gulltanni narrowed his eyes. "Shut it," he snarled, showing his blinding golden fangs. "And don't talk to me about that waste of space! I got nothing to say 'bout the guy. I'd be glad if he was ashamed of me!"

"The way you run this operation of yours… yeah," Viggo smirked. "Think he would be."

"I told you…" Gulltanni snarled between gritted teeth. "This isn't my first time! I know what I'm doing!"

As if to just insult this guy further and probably better than Aethalides ever could, all of his animals suddenly came stampeding through the camp. Aethalides even had to dodge out of the way as the animals came running, destroying equipment, trampling the camp, and trampling anyone who got in their way. Manticores were hunting and Runes men, mostly city dwelling, were quick to start leaving with their cargo.

Aethalides crawled out of the destroyed tent, pulling himself up from the sand and dusting himself down, until a large shadow fell over him.

He looked up and found Viggo's snarling face glaring daggers at him.

"Shouldda known it was you!" Viggo boomed. "You always get in the way, you're like a cockroach!"

"Wow. Rude," Aethalides said, pulling his knives out and getting ready for a fight. "You sure you want to do this?"

Hesitantly he glanced over when he heard more commotion, Boudicca and Vali were both fighting the Desert Fangs and a few arrows were striking people in the arms and legs.

Viggo burst out laughing, clutching his belly a moment as

he gave deep laughs. "What are you going to do pipsqueak?" He sniggered. "Look at you! Hardly any meat on ya'. Cyclops wouldn't even use you as a toothpick!"

Aethalides shrugged. "You clearly haven't read the story of David and Goliath have you?" He flashed his manic grin. "Spoiler alert, it didn't end well for the 'giant'."

Viggo roared and slammed his hands on the spot Aethalides had been. He'd dodged backwards and tossed his knives at him. Viggo lifted his hand and blocked the blows, before he was charging at Aethalides who called his knives back and started running as fast as he could. A member of the desert fangs tried to grab him but was immediately stopped by an arrow striking him in the thigh and he went down screaming like a sack of bricks. That would mean he'd owe Icarus one, irritating, but at least he was still alive.

Aethalides skidded to a stop, throwing his knives again, causing Viggo to slow down so he could block the blades. Aethalides used this time to run between his legs, calling his knives back and jumping for the back of Viggo's leg.

The Jotun must have been expecting it because he spun around and easily backhanded Aethalides, sending him flying through the air and smashing into the ground. The world went blurry for a second, spinning and colours flashed in and out in front of his eyesight. His ears were ringing and he felt sick.

"Ow, oh yeah… that's a concussion…" he slowly got up, wincing and groaning. "And a few broken ribs."

Viggo was coming right at him, hand raised to swat him like some annoying pest, when Vali suddenly darted forward and swung his sword up just as Viggo brought his hand down.

Vali's blade cut straight through the other Jötun's wrist, cutting his hand clean off and Viggo stumbled back, screaming in pain. He clutched at his wrist where the blood was still leaking and glared at Vali who was already prepared to parry any other attack.

Viggo huffed in breaths between his teeth, glaring at Vali with more hatred than Aethalides had ever seen. It felt like that action was just a little bit personal, he knew that Rune had gotten under Vali's skin, and maybe this was his way of getting back at him.

"It doesn't matter," Viggo snarled, spitting out the words like venom. "We have the manticore and no matter what you do, we'll get that oracle!"

"Doubtful," Vali replied, evenly spinning the sword around and getting ready to attack again. "How far are you going to be able to get with that hole in your chest?"

Viggo growled, gritting his teeth. "You... you're just like your father!"

"In all the *worst* ways, I promise you," Vali snarled, his voice turning into a growl.

An arrow suddenly struck the ground by Viggo's feet and he stumbled away, looking up to see Icarus, who was already notching another arrow. Viggo snarled, opening his mouth to say something when it turned into a yell of pain as Boudicca's sword came through his chest. He stumbled and tried to hit her, but she was quick to pull her blade out and back away from his range.

Viggo stumbled, looking over to where the rest of the gang had gone, then shot a glare back at them.

"Just you wait.." He hissed. "We'll get that oracle... and even if we don't... we sure as hel aren't letting you keep them!"

Viggo turned on his heel and ran when Vali took a step towards him, sword raised to deliver a killing blow, but the giant

311

was already making tracks quickly.

The Desert Fangs had already fled, they probably decided to cut their losses and just make it out scot-free. No doubt they had more animals kept wherever they liked to hide.

"Nicely handled…" Aethalides wheezed, slowly standing up and clutching at his ribs. "Ahh… yep… nicely done… Vali, was not expecting you to cut off his hand.."

Vali shrugged, sheathing his sword. "It's a little trick I learned from Fenris."

Boudicca waved up to Icarus and he was already shouldering his bow, running down the side of the mountain as best he could to catch up with them. All around them, Manticores were busy snacking on a few of the desert fangs who hadn't escaped, so it would be a good time to leave.

"We need to get you to the hospital," Boudicca stated as she made a move to help him, but he waved her away.

"Medea should be back… just… ah.." He sucked in a rattled breath. "We just need to get this sorted as quickly as possible. Rune's getting… too close."

"I just cut off his right hands, hand," Vali mumbled.

"Yes and while that is great, I think we can all know where he'll be heading," Aethalides sighed, looking up at the mountain. "The oracle *was* here… I'm sure that's what that cave was… but… they're long gone now."

,,,,,

"So… we're back to square one?" Icarus asked as he reached them. "What do we do now?"

In truth, Aethalides wasn't sure. They'd searched all of the places that his father had mapped out for them and got nothing. The final one was close, but… well, they didn't get much further than a few blankets and a forgotten home. Someone else had been

312

there with the oracle and… presumably taken them away. Were they already too late?

"We get the others together," Aethalides said with determination. "And we finally confront Rune. This… addition of the manticore… it's worrying. Besides," he threw his manic grin. "I'm sure Medea's just dying to get a new coat!"

Pertho: 18

"So, what's the plan?"

Xbalanque looked to Aethalides as they stood on the building opposite Rune's huge house. The whole Archives were getting ready on the roof opposite the building, looking over their supplies, getting ready for their little skirmish.

Aethalides was on his phone, texting Brianna from what Xbalanque could see. Her responses were not... well... good, especially since Aethalides kept sending emojis.

"Hehe... plan," Aethalides scoffed. "What plan?"

"You... *do* have a plan don't you?" Xbalanque frowned at him, resting his hands against his spear, glancing at the phone again. "Right...?"

"Oh come on, Xbalanque, it's us," Aethalides looked up at him with a frown. "We make plans, they also go wrong, I make a plan on the fly? Success!"

It wasn't far from the truth but that didn't mean Xbalanque was happy about it. After working as a detective for at least a few weeks now, he'd started to get used to the idea of making a plan before doing something. Hesitantly, Xbalanque reached for his own phone, opening up the text messages he'd sent to Jason, all of them read, all of them not answered. He hadn't been texting every day, but he was worried. The guy had just seen all manner of monsters in one sitting, learnt that Xbalanque wasn't completely normal and had his understanding of reality flipped on its head.

He was half tempted to send another text now, or try calling him, maybe try seeing him, but he didn't think that would be good. If he hadn't replied to him by now, well… that was pretty clear that he wanted to be left alone, but it didn't stop Xbalanque from being worried.

In their time they'd seen people go insane from witnessing less.

"Your buddy still not replying?" Aethalides asked, looking through his binoculars at the house, noting all the people on guard.

Xbalanque sighed and put his phone away. "I'm worried, honestly. He's got a kid to look after," he awkwardly tapped away at his spear. "I can't believe I messed things up… again!"

"Are you referring to your-."

"I don't want to talk about it."

"Huh," Aethalides lowered his binoculars to look up at Xbalanque with a small smirk. "Avoiding your issues? That's usually Vali's way."

Xbalanque raised an eyebrow. "Pot calling the kettle black, Aethalides?"

The ten year old, who wasn't really ten, smirked at him fully, until it turned into a full blown grin. The unsettling one that had anyone who saw it worried, well everyone except Medea, she tended to just share the grin back at him. Xbalanque would sometimes wonder if being alive so long was the thing that drove them insane or if they'd always been like that. He wasn't wrong when he implied that Aethalides didn't talk about his past in great detail.

"The difference is, my friend, I openly admit I avoid my issues," Aethalides said, then he turned back to the others, clapping his hands and rubbing them together in excitement. "So!

Who's ready to kick Rune's shiny behind?"

Medea smirked, everyone else looked rightfully nervous or irritated with Aethalides's general excitement for doing anything dangerous. Or in Icarus's case, looking two bad things happening away from passing out.

"*Confidence!*" Aethalides said, giving them all a thumbs up. "I love it!"

"Are we sure this is a good idea?" Icarus whispered. "I mean... I get it, but..." he rubbed at his arm, looking over at the large house which had multiple guards. "Rune... he's dangerous."

"Why are you complaining, Icarus?" Medea sighed in exasperation, placing her hands on her hips. "You're not even going into the lion's den. You're staying here. Out of the way."

The 'where you won't cause any trouble' went unsaid, but it was implied.

Boudicca instantly got in Medea's face, snarling at her, putting herself between Icarus and Medea. The princes of Colchis looked only amused at the attempt of being intimidating to her. There was very little that bothered Medea, Xbalanque had never seen anyone get under skin enough to really call it... fear or anger. Most of the time, her expression was nothing but contempt.

"Watch your tongue!" Boudicca snarled. "He's young, both he and Vali are children, they shouldn't even be here!"

Medea scoffed, rolling her eyes. "Yes, yes, use the excuse of youth to explain incompetence and fear."

"Medea..." Aethalides sighed. "Play nice."

She flicked her hair behind her shoulder, gliding over to her chariot and gathered up the reins. She turned to Aethalides and offered a little smile, then she turned her attention to her potions she had on her belt.

Vali slowly stepped forward, with his arms wrapped around him, carefully looking over the house. He awkwardly tapped at his arms for a moment and opened his mouth to speak, but Aethalides was quick to interrupt him.

"No, Vali, we are not going a vikingr," he quickly said. "No matter how much fun it would be."

Vali's shoulders, surprisingly, slumped and he nodded his head. He wandered away, back to Boudicca and Icarus. Waiting patiently for the go ahead.

Aethalides looked up at the building one final time, then nodded.

"Let's do it, gang!" Aethalides cried and he ran to the steps that would lead off the building.

Xbalanque and Boudicca followed him, Vali following Asterion and Medea took the sky. The guards that were there, the ones who were on Xbalanque, Boudicca and Aethalides side were mostly taken out by Boudicca and Xbalanque. This time, no killing, Aethalides had made that very clear. Though that meant there was always the possibility that they'd wake up later and become a problem.

Aethalides ran up to the door, pulling out his lock pick from inside his jacket pocket and started to work, all the while Xbalanque and Boudicca kept watch.

"I don't know why we keep that witch around," Boudicca suddenly hissed.

"Medea's been with us for a long time, Boudicca," Xbalanque replied. "And she helps."

"She is cruel and calculating," Boudicca scoffed. "With no loyalty to anyone except herself."

"A lesson I believe all of us can take to heart on occasions,"

Aethalides piped up from his spot by the door, then he glanced to Boudicca. "And... Medea has been through a lot."

"That doesn't excuse her behaviour," Boudicca spat back.

"Oh, I never said that," Aethalides sniggered, focusing his attention back to the lock, twisting and coaxing the mechanism to work with him. "But it does explain it," a resounding click came from the door and he held his hands up with a grin. "Just call me the son of Hermes, because I am the greatest lock picker in history."

Boudicca shoved the door open wordlessly, not even bothering with answering to Aethalides's ever inflated ego, not that he seemed to notice much. She had the right idea though, Aethalides's ego didn't need inflating any bigger than it was.

The radio on their hips crackled to life and Medea's voice came through, sounding every bit as bored as he could imagine she felt right now.

"The roof is taken care of," she drawled. "I'm heading into the house now, see you there."

A loud crash sounded afterwards and everyone jumped. It was heard across the whole house and the three of them shared a look. Aethalides grabbed his radio.

"Medea, was that you?"

"No."

"That was us!" Vali's panicked voice came through. "Sorry, Asterion... got the door..." There was a pause and they heard the sound of another crash followed by several screams and shouts. "Literally he got the door and... started smashing people with it."

"Vali... did you encourage Asterion to go a vikingr?" Aethalides asked sweetly and the long pause was answer enough. The ten year old gave a sigh, before taking out his knife, flipping it in the air and catching it. "Well, so much for doing this the sensible way… let's go a vikingr!"

"What does that even mean?" Xbalanque asked, raising an eyebrow.

"It means, we cause as much destruction as possible with as many casualties as you can manage!" Aethalides said, pulling out his other knife, grinning like a maniac. "All the while stealing a bunch of stuff!"

Boudicca raised her sword and yelled, charging down the corridor, where she turned a corner and the sound of battle was quick to reach their ears. An arm shot out from around the corner, splattering against the wall before it fell to the floor.

Xbalanque winced, clutching tightly at his spear and shook his head. "Yeah, I'm not killing anyone."

"Fine," Aethalides sighed, watching a guard come sprinting down from the end of the corridor, followed by two others. "Let me dance with death then."

Xbalanque watched Aethalides toss his knives, striking two of the gods in the neck, before calling his knives back.

A creek on the floorboards behind him had Xbalanque spinning around and only just blocking a strike with his spear. He shot his hand forward, and grabbed the back of their head, slamming it into the wall, knocking the guard out cold.

When he turned back to speak to Aethalides, he'd already left the corridor. Xbalanque cursed under his breath, then ran as fast as he could towards the last direction he saw him heading. As he ran past the other corridor that Boudicca had gone down, he caught a glance to see Boudicca hacking people to death with her sword, all the while Asterion was still attacking people with the door he'd ripped off the hinges and foronce, Vali seemed to be slightly enjoying himself. He was getting a piggyback ride from Asterion, sword raised high, laughing gleefully with a smile so big he could see his canines.

"Yeah! Vikingr!" He shouted, then immediately howled afterwards like a wolf. "Now let's pillage his riches and burn his home to the ground!"

"Vali, no, no pyromania!" Xbalanque scolded him.

Vali lowered his sword, shrinking in on himself. "Ah right, sorry... I was getting... a little carried away.." Asterion spun the door around and smacked another person in the face with it. Vali was quiet all but two seconds before he raised his sword up again and shouted gleefully. "Yeah, vikingr!"

Xbalanque shook his head, then turned back to running once again in the direction he guessed Aethalides had gone down. Stepping over the bodies, jumping at the door and shoving it open. It slammed in the face of a satyr that was trying to escape, knocking him to the ground.

Xbalanque was quick to kick them in the head to knock them out, as a shout rang out. Xbalanque only just had a chance to drop his spear and catch the small body of Aethalides that was thrown at him. He smacked into the wall, tripping over the recently knocked out satyr. They landed on the ground and Xbalanque clutched Aethalides tighter and he squirmed in his arms, kicking at him.

"Would you let me go!" He hissed at him. "I am not a child!"

Xbalanque screwed his face up. "I caught you because you were thrown at me!" He looked over the top of Aethalides's head, finding Viggo standing there, still missing his hand.

"You!" Viggo snarled, pointing at them. "Should've known it was you!" He pulled out his sword with the hand he still had left. "No one else would be as stupid as-agh!"

Xbalanque and Aethalides watched as Viggo suddenly got violently tackled to the ground by Vali in his wolf form. They

320

vanished around the corner, Viggo screaming bloody murder and yelling plenty of Nordic curses at Vali.

"I feel like Vali is enjoying this a little *too* much," Xbalanque mumbled, placing Aethalides down as he stood up.

Aethalides dusted himself down, glancing up at the carnage going on around him and smirked.

"Vali might be all quiet and nervous most of the time, but the boy's a Norse god at heart," he reached up and tapped his temple, almost like he was indicating that he was nuts, which was ironic. "Come on," Aethalides said, running off in the direction that Vali and Viggo had gone, Xbalanque close behind him. "Let's deal with Rune, finally!"

They ran past Vali and Viggo, reaching for the door at the end. He slammed it open and Xbalanque was more than a little surprised to see Rune sitting behind his desk, quietly writing or jotting down notes. A glass of alcohol near him, and a bunch of runes lining the front of his desk.

"If you wanted to have a conversation, you only had to call," Rune looked up and smiled at Aethalides. "You know you're one of my closest friends, Aethalides."

"Can it!" Aethalides seethed, raising his knives. "I'm protecting the oracle and my… group… people…" he spluttered and stuttered over his sentence. "My people!"

"Such an awful lot of effort put in to protect someone you've never met," Rune commented off-handedly, then smiled. "And such conviction. Which is funny, especially when you're doing such a poor job at it."

"What are you talking about?" Aethalides seethed. "I know you don't have the oracle!"

"Yes, I don't have the oracle, you don't have the oracle either," Rune continued, closing his books and folding his hands

321

on his desk, smiling. "And you've been very helpful in trimming down the search areas."

Xbalanque took a step forward, slamming his hands on the desk, and glaring down at Rune. The light elf only looked up at him with that same smile, it never changed, and he didn't look intimidated at all. If anything, he looked amused.

"Listen, you better tell us what the heck you are talking about!" Xbalanque snarled. "We've invaded your base and your men are not much against us."

Rune raised an eyebrow and laughed. "Oh, those men?" He pointed out the hall with his pen, shaking his head. "No. They're not my men. They're a bunch of Port Side Raiders who got tired of Cillian's incompetence and I offered them an opportunity," he looked down at the hall, watching Vali and Viggo still fight, then glanced at the dead bodies on the floor, clicking his tongue. "Which... worked out exactly as I expected. Why would I waste my men on this."

"Wait... you knew!" Aethalides shrieked, clutching his knives tighter.

"Of course I knew," Rune smirked. "Aethalides... you have a habit of thinking yourself... untouchable due to your background and your family. This has led to you making mistakes," he got up, walking around the desk, sitting at the edge of it. "And I'd be a fool if I didn't take advantage of that."

Xbalanque could feel a mounting dread as Aethalides stared at Rune in horror. The sudden realisation that this whole time... they thought they were one step ahead of Rune, but in actual fact...

"See I knew you were going to look for this oracle, but you tend to get distracted without a real incentive to get things done," Rune explained. "So I just gave you a little push. You always

322

have to be the best there is, no one can be better than you. Then I sat back and... *waited*."

Rune smiled, picking up his drink as he turned it in his hands a moment, in complete control despite the madness going on around him and just outside his room. In control just like always.

" You worked brilliantly," he continued, "*Especially* after I sent Phobator to give you another little push and cover my back. You're annoyingly smart, I couldn't have you working out what I was up to, that would inconvenience me heavily and to my greatest joy, that little move did the trick," he laughed, raising the drink to his lips and taking a measured sip, watching both of them carefully. "You had no idea."

A scream came from somewhere behind as the sound of swords swinging through the air and probably a door too was all that could be heard for a moment. Rune seemed to enjoy basking in the silence as he sipped his drink, placing it back on the table and folding his hands again with a smile.

"You just thought I was trying to *stop* you from finding the oracle, but all I was doing was pushing you even more to get moving and I have to say, you did phenomenally." he smiled. "You got through all of the points so quickly, discovered an old Aztec god still alive, found an old Selkie civilization, you," he pointed to Xbalanque. "Managed to stop the Port Side Raiders smuggling business from the human realm to Atlantis, probably getting your partner mentally scarred in the process," Rune shrugged his shoulders. "But, such is life."

A loud thud sounded behind them, like someone had been thrown into a wall. Rune looked past them a moment, seemed to laugh and then turned his attention back to them. Continuing his monologue. He got to his feet, doing his coat up in the process, slowly circling the desk as he continued.

"And then, *then* you, Aethalides, found me what I needed. Evidence of the Oracle. Oh yes, your… little fight with the Desert Fangs and my men was inconvenient and you almost ruined my plan with the manticore, but… all in all, you gave me what I *wanted*, what I needed," Rune pocketed his hands and smiled at them, showing off the small fangs in the corner of his mouth. "You've narrowed down the search to *one* area. The desert, in hindsight," he laughed, picking up his drink again to finish it. "Should've been the first place I looked, but… I can't complain too much. Especially when you worked so hard *for me*," he turned and plucked something up from his desk, holding it out to Aethalides with a smile. "I really do feel like I should repay you."

Xbalanque could feel his blood boiling just listening to Rune and looking at what he had in his hand. A cheque was made out to Aethalides with a hefty payment.

"So I *thank you,*" Rune said, still holding the cheque out, still smiling that smug look. "But your services are now no longer required."

Aethalides snapped, smacking the hand away and glared at Rune. He was practically foaming at the bit to start slicing, with Xbalanque quickly pulling Aethalides away from Rune. He was yelling all kinds of curses at him, some Xbalanque had heard before, others he didn't. They were all in Greek and he had no idea what he was saying.

There was more shouting and crashing behind them and Xbalanque spun around, still holding the feral man child in his arms and there was Brianna with her rookie.

In the background, there were two big Jötun guards taking Vali away, as he was still in his wolf form.

Brianna pulled her handcuffs out, looking him over with a

grim expression.

"Let's not make this difficult, Aethalides," she said, holding the cuffs up. "Drop the knives."

"You can't be serious!" Aethalides spluttered, pushing himself out of Xbalanque's arms. "It's Rune- it's."

"Aethalides," Brianna hissed, giving him a warning look. "Don't make this any harder."

Xbalanque sighed, dropping his spear and ignoring the glare Aethalides shot him, then reluctantly dropped his own knives.

Brianna handcuffed him, while the rookie handcuffed Xbalanque, taking the pair away after picking up their weapons.

Once they were taken outside, there was a prison cart with members of the Archives already handcuffed and inside. Brianna led them onto the cart, slamming the barred door shut and then it started moving.

No one spoke. Aesthalides was clearly seething. Gritting his teeth, not focusing on anyone, glaring down at the floor.

The trip to the guard station was short, then they were dragged to the jail, shoved inside with the cuffs removed and left. Aethalides didn't stop moving, he paced back and forth in the cell, all the while the rest of them sat on the seat of the floor.

Xbalanque didn't know what to say and looking at everyone else they didn't know either. They shared looks, then glanced worriedly at a seething Aethalides. Xbalanque had never seen him so mad, he didn't know if he was angry at Rune or himself. Knowing Aethalides it was probably both.

Finally, after waiting for who knew how long, Brianna came up to the cell and opened the door, she hooked a thumb. "Come on. Your bail has been posted."

"Finally!" Aethalides threw his hands up in the air. "My father will be hearing about this."

"Your father already knows."

Aethalides froze a second and tilted his head. "Was he the one who posted our bail?"

"No. That was Anansi," Brianna crossed her arms. "Your father was the one who gave me permission to arrest you all. He wants to speak with you."

If looks could kill... Brianna would certainly be a missing person right now. Still, Aethalides dutifully walked through, collecting his stuff on the way as did the rest of them, he only dropped the attitude the moment he saw his father and there was a good reason.

Hermes looked *livid*. Even Anansi backed away from him and Aethalides bowed so quickly that Xbalanque thought he'd get whiplash.

"Save it," Hermes bit out and Aethalides shot up quick, opening his mouth to say something, but once again his father beat him to it. "What were you thinking? How did you screw up so badly!?"

"I was just-."

"*Silence!*" Hermes roared and Aethalides snapped his mouth shut, dropping his head. "You are not the one speaking right now, you are the one *listening*. You, my son, have an unfortunate character flaw that has only gotten worse the older you've gotten and that's your ego. Your arrogance rivals us gods and now it has come to bite you."

"You're arrogant too," Aethalides awkwardly muttered, still keeping his head down.

Hermes's nostrils flared and his eyes sparked for a brief moment with magic. "Unlike you I have the *skill* to back up that arrogance! You were discussing sensitive information and forming plans in the *streets*, where anyone could hear you!" He gestured vaguely around himself, stalking up to Aethalides and only now, did Xbalanque feel like Hermes really was a god. A very powerful, very scary, very angry god who was holding on to his temper just barely. "What on Gaia's earth were you *thinking*!?"

"Rune still doesn't have the oracle," Aethalides pleaded, looking up at his father expectantly. "He doesn't have them, we can still find them before he does!"

"No, no you need to stop talking right now," Hermes scowled, holding up a finger to silence him. "You know as well as I do, that Rune isn't the *only* issue. You let Loki travel with you on that boat trip and I had to find out that piece of information through *Heimdallr!* You let that maniac close to discovering the oracle, do you have any idea the type of damage he could've caused!" Aethalides didn't say anything, just looked down at the floor again. *"Did* you think- were you so confident in yourself that you believed you could handle him if you did find the oracle? If you did, then your arrogance is worse than I thought."

"Why did you let Brianna arrest us then?" Aethalides shot back. "We could've spent the time we've spent here looking for the oracle in the desert!"

"Oh, you mean like the time you spent invading Rune's home to prove a point?" Hermes raised an eyebrow, crossing his arms. "I get it, your ego took a hit, as a god I can hand on heart say I don't like it when that happens to me, but I expected you honestly to be better."

"Well, when I'm so much like you, *father,* how could I *possibly* be better," Aethalides replied sarcastically.

Behind Hermes, Anansi winced, flicking a worried look to the back of the other gods head. They'd attracted the attention of the rest of the guards and all of them flinched or winced at the words, eyeing Hermes up wearily. Brianna looked like she was trying to calculate if she should protect a civilian should the worst happen and exactly how she was going to do that.

Hermes set his jaw, his face turning stony and his eyes flickered with a flash of purple again.

"You… you are so stubborn, just like your damn mother," Hermes grumbled, rubbing at his temple. "And as she would say, I have been babying you for too long, no, no… from now on the rules apply to you too. I'm not covering any more. You break the law of Atlantis from here on out? Brianna has every right to arrest you."

Aethalides gaped. "What? But… but we can't stop Rune if we have to obey the law!"

"Well you haven't been able to stop him *breaking* the law so what difference is it going to make?" Hermes shouted at him. "And now because of all the carnage you've caused, the rest of the pantheons have found out about this and oh boy… you would not *believe* how much work that's going to mean for me! So no, you are not going to do anything, you and your band of miscreants are going to go home and stay home, while I fix this mess," Hermes hissed at him. "Like I always do! So you don't end up in worse trouble than you already are!"

"What about the oracle?" Aethalides shouted in protest. "You're just going to leave them to Rune!"

"Brianna and her guards and the other captains will be dealing with finding the oracle in official capacity," Hermes snapped. "Which, as Athena so *beautifully* screamed at me earlier today, should've been the course of action I took in the first place. So, that's what's happening. Her men will be looking for the oracle and bringing them to the council of pantheons after."

"To the council of pantheons- you know that's a bad idea!" Aethalides snapped at him. "Their presence is just going to cause another in-fight with the pantheons and maybe another war, all of them are going to want a new oracle-."

Hermes had been pacing, rubbing his forehead looking like he was on the verge of a headache. With Aethalides's words it looked like the vein in the side of his head was going to burst, eye twitching and finally the god snapped completely. His eyes were glowing, his body had a light to it and suddenly shot up a few feet nearly crashing through the already very high ceiling.

"You think I don't know that!" Hermes yelled, his voice shook the room. "Why do you think I came to you in the first place? If a band of misfits happened to come across an oracle, fine, but if the other pantheons find out that one of their own knew about them the entire time? Different story! Do you have *any* idea the position you've put me in?" He was seething, form flicking between human and something else entirely. "My loyalties and alliances are being called into question now. As well as the peace treaty *I* helped create! So please, will you just go home!" Finally he shrank back down to his normal human size, his eyes stopped glowing and Hermes... he just looked tired. "Just... go home."

Aethalides opened his mouth to protest more, when Anansi stepped forward, placing one of his hands on Hermes's shoulder, shooting a look at Aethalides that had him snapping his mouth shut again.

"Have no fear, I will make sure they all get home and stay inside," Anansi assured him. "You go home and fix that pantheon of yours."

Hermes nodded, fixing Aethalides with another stern fatherly expression. "I am very disappointed in you."

And with those parting words, Hermes was gone.

Silence greeted them, Aethalides looked like he had the wind completely knocked out of him, bowing his head.

"We aren't just going to let that happen, right?" Icarus, surprisingly, was the first to speak up. "I mean… come on… it's us, we-."

"Of course we're not-," Aethalides began but was interrupted by Brianna.

"You are going to do no such thing or I will personally see to it that you are back in that cell" she snarled, pointing in the direction of the holding cells. "Do not push me on this, Aethalides! I've been convinced that your people shouldn't be allowed to operate at all, you put people in danger and you take no responsibility. You're dangerous."

"Right, yes, because the guards are so much better," he rolled his eyes. "You heard what my father said about the pantheons, do you honestly think-."

"The gods know best. They make the rules, we do what they say, that's how it's been for years!" Brianna hissed back. "That's how it's always been and we would be very arrogant to suggest we know better than the gods."

"You haven't spoken to a lot of gods in your time, have you?" Vali was surprisingly the one to speak up, crossing his arms and glaring at her. "I've been at their mercy before, are you honestly going to stand there and tell me they were justified and correct in their actions against my family?"

Brianna pursed her lips. She looked away awkwardly, the rest of the guards looked just as awkward given Vali's history. It was certainly an event that would make you question the gods ability to make wise and rational decisions. Hades, any of Aethalides's family had at least one myth depicting them as less than rational beings. Some more than others and some had no rational thought process in them at all.

"That... was a special case," Brianna worded herself carefully, Vali scoffing and rolling his eyes at her comment. She quickly cleared her throat and continued. "But this isn't."

"Are you joking me, right now?" Aethalides asked her, his face contorting into a glare. "This is one of the most dangerous and delicate situations we've been in since Eris took charge of the gossip column!"

"Aethalides!" Brianna snapped at him, standing over him and glaring. "Do yourself a favour and go home. Take your band of misfits with you." She leaned down and jabbed him in the chest. "Stay out of it! Before you get yourself killed or worse."

There were shared looks amongst the archives, all turning to Aethalides expectantly. He was staring at Brianna with a somewhat enraged snarl on his face. Looking like the age he actually was. His eyes... looked old. Filled with god knows how much experience and knowledge, over crowded and pushing past breaking point. He often looked down on people for being foolish and honestly? He had every right to considering his age.

He took a glance at Anansi, the spider god who had walked forward, placing one of his hands on Aethalides's shoulder. He gave a smile to Brianna, charming as always, a gift all tricksters seemed to have.

"Hey, no worries, Brianna!" Anansi purred, tiny fangs poking out the corner of his mouth. "I'll make sure they all get back to the Archives safe and sound, yeah? No need to worry further."

Brianna looked like she didn't trust him, but... well, she had little choice in the matter. Besides, what was she going to do? Question the word of a god? She already made it very clear her stance on that.

"Make sure they do," Brianna hissed, fixing Aethalides with another glare. "There are rules and we all have to follow them."

"Sure..." Aethalides smirked back, cold... calculated, honestly a little terrifying. "How often the gods do bend them."

Brianna narrowed her eyes. "Go home, Aethalides."

They walked out of the guard station, Anansi staying close to them the entire walk back. All around them guards lined the streets, there wasn't a single turn you could take without them making an appearance and whenever they did, they sent glares at the group. So did the everyday citizen too, not surprising considering they basically turned their home into a war zone. Or at least, it was on the verge of becoming one.

Everything felt tense, Xbalanque couldn't help but feel like they were being judged and assigned execution by every single glare that went in their direction. If they didn't get themselves out of this... well, he was certain that they'd be executed, or lynched.

Finally they got back to the Archives, he was happy to be home and off the streets. Things were going to be tense until that oracle was found and when they were... that would be the straw that would break the camel's back.

"Ugh!" Aethalides shouted and tossed his staff far away from himself. "Idiots! All of them, ilíthioi! Who blindly follows the gods and believes in everything they say?"

"Icarus," Medea mumbled under her breath, but quickly and surprisingly snapped her mouth shut when Aethalides hit her with a particularly ugly look.

"Not... now..." he snarled out. "We have to get back to that desert!"

"You heard what they said!" Boudicca snapped at him. "Do

you think disobeying the gods would be a good idea?"

"Yes," Anansi's voice cut through the impending argument. All eyes fell on the spider god as he straightened out his clothes. "It is exactly the type of thing you should do."

Icarus screwed his face up, looking to Anansi in confusion. "You're a god. Why would you want us to go against... you?"

"Ha!" Anansi laughed, crossing one set of arms in front of him, the other set were clasped behind his back. "I'm a god, sure... but a god without a pantheon and I couldn't be happier. All that drama... no, no, no... too much," he shook his head. "And this might come as a surprise to you, but I like the world. Could it be better? Of course! There is always room for improvement, but that would not come from a bunch of oldies throwing hissy fits and tossing their spades around in their sandbox. Especially when all they're going to do is break everything in said sandbox."

The spider god walked to the stairs, leaning on the bannister and gesturing with his hands as he looked at them all.

"Look, I'm a trickster god at heart, stories may be my deification, but I even used trickery to get that title. If it weren't for me bending the rules, using trickery and going against the grind, we would never have stories in the first place," Anansi explained, grinning. "Sometimes you gotta break stuff, sometimes you gotta bend the rules and cause a ruckus to get the right thing done. Sometimes... It's the only way you can make the world a better place."

"But the gods-," Icarus tried to protest, but Anansi interrupted him.

"*Screw* the gods!" He waved him off. "They sit there in their ivory towers making rules for people they don't even mingle with any more!" Anansi pointed to all of them as he began to circle them slowly. "You are all the losers of your stories, the ones who end up with the short end of the stick, vilified, laughed at, forgotten. You don't fit into the god's narrative because you break their perfect world! We don't even know why any of you, bar Aethalides, are back from the dead. You even break the very laws of *nature!*" Anansi grinned at them. "So quit feeling sorry for yourselves and get out there. It's time you live up to your reputation of being troublemakers."

Very slowly a grin started to spread across Aethalides's face. It was the grin that would usually scare him, but right now, he was grateful to see it. It was contagious too because the others started to share it, even Icarus offered a small smile, still looking nervous, but ready to follow the others.

"What I'm hearing," Aethalides started slowly. "Is a *god* giving us permission to go and look for the oracle…"

"That's what I'm hearing too," Xbalanque smirked at him.

"Oooh, breaking the rules, Xbalanque?" Medea teased. "What would your police buddies think?"

"Well, it's like Anansi said," he shrugged and offered a grin. "Sometimes you gotta break some rules."

"Everyone in on this?" Aethalides asked, turning to the others. "No shame in backing out, but I have to hear it, are you all in?"

They shared looks between each other, silently agreeing and nodding to Aethalides in confirmation. They were going to do it. They didn't care how much trouble they got in, they were going to find that oracle one way or another.

"All right…" Aethalides grinned. "It's settled… First thing tomorrow… It's back to the desert, so get some rest. We've got an oracle to find."

Dads, can't live with them, can't live without them: 19

Vali slowly crept through the halls of the Archives, plenty of people here were light sleepers. Survival instincts kicked up to the max, even when they slept in a place that was safe. Boudicca was the worst, it was very rare he could slip past her door, but this time he hadn't disturbed her.

Sneaking downstairs, Vali headed to the kitchen, the Archives at night was very strange. It looked more like a museum or some kind of old library. The funny thing was, he could remember when some of these things came into existence and had been state of the art. Now they were either old or considered retro and that was when he excluded the ancient things.

It was late into the evening or early in the morning? Vali wasn't sure, but after getting some sleep, like clockwork, he was struck with a nightmare again.

It all happened so fast, there's just the feeling of flesh tearing, a flash of sharp teeth, crimson everywhere and screaming. So much screaming, but it's the quiet at the end that's always the part to wake him up. The silence of death that weighs heavy in the air and that, that is the part which Vali hated the most, because he knew that no matter what; his brother is dead. Narvi is gone and only silence remains.

So like always, after being hit with a nightmare like that he got up to go to the kitchen and make himself a cup of warm milk. He didn't get that far though.

When he made it downstairs, a light coming out of *that* room and it made him feel a little uneasy.

The memorial room wasn't a place that was visited often by any of them. It was there and occasionally he'd pop his head in and stare at the pictures and photos. Some of the people had passed on so long ago that the only thing they had were their names on little pieces of paper. Aethalides had always insisted that he'd end up drawing them, he could remember what they looked like after all, but there was always something else that would come up. A monster needed to be fought or a natural disaster needed to be curved by calming down whichever god was throwing a bit of a tantrum.

Bottom line, the room was usually just left to collect dust, until a new person needed to be added to the wall.

No one had died tonight, so Vali was a little surprised to find Aethalides, the biggest avoider of the room, standing in it and staring at the wall of pictures and names.

He didn't acknowledge Vali's presence, his eyes were fixed on the wall and he was fiddling with his necklace bearing his father's symbol.

A lot had happened and while he was acting like he was okay, it was clear that what his father had said, had gotten to Aethalides. As always, Aethalides dodged and weaved any conversations in regard to his father. It was clear that this time had gone differently, this time, Hermes had been annoyed at his son's attitude.

Vali didn't know what to make of everything, but he couldn't say he was that surprised. Gods would be gods after all.

"What are you doing in here?" He asked softly, but Aethalides didn't answer him.

He frowned, glancing back at the door before turning back

to Aethalides. If he was having a memory episode Vali wouldn't be the best person to pull him back from that. He was just getting over his own unwanted trip down memory lane.

"Aethalides?"

"Do you remember the day we met?" Aethalides asked, his eyes still firmly set on the wall.

"Yes…" Vali trailed off, walking slowly to stand next to him. "You told me you understood what it was like to be a child of a god and you said I'd be safe."

Aethalides laughed softly. "A warm bed, fresh food and above all safe," he repeated the words he'd said to him once all those years ago. "Can you believe I promised all these people the same thing?" He gestured to the wall before letting his hand drop.

Vali knew where this conversation was going. It was one that Aethalides usually had with Medea mostly because it happened after one of *those* nights, which then turned into one of *those* sessions.

"Have you been drinking?" He found himself asking and immediately regretted the words the moment he'd said them.

Aethalides threw him a look but sighed and gave a slight nod. He sounded more exhausted than upset though.

"Yes, Vali, I have been drinking," he replied, tapping at his temple. "Sometimes it's the only way to get this old thing to just stop," he grimaced a little, clearly uncomfortable with how personal the conversation was going. "I wanted to try and get some sleep tonight but once again Hypnos eludes me. At this rate I and anyone else won't have to worry about me getting trapped in a memory, I'll be hallucinating pink elephants or something."

"It's not your fault you know," Vali said, glancing up at the wall again. "People make their own decisions, it's not your responsibility to look after everyone and we were all there

337

tonight. We could've said no."

Aethalides was silent for a moment, he'd looked away from the wall, staring at his feet now. Vali could only imagine what was running through his head, finding out that Rune had simply used them this entire time, how they were now considered public enemy number one if they so much as stepped a toe out of line. Not to mention the complicated feelings he had surrounding his father.

From what Vali could gather, Aethalides was close with his father, but after tonight something had changed. Fractured and broke. A relationship between father and son was complicated at the best of times without adding the whole divine elements to it.

"You could also apply that logic to your own situation, Vali," Aethalides said, glancing up at him and Vali felt himself freeze.

He hadn't expected Aethalides to turn his own words against him like that. Not with the subject that he himself would avoid as much as he could.

"I killed my brother."

"While you had no control over yourself thanks to a curse the gods put on you," Aethalides replied, giving a small smile. "You put too much responsibility on yourself sometimes."

"Right back at you."

He laughed, eyes glued to his feet, then he looked back to the wall, the laughter dying on his lips. There was a haunted look in his eyes as they roamed the images and names. Vali wondered how many of these moments Aethalides re-lived against his will when the memories came back.

No wonder he couldn't let go of the guilt.

"You should get some sleep, kid," Aethalides whispered, his fingers touching the necklace again. "It's... gonna be a long day tomorrow."

"We'll beat Rune, Aethalides," Vali promised, reaching to put a hand on his shoulder but stopped himself when he saw Aethalides tense up slightly.

He visibly relaxed after Vali lowered his hand.

"Thank you, Vali," he whispered and gave a little smile. "Just... after being manhandled today... I... it's just a bit much right now."

"No worries," he returned his smile with one of his own. "I'm going to make myself some warm milk, do you want some? Helps me sleep... it might help you?"

There was a long pause, clearly, he was weighing up the pros and cons before sighing. Aethalides flashed him a tired smile.

"Sure, why not. It's not like my medicine is helping anyway."

"That's not medicine, Aethalides," Vali replied walking to the door and he heard him huff, still sounding slightly amused.

"You're starting to sound like Xbalanque and I don't mean that as a compliment."

Vali rolled his eyes but didn't reply to him.

Finally, he made it to the kitchen and made himself a glass of warm milk, a guilty pleasure he'd gotten himself into after Anansi introduced him to one time when he found it difficult to sleep.

The little spider wasn't around at the moment, he was probably asleep, which is where Vali should be. Nightmares had other plans though, at least it wasn't as bad as Aethalides had it when Phobator had popped up.

Another thing that Vali had noticed was since that night, Aethalides avoided the memorial room more than usual, even opting to not walk down that corridor at all. Another reason he was so surprised to find him standing inside, staring at... what Vali could only assume was a room of Aethalides's past failures. At least, that's how Aethalides viewed it.

It wasn't a room of memorial and honour for the dead, it was a room of lives and mistakes he could've prevented if he hadn't messed up.

He got there and started the process of warming up two cups of milk, standing at the stove and watching it carefully so he didn't overheat it. A sudden noise of the fridge opening made him jump, almost dropping the cups in hand.

Spinning around he came face to face with Arachne, a pink dressing gown, with eight pink fluffy slippers and her hair in rollers.

They stared at each other for a beat, before Arachne carefully lifted up a small helping of tube yoghourts.

She shut the fridge slowly as they continued to stare and after a moment, with one of the yoghurts in her mouth already, she wordlessly handed him one. Vali accepted it and raised an eyebrow at her, Arachne raised a finger to her lips in a shhhh motion before she scuttled off.

So she was still being the yoghurt thief then. Probably should let Icarus know... but, oh well, what he didn't know wouldn't kill him. At least this time.

Vali shook his head and turned back to the milk, pouring two cups full, then he went back to the room, but the light was off and Aethalides wasn't there.

Sneaking back upstairs, he felt his ear twitch slightly at a noise upstairs, probably Aethalides, might be in his office.

Once he reached the office, he found light streaming out from under the study door.

Shaking his head, Vali gently pushed the door open, finding

the current ten year old sitting at his desk, a cup of coffee on his desk, writing away. His old herald staff was actually off the wall and resting on his desk, alongside several open books.

He didn't even look at Vali, continuing to write, but somehow he still knew it was him. It wouldn't surprise Vali if Aethalides had their individual footsteps memorised.

"Drop off the milk and go back to bed. You should be resting," Aethalides stated matter-of -factly, still writing, while other books lay open on the desk in front of him. "Shifting between human and wolf takes a lot of energy."

"I could say the same thing about you," Vali replied softly, walking up to the desk after he closed the door.

Scattered across the top were books upon books about Aztec myths, their culture, even notes on the weapons used. He had to wonder if this had anything to do with the reappearance of Itztlacoliuhqui. Another issue for them to deal with later maybe? Looked like Aethalides was trying to cram as much information as he possibly could in one space, while also writing his own book that he seemed to be half way through already.

Vali wondered how long he'd been sitting here working like this before he made his way to the memorial room.

He gingerly placed the cup down in a section that was free of any objects. The cup only just fit in the gap.

"I couldn't sleep," Vali said when it became apparent that Aethalides wasn't going to say anything.

The writing slowed to a stop and he finally looked up at him, scanning over his entire body, a little frown fell across his face.

"And why is that?"

"Nightmare," he shrugged, looking down at his milk. "Same old same old. What about you?"

Aethalides shrugged. "Couldn't switch my brain off, I

341

guess," he looked up at Vali, then went back to writing. "Maybe I could invest in a dream catcher for you. I hear those are good. It might help you sleep," he paused again, writing stopping once more as he seemed to think. "Or lavender. I would offer you the Greek secret ingredient but you're a little too young for that."

Vali raised an eyebrow. "What's the Greek secret?"

Aethalides sighed and placed his pen down, sitting back to look at him. He seemed to have given up on his writing and studying like he knew Vali wasn't going anywhere until he either forced him to go to sleep or he went voluntarily. The problem was, that Aethalides could be very stubborn, so Vali was going to have to wait it out.

He sighed again, rubbing at his bloodshot eyes, then leaned back in his seat, resting his hands on his lap.

"Hypnos, the personification of sleep," Aethalides began. "Twin brother of Thanatos, a being I am all too well acquainted with," a slightly bitter tone crept in at the edge of his words, but Aethalides continued anyway. "Has a symbol to recognise him. That being the poppy flower."

"Opium?" Vali guessed and Aethalides gave a small nod. "And I thought the Victorian era was bad."

Aethalides snorted, rolling his eyes. "Oh please, they were tame. Dionysus' parties could get even worse," he paused again, looking to Vali, scrutinising him. "Why are you really here, Vali? What do you want?"

"I was concerned after what happened today..." he said slowly, treading carefully with his words. "In regards to your father."

"My father..." Aethalides trailed off and then groaned, he pinched the bridge of his nose. "Oh boy. It's gonna be one of *those* conversations isn't it?"

"Your father really is trying-."

"I think you mean he *is* trying."

Vali sighed, taking a sip of his warm milk to keep himself steady and to bite back the retort that was on the tip of his tongue. Oh, Aethalides thought his dad was bad, and Vali's entire family were prophesied to end the world at some point or at the very least be part of it.

Instead the fifteen year old invited himself to sit on the seat opposite Aethalides and he ignored the way the ten year olds shoulders slumped, because he knew there was no getting out of this conversation. Not unless he went to bed, but that wasn't going to happen either. Aethalides was just going to have to sit through it all and bare it.

Besides if anyone was going to understand how tricky immortal families could be, it would be Vali.

"I get it," he stated, looking back at Aethalides who looked mildly uncomfortable. "It's easier to ignore a problem than admit there is one. You said it yourself, I avoid my problems."

"That's not what I-."

"It is and we both know it. You are a horrible liar."

Aethalides apparently didn't have anything to say to that, snapping his mouth shut and looking away from him. He was shifting in his seat and tapping away at his desk, Vali imagined he was probably kicking his legs too and cursing him with every word under the sun.

"I also get the whole... being related to a trickster god," Vali went on. "People judge you because of what your father is or what he did... or what he's going to do, in my case," he placed a hand on his chest and shrugged. "Then you have your own actions to account for and suddenly it's to be expected when we do a bad thing because of who our parents are. You have it worse

343

than I do, because you have a unique gift that's turned into a curse."

"I'm being lectured by a fifteen-year-old…" Aethalides said slowly, clearly to himself and while he was still not looking at Vali. "What has my life become…"

"My point is," Vali raised his voice, but only slightly, just enough to get Aethalides's attention. Finally the other looked at him, now very uncomfortable. "Your dad's trying. He's not perfect and… sure.." He laughed. "He's going to mess up, probably all the time. But he's trying and he cares about you. That's why he was so mad today."

"Vali…" Aethalides began looking away from him and sighed. "It's not that simple…"

"Oh I know, You said it yourself that you understand what it's like to have a trickster god for a dad too," he smiled and gave a little shrug. "It's never easy and they fix things for everyone else, but go under-appreciated-."

"My father is not underappreciated, he's an Olympian!"

He frowned softly, looking down at his glass of milk. "Yeah, but… have you ever heard the gods thank him?"

"He… doesn't mind. He's okay."

Vali raised an eyebrow. Aethalides didn't sound too convinced, in fact, his tone was more like he was trying to convince himself than Vali.

The conversation that had happened earlier, the way Hermes had criticised something that he himself was also guilty of, stating that he was careless, had clearly hit Aethalides. It was a gut punch. Sure, Aethalides had disappointed people in the past and he'd been told so, but it was different when it came from your father.

"Maybe at first but it's been over six thousand years,

Aethalides," Vali said gently. "Working so hard with nothing to show for it, not even a thank you? It can get to people after a while."

Not to mention, Vali could easily remember all the things that his own pantheon used to say about Hermes when the god wasn't there. Nothing good that was for sure and the rest of the pantheons... often referred to him as the 'olympian lap dog' though Vali never quite knew why.

Aethalides apparently didn't have anything to say to that. Looking away again, tapping a beat on the desk before he wrapped his arms around himself and started to rub at his arm. He grimaced slightly and then let out a breath, finally looking back at Vali with an odd expression.

"You're very mature for your age."

Vali laughed. "Well, like you, I've been around for a while and... and I lost everyone..." he glanced to the side, the place where his brother would've been standing when he was still alive.

His expression fell when all he found was an empty space. No brother. There hadn't been a brother there in a very long time, he'd of thought he'd be used to it by now, but it still hurt. Like a piece of himself was missing.

They hadn't even done anything, it had all been their father, but no... the gods decided that the way to punish Loki was to punish them too.

"You still have family, Aethalides," he said slowly. "Don't lose it because you're bitter."

He breathed through his nose and gave a small nod. "I shall... take your advice under recommendations," Aethalides replied, giving a shrug and then looked him dead in the eye, clearly uncomfortable from doing so. "Now go to bed. It's too late to have a therapy session and we need to be ready for tomorrow."

Vali knew he wasn't going to get any further, at least not tonight, so he gave a little nod and got up to his feet to leave.

The moment his back was turned he heard the scratching sound of a pen gliding across paper again, finding Aethalides had gone back to writing again. His eyes firmly fixed on the books and not even giving Vali a glance as he reached the door.

He paused, hand hovering over the door handle and went to say something, but Aethalides beat him to it.

"Bed, Vali," he said firmly. "Now."

"What about you?"

He could almost picture the grimace on Aethalides's face as he replied. "Sleep isn't going to be gracing me tonight. I'll be fine. Go to bed."

With a defeated sigh he left his office, gently closing the door on his way out. He stared at it for a moment longer, before giving up and tiptoeing down the hall again, back to his room downstairs.

As he went down the hall he found another light coming out from under a door.

He frowned, looking up at Icarus's door, shaking his head.

"Does no one sleep in this place," he mumbled to himself, walking up to the door and gently pushing it open.

Inside Icarus looked startled to see him. His head shooting up as he sat on the floor surrounded by papers and even a few marble tablets.

Icarus's room had no end of bits and pieces in it. Shelves lined the wall filled with little trinkets he'd collected over the short period he'd been alive again. Even a few of his own things from ancient Greece. A chest was sat, opened, next to his bed

346

which is where all the papers came from. Around his room, pinned to the walls, were posters for various places around the world and a few of the tv shows Icarus had liked over the years. A few clothes were scattered here and there on the floor or resting over the back of his chair that sat at his desk.

Icarus blinked at his sudden appearance and gave a sheepish grin. "Oh, uh, hey Vali," he rubbed the back of his neck, dressed in a vest top and pyjama bottoms Vali could see the burn scar easily that ran up his arm. "What are you doing up?"

"I was getting milk," he replied, then narrowed his eyes at him. "Why are *you* up?"

"I… couldn't sleep," Icarus admitted, looking back at the papers. "So I decided to look through the old trunk again," he offered a little awkward smile, lightly patting it. "Ya know, try and figure out what the old man was thinking…"

Vali took a seat on the floor, just in front of the notes and tablets. His eyes scanned over the various pieces he could see, but he couldn't read any of them. It was all in Greek, but there were a few draws, sketches that looked like inventions of some kind.

It didn't take a genius to work out who these used to belong to.

"These… are your father's notes…?" He asked and Icarus gave a slow nod.

"He wrote so much," he admitted. "Too much, pater- I uh, I mean dad, he just kept going."

"Do you understand it?"

Icarus looked startled and once again smiled at him. "Yeah… yeah! Of course I do, I mean… he was my dad, clearly I… I mean, I'd obviously…" he trailed off and gave a defeated sigh. "No. I… I'm *trying*, but…" Icarus looked down at the papers in his hand and threw them away. "Gods, this is so stupid! Why don't I *get* any of this, he was my father I should be able to understand just what the hades he was talking about!"

Vali gave him a soft look. "Icarus, just because he's your father doesn't mean you're going to understand everything he does. *Believe* me," he picked up one of the pages and gave it a look over. "I can't work out half of the reasons my dad did what he did."

"That's different though! That's not inventions... or living up to your father's reputation and potential! You... you have a purpose!"

"What?"

Icarus sighed and buried his head in his hands. "Oh gods, that was so stupid, why'd you say that, Icarus... You're an idiot..."

"Icarus!"

"Gah! What? *What?*"

Vali shook his head, placing the paper he'd picked up back on the floor with the rest.

They should both be in bed and asleep, but here he was, playing therapist, because all of these loveable idiots were too emotionally constipated to deal with their issues by themselves. Or they just ignored their issues all together, like Vali did, but he was more of a do as I say, not as I do kind of guy.

"Do you really believe you have no purpose here?" He asked softly.

Icarus looked uncomfortable, shifting in place and looking away from Vali like he couldn't face him. His face had gone a little red and he pouted, clearly embarrassed and a little bit frustrated at the same time.

"Kinda," he muttered. "I mean... I don't really do anything

here and you know what everyone says every day... I'm the screw-up!" Icarus gestured towards the door. "I say the wrong thing or I'm clumsy and cause another problem... for crying out loud Vali, I can't even be bait correctly! Remember that time with the harpy? Aethalides got taken and not me!"

Vali raised his hand and shook his head. "Okay, first of all, you're not a screw-up. So you make a few mistakes and occasionally, put your foot in it, but come on, who hasn't?"

"Everyone."

"Seriously?" He raised an eyebrow. "Okay, let me lay it out for you... Aethalides has had his fair share of screw ups. He's gotten things wrong before. Xbalanque's mistake cost him his brother's head, Medea abandoned her whole family for a guy that turned out to just be using her and Arachne challenged the goddess of weaving to a *weaving competition*," he ticked them off his fingers as he went. "And don't even get me started on the trouble Anansi has got himself into."

Icarus was silent, pulling his knees up to his chest and wrapping his arms around them, looking away from him. He was frowning still, looking like he didn't want to believe him or listen.

"My point is," Vali went on. "Is that yes, you make mistakes... but none of them have ever been quite as dire as *those* mistakes."

"Yeah, but those all happened thousands or hundreds of years ago!" Icarus argued, throwing his arms up in the air and letting himself fall backwards so he was staring up at the ceiling. "Everyone's so much cooler and... and better now. They don't make so many mistakes, not like me. Plus, everyone else has a... *purpose* here. Not me."

"What are you-?"

"Aethalides is the genius, Medea is the badass sorceress, Boudicca is the stone cold warrior queen, Xbalanque is the hero," Icarus raised his hand, ticking them off. "Arachne is the housekeeper, Asterion is the strong man and the freaking Minotaur, Anansi is a literal god and *you* can turn into a wolf!" His hands dropped to the floor again and he let out a sigh. "But me? I'm just the stupid kid who flew too close to the sun and literally crashed and burned. I'm a *cautionary tale!*"

Vali was silent, now sitting with his knees against his chest and his own arms wrapped around them as he listened to Icarus tick everything off. He could see the point Icarus was making, even if he didn't agree with it.

"You know…" he started slowly. "I couldn't always turn into a wolf right?"

Icarus lifted his head to look at him with a dull expression. "Can you use a sword?"

"I'm a norseman, of course I can use a sword."

"Well, there you go then," he gestured, flopping his head back down. "Still more badass and useful than me. Unless you count me as cannon fodder."

He bit his lip and looked around at all the pages on the floor, eyes scanning over the notes and could see a few had been made in different coloured ink. Even though it was written in Greek, he could still recognise Icarus's handwriting.

"Is that why you're trying to understand your dad's notes?"

Icarus exhaled through his nose, he didn't sit up, he didn't even lift his head to look at Vali, but he did answer him.

"I just thought… that if I could… you know, understand my dad's notes, start inventing like he did… maybe… maybe I'd be more useful," he admitted. "Maybe I could make a more worthwhile contribution instead of being the screw up," Icarus clenched his hands by his side and muttered bitterly. "But knowing me I'd probably screw the inventions up and end up killing someone anyway, so it's probably a good thing I suck at this too."

Vali honestly didn't know what to say to that. He looked down at all the notes and the huge chest, noticing some scorched and burned feathers poking up out the top of it, but he couldn't tell what they were.

"Where did you even get the notes?" He asked.

"Aethalides had them," Icarus explained, a smile creeping into his voice. "He met my dad… in Athens and after he died Aethalides kept his notes so they wouldn't get lost to time. When I… came back, he gave them to me," he laughed softly. "He said they were mine. That I deserved them, then he told me my dad was the greatest mind he'd ever met in ancient Greece and one of the greatest inventors of all time. I mean, I already knew that," he gave a shrug. "But it was nice to hear someone else say it."

Ah. Now things were starting to make sense.

"And is it because Aethalides knew your father that you feel the need to prove yourself more?" Vali asked gently.

Icarus was silent, but he slowly sat up and looked to Vali with an unreadable expression on his face. Like a wall had just gone up.

"You know what, you're right… it's late," he began to shuffle the papers back into order. "We should probably get some sleep. Big day tomorrow, breaking rules set by literal gods."

"Icarus?" Vali frowned, reaching out for him. "I didn't mean to upset you-."

"I'm fine, Vali."

"You don't seem-."

"I said, I'm *fine*!" He snapped, glaring up at him. "Go to bed.

I'm gonna be once I put all of this away."

Vali frowned and looked down at the notes. "Do you want me to help?" He asked, reaching for the chest, he leaned on his knees to get a better look inside and found more scorched feathers that stretched down and- "Wait, are those your wings?"

The lid was suddenly slammed down on the chest and Vali had to snatch his hand away otherwise he was going to lose fingers.

He looked to Icarus who had a haunted expression on his face, but he quickly covered it up with a scowl.

"Good*night*, Vali," he hissed between clenched teeth and Vali took that as his cue to leave.

He reached the door, looking back at Icarus who was busy cleaning up the notes and tablets, shuffling them together in a rush.

"Goodnight, Icarus," he whispered softly, before he left, gently shutting the door behind him.

Diamonds in the Rough: 20

"All right, so we know that the oracle was here," Aethalides stated, pacing back and forth at the edge of the cave, while Vali, in wolf form, sniffed around inside.

It was only himself, Vali, Boudicca and Xbalanque that were out, the others had stayed back at the Archives, Medea with the job of running a spell that would keep an illusion up like they were actually there. Hopefully, it would work long term and not draw too much attention.

Vali looked over at Aethalides, giving a small whine and a bark.

"What is it, boy?" Aethalides replied, mimicking how people spoke to their pets. "Timmy stuck down a well?"

Vali threw him an unimpressed look, with Boudicca smacking him on the back of the head at the same time. Then he morphed back into his human form, crossing his arms and glaring at Aethalides.

"I know why I can't track the scent..." he grumbled. "Because it's a god."

Xbalanque, who had been keeping a lookout for any said gods, looked back at him in confusion. Hel, all of them were looking at him in confusion, which was understandable. None of them had heightened senses like he did, they wouldn't know the difference between a god or a human or a satyr... though the latter tended to smell like a wet farm animal ninety per cent of the time.

"Gods smell different because they have different domains and can change their form…" Vali explained. "It makes them incredibly hard to track."

"That… oddly makes sense…" Aethalides said slowly and then shook his head as he seemed to catch up with what Vali had said. "I'm sorry, *god?* A god was here?"

Vali gave a small nod.

Uncomfortable looks were shared between the group. This wasn't good. If it was a god, then which one and for which pantheon? Also, if they did belong to a pantheon, then… why hadn't they given them to said pantheon or told the others? Maybe they had… and they were just keeping it a secret.

Either way it wasn't good. It could mean war between them all, especially if they found out about it and it became public knowledge, worse yet the gods would find out and… well… Vali could speak first hand that they didn't always follow logic. Plus, if the way Hermes had talked about them was anything to go by, the gods were just looking for an excuse to have a fight. Seriously, what have they got against peace?

Sure, Vali was a norse god first and a peaceful god… second, but he didn't see the point in fighting for fighting's sake. Maybe that was also why he didn't always fit in with the others, Thor had regularly gone to the realm of the giants looking for a fight and every time an idiot would step up to try and be the one to kill the giant slayer. It was like they forgot about his name.

"Fine, great, terrific!" Aethalides threw his hands up. "A pantheon is either hiding the oracle or a god is hiding the oracle from their pantheon… this…" he pinched the bridge of his nose. "This just got a whole lot more complicated."

"But why?" Xbalanque raised an eyebrow. "Why would they hide them?"

"Could be a peaceful god?" Boudicca suggested. "Perhaps they know what might happen if this oracle is found, so they are hiding them."

"It's an idea…" Aethalides agreed. "But… I don't know-."

"It's not a peaceful god," Vali stated.

The three of them looked at him again, Vali awkwardly shifted in place. He felt like they sometimes forgot that he himself was a god, though he didn't flex that side of his powers..Hel, he didn't know how to use all of his powers, never trying them out. Never practising, despite it probably being a good idea.

Still, there were some parts that he knew because… all gods just knew them naturally and… magic was something that Vali was reasonably in tune with. At least enough to know what kind of magic was used here.

"I know I'm not going to like this answer…" Aethalides said slowly, a wince already forming across his face. "But what kind of god is it?"

Vali shrugged. "Chaos… or chaotic… that's about all I get from it… which means-."

"Which means it's either a trickster, war, storm or discord-infused god!" Aethalides threw his hands up in exasperation. "Either way, not good!"

"I'm sure a nature god wouldn't want to do it," Xbalanque mumbled. "What would they get out of it?"

Aethalides gave a little broken laugh, sitting on the ground now and pressing his hands to his eyes. Right, maybe asking the guy who was connected to the Greek pantheon, a pantheon that practically lived on drama, wasn't a good idea.

When Vali was a boy, when things were… good, Hermes would come by and speak with his father and the other gods. Out of all the Greek pantheon, he was the one that Vali saw the most. That might be why he felt so at ease with Aethalides, being a son of Hermes, he at least understood him a little better than most.

Well, when he was a child, Hermes would come and tell stories of his pantheon, really it was just over glamorised family gossip and drama. He'd paint them as some kind of epics, describe them as true issues of the heart or mind, real problems. Vali would listen, despite his father dismissing him, saying something to Hermes along the lines of 'kids, in one ear out the other, speak your mind, friend' with a charming smile that would work wonders on anyone that wasn't Hermes.

So, Hermes talked and talked, he spoke about every little detail, except for the really important ones, but it was just drama after drama. Like the Olympians fed off it more than prayers.

Even now, he could hear the Greek gods' voice in his head; 'And then Aphrodite was sleeping around with Ares', 'Father has found another mortal and step-mother is already plotting the poor kid's demise, honestly, if I wasn't a bastard myself I'd say I can't say I blame her-', 'So, another one of Apollo's lovers bit the dust, might I introduce you to our latest flower?' 'Anyway, Hephaestus found out and then got Aphrodite and Ares stuck in a rather… compromising position should we say… it was hilarious!'. Nothing but non-stop drama that could easily be avoided.

So yes, he could see why Aethalides was having a mini breakdown in the middle of the desert.

"I… might… have an idea," Vali said slowly, looking away awkwardly. "It's risky…"

"How risky?" Boudicca asked, narrowing her eyes and he resisted the urge to flinch at the look.

Aethalides had poked his head up from behind his hands,

looking at him like they had nothing really left to lose, they just had to find this… oracle.

"I could… ask Heimdallr."

"No. No," the ten year old that wasn't really ten, was up on his feet in an instant. "That is a *terrible* idea, why would you suggest such a thing?"

Vali shrugged. "Heimdallr sees more than most. He would be able to see the magic trail this god left behind, I'm sure."

"Yeah," Xbalanque raised an eyebrow. "And then he'd probably hand us over to the council of pantheons. I've heard stories about him, Vali, he's loyal to a fault."

"It's Heimdallr's job to protect the realms, all of them, not just Asgard," Vali hissed. "If anyone will want to avoid a war, it's him."

"You are right, I would."

Vali yelped and the others jumped, spinning around to find Heimdallr standing there, he looked… odd amongst the desert. His clothes and complexion made him shine in the hot sun, rainbow eyes spinning wildly as they glared at the group. He didn't look impressed and when that glare fell on Vali, he felt himself shrink away from the disappointed expression.

"What in the nine realms do you think you're doing?" Heimdallr snarled. "Are you trying to live up to your father's reputation?"

He shrugged. "No matter what I do I have that reputation…"

"So you decided to just prove them right?"

Boudicca pulled Vali away from Heimdallr, putting him behind her as she took her sword and shield in hand. Despite facing down a god, her conviction for protecting him was unwavering.

"How did you find us?" She snarled, pointing the sword at

him. "Were you watching us?"

Heimdallr's eye twitched slightly. " When you say someone's name enough you are bound to catch their attention."

"Your hearing's that good?" Xbalanque raised an eyebrow.

"Boy, I can hear the sound the grass makes as it grows, yes, my hearing's *that* good," Heimdallr hissed. "Now, to the matter at hand, you are clearly looking for the oracle, something I know you were told not to do."

"Actually," Aethalides interrupted. "Anansi gave us permission."

"Anansi?" Heimdallr sighed and pinched the bridge of his nose, muttering in Norse under his breath. "You honestly trust Anansi's word over all of ours? He's a trickster god first and foremost. They only care about themselves and do nothing but cause trouble for everyone else. They're nothing, but good for nothing troublemakers."

"Riiiight..." Aethalides drawled with a sarcastic smirk. "That's why my father was the only one to start working towards peace."

"And why you always asked my father to fix your problems," Vali stated with a glare.

"Loki- ughhhhhh..." Heimdallr growled under his breath and took a moment to calm himself. It was weird to see him so riled up and annoyed. Usually, Heimdallr was so impassive that this... was weird. "Enough. You all need to go back to the Archives and maybe... maybe you'll get off lightly."

"Lord Heimdallr, please, you know how bad it'll be if they get their hands on the oracle, the fights, the wars-."

"Do not speak to me about the war between the gods, Hermesson," Heimdallr growled out, suddenly looking deeply haunted. "You weren't there and you know nothing of the pantheon war."

"Oh, you mean the war that happened between you all during the Roman Empire?" Aethalides replied sarcastically. "I *was* there. I saw what all your… temper tantrums did. Pompeii, the earthquake in Crete, the tsunami that came after, the plagues, the famine, the infighting!" He pointed at Heimdallr angrily, stepping forward. "I was there! I saw what you gods do when you have your wars and how we get stuck in the middle of it! So yes, I'll break the rules to save people that you *clearly* don't care about!"

"Silence, boy!"

"I'm pretty certain I'm a few thousand years older than you, Heimdallr!"

Heimdallr gave a low throaty chuckle. "Oh… son of Hermes… I am *far* older than you could imagine," he replied calmly, his eyes suddenly glowing with a blinding white light and then going dim, back to his usual rainbow ones. "Go home. All of you."

"Heimdallr, please!" Vali quickly stepped forward despite Boudicca's protest, standing in front of Aethalides and blocking Heimdallr's view of him. He understood why Aethalides was angry, but this wasn't going to help matters. "You know we're right. We need to find the oracle before the gods or the guards or Rune."

"I already left my post for you once, to find this oracle when I wasn't aware," Heimdallr stated. "Do you have any idea of the awkward position you put me in after that?"

"No, I don't, but I'm sorry if we did," Vali looked away. "Look, I get it, you're loyal and have a job to do… and Odin is your father, but… you know what he's like. Even you admit that what he did to me and my brother wasn't right… do you think he'll be any better with this?"

Vali could only pray that he'd get through to him. They needed Heimdallr's help, they needed him to see where the god went and took the oracle. Magic left a trail after all, especially if it was used like this. Vali couldn't see it, he wasn't skilled enough in his natural magic to be able to. He'd only just started carrying around rune stones to use and even then he wasn't very good at it.

Heimdallr pursed his lips, looking away for a moment, face screwing up. He looked like he was having a war with himself, over what was the right thing to do and following your duty. Vali got it. You make an oath, you keep it, Heimdallr had sworn to protect the realms and serve his king. Sometimes those were not the same thing.

"The ant nests…" he finally said. "That's where they went."

Vali blinked in surprise. "The… old myrmekes nest?"

"Yes," Heimdallr finally looked at them with a grave face. "That is all I'm doing, all right? You'll have to work from there."

"Thank you," Vali bowed to him. "Bifrostens herre."

Heimdallr screwed his face up. "Don't make me regret this."

"You won't tell anyone?" Aethalides asked hesitantly.

Heimdallr was silent for a moment. His back turned to them and then he glanced over at them. His expression was unreadable, like it usually was whenever he was dealing with people. Neutral, unmoving, never giving anything away. Vali remembered that it was the thing that drove his father up the wall, why he constantly tried to upset him.

"I will not go out of my way to say anything…" Heimdallr said slowly. "But if someone asks, I will not lie."

Well, that was as good as they were going to get.

Heimdallr left them, in a swirl of colours and light, leaving them alone in the desert. Now they just had to get to the nest.

"We should probably move quickly," Aethalides muttered. "We don't know how long it's going to take... for someone to ask Heimdallr about us. I imagine Odin is using him as his own security camera right now."

He wasn't wrong. Vali remembered what Odin was like.

Crossing the desert was just as hard as it had been the first time, only this time they had to dodge everything else that came with it. Like gods keeping an eye on things or the intense heat. Gods the heat!

Vali hated the desert, he hated any of the warmer climates, enjoying the cool and the colder temperatures than the hot weather of Greece or Egypt. The northern side of the desert known as the 'Land of Apophis' was nothing if not unforgiving. It felt like he was in the middle of a dwarven forge at Svartalfheim or worse, walking through the fire giant realm of Muspelheim, a place of fire and magma. The parts of the world tree surrounding that realm were usually burnt and blackened, with tiny bits of ash that clung to the charcoaled parts of the still living tree.

He paused and looked up at the sun, unforgiving, beating down on them, it made him sweat. Nowhere in this desert was there actually a place of shelter. It was mostly a barren wasteland, save for a tiny village and the surrounding mountains from afar. The biggest part of this side of the desert was Mithra's Gold, a place filled with huge and beautiful stone carvings and complicated building structures that looked straight out of someone's dreams.

It was impressive, not that Vali gave much attention to architecture, he still favoured writing poetry over carvings. They didn't go close to Mithra's Gold as they walked, but even from the distance they were at, he could see the complicated buildings and beautifully ornate structures that seemed more about form than function.

Vali turned his attention back to the mountains ahead of them, Ra's mountains that made up the border at the top between the desert and one of the more lush and green areas that surrounded Njörd's Harbour. At the foot of the mountains were several giant ant nests made by the myrmekes. A giant ant species that could range in size from dogs and giant bears. Really big ants in other words.

"Come on," Aethalides insisted, trudging through the sand and trying not to fall over at the same time. "We better hurry and get there before it gets dark. The myrmekes will come out then."

"Isn't that what we want?" Xbalanque raised an eyebrow. "What if they're in that nest?"

"This one is abandoned," Aethalides insisted as they got closer. "But the ones surrounding it aren't. We just gotta hope that the myrmekes haven't decided to perform an extension by connecting the tunnels to the old ones."

"And if they have...?"

Aethalides sniggered. "Let's hope that won't happen," he flashed them the crazy grin. "We'd be in a lot of trouble if they are. Then again, I've never died by giant ant before, certainly one to add to the books."

Xbalanque pulled a face. "Okay, yeah, no, we're not doing that."

Aethalides laughed softly, evolving into a full giggle as they continued to walk. So many hills and dips in the desert, a few times they slipped down them, eventually getting closer and closer to the nest. As they got closer, it seemed that some other people were there, people that were... riding the ants...?

"Oh you have to be *kidding* me," Aethalides mumbled, coming to a stop as he watched these people, dressed in brown armour, riding the giant ants back and forth, coming out of the abandoned nest.

It looked like they'd only recently decided to settle there. Walking back and forth, carrying boxes, taking them off the ants as they used them to drag carts or just carry the supplies themselves. They were covered in head-to-toe brown armour that almost matched the ants themselves, but the designs were undoubtedly Ancient Greek, with a few little tweaks to it.

Aethalides seemed to be cursing under his breath in Ancient Greek, starting to pace back and forth, grumbling under his breath continuously.

"Um, Aethalides?" Xbalanque raised an eyebrow. "What's the matter?"

"Do you know them?" Boudicca questioned as Aethalides made a small noise that sounded a little like a whine.

"Know them? Of course, I know them!" He gestured at the soldiers who had bravely tamed ants. "They're Myrmidons. See, Zeus had been Zeus again and Hera found out, like always, so she sent this plague to kill off Aegina and her son. She didn't succeed, only killed all of their people instead," Aethalides explained. "Anyway, her son, Aeacus, asked Zeus to give him his people back, I mean Zeus was his father so... not the most outlandish thing to ask."

"But you can't bring people back from the dead," Vali stated, screwing his face up. "At least... not *that* many people."

"No, you can't so... Zeus made him new people out of the ants since they were the only creatures other than Aegina and Aeacus who survived the plague. Thus the Myrmidons were born," he gestured to the soldiers. "They're as strong and sturdy as ants, also equally as aggressive, extremely loyal to their king and they wear their brown armour in memory of their origins," Aethalides screwed his face up as he placed his hands on his hips. "Looks like they've added riding giant ants to that list, as well as living in old ant nests. Why are they here? I thought…"

"Thought…?" Boudicca prompted when Aethalides had trailed off.

He rubbed his forehead and kept his face screwed up in confusion. "I thought they weren't around any more… the last time I saw them was at the battle of Troy. Achilles brought them with him."

"Are they dangerous?" Vali asked as he watched the army continue to work together to make their new home… well, more homely he guessed.

Aethalides laughed. "Are they dangerous? Of course, they're dangerous! They're human beings with the strength of ants!" He looked over at them and screwed his face up. "This has complicated things… we need to get past them somehow…"

"Without being seen, huh?" Xbalanque suggested, spinning his spear around in his hand with a slight smirk. "I'm good at that. Leave this to me."

"Oh, like how you went down to the underworld?" Aethalides raised an eyebrow. "So impressive."

"You don't have to get mean about it, Aethalides," Xbalanque scowled. "I know you're stressed, but that was a low blow."

"Right, right…" he waved him away, placing a hand to his chin as he started to pace back and forth. "Okay, we can't be seen… so we need to come up with some kind of plan… a way not to be seen…"

Vali sighed under his breath and looked over at the mess that was waiting for them. Well, he couldn't wait around for them to do something, it would take too long and he was a norse god. Sure, they made plans... but it was easier to just... run headfirst into it, with an element of fines.

Slowly, Vali side stepped away from them as the adults of the group discussed plans and strategies that would get them past this. He had a better idea, but he knew that if he tried to voice it, they'd say no, probably stating it as too dangerous. Yeah, like breaking into Rune's place was any safer?

Vali quickly took on his wolf form and scampered over to the ant nest. He snuck around the edge of some boxes, the soldiers and ants barely paying any attention to him. He was just a wolf after all and while they didn't always show up in the deserts, there were odd occasions when one would get lost.

Besides, what would they have to worry about a wolf sniffing around? They were riding giant ants, a lone wolf was probably of little concern to them.

Quietly he snuck inside the abandoned nest and made a break for it, running as fast as he could down the corridors, sniffing at the ground for any scent of the oracle or the god. It would be a hel of a lot easier if Heimdallr was with them, but the god just helping out in general was more than he was expecting or could hope for.

He ducked behind a pile of boxes, keeping his head low as he looked around, the smell was thick and it was moving deeper into the nest. For now nothing and no one seemed bothered by his presence. They'd just think him some kind of wolf, not that he was secretly a god.

Vali caught a scent of the oracle and followed it quickly, running down the path and finally coming to a part of the place that obviously hadn't been searched or cleared out by the myrmidons yet. There were piles of rubbish from Demeter eats, left behind and dropped, almost like they'd been left here in a hurry.

Glancing behind himself, he didn't see anyone coming down the corridor and slipped back into his real form, looking over the pieces carefully. There had to be something here, obviously the oracle wasn't here any more, but there had to be… some kind of clue that would lead to them. He picked up pieces of trash, flipping them over, sniffing at them and he couldn't help but grimace. Ugh… vegetarian meal… fair enough if you liked it, but it wasn't Vali's thing. He was undecided if that was down to being a norse god or the wolf side of him.

Vali continued to look through the garbage, flipping past pieces of trash and not coming up with anything. Come on, there had to be something, surely the Norns wouldn't be so cruel- oh, who was he kidding?

He desperately kept a growl from emitting from his mouth as he continued to search through the leftovers. All of it was vegetarian, not a single piece of meat and what smelt like tea had been cooked up. Okay… interesting… Vali's knowledge of Mesopotamia wasn't great… it wasn't a pantheon his own had really interacted with much, literally on the other side of the globe and as old as they were… Well, the Olympians liked to think they were the ones in charge, but everyone deep down knew that the Mesopotamian and Persian gods were the ones who actually ruled the roost. Their age was not something to be scoffed at.

Finally after scrounging around in garbage for ages, he found something that didn't belong amongst the garbage. A leaf. A leaf that wasn't one you would or could eat and not something that was found in the desert either. It was dried up, had been there for a while, but it was at least something.

Vali sniffed at and nearly sneezed. He felt like the god that had their oracle or one of their smells, and he could taste the chaos magic in the air. He really needed to learn how to recognise magic signatures, it would be useful in times like this.

He felt his ear twitch slightly at the sound of footsteps.

Carefully and quickly, Vali slipped the leaf away in his pocket and shifted forms again. He needed to get out of here and quickly. He'd spent too long in this place and without the aid of his wolf form. Who knew who might-

Vali froze at the sight of a Tyr walking down the tunnel towards him. Heimdallr must have said something.

He gulped, taking a few steps away from where Tyr stood, his eyes fixed on Vali in an instant, recognition clearly flickering in them. He knew, of course, he would and Vali wouldn't be able to talk himself out of this one. Tyr, was a war god first and foremost, his hand was already on his sword hilt.

"You shouldn't have come here, Vali, son of Loki," Tyr spoke slowly, eyes going over him. "The norse pantheon will not stand for this."

Vali changed forms again, drawing his sword and holding it out in front of him. Tyr looked surprised by the action, but a flicker of a smile twitched at his lips. He drew his own sword, holding it one handed, as his other hand was lost to Vali's brother years ago.

"I'm glad to see you act like a real vikingr and not like a snivelling coward like your father," Tyr complimented as he widened his stance. "You must know that you can't win this fight."

"Maybe not…" Vali agreed, baring his teeth. "But I'm no coward."

Tyr smiled and then charged. Vali would admit that maybe he slightly underestimated him, but even with his lost hand, Tyr still moved quick and with brutal swings. He couldn't help but feel that he was going easy on him, not fighting as hard as he could, giving Vali a few openings to strike, only to easily block and counter them.

He wished it was someone like Forsetti who had found him, someone he could talk to, not Tyr. Yes, out of all of the gods, Tyr was one of the most calm and reasonable, but he was also one of the quickest to action. If he saw no way of talking out of a situation, Tyr would be right by Odin's side, leading into battle.

It was always funny to Vali that Tyr was favoured over Odin. No one, not even the people who worshipped them liked or trusted Odin. But Tyr? He was a warrior, honoured, prayed to before every battle to give strength and courage to the vikings and norsemen. Odin was often avoided.

Vali ducked a swing, blocking the counter just barely and Tyr leaned all of his weight on it, sending him down to one knee and still pressing. His eyes lingered on Vali's blade a moment, widening in surprise, before looking at him.

"A gift from your sister?" He asked and Vali scowled.

"Hardly. I ripped this blade out of the river myself!" He snarled, shoving back with all of his might, finally sending Tyr back from him. The god actually stumbled slightly, but was able to correct himself easily.

They circled each other, Tyr didn't bother with any fancy tricks with his sword, he still held it ready to fight, unlike his father. Loki took whatever chance he could get to show off his sword skills, even when it wasn't needed and even when they weren't very good.

"Impressive," Tyr commented with a nod. "But if you

wanted to change people's opinions of you, perhaps swinging a necromantic blade is not the way to go about it."

"You didn't give me much of a choice," Vali snarled. "I was an enemy and no one would make me a blade, so I had to find one."

"So you took one from the realm adjacent to your sister's?"

Vali let himself smirk for once, giving the blade a small flourish but keeping himself ready to dodge at any time. "I like to keep the family I've got left close."

"Is that why you adorn yourself in their imagery?" Tyr questioned as he lashed out at Vali again, the two blocking and dodging, striking out with their blades and swinging at each other. "I see your siblings and nephews, but no sign of your father... or Narvi-."

"Keep his name out of your mouth!" Vali roared, his teeth growing slightly into points. "You do not have the right to think his name, let alone *say* it! You oh so called god of justice, sat back and watched as Odin condemned innocents to punishment! There was no justice that day!" He swung his sword above his head and brought it down over and over again. "There was just revenge and you did *nothing!*"

Tyr easily manoeuvred his sword, disarming Vali in an instant before elbowing him in the face. He swore he felt something break in his nose, blood was trickling down his face as he was knocked to the floor. He growled and tried to sit up, only to be met by a sword pointed at his throat, Tyr's steady hand and gaze behind it.

"Go on then..." Vali snarled, glaring daggers at him. "Finish it. Give them something to cheer about back home, I'm sure the halls have been quiet of celebration for a while."

Tyr's eyes flickered over him, studying is what it felt like.

He felt like a fly caught in a jaw, being watched by its captor as it decided its fate. Would Tyr go through with taking his head or would he let him go? Worse, would he bring him back to Asgard. Odin did not suffer fools well and Vali knew he suffered any one that disobeyed his orders even less.

He hoped Heimdallr would be okay.

"Heimdallr was right," Tyr said quietly, pulling the sword away and slipping it back in the scabbard. Next thing he had his hand held out to Vali, to help him up.

Vali's eyes flickered from the hand to Tyr's face several times. Was this... some kind of trick? No, Tyr wasn't the kind, he wasn't Odin or his father. This... was genuine.

Hesitantly, Vali reached out and grasped his hand, easily being pulled to his feet. Then Tyr stepped away, picking up his sword and holding it up in the small amount of light, looking it over.

"What's it called?" He asked, not looking at Vali at all, eyes still studying it.

"Hel taka," Vali said quietly and Tyr nodded.

"Good name," he held the sword out for Vali to take and he did, though he was hesitant about it, before slipping it away on his scabbard. "Your friends are still outside trying to devise a plan of getting in without being seen. Should've known that a child of Loki is more than enough to achieve that."

"They saw me..."

"But they didn't know it was you. They thought you were a wolf," Tyr offered a smile. "The myrmirods hardly care for wolves walking freely around here. They're sturdy people, perhaps they'd hope to try and tame you."

Vali shook his head. "Why are you doing this? You... you're really just gonna let me go?"

Tyr was quiet for a moment, folding his hand behind his back, pressing his other arm there too as he turned away. He walked a little further down the corridor so he stopped in front of the mess of garbage left behind. Idly he kicked some with his feet, not saying anything.

"Do you know much about the war?" He finally asked.

Vali looked back at him confused, hesitantly askingAre you talking about the pantheon war?"

Tyr hummed, nodding his head. "So many died. I am a war god, but I do not believe in fighting for the sake of it. I am a god of justice after all. Forsetti and I... we were the ones of our pantheon that joined in Hermes's cause. Who stood against our own pantheon to stop... the constant fighting and... essence stealing between us gods."

Vali didn't know what 'essence stealing' was and he didn't want to know. It sounded horrific, just thinking about what it could mean had him squirming in place.

"I serve Havi, but for too long I have stood idly by and let injustice spread in our pantheon... to our followers. It's time it ends," Tyr turned back to him, taking a steps forward as he continued to speak. "Forsetti and I have been speaking about... rekindling the original council back together, minus a few members of course.." He suddenly looked sad, looking away. "May their souls find rest in Mictlān, Xibalba and Hanan Pacha. Still, we've been... distant. I think it's time to change that, but it's not going to be easy. Finding this oracle and keeping them away from the gods," Tyr placed a hand on Vali's shoulder giving it a squeeze. "Might be a step in the right direction."

"Odin won't like this..."

"He doesn't have to like it," Tyr responded. "But sometimes we have to live with things we don't like. Now, go. Your friends are waiting on you and you've already hung around here long enough."

Vali took a few uncertain steps away, half expecting Tyr to do something and attack him when his back was turned, but the other god did nothing. He stood and watched him leave, hands once again behind his back. Maybe Vali had more... allies in Asgard than he previously believed. He wouldn't call them friends, there were no friends in Asgard for him, never could be, not after what they did.

He slipped back into his wolf form and ran, scampering through the long corridors and running through the maze of tunnels. The guards and ants paid him little mind, he was just a wolf to them.

Once he finally reached outside, he was climbing up the dunes, the sand was hot on his paws and he flicked every time he put his paws against the sand. Then he reached the others, who were still arguing over what they were going to do and how they were going to get past the giant ants and the guards.

Vali slipped back into his other form, standing next to them and looking back and forth. Aethalides was arguing with Boudicca and Xbalanque was mumbling something about being able to use some of his magic and then wincing at the idea.

"Ummm... can we go?" Vali asked, raising an eyebrow. "It's... getting kinda hot."

"We still have to get inside-."

"Tyr's here."

Aethalides stopped in his tracks, looking at him and then looking back at the ant nest, seeing Tyr himself walking out. The way he paled was... well, it was almost funny. Then, he quickly turned away from him and gestured frantically for them to start running.

Boudicca opened her mouth to protest, but Xbalanque shook his head. She sighed but nodded and they started running again. They just had to get as far away from the nest as possible and then he'd show them what he got. Preferably when they got back to the Archives.

"What do we do now?" Boudicca asked.

Vali smirked and patted his pocket. "Don't worry… I got it in hand…"

Dagaz: 21

"Sometimes I forget that you can be sneaky, Vali," Aethalides mused as he looked over the leaf that Vali had brought back to the Archives.

It was late, the whole Archives were back together, there was a better chance that they could still wrangle this in their favour.

The leaf wasn't one that Aethalides knew, but then again, botany was never his strongest subject... at least non magical botany. The most he could work out was... it wasn't a leaf for anywhere in Europe, but that didn't help. The way Atlantis was... there were jungles, forests, plant life from all over the world in one place. It was as lovely as it was infuriating.

"We could do with talking to a nature spirit... or god.." He mused.

"And darling, which nature spirit or god is going to help *us*, considering that your father has probably blacklisted us?" Medea asked.

Aethalides paused, looking over to her. She was lounging on the chaise lounge in the main library, reading one of her latest fashion magazines, with a few gossip magazines laying on the table next to her. The glass of wine just added to the whole scene. Medea herself was dressed in her silk dressing gown, her hair elegantly done up so she was ready for bed.

"I... hadn't figured that out yet, but I will," he reasoned, looking her over with a smirk. "And your addiction to the gossip column is honestly concerning."

"Blame my grandfather, Helios," Medea chimed back, picking up her wine and taking a sip as she smirked. "He's the biggest tattletale since Ares and Aphrodite got their little affair brewing…"

Aethalides waved her off, the last thing he wanted to do was start discussing his family's dirty laundry. He got enough of that whenever he read a new mythology book to see what groundbreaking differences they were going to come up with. Ninety five per cent of the time, it was just the same stories being told in a slightly different way. That didn't mean he wasn't going to stop buying them.

He looked back at the leaf, it would be so helpful if he could go to someone… anyone… oh… Aethalides winced, he had an idea, but he was loathed to do it. There was a nature god he could turn to and ask for help, but he really didn't want to. Mostly because it would mean… he'd have to owe him and that god was… the last person he wanted to owe. Not nearly because of what this god would ask for in return, but…

"I'll be right back…" Aethalides mumbled, picking up the leaf and leaving without another word.

It was late, most of Atlantis was tucked in bed and asleep, only a few places were still open and all of those would be in the theatre and entertainment district, filled with arts and performances, restaurants and clubs. He unfortunately had to head there and that was… what could generously be described as dangerous. Not for the patrons, but… down to the alcohol and Aethalides… issues.

He shook his head. Nope, he didn't need it… even if he was going to meet… his brother..

Aethalides made his way up to the aptly named 'Club Bacchus', owned by his uncle Dionysus, the god of wine, merriment and parties, but he wasn't who he was here to see.

Inside the club, the carpets were leopard print, and grapes and grapevines hung from the ceiling and along the wall, everything was gold, purple and wine red. Plush crisp sofas of leopard fur, patrons were dancing the night away, in the main hall there was no ceiling and grass grew, with trees scattered around. Little string lantern lights of various colours were lining the trees and hung between them.

There were games and parties, music blaring, glow sticks aplenty and a bar lined one wall. Amongst the trees were bean bags, chairs and benches, all decorated with either purple fabric of leopard skin. There were even real leopards wandering around the edges of the party, or lounging in areas with some of the other patrons.

Most of the members of Club Bacchus were satyrs, nymphs and humans, with a few odd exceptions, but Aethalides ignored them, looking for one satyr in particular.

It didn't take him long to find him, standing on top of one of the tables, arms in the air, crying out and shouting as he drank from a large bottle that was being poured down his neck. The wine got splattered across his body, staining the clothes he wore, making the green cloth look like it had been blood stained.

"Pan!" Aethalides shouted over the music. "Pan!"

The satyr paused and turned to look down at him. Dressed in his green tunic, decorated with gold, leaves and grapes, his long horns curled around his head and his beard had been neatly combed and platted at the front in a single plait with beads running through it.

Pan's horns were by far the largest of his kind, one of the benefits of being a god, along with all the classic Ancient Greek look, a pair of purple sunglasses over his eyes with little peace symbols in the glass, multiple pin badges decorated the green cloth going over his chest. A smiley face, a peace symbol, a little goat, a herald staff and many recycling symbols from all over the world.

"Aethalides!" Pan cried out, arms outstretched towards him. "Well, look who it is! If it isn't my baby half brother! Man, it's been an age!" He jumped down and made his way to him, placing a hand on his chin in thought while looking Aethalides up and down. "Huh. Is it just me, or have you gotten shorter?"

"It's a new body, Pan. I'm ten again."

"Again? Oh, you poor thing!" Pan reached forward and patted him on the head. "Never mind, yeah little bro? Doesn't matter how old you get, you'll always be younger than me!"

Aethalides blinked and nodded slowly, as he shoved Pan's hand away. "Yes... that's how age works..."

"Ha! And there's funny ol' Aethalides," he slapped him on the back hard. "You were always the smart one, right?"

Pan had leaned down into Aethalides's face, grinning from ear to ear, his brown eyes were sparking with power, hands placed behind his back. It wasn't a *nice* smile, it was nothing but smug and Aethalides could already feel the temper he usually kept a good check on starting to pitch towards the red zone.

He shouldn't have come here, but he needed the location and identification of this leaf.

"Look, *I* don't want to be here," Aethalides stated and flashed a strained grin. "*You* don't want me here."

"Too damn right, you're really cramping my style," Pan waved him away with a smirk. "Man, that sounds like something Hermaphroditus would say! Maybe I've been spending too much time with them..."

"Besides the point," Aethalides continued through gritted

377

teeth. "I need you to just take a look at this leaf and tell me what plant it's from and where this might be in Atlantis..."

Pan stood up, snatching a drink from a waiter who happened to be walking by. He took a gulp, before pausing and swirling the rest of the drink around in the glass as he thought about for a moment or seemed to think about it. Aethalides didn't have his hopes up, he knew what Pan was like and-

"Ummm... how about, *no!*" Pan sniggered, shoving Aethalides backwards so he landed on his backside with a grunt. Aethalides glared up at his half brother who gulped his wine down, some even dribbled out of the corner of his mouth that he wiped away with the back of his hand. Pan grinned. "Pops told all of us about your screw up. Ooooooh boy, Aethalides... you're in *trouuuuble.*"

"Oh gee, really? I never would have guessed!" He rolled his eyes, getting back to his feet and dusting himself down. "Listen, you goat headed moron, if my group doesn't get there first and find the oracle before the guards or gods forbid, Rune, then it's going to be trouble for everyone!"

"Well, shouldda' thought of that before you got yourself in trouble, huh?" Pan smirked. "Now get gone. If dad catches you talking to me... no end of the lecture I'll get for letting a child in here."

Aethalides was fuming, he had half a mind to go tell his half brother where to stick it, but there was no point in drawing attention to himself. He'd already done that too many times which got him into this mess in the first place.

He turned abruptly on his heel and stormed out of the club, shoving anyone that got in his way out of the way, finally making it outside in the fresh air. Aethalides pulled out his packet of cigarets and quickly lit it with his new lighter. Taking a drag and blowing the smoke up to the sky as he thought. Who the hades could he go to now? His brother might even alert his father of... this little moment.

With a grumble under his breath he marched back to the archives, still smoking, keeping his head down and avoiding the guards as best he could. If they saw him now, they might start asking questions, like what was he doing out at this time and was he doing anything he shouldn't have been, like... say, continuing a case when everyone had gone home.

Finally making it home and slammed the door shut behind him. He took out his cigarette and sighed out the final bit of smoke, making his way up to his office. He didn't want to speak to the others after this mess, maybe he could use his books to identify the leaf... that's if he actually had any botany books. Sure, Aethalides liked information, but there were some subjects he didn't... dabble in as much as others.

"Really starting to regret not paying attention to my farm hands back in the day..." he mumbled, rubbing at his forehead. He could feel a headache coming on and not because of his memories threatening to overspill in one collective mess for once.

"I've got it! I've got the answer!"

Aethalides lifted his head at the voice, raising an eyebrow as it got louder and louder, closer and closer. He could hear running footsteps, the shouting of a boy coming back with a victory, the bizarre thing was it was Icarus that was shouting.

Oh, they weren't playing football down the corridors again without him, were they? That's so uncool.

The door slammed open and Icarus held his phone out triumphantly, a grin on his face. "I got the identity of the leaf and I know where the oracle is!"

Aethalides blinked several times, reaching up to rub the ear wax out of his ear. "Umm... come again?"

"I got the answer! This leaf grows in the Forest of Stories just east of here," Icarus explained with a grin. "It's a jungle plant, no wonder we didn't know it."

"I didn't know you were putting botany on your list of things to do, Icarus..."

"Huh? Oh, no, I went to Demeter Eats with a picture on my phone, spoke to Petal," he explained. "They fixed the roof ya' know? Got all new furnishings too."

Aethalides rubbed at his forehead. "Well, that's good to know on the Demeter Eats side. but... you said this is from the Forest of Stories?" He held the leaf up in question. "Positive?"

"Yeah! She was positive and I'm not going to be doubting Petal.." Icarus went a little pale, laughing nervously. "She's... terrifying."

Yeah, Petal was the definition of... terrifying.

Suddenly Aethalides's phone rang and he pulled it out of his pocket. His father's name flashed on the screen and Aethalides screwed his face up. This couldn't be good. Probably Pan had gone taddel told him about his private investigation. The gods knew the Archives were helping the guards, working jointly and under an official capacity, with Brianna using the excuse that they'd know the most about the case so far. The gods didn't like it, but there was nothing they could do about it.

Icarus looked over the phone, wincing and looking at Aethalides like he was going to get blown up to a million pieces.

Aethalides glared at the name for several minutes before hanging up the call and placing it on the table. "Let's go," he said, getting to his feet.

"You're not gonna... answer that?" Icarus said awkwardly.

"Nope!" Aethalides brightly replied, smiling up at him. "I'm getting this oracle and proving a point."

A point, a *stupid* point, a very *self centred* point, but he was the son of a god. They did it all the time.

So about an hour later, he'd gathered those who wanted to go to the forest, Xbalanque, Boudicca and Vali, while the others stayed back at the Archives not to raise too much suspicion. Aethalides had even left his phone at home, he wasn't taking that with him because he knew his father could find him with that if he wanted to.

The forest of stories was mostly wild, but in the centre was a small village, made up of African huts that were decorated and painted with west African patterns, all of which meant something. The forest itself was more like a jungle, filled with plants and insects and animals that no one outside of Atlantis or even in Atlantis would have ever seen before. Anything was possible in the forest, every story that has ever existed was brought to life in this place, dangerous for multiple reasons and also one of the safest places in existence because the forest had one protector who had power over stories itself.

The trees were a cacophony of colours and smells, various flowers and plants were popping up everywhere along the path that would change between dirt, pavement and even a yellow bricked one. There fruits of various species hanging from the trees, even the water looked different, multiple rivers flowing through. Some crystal clear, others dark and murky, many were made of different coloured water, almost like juice was being poured down the stream instead of water itself.

The animals that also inhabited the forest were a range, some of the ones that Aethalides recognised others he was seeing for the very first time. There were flying rainbow fish that looked like coy carp or fighting fish, a phoenix here and there, and other birds that came in a range of different colours.

The forest at night seemed to glow with various colours, the trees lighting up like Christmas, with fluffy clouds made of candy floss at perfect head height to be grabbed and eaten from and bubbles seemed to just appear out of nowhere and blow about in the wind effortlessly.

It was like walking through a living dream, if you thought it and wrote it down as a story, it was here. Of course that meant it wasn't all sunshine and rainbows and Aethalides was aware of the very real dangers the forest presented, but this part of the forest was safe. Lucky for them.

They followed the path through to the village, along the various different types of road, from starlight, to rainbow, back to dirt and bricked.

Finally they reached the village, equally as beautiful and stunning as the forest itself. There were the traditional African huts, but then some of the other buildings were physically impossible for anywhere but here. They wouldn't exist out of the forest, painted in various colours, beautiful patterns painted along the side of them, some even seemed to be based around animals and everything about the village was bright, vibrant, filled with never ceasing energy.

There were still people out and about, chatting and talking, it seemed like this place was a never ending celebration with dancing and singing. Though the moment the Archives came into few everything stopped and all eyes landed on them. The people suddenly looked nervous, glancing amongst themselves, with a few whispers here and there.

Yep, they were definitely hiding something or more likely someone.

"Can we help you with anything?" One man asked, dressed in a big shirt with west African patterns and loose fitting trousers, walking up to them, practically trying to stop them from entering the village in the first place.

Everyone in the village was the same, a mixture of traditional and modern wear, the various patterns meaning different things, decorated with beads.

"Yeah," Aethalides crossed his arms and frowned. "We know the oracle's here. Please don't mess us around, this is important."

The man laughed. "You'll need to speak to our protector if you want to speak with the oracle."

Aethalides paused, looking a little dumb founded, glancing at the others who seemed just as surprised and shocked by the blatant admission of the oracle being here, without much hesitation. Must have a lot of faith in their protector if they were betting that the Archives themselves couldn't do anything. He didn't want to go muscling in, but they were running out of time. If Rune was coming, he wouldn't hesitate to just tear through the village, regardless of who he hurt or killed.

"You're just... admitting that... the oracle is here...?" Xbalanque said slowly.

"You've clearly already figured it out," the man replied with a smile. "It'd be foolish of me to deny it. Anansi said you'd work it out eventually."

"Anansi... said..." Aethalides trailed off before cursing in Greek and slapping his hand to his face. "I'm an *idiot!*"

A deep chuckle came from behind the man and it grated on Aethalides's nerve as Anansi, in his spider form slowly crawled onto the man's shoulder. He didn't have a human face, but Aethalides knew that he was flashing his famous grin, with his tiny spider fangs poking out as his eight eyes looked down at them.

"Took you long enough," he smirked. "I sure cut it close…"

With that being said he jumped off the man's shoulder turning back into his human form, stretching out his four arms, the smile still on his face and eight eyes staring intently.

Anansi, as usual, was dressed in his traditional tribal look, with face paint decorating him like an African jumping spider and he shoved his dreadlocks out of his face.

"Thanks, Obi, told you it would be funny to see the looks on their face," Anansi said, patting the man's shoulder.

Obi grinned. "You weren't wrong."

"*You* have the oracle?" Vali blinked. "Why didn't you say *anything?*"

"Vali, you've met the gods, why do you *think?,*" Anansi screwed his face up at them, turning to Aethalides and sighing. "Don't give me that look. I found the oracle long before Apollo ever had his visions of the future, so much for god of *prophecy* huh?"

"You knew where the oracle was the whole time and you didn't think to say anything!" Aethalides yelled. "You could've fixed this whole mess from the start!"

"You think I'm gonna trust those bunch of yahoos up there?" Anansi hooked his thumb up at the sky, placing his three other hands on his hips as he cocked an eyebrow. "I wasn't born yesterday, boy, I know for a fine fact you can never trust the man in charge. Plus, it's my job to protect those who ain't in a good place, look after the underdogs. Why'd you think I spend so much time with you?"

Aethalides' eye twitched slightly at that comment before he pinched the bridge of his nose and muttered more curses under his breath. Now he definitely knew a headache was coming on. All this time Anansi knew! Anansi knew and he never said anything, not a word, didn't even report it to the other gods.

"Anansi, since you know how nuts and paranoid they can be, that's exactly why you should've said something to us-."

"That's exactly why I *shouldn't* and *didn't* say anything to you at all," the spider god snapped back. "I am the god of stories, and every life is a story, no matter how short it is. I knew when that oracle was born the moment I opened my story book and their tale started to be written out. Which is why I also had to get them somewhere safe! They were perfectly fine living out in Innana's Haven before the 'great' Apollo had his freaky vision of the future," Anansi sighed, pinching the bridge of his nose and glared over the tip of his hand. He clicked his tongue at them, standing straight. "I don't belong to a pantheon, which is why I was the perfect person to find them."

"They're not safe here," Boudicca said, crossing her arms. "You left clues back at the ant nest. The guards will know they're here and be on their way. Plus, it is likely that Rune has informants in their ranks."

"Well, *obviously*," Anansi huffed back in return, crossing his multiple arms in front of himself. "Another reason I didn't say anything, but who also likes to stick their shiny backside on Archives ground more often than not? Oh yeah! *Rune!*"

Aethalides really wanted to protest that. Sure, Rune did come and go sometimes... frequently from the Archives, that didn't mean he was going to let the elf walk in and leave with the oracle. What the sweet tartarus was Anansi thinking?

A rustling in the bushes caught their attention and one of the villagers came running through looking panicked. They stopped at Anansi, pointing in a vague direction of the trees and part of the forest that would lead to some fields and a meadow that once was taken care of by the Aztec gods until they vanished.

"Rune! Rune and the Hel Raiders! They're coming this way!" He shouted, reaching for Anansi. "They're here for Meania!"

Anansi grit his teeth, fangs poking out and eyes glowing in annoyance as he fixed a glare on Aethalides. He had the decency to at least shrink in on himself and offer a little nervous smile. Getting on Anansi's bad side was no easy task and he couldn't help but feel like he'd succeed brilliantly on doing that, just like his dad.

"Can't you do *anything* right?" Anansi yelled at him, waving his many hands in the air. "Come on, we need to protect the village and then get Meania out of here."

"I'm sorry, protect the village?" Aethalides spluttered. "The main priority is the oracle not-."

"You brought Rune and his men here, to my people's homes, you are staying to help defend them before you go galavanting off," Anansi hissed.

"I never intended to lead Rune here!" Aethalides protested. "I was just trying to find the oracle and get them somewhere safe!"

"Ughhh typical ancient Greek! Believing that only their place of residence is safe because they're so above everyone else!"

"Hey, that's not fair!"

"Never said it was fair," Anansi hissed, turning to glare at him, clicking his tongue. "But it is the truth."

Aethalides turned to the others for help, but they looked content to let him suffer and splutter through his words. He was not having a good time today, was he? Really off his game.

"Anansi, I promise I didn't mean to lead Rune-."

"But you still *did!*" Anansi extended out his arms and glared at him, a mocking grin spreading across his face. "Here are the consequences of your actions, Aethalides! I know the concept of accepting responsibility is new to you, but you're always complaining about not experiencing anything new, so here you go! Something new! Don't squander it now," he wagged his finger at him with a mocking stance, hands on his hips. "You and your conscience aren't exactly on regular speaking terms."

Aethalides felt his face crumble. That was a bit of a low blow, but... all right, fine, not *exactly* untrue.

Anansi led them out to the forest, where yep, there were various members of the Hellaiders. More than likely they were Rune's best men, sent to raid the village. He couldn't say he was surprised that Rune knew they'd come here, probably someone had said or seen something from him visiting Pan or even Icarus talking to Petal.

Xbalanque spun his spear around in his hand as he narrowed his eyes through the glowing jungle, the dark dressed figures of the Helraiders standing out against the rainbow glow of the trees.

"Time to teach these trespassers the true meaning of a horror story," Anansi chuckled, jumping to a tree and turning back to his spider form. "Do me a favour and keep them busy..."

Boudicca had already drawn her sword, shield in hand and she charged headfirst into the incoming fight, swinging at one of Rune's satyrs, nearly taking the head.

"I... can't believe I'm saying this, but don't kill anyone!" Aethalides yelled, earning a glare from Boudicca. "We're in enough trouble!"

"You're scared of them?" Xbalanque raised an eyebrow, for a brief moment not looking impressed. "The gods I mean."

"If you haven't noticed my extended family happen to be *uncomfortably* good at coming up with inventive ways of punishing people," Aethalides bit out, pulling his knives out as Vali drew his sword. "So yes, I'm playing it safe!"

Xbalanque didn't look impressed, but it was hardly surprising considering how he literally killed three of his gods with the help of his twin brother. Pity Hunahpu wasn't here, maybe if he was, Xbalanque's strength might double.

Aethalides watched as the three that were bigger than him easily entered fights, ducking and dodging any attack, Xbalanque used the other end of his spear to crack a fae across the face, easily breaking his jaw before he could utter any kind of magic. A few teeth even went flying out of his mouth from the impact.

Boudicca was using her shield as a weapon, nearly steamrolling into a group, smashing the final one against a tree, knocking them out. Another she kicked backwards, spinning her sword in hand and striking at their hand, causing them to drop their own sword.

Another came running up behind her, only to be stopped by Xbalanque, who used his spear to pole vault himself over and kick the Helraider into another tree.

They groaned and pulled themselves up, getting ready to attack, when suddenly the tree twitched and moved, eyes appearing in the dark bark and a pair of long arms snatching the figure around the arms and middle. Everyone froze, watching in mild fascination and utter horror as the tree then opened up a truly monstrous mouth and shoved the screaming Helraider into its mouth whole. Then the terrible wooden jaws snapped shut, glowing eyes focusing on the rest of the fight. Aethalides realised too late that this tree wasn't glowing like the others, its wood dark and rotting, with mushrooms growing across its back, dead leaves falling from its branches that looked more and more like elongated arms than branches at all.

A chuckle came from the trees, the lights began to dim around them, a breeze came through, cold and biting. The dark chuckle from before seemed to flow with the wind that took up a more monstrous appearance. A face appeared in the air with a grin and then the rest of the trees sprang to life, their roots rushing out from under the ground, trying to snare and snatch around the Helraiders legs.

The gang members yelled and screamed, running away from them, trying to escape and only succeeding in smashing face first into multiple spiderwebs, getting caught and tangled. Stuck to the many strands and unable to pull themselves away. The light around them took on a crimson red, the spiderwebs seeming to glow a bright white or silver, drumbeats picking up around them while they struggled.

The laugh came back, this time Aethalides recognised it as Anansi's and he turned in the direction it was coming from, finding the spider god sitting on a makeshift throne made with wood and elephant tusks framing him. A leopard skin decorating the throne. A stick with a snake tied to it sat on the right side of him, which had a gourd that seemed to be buzzing hanging from it, as well as a wrapped up ball of spiderwebs that seemed to be glowing.

Behind the throne was a huge spider web, glowing just like the rest against the crimson-red light that matched Anansi's glowing eyes. The spider god himself was relaxing against the throne, one leg swung over the armrest, the other swinging idly by. He held a storybook in one hand, a drink in the other, while his third hand held the strings of a puppet covered in tar.

"Step into my story, said the spider to fools," he purred, a deep rumbling and mocking laugh leaving him that echoed around the forest.

That's when everything clicked for Aethalides. He was ashamed to admit that he had mostly written Anansi off, down to him being the god of stories, because what could he do? Read a story and put someone to sleep? Know every single story that ever existed? He understood now though, watching the way spider legs seemed to appear out of his back, reminding him for a brief moment of Phobator, Anansi wasn't just the protector of the forest of stories... he *was* the forest.

"Let's see..." Anansi said as he thumbed through his storybook. "Should I have you eaten by a giant snake? Consumed by a Jöroguma? Perhaps simply ripped to shreds with a simple pull of those threads..." he hummed to himself, his only free hand pulling out a pen from thin air. "Decisions, decisions... so many choices and not enough time.."

"Y-you can't do that!" One of the gang members spluttered out. "There are rules!"

"Yes, there are rules... but... not to overuse a narrative... I am a god," Anansi grinned, letting his fangs poke out. "The rules do not apply to me."

"Anansi!" Vali cried out, eyes wide. "You... you can't!"

"Why can't I?" Anansi raised an eyebrow. "I am a god and on top of that, a spider. We are predators after all," he grinned showing his fangs. "But, you're right. Why be hasty? I'll just leave them here and think it over. Come," he beckoned them to follow, the throne suddenly vanishing and the forest returned to normal except for the captured men.

They followed Anansi through the forest, back to the village and to a home, which was painted and decorated with African art and a few new pieces that were clearly Mesopotamian inspired.

"Do you think that was all of them?" Xbalanque asked, looking back towards the forest. The once vibrant town was now almost like a ghost town, everyone had disappeared inside and locked their doors.

"Unlikely. Men like Rune don't stop until they get what they want. It isn't safe for the oracle to be here any more," the spider god sighed. "Best you take them now."

Anansi pushed the curtain back, disappearing inside and indicating that the others stayed outside. They didn't have to wait long before Anansi came back outside accompanied by the oracle... who was just a kid. No older than thirteen by the looks of them.

Dressed in various shades of yellow and orange, an orange shawl wrapped around them and over their head, dark olive skin and dark hair that was brushed off their face, held back by a gold band, a few dark curls framing their face. They looked terrified, picking up a worn bag and throwing it over their shoulder. Wearing a necklace of blue and orange beads with thin golden leaves hanging off it.

They looked up to Anansi who placed a comforting hand on their shoulder, offering a smile. "It's okay, these people are here to help you. Get you somewhere safe."

"But you said here was safe..." the oracle whispered, then glanced at Aethalides and the others.

"I know... I know... but.." Anansi winced. "The people that are after you are here now and-." A shout and a warning bell going off had all of them looking in the direction as a few of Rune's men ran into the village. "We're out of time! You need to go," Anansi was gently pushing them to Boudicca who instantly wrapped her arm around Meania, leading them away with Xbalanque and Vali in tow.

"Anansi, come with us!" Aethalides said, turning back to Anansi. "We'll need your help."

"I'm not leaving my people to deal with Rune and his goons," Anansi said, placing a hand to his chest while he gestured to the chaos. "Besides, who else can stall Rune than a god? He knows better than to mess with me for long. Now get out of here! And hurry!" Anansi turned back to the chaos happening around them. "You're gonna have bigger problems than Rune coming down on you, Aethalides.."

Aethalides sighed, nodding and quickly running away to catch up with the others. He ran through the forest, they were going to come out on the other side where the flood plains were, hopefully that would be a perfect place to lose them. Running through the woods, battering trees out of the way, pushing through until they all finally got to a clearing that was circled by marshes.

"Okay, okay, this way," Aethalides pointed to the right. "Don't worry, Meania, we're going to get you somewhere safe, I prom-."

His sentence cut off as a bright light appeared in front of them and standing there was his father... who looked... less than happy. Hermes's eyes were glowing a startling purple, a snarl on his face, looking at the oracle. The poor kid shrank in on themselves, huddling closer to Boudicca who instinctively pulled them closer, protectively wrapping her arm around them.

Hermes sucked in a breath, as he pressed a finger to his forehead in annoyance. "Why... why do you never *listen* to me!? Do you have any idea what you've done!?"

"Found the oracle?"

"Aethalides!" Hermes shouted, glancing at the oracle who flinched at the raised voice. His face softened for a mere moment

392

before hardening again and narrowing on Aethalides. "Hand over the oracle, right now."

"Since when do you listen to orders?" Aethalides countered. "You know better than anyone what will happen!"

"My hands are tied, why can't you understand that and why can't you understand that I'm trying to protect you and Atlantis at the same time!" Hermes gestured to the oracle. "Got any idea what the others are going to do when they find out that you found the oracle when you were instructed not to?"

"Yeah, they'll throw a hissy fit," Aethalides rolled his eyes, sounding braver than he felt. In truth he was tired to his families over dramatic nature. "Meania is coming with us."

"No... they're... not..." Hermes said slowly. "We can still fix this... but that means you have to hand the oracle over to me."

"So a bunch of gods can argue over their fate?" Vali growled out, hand reaching for his sword. "So they can make choices they have no right to make? Like you did to every single one of us?"

Hermes's lip pulled back in disgust. As a god who liked to pride himself on being a god of freedom and bending the rules, to have him now enforcing them... like this? Worse, being accused of conducting peoples fates, directing them like puppets on a string? Well, insulting was an understatement.

"Vali..." Hermes said slowly, a low growl that Aethalides had never heard from him before. "We aren't the norse pantheon. We, the Greek pantheon, are pioneers of justice and democracy-."

"Oh shut up!" Aethalides yelled at him, watching his father flinch, then stand his ground again. "I was there! I *lived* that era, I lived all those eras after that! Ancient Greece was just as corrupt as everywhere else! So are all of you," he accused, pointing at him. "Aphrodite tried to kill Psyche because she was prettier than

her! Leto had her children, Apollo and Artemis murder all of Niobe's children, just because she insulted them!" He waved his hands in the air in exasperation. "You turned someone to stone because they lied to you!" Aethalides reached back for his herald staff. "Does that sound like *'democracy'* and *'justice'* to you?"

Hermes was quiet, too quiet. His face was neutral, eyes still glowing a bright purple as he looked them over. He took a breath, closing his eyes a moment, then a determined look crossed his face as he summoned his own herald staff, holding it in front of him.

Aethalides responded by drawing one of his knives and his own herald staff. He grit his teeth and glared right back at Hermes who seemed stunned by the turn of events.

He narrowed his eyes. "What are you doing?" Hermes hissed at him.

"I'm going to fight you, because I know you won't kill me!" Aethalides snapped back. "And I can't say the same about them."

Hermes looked taken aback for a moment, before settling into an expression of acceptance. "Fine…" he ground out. "Have it your way."

Aethalides turned to the others. "Get them out of here, back to the Archives or… hades, somewhere safe!"

Xbalanque looked surprised and nervous, glancing between Aethalides and Hermes. "Are you seriously.."

"Yes, I'm seriously about to do this! Now go!"

They nodded, running with the oracle away from Hermes and Aethalides in the direction of the road. What surprised Aethalides was that Vali took a stand next to him, drawing his sword and glaring at Hermes. He glanced at Aethalides and offered a smile, nodding.

Aethalides blinked, then nodded back with a smirk. It looked like it would be both of them dealing with this then. Good thing too. Aethalides was confident in his abilities, but he knew that he wouldn't stand a chance against his father, not for long enough. Hopefully with Vali at his side it wouldn't be over in seconds.

Hermes moved in a blink, suddenly standing in front of Aethalides and swinging his staff down at him, but was blocked by Vali's sword as Aethalides threw his knife. Hermes dodged it, then blocked another strike from Vali as he swung out at him, spinning his sword in his hand easily. Vali was the one leading the charge, having his strength backing him up and Aethalides had his back, throwing knives and then using his own herald staff to block a few attacks that Vali missed.

Aethalides knew that his father was holding back on his power, otherwise this fight would be over in seconds. Maybe not for Vali, but it would be for Aethalides.

Hermes swung the staff wide, nearly catching Aethalides, who stumbled backwards and fell to the ground. Vali ducked the hit, then struck upwards with a shout. Everything happened so fast and the next thing Aethalides knew, Hermes cried out in pain and shock, stumbling backwards. He reached for his cheek, pulling his hand away to show gold dripping down his face and running along his finger tips.

Hermes stared in bewilderment for a moment, Aethalides was equally as surprised and then Vali launched another attack. He charged at him, sword raised and Hermes glared clenched his fist in anger, his whole body starting to glow. Just as Vali swung his sword at him, Hermes snapped his eyes open, glaring at Vali.

"Enough!" Hermes shouted, easily catching Vali's wrist and throwing him across the ground. Vali even smashed into the marshland, falling into the water with a yelp. "That's it! I can't help you any more, Aethalides!" He turned to him, glaring at his

son, but there was a deep-seated pain in his eyes. Aethalides could see it even with the glow. "I have to bring you to the council, the gods-."

"What are the gods going to do to me?" Aethalides smirked. "With the life I live every day? What can you possibly do?"

"Aethalides, you don't understand! They'll use you to get to the Archives, to get the oracle!" Hermes explained. "They know about your memory!"

"I can only use that if I actively already know it! You know that!"

"I know that, but some of them think it could... work definitely, because... because.." Hermes looked like he was struggling to think of a polite word and eventually gave up. "they're idiots!" He shouted, gesturing with his hand, then he pressed a finger to his forehead. "Gods, this is such a mess! Usually I can talk my way through things but no one is listening to me!"

"Dad," Aethalides got to his feet, walking to his father and looking up at him. "You know that we can't trust the others with the safety of the oracle... it'll all go wrong... Atlantis... everything you did would fall apart, that's why you asked us in the first place."

"No? Really? You don't say!" Hermes yelled at him, before taking a breath and calming down. He finally sat down on the ground, pressing the heels of his hands to his eyes as he let out a frustrated groan. "Every pantheon is just so godsdamned paranoid. They think that each other is out to destroy or conquer the other, just because of the past and us old gods are many things but forgiving is sadly not one of them. Nor is forgetting now that I think about it."

"Heh. Yeah, I know what that's like," Aethalides laughed as

he took a seat next to his father. "But there's got to be another way, someway to fix this…"

"I've been rattling my brain trying to figure out what that could possibly be," Hermes mumbled. "But I told you, they don't listen to me any more. They're not going to hear what I have to say… my own family is contemplating labelling me a traitor, just because I didn't want to have another war," he lifted a hand and dropped it. "It's like they forget I'm the god of peacekeepers…"

Aethalides sighed and looked away. This whole thing was a complete mess. The gods didn't make things easy. They never made things easy. His whole existence was usually built around chasing monsters they created that then threatened people, people who didn't even know said monsters existed. Doing that was easy in comparison to… this. Gods he hated getting mixed up in politics. Especially godly politics that nonsense never made sense.

"Before… how did you create peace between the pantheons?" He asked, looking up at Hermes who sighed.

"Wasn't easy. I mean, you know what we were like back then, completely ruthless and you remember how many natural disasters happened during Rome's era! That was us just… throwing our weight around," Hermes screwed his face up. "Not to mention all the essence stealing…"

"I'm sorry the *what?*" Aethalides yelled and Hermes winced, looking away.

"You know we don't have physical forms, at least not unless we want to have them. Well, we worked out that if you found a god that matched you from a different pantheon to a degree, we could rip that part of their essence from them and just… attach it to ours," Hermes explained. "Sometimes even gain some extra powers along with it. It was like… sewing on an extra limb, but actually being able to use it and maybe getting an extra eye at the same time. Gods, everything was so messy…" he trailed off and let himself fall back against the grass so he was staring up at the sky. "In the end it was too much. The mortals were dying, we were suffering just as badly… so at least one god or goddess from every pantheon formed a little group, discussing peace, finding common ground… In the end it took all of us, our group, standing up against the rest of them for the other gods to realise that this fighting really wasn't working. We were all equally matched… the fight would last forever."

"And… it all just stopped? Just like that?"

"Eh, no… not completely. There were and still are arguments, grudges, pantheons not forgiving other pantheons for certain atrocities…" Hermes placed his hands behind his head as he continued to look up at the sky. "But once we made up Atlantis and started to work together, actually have a council, things started to get better. Heh, it was only until after all the dust settled and we stopped slapping each other that we realised… the people who hadn't moved down to Atlantis… well most had already moved on to other beliefs by then. The Roman Empire became the *Holy* Roman Empire and out all of us old gods went," Hermes pulled a face. "And I know for a fact the other pantheons *loved* watching our fall from grace, that was until it happened to them of course."

Aethalides placed a hand to his chin, glancing over at the marshland, worried about Vali until he saw him standing at the edge, wringing his coat out. Looked like he'd seen the fighting had stopped and was keeping his distance while they talked.

"There has to be something," Aethalides muttered. "There's got to be something we can do to stop the pantheons from… wait… what about the other gods that helped you with the peace?

Won't they want to keep it too?"

"Well, sure… but… we don't have as much sway now," Hermes frowned at him. "It's peacetime at the moment, the others listened to us because they were desperate to stop the fighting, but now? They don't care."

"But you had sway before. Maybe reminding them what happened will get them to listen," he let a crooked smile spread across his face. "You said it yourself, you guys don't forget…"

Hermes glanced to the side. "I mean… I can try… but they're not really in the listening to me mood much either."

Aethalides let himself grin, reaching up to place a hand on his dad's shoulder. "I have faith in you, now all you need is to have faith in yourself."

For the first time in a while Hermes actually laughed, throwing his head back and getting to his feet. "You can't throw my own words back at me, that's simply too cruel… though, you might have a point," he placed a hand to his chin in thought for a moment, then shook his head with a growl. "Ah! I've been listening to my melodramatic family too much. Doom and gloom? That's not me! Okay, you're right… never thought I'd say that about a mortal, but you are," Hermes looked down at Aethalides and smirked. "I have to talk to the others, get the old gang back together and… arrange to make some changes around here. I think Atlantis has grown a bit too wild, even for me."

"Uhhhh… other arrangements?" Aethalides asked nervously.

Hermes placed a hand on his shoulder. "Don't worry about that. We'll handle it, 'cause they're going to listen… one way or another. You need to get that oracle somewhere safe… give me some time," he winced and awkwardly looked away. "I know that's a lot to ask, but-."

"Don't worry, father, we'll handle it," Aethalides waved to Vali who slowly made his way to them. "Just gotta find Boudicca and Xbalanque now."

Hermes nodded, looking back towards the forest of stories. "Rune's men are leaving, but they're looking for you... I can buy you some time. Get back to the Archives now."

Aethalides nodded, turning to Vali and pointing in the direction they needed to run. When Aethalides looked back, his father was nowhere in sight. Must be off messing with Rune's men, they'd have time to get back to the Archives that much he was certain.

They finally reached the road and began running up it, the heart of Atlantis was in the distance, getting closer. Hopefully, the village in the forest of stories wouldn't have gotten too damaged, but he doubted Anansi would let something like that happen. The spider god was too tricky.

"You think Hermes will be able to get the original council back together?" Vali asked as they continued to run. "And what are we going to do with Rune? I doubt he'd be back there."

"If anyone can, it's my dad. He'll do it, as for Rune..." Aethalides frowned. "We need to keep the oracle away from him, that's the priority."

Vali nodded and they continued to run. They had to be sneaky once they finally reached the heart of Atlantis, just to get past the guards and dodge them in the streets. Aethalides knew the heart better than anyone, easily guiding Vali through the many different alleyways and secret passages that many wouldn't be alive to remember being made, but Aethalides knew like the back of his hand.

After several more twists and turns, a few backtracks when they crossed paths with the guard shifts, until they reached the

Archives, but Vali stopped him from approaching.

"Something's not right," he mumbled, then sniffed the air, letting out a low growl. "Viggo's here... as well as a bunch of Rune's men..."

"Is Rune here?" Aethalides asked with a grimace.

Vali shook his head. "Not here. I don't know where, but he's not here."

"Thank gods for some silver linings..." Aethalides's eyes widened in panic. "What about Xbalanque and Boudicca?"

Vali sniffed the air and once again shook his head. "Not here."

Aethalides let out a breath he hadn't realised he'd been holding. "Huh... so the fates are being kind today. Weird. Whelp! No time like the present!" He pulled out his knives, throwing one up in the air and catching it with a grin. "Let's see our uninvited guests out... shall we?"

A little help from your friends: 22

So things had gone from bad to worse. Xbalanque had slightly panicked when he saw all of Rune's men circling the Archives. They couldn't stay there, but where could they go next? It wasn't like they were popular in Atlantis, most of the time people thought they were a nuisance who got away with damaging property because of Aethalides's father... which... wasn't completely untrue.

Still, that left them with little options and they definitely couldn't go to the guards, Brianna would blow a gasket and then be less inclined to help.

Xbalanque glanced over at Boudicca and the oracle. Boudicca hadn't let the kid leave her side, holding them close and telling them everything was going to be okay. If there was one thing Xbalanque could be certain of, it was that nothing and no one was going to get the kid while Boudicca was alive.

"We need to get out of Atlantis," Boudicca hissed. "It'll be harder for Rune to mobilise anything in the human realm. That's where we need to go."

"Human realm..." Xbalanque mumbled, thinking about it. "Yeah... yeah okay, I think... I think I know somewhere we can go. Come on!"

Boudicca followed, taking the oracle along with them. It was a long shot, Xbalanque knew that he had no idea if Jason would help or not. He hadn't spoken to him since... that day on the canal, Jason hadn't even been in work, taking leave for health reasons. The poor guy probably thought he was going crazy.

They quickly ran through the streets, dodging any of the guard routes, it wouldn't surprise Xbalanque if they were being directed to the Archives now after hearing the commotion. It was unlikely that the group would take care of Rune and his men quietly. Aethalides did enjoy making a racket when he dealt with an issue. Loud and obnoxious, yeah that sort of summed him up perfectly.

They took the many twists and turns, eventually coming to the many entrance ways that would lead to different parts of the human world and unsurprisingly they were being guarded by Rune's men. He mustn't be leaving anything to chance. By Xibalba, even some of the port side raiders were here, along with Cillian. The baby-faced fae was pacing back and forth, crossbow in hand, looking ready to shoot anything that moved, even if it was one of his own men, which was probably why they all stood with shields on their backs.

The only one who didn't was the Jötun giant turned little chihuahua that scampered around Cillian's feet, barking at other members like it was giving orders. Most of the others seem to just ignore him, though one of the other fae knelt down to straighten out the tiny sailor hat it was wearing.

Suddenly the chihuahua stopped and slowly turned in their direction, growling.

"That is a very strange rat," the oracle whispered. "Why does it have clothes?"

"Long story," Xbalanque mumbled and then threw a bewildered look at the kid. "And that's a dog, not a rat."

The kid looked up at him, blinking owlishly, then looked back at the Chihuahua. They did this several times, before finally looking back at Xbalanque and shaking their head.

"No, that's definitely a rat," they replied.

The Jötun turned chihuahua did not like that statement apparently as he suddenly started to bark angrily at them. Well, it was more like a little yipping noise, but it got the attention of the others. Cillian especially dashed forward, his crossbow raised.

"He's going to miss," the oracle whispered and sure enough not a moment later the bolt went flying past their heads and struck a shop window behind them.

They hadn't even moved.

Well, it was good to know that in the time spent away from Cillian he hadn't magically improved. Like that was ever going to happen, but they did live in a world of gods and nearly every day there was a small miracle.

Boudicca pulled out her sword as Xbalanque got his spear, but she placed a hand on his shoulder and shook her head.

"You need to get them out of here," she instructed him, gesturing to the oracle. "I'll handle these pests."

"I'm not just going to-."

"This isn't open for discussion," Boudicca hissed, ushering the oracle to him. "Now go!"

She charged towards the fight and Xbalanque moved quickly, taking the oracle with him as they followed behind her. Boudicca easily bashed the port side raiders away, but Rune's gang were playing for keeps. Trying everything to get past her and at Xbalanque and the oracle. Boudicca smashed her fist into the side of a satyr's face, looking back at Xbalanque with a fierce glare. There was going to be no argument on this, he had to get them away.

He stuffed his hand in his pocket, pulling out the key and holding it up to the exit he knew would lead to Derby. It opened and he pulled the oracle along. One of Rune's men tried leaping at them, but Xbalanque quickly pulled the oracle behind him and kicked the guy back just as the portal closed.

"Okay… are you okay?" He asked, turning to the oracle who stared up at him and glanced back to the entrance. "Boudicca will be fine," Xbalanque assured them, placing his hands on their shoulders. "Now, are you okay?"

Slowly the kid nodded their head, looking nervous, their attention was quickly taken by the world around them. Gazing at all of the tall buildings. It was early morning, the sun was only just rising, lighting up the small English city to another dull grey day. Of course, the kid had never seen anything like this before, they'd only seen Atlantis. Xbalanque wondered if they even knew about the human world until now.

"I never asked, what's your name?" He said, desperate to get the kids attention off… whatever he could maybe start to worry about. The last thing he needed was the oracle to go into a panic.

"My… name is Meania," they mumbled, shrinking in on themselves. "Are we… going to be safe here?"

Xbalanque screwed his face up, looking around the streets of Derby where they'd ended up. He could… always pay Jason a visit. They wouldn't be expecting him to take the oracle there, it had to be a safe place for them and Jason was… he would help, wouldn't he?

"I know a place up here," he mumbled, placing a hand on Meania's shoulder. "We're going to be fine, I promise. I'm Xbalanque by the way, you can call me 'X' if it's easier."

"O-okay," Meania nodded and Xbalanque guided them through the mostly quiet streets.

He wondered what they both looked like. Xbalanque hadn't changed out of his mayan leather jacket, which didn't look

405

strange in Atlantis, but up here... it was definitely a fashion statement. Actually his entire look could be described as that. Meanwhile, Meania was staring around at the human world with big wide eyes. They looked so young, sure they were, but right now they looked younger than they were.

Xbalanque himself, being born first in the human world before... events happened... with his brother, he didn't find it all that fascinating. More alien since the changes and updates in technology and styles. Meania on the other hand was looking around at the quiet derby streets like they'd just entered a brand new wonderland. In Xbalanque's opinion, nothing topside came anywhere close to Atlantis.

He guided them out of the main city centre, they could catch a bus, but he had a feeling that would be a bad idea, even if it was quicker. They'd be trapped, nowhere to go and Xbalanque wasn't taking any chances, at least with the layout of the city and surrounding areas he could weave in and out of the streets. If he didn't get lost. Damn, British houses and cities were laid out like a rabbit warren, he was used to cities being built on a grid.

"Where are we going?" Meania asked as they stayed close to Xbalanque the entire way.

"I have a friend up here. He'll help, I know he will..." Xbalanque mumbled the last part. At least, he hoped that Jason would help. He really was depending on his better nature.

Xbalanque quickly guided them down a small jitty, then up towards the pentagon island. Roundabouts, another thing that Xbalanque was still getting his head wrapped around at times, so Jason mostly drove the cars.

"We gotta get to Oakwood, it's at the top of a hill," Xbalanque explained, looking at a bus that passed. It would be quicker... "We just gotta follow that street up there, head into chad and then go up the hill…" he trailed off and looked behind them, feeling a chill go down his spine as that familiar Chihuahua came around the corner, dressed in his little sailor outfit. "I'm… really starting to hate that dog…"

The chihuahua snarled and started barking, yapping away and running at them, followed behind by Cillian who had also made his way around the corner.

"What do we do…?" Meania asked, backing away.

"Run! Run right now!"

Meania did as they were told. Running as fast as they could, Xbalanque close behind them. He could hear the sounds of Cillian and the chihuahua chasing after them yelling and cursing, though the dog was mostly barking angrily at them. To any outside observer it probably looked hilarious, a grown man and a teenager being chased by a baby-faced redhead and his little dog.

"When I get my hands on you, I'm gonna make you regret you ever crossing me and the Port Side Raiders!" Cillian yelled, the chihuahua yapping away in agreement.

"Port Side raiders, *port side!* Don't you think you're a little… inland!?" Xbalanque shot back, throwing a glare in Cillian's direction. "Like, literally you are in the centre of England!"

"Port side raiders are free to go wherever we please! No land is out of our reach!" Cillian yelled back.

"Except for any land in the heart of England? Like say… the midlands? Which is where you are?"

Meania glanced back at him with a frown. "Is irritating him a good idea?"

"Oh, trust me, you get Cillian angry enough he'll always make mistakes."

407

"I can hear you!" Cillian screeched.

Xbalanque glanced back at him and decided to shout up. "He's just a crybaby toddler man-child with a temper tantrum issue!"

The inhuman screech of rage that Cillian shot back at him only further proved his point.

Xbalanque ran up the way, gesturing to Meania to follow him up a small road once they got to chaddeston, finally reaching a hill. He carefully pulled the kid forward so they were in front of him. That way he could at least protect them from the back while Cillian and the Chihuahua chased after them.

There had to be something he could do. Something he could do to help keep them safe and stop Cillian and the chihuahua at the same time. Not an easy task. Especially since from the outside, they wouldn't know what was really going on and it's not like Xbalanque could just drop kick the Jötun chihuahua out in public. It wouldn't come across well and he did have a job to attend to up here.

"Just keep running up the hill, Meania, keep going!" He yelled at them. "You got this!"

Meania paused and looked back at Xbalanque. Their eyes were glowing a soft yellow light and they glanced over down the road they were just crossing.

"Van…"

Xbalanque squinted in confusion and then heard the sound of a horn going off. A van that was definitely going too fast for that road was heading straight for him. Xbalanque blanched, launching himself across the gap, with Cillian and the chihuahua close behind.

Xbalanque heard the sound of the van screeching to a halt, with Cillian yelling something at the Chihuahua that went something along the lines of 'you're not a Jötun any more! Get out of the way of the van!' Followed by a loud yelp.

"Are they okay!?" Meania cried out.

"You tell me, kid!" Xbalanque shouted back, taking their arm and running them up the hill quicker. "Come on, keep going, we're almost there!"

Finally, after running up the hill and feeling very out of breath, they made it to Oakwood. Xbalanque leaned on his knees while Meania stood to the side seemingly unfazed by the hill they just ran up. He remembered a time when he could run up hills and not get tired. It turned out even immortals got old with achy joints, except for gods. They have all the perks with none of the drawbacks.

"My... powers don't work like that," Meania muttered suddenly, looking away awkwardly. "I can't control what premonitions I get..."

"So... you have no control over that power of yours whatsoever?" Xbalanque huffed, looking them over. "You can't call on visions at will, like by command?"

Meania shook their head. "I don't know how to. They just... come to me at random, why?"

Xbalanque slowly stood up straight, mind racing. "It means... that Rune won't have a reason to go after you and neither will the other gods."

"The gods! Why do they want me? I'm just an oracle!"

"Yeah, you can tell the future," Xbalanque placed a hand on their shoulder. "Listen, I don't think you understand just how valuable people like you are and... your kind... you have healing powers alongside your ability to access prophecies."

"But I told you, I can't do that on command, I just get... flashes of random pieces of information," Meania looked up at him with big frightened eyes. Far too innocent for this world, kid was starry eyed individual he'd ever met. "And what good is knowing the future anyway? If you know what's going to happen and can't change it... wouldn't that be... worse?"

Xbalanque laughed softly. "Look," he hooked his arm around their shoulder. "As much as you are right, there are still people out there who would want to have you... just so you could tell them what was going to happen and they could avoid it."

"But that's not how prophecies work!" Meania complained. "If I see it, it's going to happen, no matter what you do."

"People like to try and cheat fate."

"But you can't! I... I hate my gift," Meania cried. "Do you have any idea what it's like... seeing what is going to happen, knowing you can't do anything about it? Anansi told me that once an oracle sees a future event it means that line in the story is set in stone and you can't change it, no matter what you do."

"Huh... someone should tell the Norse gods that," Xbalanque mumbled under his breath. "They're all about dodging their destiny and taking control of their fate."

"Uh-oh."

He paused and looked down at Meania who had gone very still, eyes glowing a soft yellow again.

"What's uh-oh, what did you see?"

Meania looked up at him worriedly. "You'll get me to your friend... and he'll help, but..."

Xbalanque scrunched his nose up. "I'm gonna guess I'm not going to be along for the rest of the ride, huh?"

The Mesopotamian oracle shook their head.

Well, he had a feeling that might happen. Risks like this... came with the territory... still...

"Just answer me one thing," he gave Meania a serious look.

"Please tell me it's not Cillian or the damn chihuahua that gets me?"

"Ahh…"

"Oh man, come on, seriously?" He complained. "I get taken out by the baby-faced leech of Atlantis?"

Meania shrugged.

Ugh. Xbalanque wouldn't say he was particularly prideful, but come on, that just hurt.

"Okay, fine, whatever," he pointed at Meania in a warning. "Just don't tell Medea or Aethalides, they'll never let me live it down…" Xbalanque trailed off as Meania's face slowly began to wince and cringe, making his own face drop to a flat expression. "Why do I get the feeling eternity is about to feel a Xibalba of a lot longer?"

"Ah… I… who knows…" the kid awkwardly laughed, looking away with a strained grin. "I certainly don't."

"You are a terrible liar," Xbalanque sighed, pinching the bridge of his nose. "Whatever… like I said, let's just get you to safety…"

They went back to jogging again, Xibalanque checked his corners this time when he ran, just on the off chance there were any surprises like small yappy dogs and a baby-faced wannabe bad boy. Good gods, did it really have to be Cillian to take him down…? That was just embarrassing. The guy would have to get lucky, there was no way around it.

Finally, they made it to Jason's house. He doubted Jason was going to be happy about being woken up this early… oh well, he'd add it to the list of things he'd apologise for.

He slammed his fist on the door knocking loudly and rapidly, he could hear the sound of someone getting up and moving. He hoped it was Jason, he didn't know how he was going to explain this to anyone else in the house, it was madness.

Finally, the door opened and Jason was on the other side. The police detective was dressed in a dressing gown, hair mussed, face filled with tired lines and his eyes were squinting at Xbalanque like he hadn't gotten them to focus yet. He stared at him, then he looked to Meania who was hiding behind Xbalanque, poking their head out cautiously.

Jason looked between the two for a moment, then sighed and pinched the bridge of his nose mumbling under his breath.

"I'm gonna need coffee for this," he muttered and stood to the side, gesturing limply for them to come in. "Come on, I can't turn you away. you look… terrible."

"Thanks, man, good to see you too…" Xbalanque glanced at Jason, who admittedly looked… rough, but that might be down to the time of day and less to do with stress thanks to finding out about the alternate world that existed under his nose. "Are you ok-?"

Jason raised his hand to silence him. "Coffee first, Xbalanque, then you can talk to me about… whatever the hell kind of mumbo jumbo magic issues are going on…"

"Right…" Xbalanque gave an awkward smile and then rushed to guide starry-eyed Meania to the kitchen.

Jason sighed, shaking his head, closed the front door and followed them through.

It was quiet as the kettle boiled, Xbalanque watched Jason slip coffee into his cup, and then make his way to the fridge. He took out the milk, paused and looked back at the pair of them. Jason's eyes scanned over them for a second and then he turned back to the fridge placing the milk back inside, before trudging back to his coffee.

Meania was staring at the kettle and some of the other

412

gadgets in wonder, then sat up straight after Jason took his now full coffee cup of black coffee and sat down opposite them. Xbalanque still waited quietly, watching as Jason took a sip of his piping hot drink, wincing at the same time as he predictably burnt his mouth.

"All right…" Jason mumbled after a moment and placed his cup down on the table, holding it with both hands. Xbalanque suspected he was doing it more to ground himself than for any kind of warmth. "Start from the beginning, what's going on?"

So, Xbalanque told him everything. About the oracle, Meania, who he also introduced, about Rune, the gods, the council, and the mess that they were all in. A brief explanation of Atlantis and even brushing up on Cillian who was on his way this moment. Jason listened quietly, his face going through a range of emotions that went from bewilderment, and astonishment to utter existential horror, which was understandable. It wasn't every coffee morning you got your entire worldview thrown out of the window and replaced by an over complicated multicultural dramatic and confusing reality.

"…Annnnnd that about covers all of it," Xbalanque finished, looking to Meania for confirmation, but the kid shrugged at him. Right, they wouldn't know they hadn't been there for all of that. "Umm… do you have any questions…?"

Jason stared at him like he was an idiot for a moment, then took a breath and another gulp of his coffee, slamming it down on the table.

"So many, but now isn't the time," he pointed to Meania as he looked at them. "You can tell the future?"

"Yeah… but… not really on command…" Meania rubbed the back of their neck, looking away awkwardly. "It's complicated…"

Jason gave a high-pitched, strained laugh. His face contorted to one that was barely withholding a full freak out. "Yeah… yeah, that is absolutely right, it's complicated all right… oh sweet… wait does that mean all of the religions are real!?"

"Ummm…" Xbalanque looked to the side awkwardly. "Yeah… but us older belief systems don't really like to talk about the new ones much… there's still a bit of bad blood between them on that front.."

"So… like, *all* of them? Every single one?" Jason clarified. "All… coexisting?"

"Ah… coexisting is… pushing it, but yeah they all exist and are all very real and we are getting off-topic right now," he turned to Meania, gesturing to them. "We have to get them to safety. Rune wants them for their ability to tell the future, he thinks that way he can dodge the law."

"And the gods want them because…?"

"The gods are the gods and they will take any excuse they can get to throw a fight," Xbalanque explained with a shrug. "Plus, a lot of them are obsessed with fate and avoiding it. They'll want to get their hands on Melania too."

"But you just said," Jason turned to Meania again. "That you can't see the future on command… so… wouldn't that render their whole reason for wanting you… pointless?"

"Yes, yes it does… but they don't know that," Xbalanque explained. "Heck, I didn't know that until… a few minutes ago… look, Jason, I know I'm asking a lot, but-."

"You literally have no one," Jason finished for him, glancing at Meania again who was now staring down at the table. Their expression was grim and frightened. It must be getting closer to the time when Xbalanque was going to end up captured. "Damn it…all right, all right, I'll help," Jason looked to Xibalanque.

414

"What do you need me to do?"

"I need you to get them somewhere safe," Xibalanque said, as Jason got up and placed his cup on the counter, rushing to the hallway and getting to the stairs, he followed behind him. "Somewhere that only you know, somewhere I won't."

"Is that even possible?" Jason threw him a look as he was halfway up the stairs. "You've been alive so long... wouldn't you know everywhere?"

"No, I mean, like somewhere I wouldn't know you'd go. Somewhere that's special or important to you, preferably out of the way of people."

Jason seemed to think about it for a moment and slowly nodded to himself. "All right... yeah... I know the place, let me just get dressed."

Jason rushed up the stairs and it wasn't long before he came back down in jeans, boots, a shirt and a jacket, straightening out his collar. His hair was still mostly a mess, but he seemed to have attempted to calm it down. Once he got to the bottom of the stairs, Xbalanque held out his phone to him.

"I... already have a phone..." Jason said slowly in confusion, but Xbalanque shook his head.

"This has the numbers of the others on it. Call Aethalides when you get somewhere safe or if you need help," he explained. "Plus, it'd be better if the people that are coming don't find me with this on me. They might use it to track our conversations."

"Right..." Jason took it and quickly stuffed it in his pocket, turning to Meania as he picked up his keys and his own phone. "All right kid, let's get you somewhere safe."

They went outside, walking to Jason's car and Meania got inside. Jason was just about to open the door when Xbalanque stopped him.

"Look, Jason... I'm... really sorry to drag you into this-."

"Why?" Jason screwed his face up.

"Because... it's dangerous and I know-."

"X'," Jason sighed, leaning on his car and crossing his arms. "I'm a detective, I'm supposed to look after people and keep them safe... sure this whole... magic world and gods feels a little above my pay grade... but oracle or not," he hooked his thumb at Meania who was watching them through the windows. "They're just a kid and they need help."

Meania suddenly poked their head out of the door, wide eyed and panicked. "They're here! They're going to come around the corner in moments!"

"All right, you gotta go," Xbalanque said and held his hand out to Jason to shake. "Good luck."

Jason quickly reached down and shook his hand, nodding. "You too. See you at the finish line, yeah?"

"Yeah, now get out of here!"

Xibalanque took a few steps away and watched Jason get in the car and drive off. No sooner had their car turned the corner than Cillian and the chihuahua came around the corner. Cillian had a feral expression on his face, crossbow raised and ready, the chihuahua right behind him, barking and yapping.

"Seriously?" Xbalanque sighed as he took his spear out, spinning it around in his hand. "I thought your little rat there got hit by a truck?"

"You'll regret crossing me and the Port side raiders!" Cillian yelled. "The Archives have had their time in the sun, it's our time! And once I take you out, Rune will finally see who I am and so will the rest of Atlantis! I'll finally get the respect I deserve!"

Xbalanque sniggered. "Sorry, Cillian, you could defeat all

the gods and goddesses from all the pantheons… and you'd still be that baby-faced crybaby to everyone."

Cillian let out an enraged shriek, then his eyes started to glow a luminous pale green… which was weird… he'd never-

"Xbalanque *stop moving,*" the fae spoke and it was like his entire body locked up. He couldn't move, he couldn't speak, he could only breathe and move his eyes around. What was this? "Since none of you would respect me before, I'm… finally using my powers!" Cillian cried out proudly. "Not so much of a joke now, huh? Don't worry, Rune is coming, he'll want to see this and when he see's that I got you… by myself-," the chihuahua yipped at him and Cillian flinched. "Uh, I mean *we,* when he sees that *we* got you all by ourselves, he'll see me as his equal!"

Xibalanque wanted desperately to tell him that would never happen, not in a million years would that happen. Rune only looked at Cillian with contempt and used him, this entire time that was all he was doing, using the idiot and his gang for his own advantages. Cillian was just too blind to see it.

He couldn't say he blamed him. Rune was very good at using people and making sure they didn't know about it. He'd sure had the Archives wrapped around his finger without their knowledge.

True to his word, Rune did make an appearance with the more human looking of his group and they came… in a really big truck that seemed… to be growling… That wasn't a good sign.

Rune himself even arrived in flashy cars. Looks like they hadn't completely taken out Cillian's operation in Derby.

Rune looked surprised to see Xibalanque, then glanced to a proud Cillian who gestured enthusiastically at his captive with a grin.

"I got him! See!"

"I do see, thank you, Cillian," Rune looked Xibalanque up

and down. "But what I do not see is an oracle."

"Uh ah... oh... umm.." Cillian's bravado quickly evaporated and he glanced to Xbalanque, almost like he was looking to him for advice on what to do. "Umm... well, that's fine! He had the oracle with him, we can ask where he took it, yeah... here allow me," Cillian cleared his throat and puffed his chest out again. "Xibalanque, tell us where the oracle is."

"I don't know."

It was almost worth being caught by Cillian to watch the way he fluctuated between overconfident to internal panic in a matter of seconds. Glancing to Rune, the fae quickly collected himself, marching forward until he was nose to nose with Xbalanque.

"I will ask you again and you will answer me!" He growled, eyes glowing. "Xbalanque where is the oracle?"

"I told you, I don't know," he replied with a smirk. "Don't worry, it's not you... really. Your magic is working, I just generally don't know where they are."

"How can you not-? They were just with you!"

"Yeah, they were."

"So where have they gone?"

"Dunno."

"Aghhhh!" Cillian yelled, raising his hands up to the sky and letting out a string of curses. He turned back to Rune and quickly composed himself. "I assure you, Rune, they really were just-."

"No, I believe you," Rune replied, looking back at his men and nodding. They nodded back. Moving to the back of the truck where the growling was coming from.

"If you just... give me some time, I'll be able to find-." Cillian began but was interrupted when Rune chuckled. It was horrible and mocking, for a brief moment Xibalanque even felt bad for Cillian. The fae's ears dropped at the sound and Rune turned to him, walking over and towering over Cillian. The contempt had turned to amusement and he smiled down at him.

"You? No. You've played your part, I have no further use of you."

"What? But I-."

"Are an inadequate little nothing. A pawn in a much larger game and now. I, much like everyone else, have no further use for you."

Xbalanque winced. "Ouch, dude… little harsh."

Rune turned to him with his cold smile in place. "As the saying goes, truth often is."

"B-but.." Cillian stammered, staring up at Rune with a broken expression. "I thought I was-."

"Special?" Rune beat him to it, not even bothering to turn to him properly and address him, he only glanced and raised a mocking eyebrow. "Yes, you tend to think that about yourself a lot."

From behind him, more growls could be heard and finally, the creature that had been in the truck was brought forward. It was a manticore. One of the Mesopotamian kinds, which meant it had to be the one that Rune had perchased from the desert fangs not long ago. He'd been saving it all this time, just for this special occasion. A Mesopotamian manticore to hunt down a Mesopotamian oracle… oh gods, what had he just signed Jason up for?

"It was a valiant effort, truly it was," Rune said, smirking up at Xibalanque as he watched the manticore sniff around the streets, finally catching on to Meania's scent and letting out a roar. "But you see, you Archives have shot yourselves in the proverbial foot. You have no one. The gods have turned on you, Atlantis has turned on you, you're all alone," Rune laughed, shaking his head. "And here I thought this was going to be a challenge."

"He's got the scent, sir!" Rune's guy shouted.

"Let him go, we follow him and get our oracle," Rune ordered and the manticore was unleashed, quickly running off at pace, the van chasing after it and a car pulled up next to Rune, waiting for him to get in. "I really have to thank Heimdallr's son for that thing. Oh what spite can do to the youth."

Xbalanque frowned. "What are you talking about?"

"Another mystery I suppose you'll just have to solve," Rune smirked, reaching up to lightly pat at the side of Xbalanque's face mockingly. "That's if you get to live after this. I've heard that the gods aren't kind to those who disobey them."

"You're wasting your time, Rune. The oracle can't pull up prophecies on command."

"Maybe not now, but I tend to find… a little encouragement goes a long way," he smiled at him, showing off his fangs. "I hear the threat of death is very motivating. Now, if you'll excuse me, I've got an oracle to procure. Oh, Cillian," he turned to the fae and smiled. "Xbalanque's all yours. Consider it… payment I suppose for all your… well, I hesitate to call it help, but… it's for your uses."

Without another word, Rune got in his car and it drove off, leaving Xbalanque with Cillian and the chihuahua, the latter of which looked like his whole world came tumbling down around him. The chihuahua on the other hand looked ready to rip his throat out. Jötun, chihuahua, the only real difference between the two was the height and use of opposable thumbs.

"Cillian," Xbalanque hissed. "Come on, you just gonna let Rune say those things to you and get away with it? You never let us do that."

"That's because it's you *guys!*" Cillian hissed at him. "You're not *Rune* and besides he's right!"

"Wow, it only took Rune saying it for you to finally realise," Xibalanque mumbled and then flinched when the chihuahua barked at him. "Look, I get it, okay? It's not easy screwing up and then being *told* how much you screwed up or how… useless you are to someone. Believe me, I *get* it!" He cried out. "But… you have the power here. Rune's gone, you can make the difference."

"By doing what?" Cillian scoffed. "Freeing you? Even if I did do that, you don't know where the oracle is and we have no way of tracking them. Face facts you guys lost this one and the only way I'm gonna get out of this is if I don't help you. Rune's gonna be top dog more than ever after this."

"Hey now… where's that stubborn fae I'm used to?" Xibalanque flashed a grin. "Don't you want to kick Rune's shiny behind all the way back to Alfheim?"

"Of course I do, but I'm no match against him!"

"Really?" Xibalanque raised an eyebrow. "You sure about that? I mean… you do know his name after all," he smirked at Cillian 'whose eyes seemed to be flashing with realisation. "All it would take is some magic words from you and you could easily put the guy in his place."

"You… you'd let me do that?"

"I think the whole of Atlantis would *thank you* for it," he flashed Cillian a grin. "What you say? You help us out with this and the Archives will put in a good word about the Portside Raiders…?"

Cillian looked down at the chihuahua for a moment, contemplating and then a smirk crawled up his face. His eyes glowed green as he looked at Xibalanque. "I release Xibalanque from my spells."

He could move again. God that was nice, he didn't want to go through that experience ever again.

Cillian walked over to him as he rubbed feeling back into his wrists and shook out his legs and arms. The fae was grinning, showing his fangs and his ears had perked up.

"Let's get your band of Archives and kick that shiny elf back to where he came from! It's about time people took the port side raiders seriously!"

The Lost Oracle: 23

Jason couldn't help but keep glancing at the kid next to him. The thirteen year old who was… apparently the magical world's most wanted for their gift. Magical world… what had his life come to?

He didn't want to be doing this, but he couldn't just leave the kid in danger, they were only thirteen and being hunted down by gods, street gangs and god knows what else. Jason didn't know what was down there, but he had a feeling that it wasn't anything good and this kid was on their own. They needed help and… well, Jason couldn't leave well enough alone.

Meania was staring out the window with big eyes, watching the English countryside go past them, fields and trees, the grey sky making them stand out as a flash of colour. It was like the kid had never seen anything like this before, could be that they hadn't and Jason had no idea what Atlantis looked like whatsoever.

He flexed his fingers on the steering wheel, letting out a breath he didn't realise he'd been holding. Jason could feel the sweat building on his hands, clammy and tense, he'd never been scared like this before. People he could handle, criminals, sure, he knew what he was doing, but this? This was crazy! This was… magic and gods and whatever the hell else came with it. He wasn't trained on how to deal with this, what the hell was he supposed to do if he did come across a magical being that knew who Meania was?

"So…" he started awkwardly, glancing to Meania who took their attention away from the countryside. "How are you feeling kid?"

"I'm... okay... just worried," they looked back out the window. "I haven't seen the future so... I have no idea who is going to win or what will happen."

"Right, right... yeah... seeing the future..." Jason trailed off and gave a high-pitched laugh. His grip tightened on the wheel as he shifted in his seat. "Man, that... that must be... intense.."

Meania smiled at him. "It can be, it's... mostly disappointing if I'm being honest. Everyone's disappointed when they hear what their future is going to be."

"But you can't... um, call it up whenever you want?"

Meania shook their head. "No... I... I don't know how to do that," they looked down at their hands, fiddling with the shall they had wrapped around themselves. "Anansi said I'd learn eventually, but it would take time and I'm still young. Are... you okay?"

"I'm gonna be real honest with you kid, I'm freaking out," Jason laughed, driving the road he knew well, it was a part of the countryside he liked to go for some peace and quiet, helped him think. He didn't tell anyone about it, because he liked having a place that was just his. "But, this isn't about me. I gotta get you somewhere safe, that's the important part."

"You don't really want to be here do you?"

Hit the nail on the head with that one, he thought to himself, giving a slow nod.

Meania looked out the window again, seeming to be in deep thought for a moment. "If you didn't want to help, why help at all? I don't understand that..."

Jason let out a sigh, tapping an idle beat on the wheel for a moment. "I... can't leave it alone when I know someone's in trouble. You're just a kid, I don't care what kind of... I don't know, crazy super powers you got," he moved his hand flippantly, like a gesture of magic that he had a feeling would be completely wrong. "It's my job to help people, that's the whole reason I wanted to be an officer... I thought it was the best way I could help people..."

"Oh, so you're like the guards in Atlantis?"

"I... suppose? I got no idea, but my job is to stop bad people from doing bad things to good people," he paused and thought about it. "And to stop good people from ruining their lives and doing a bad thing... it ain't easy and... we get it wrong, we make mistakes and we shouldn't..." Jason paused and screwed his face up. "Sometimes I feel like I do more harm than good... but... that's not important right now. I'm here to help you, get you somewhere safe."

Meania smiled at him. "Thank you. I think... that's brave of you."

Jason laughed. Yeah, brave, sure. He thought it was more *stupid*. He didn't know what he was going to do if someone or something magic came along. Hell, he didn't know the first thing about magic, he was just... an average guy. Man, he wished he'd paid attention to what his daughter talked about, she was the one that was into magic and mythology, would talk about it non-stop and he... well, he *tried* to listen, but he was mostly... half listening. He tried, but his mind was usually occupied by a case.

After he found out about Xbalanque and this... crazy world, he'd sat with her and asked questions. The way her face lit up... how excited she was to talk to him about a subject she liked, just her enthusiasm... it made him realise those were the questions he should've been asking a long time ago and not just so he could make sense of what he saw.

Jason took a breath and finally pulled the car in to the small car park that was out of the way. They would have to walk from here, but at least it was safe and out of the way of people for the most part. He doubted there'd be many visitors up here, at least not at this time.

"Okay kid, we're walking from here, follow me…" he said as he got out of the car and Meania was close to follow him.

"What is this place?" They asked, looking at the sign and tilting their head. "I… um… I can't read that…"

"Huh?" He looked at the sign and then looked back at them. "Oh it's called Straws Bridge, but if we go this way, we'll get to the Nutbrook ponds. It's out of the way, people don't come down here at this time, we should be okay."

At least, Jason hoped they would be okay.

It was quiet, the bird song the only noise as they walked through the trees. Already he was starting to think calmer, like this he could almost imagine that he was just going for a walk and not hiding away from some magical beings. Of course, that mirage was quickly broken as he pulled out Xbalanque's phone and went through his contacts to one that read 'Aethalides'.

Hesitantly he hit the call button, placing it to his ear and waiting. He heard the number get dialled and then it was ringing. Wasn't long before it was answered.

He was hesitant to say anything at first, but eventually, he found his voice and spoke.

"Umm… hello?"

"Hi, Jason right?" Came the chipper and young voice down the line. Really young, sounded like a boy 'whose voice hadn't broken yet and wasn't anywhere near to breaking. "Heh, it's funny, I used to know a Jason, hope you're not like him though. Anyway, you good? The oracle safe?"

"Umm..yeah… .yes… we're… okay.." He glanced to

Meania who was looking around the woods with big eyes, a grin on their face. "We're at a place called Straws Bridge... heading to the pounds round the back.."

"Oh, the woods! Wow you couldn't have picked a more cliche place to be hunted down by a rabid beast."

"By a... what?"

Aethalides chuckled. "You got a manticore on your tail, quicken the pace and run, we're coming as fast as we can."

"Well... how the hell do I stop a manticore?"

"Oh, you just worry about keeping away from it and watch out for its spines! They shoot out and they're highly venomous, like... *certain death* venomous. Anyway, good talk ba-bye!"

"*Good talk-* hey wait!" Jason pulled the phone away as nothing but a dial tone reached his ears. He looked to Meania who's eyes were glowing a warm yellow and their face took on a fearful expression. Jason slowly lowered his arm. "Kid, what is it?"

"Monster..." Meania whispered and pointed in the direction that's just come. "It's coming this way."

Jason mentally cursed, quickly taking the kids hand and running down the path as fast as they could go. He didn't want to look behind him, to see just what the hell a manticore was. Turns out, he didn't need to turn around to see it, because the thing suddenly leapt out of the tree line to land in front of them.

The manticore was huge, the size of a lion with a body of one. A scorpion-like tail that had hundreds of venomous quills at the end of it, but the most disturbing thing was the human-like face that was snarling at them. Drool dripped to the floor, fangs poked out between the human lips, but the mouth was too big to be human. Its massive paws already had the claws out as it stalked towards them, snarling and growling.

Jason backed up, keeping Meania behind him, he could feel his heart beating rapidly in his chest as the thing continued to get closer and closer.

"Kid, you need to get out of here…" Jason hissed, urging him to run. "Go, I'll… I don't know, I'll hold this thing off for as long as I can."

"But-."

"No buts! Get going!" He glanced at them and gave a comforting smile, but it probably came across more as a grimace. "I'm going to be fine, okay? Now go! Run!"

Meania looked uncertain, but nodded and started running. Jason snagged up a large branch that had fallen off a tree and held it like a baseball bat, glaring at the manticore. He desperately tried to ignore the way his hands shook, the way he was sucking air between his teeth.

The tail flexed and that was the only warning he got before the barbs were shot out at him. Jason dived behind the trees, a few of the spikes embedded themselves into the trunks. The venom that dripped from them caused the bark to melt away and smoke to rise up. The stuff was so damn potent it was *melting* the trees.

A flurry of curses flashed through his head as he stared, but he didn't get long to marvel at the certain death those spikes would cause when the manticore pounced at him. He scrambled to his feet, not getting away quick enough to avoid the huge claws of the monster ripping through his arm and tearing it to shreds.

Jason let out a cry, stumbling away from the beast as he gripped at his arm, the branch was still clutched tightly in hand of the arm that had been cut to ribbons with just one swipe. He could feel his blood running down his arm, seeping between his fingers and he sucked in air between his teeth. The manticore was

428

getting closer, lunging at him again and he jumped backwards, ducking behind a tree in the nick of time when it struck at him once more.

He was way out of his depth, what the hell was he supposed to do against this thing!? The branch was still in hand, but... he doubted it was going to do much if anything against it.

He couldn't outrun it, he wasn't stronger than it, the thing was built like a lion and had a scorpion tail. Still... he doubted it would enjoy being smacked in the face with a large branch.

Despite the pain, Jason pulled the branch up, readying it up for a swing and when the manticore attacked him, he jumped back before lunging forward and striking it on the nose. It let out a yowl and shook its head, the snarl pulled across its face and it jumped at him, taking Jason to the ground.

Jason screamed, lifting up the branch and holding it in front as a block, only to watch the manticore snap its jaws around it and then break it with one crunch. Wood and splinters went everywhere, Jason tried dragging himself backwards as the creature opened its inhumanly wide mouth to clamp its teeth on him. He desperately sorts out a weapon, a piece of wood, a stone, a rock *anything!* Finally landing on what had to be a brick someone had carelessly dropped them.

With a cry he swung the brick and smashed it across the manticore's face, clawing his way to his feet while it was distracted and shaking its head. He couldn't help but feel like the damn thing was playing with him.

He tried crawling backwards away from it as the manticore drew closer and closer, a snarl on its face, drool dripping down and now a bloody mark across its head.

Jason's back hit a tree and the manticore growled, the only warning he got before it pounced. He flinched, covering his face with his arms and let out a shout, but he didn't feel any teeth biting into his body, no claws, it sounded like the monster was snarling and choking.

He hadn't even realised he'd closed his eyes until he was opening them and peeking through his arms to see the manticore now had a spear shoved down it's throat by Xbalanque. The thing was still alive though, in pain clearly, but it didn't look like it was any closer to slowing down.

Xbalanque yanked his spear out and went to stab at it again, but the manticore jumped back prowling back and forth, 'its scorpion tail raised high and flicked. The spines were back, long inky black quills with venom dripping off them. Jason knew what the twitching meant; it was going to shoot the quills out.

With strength he didn't know he still had in him, he scrambled to his feet and tackled Xbalanque to the ground just as the quills fired. They struck the trees and plants behind them, melting away the bark like before as the acidic venom dripped and spread through the tree, turning part of its trunk black.

"You, okay?" Xbalanque asked as he helped him up, pulling Jason behind himself and fighting off the manticore, keeping it at bay with the spear.

"Where's the kid?" Jason asked, completely disregarding the question.

"Rune's got them," Xbalanque hissed. "The others are dealing with him, they're still here though, we just got to deal with this thing."

"And um… how do we do that?"

"The tail," Xbalanque explained. "Manticores can recover from anything, but if we cut off the top of its tail it's done."

Jason blinked, clutching at his arm as he watched the manticore leap at them, scrambling away while Xbalanque moved with practised ease. His footing was sure and even, like he was a dancer or a professional fighter, there was almost an elegance to it.

The manticore reared up on its back legs swiping at Xbalanque, who dodged and kept out of the way, up until it leaped at him and he had to use his spear to hold it back. The manticore forced him to the ground, trying to bite at him and Xbalanque used the spear to block its biting jaws.

"Get out of here, Jason!" He shouted. "I got this!"

"Oh, yeah, sure…" Jason grumbled as he picked up a rock and raised it above his head. "Sure, looks like you do!"

His arm was screaming at him to drop the rock, but he didn't, charging at the and slamming the rock across it, actually causing part of it to split. The scorpion-like exoskeleton splintered and split revealing a fleshy, gooey like substance underneath it.

The manticore let out a yowl of pain, swinging its stringer to try and hit him, but he was able to back away just in time, giving a half-hearted throw of the rock at the tail. It smashed into the regrowing quills, breaking and snapping them. The manticore yelled, it was almost human-like and then it turned its attention to him.

Jason backed up, getting ready to dive out of the way, when an arrow suddenly shot through the air and straight through the manticore's tail, through the splits and cracks that Jason had caused by the rock. The end of the scorpion tail was hanging on just barely and the manticore was writhing around, crying out in pain, barely able to keep itself standing.

Xbalanque ran forward with his spear and swung it around, knocking the entire thing off, it sailed through the air and landed on the ground with a splat. The manticore let out one final cry and finally fell to the ground silent and dead.

"Oh, my gods!" A young voice shouted and Jason turned to look up the path, finding a kid dressed in a white hoodie with a bow in hand, sandy blonde hair falling across his eyes. His mouth was agape and he was staring at the dead manticore in shock. "I *actually* did it!"

Xbalanque gave a breathless laugh, giving a thumbs up to the kid. "Nice one, Icarus!"

"I actually hit it!" Icarus continued, jumping up and down. "Whoo! I did something without screwing up! *Oh gods!*" the celebration was short-lived as a look of horror crossed his face. "Isn't killing a manticore illegal!? Am I going to be in *trouble?*"

Xbalanque gave a crooked smile. "Technically this whole operation is illegal, including our side of it."

"But-."

"Go and help the others, 'Icarus, we'll be right behind you!"

Icarus nodded, though it looked like he wanted to protest more, but didn't and quickly darted away, running back up the path with his arrows on his back.

Jason stared after him in silence for a moment, stunned and pointed in the direction the kid had run. "Icarus…" he said slowly, turning to Xbalanque with wide eyes. "As in… *Icarus* Icarus?"

Xbalanque nodded. "Yeah, that Icarus."

"But didn't he… die?"

"Yeah."

"Then…" Jason glanced in the direction the kid had gone, before turning back to Xbalanque. "How's he here?"

Xbalanque shrugged.

Right, well… that's something for later he guessed.

Jason gripped at his arm still, giving it support and Xbalanque screwed his face up in concern, looking him over for a few moments.

"You didn't get hit by one of those quills, did you?" He asked.

"I'm fine, I'm fine! Come on, we got to help the others right? You said this Rune guy was here…"

"Jason," Xbalanque placed his hand on his shoulder. "You've done enough, sit this one out, we got-."

He batted his hand away with a scowl. "The hell I am! You got me into this, you think I'm just going to back out now!" He snapped at him, clenching his fist. "I'm not leaving until I know that kid's okay and safe! Besides, I'm fine!"

"You just took on a manticore… I really think-."

"And I'm still breathing!" Jason started running down the path, his arm was screaming in pain, he could hear Xbalanque running after him, easily keeping up. He guessed the guy would be fitter than him.

Even so, he wasn't just going to walk away, just because things got… dangerous. That kid needed help and he wasn't going to just abandon them. Sure, he was injured and could do with medical attention, but he'd be fine, he could get through this. He knew he could.

The others weren't that far away. Rune had brought a lot of guys and he could see the kid was being shielded by a red headed woman with a sword and shield. Any of Rune's guys got too close; they were being met by that sword and… well, Jason was just glad that lady seemed to be on their side at least.

There was… there was a minotaur that had him rubbing at his eyes and blinking several times. He almost questioned reality when he mentally slapped himself because he literally just fought a manticore.

Jason and Xbalanque quickly made their way to the oracle,

who immediately gravitated to Jason, hiding behind him as he did his best to shield them. God, he really hoped no one came down here for a morning jog, they'd… certainly, be met with a sight.

Finally, as he looked through the crowd of fighting monsters and… different peoples, he saw who he had to guess was Rune. He looked like the guy that would be in charge and he was fighting off a… ten-year-old. The same ten-year-old that had visited Xbalanque that one time at the workplace. He spotted Vali too, fighting left and right with a sword, but the kids' eyes were fixated on Rune. Behind him was Icarus, giving him cover and Jason had never seen two people more opposite than those two.

"Do you really think you can win this one?" Rune smiled, easily dodging each one of Aethalides's strikes. "How many times have you beaten me, Aethalides?"

Aethalides took a breather, spinning the blades around in his hands as he offered a crooked grin. "There's a first time for everything," he joked and then tossed one of the blades at him, Rune only sidestepped the blade, then it was immediately back in Aethalides's hands.

"He'll get stuck…" Meania whispered next to Jason. He jumped a little, not expecting the kid to speak, but Meania's eyes were glowing and fixated on Rune and Aethalides.

"What? Who will get stuck?" He asked.

Meania looked up at him. "Rune. The child of Loki has many tricks…"

Child of… *who* now?

Suddenly Vali launched himself forward, dodging anyone that tried to stop him to strike at Rune. He leaped into the air and brought his sword down, aimed straight at Rune's head. The light elf carefully dodged out of the way, only just dodging the second strike that was aimed at his neck. The smile had left his face and now he looked angry. That was probably a little too close for comfort.

Jason had met humans like Rune. People who thought themselves untouchable and they lived up to that reputation through and through. Rune was just like that. Everything about him was pristine and clean, not a single mark on him, he wasn't marred by any kind of scar or supposed imperfection. He was perfect, too perfect, it was almost sickening.

"Has the little wolf come out to play," Rune growled, baring his own fangs. "Remember how this went for you last time, Vali?"

"Then why do you look so nervous?" Vali challenged.

Rune flexed his fingers and a beam of light appeared in hand, taking the form of a thin blade almost looking like it was made of glass. He spun the blade in his hand a moment and struck out at him, slicing the blade through the air in rapid succession, some hits did land on Rune, but he didn't seem that bothered by the slices and cuts.

There was a singing sound of a blade flying through the air was heard above the ongoing fighting and Jason watched in mild satisfaction as one of Aethalides's blades shot passed Vali's head and sliced across Rune's cheek.

Rune let out a cry, backing away and slowly raised a hand to his cheek. White light was leaking down his face, he touched it with his hand and pulled it away, staring at the glowing blood on his fingers in clear shock.

The surprise and astonishment left his face quickly, morphing into one of rage as he clenched his fist and snapped his head in Aethalides's direction.

The blade had returned to Aethalides's hands and he was

spinning them around his hands with a grin on his face. He stopped spinning them to point a blade in Rune's direction before using the blade to beckon him to try and hit him.

"You little... You're going to pay for that!" Rune yelled. "I'm untouchable!"

"Clearly not."

The light elf let out a feral scream and charged forward, swinging his blade at Vali. Vali had taken his time to drag his foot through the dirt and then jump back, the moment Rune's foot landed on the mark Vali had made in the ground he was frozen. He couldn't move. Rune stared down at the floor in clear shock.

Slowly those cold eyes looked up at Vali who smirked at him. Jason was slightly taken aback at the look on Vali's face. When he met the kid, Vali was shy and basically hiding in his clothing, now he was standing tall with a look on his face... that could almost be described as... cruel.

"Did you forget about Isa?" Vali mocked.

Rune blinked and then started to chuckle, clasping his hands behind his back as he stood still. Most of his men were down, it didn't stop them from trying to attack and take swings, but not a single one of them would come to his defence.

The light elf smirked right back at Vali, looking vaguely impressed. "Well played, Lokison. I tip my hat."

"Ha!" Another... elf like being, shot forward, baby-faced with curly red hair and pointed at Rune, trying to appear big and tough. "How's it feel to be beaten by the Port Side Raiders?"

"Oh, I really wouldn't know," Rune replied calmly with a smile. His hand moved lightning fast as he pulled what looked like a stone from his pocket. "Lögr!"

The moment the stone hit the ground, water erupted and washed away the symbol Vali had drawn with his foot. Then he waved his hand, the water seeming to follow his movements, sending it flying at Vali and Aethalides. They were smacked in the face and sent flying, hitting the ground hard.

Rune turned his attention to the other elf as he leapt forward, a bright beam of light turning into a spear coming from his hand and he spun it around so it was pointing forward. He drove it straight into the shoulder of the other elf, who hadn't had time to move and he let out a shriek, clutching at the spear that was still being driven into his shoulder. Rune had a feral grin on his face, twisting the spear in his hand.

"Did you really think you were ever going to be anything?" Rune mocked. "You're a *joke*. To everyone. The only person who doesn't see it is you," he yanked the spear out and spun it in hand, using the end to crack the other elf across the face and send him to the ground. "In fact, if you ask me, you're an overused joke. *Stale,* " He raised the spear above his head. "It's about time someone put you out of your misery."

Rune brought the spear down, only for it to be stopped halfway when a whip of golden, what looked like sunlight, wrapped around the spear itself. He snapped his head in the direction of the light, finding Medea at the other end of it. The golden light was wrapped around her hands as she held it tight, gritting her teeth.

"Always forget that the women in Helios's line are so gifted in magic," Rune snarled out, tugging at the spear, pulling against the light.

Medea snarled and moved her arms, flicking the whip off the spear, sending Rune stumbling backwards, before she snapped and cracked the whip at his face.

Rune hissed, conjuring up more sharp pieces of light and throwing them in the direction of Medea, only to be blocked by

437

Boudicca who'd dived forward with her shield raised.

The light elf didn't even get time to readjust for another attack before the minotaur came barrelling into him, head first, sending Rune flying through the air.

He landed hard, Xbalanque's spear came inches from striking his neck and he followed up by swinging up again, ready to catch him. Rune blocked the hit with his wrist, hissing as the blade sliced across the back of it, cutting the coat and tearing the sleeve.

'Xbalanque kicked him in the chest, sending Rune sprawling across the floor. He was quick to get up to his knees, flinching again from another strike from Xbalanque, ducking an arrow from Icarus, working up to stand as he backed away from them.

Rune looked around and his eyes landed on Jason and Meania. A grin was on his face in an instant, despite the blood running down his face and his shoddy appearance.

His men were all on the floor, either unconscious or in what could be generously described as 'critical condition'.

The elf pulled another stone from his pocket and slammed it against the ground, shouting out 'Kaun'. A huge fire erupted, which he used to create a wall on either side of himself, leading all the way to them.

Rune pulled up more blades of light and ran straight at Jason who put his hands up to shield himself, standing in front of Meania. He braced for impact as he heard Rune yell, swinging the blades down.

"Rune stop!"

The blades never made contact with his arms and Jason slowly lowered them, staring at a bewildered Rune. His arms were shaking and he was wearing a feral expression, eyes flicking to the left as a figure came up to the wall of flame,

438

clutching at their shoulder.

It was the elf from earlier and he was glaring at Rune with such hatred, a look of concentration on his face, eyes glowing green.

"Rune, *drop the blades,*" he snarled out and there was a resounding bell-like noise as the blades of light hit the floor.

"You little…" Rune began to growl out, glaring at the other. "You think this means *anything!*"

"Put the fire out, Rune," the elf replied in annoyance and Rune did some kind of hand movement, extinguishing the flames in the process.

"I'll have your head for this, Cillian!" Rune yelled, spitting out venom as spittle ran down his chin. "Do you really think you've won?"

"You do know you're going to prison right?" Aethalides said slowly. "I mean, Viggo and the rest of your group are already there, Brianna's just waiting for us to bring your shiny behind to her."

At this, Rune just chuckled. "Yes, and I dare say you lot will be accompanying me," he smirked at Aethalides. "You did break so many rules. Doubt your father can help you now, Aethalides, so enjoy this freedom while you have it."

"Oh, it's so funny you think I had any freedom in the first place," the ten year old gave a manic grin. "Even so… best leave now, don't want to attract too much attention. Asterion! Could you pick up the package for us, the rest of you, use your legs, oh and Detective," Aethalides turned to Jason and grinned at him. "You better come with us."

So, after a trip in the cars and a… campervan, a quick heal from Medea and walking through a wall… which… what the *actual* hell, they were in Atlantis.

Jason had to take a moment, leaning against a wall as the rest of the discussion went on around him. A lady dressed in armour with several other creatures and beings dressed in the same kind was there to take Rune and his people away.

She didn't leave right away after, instead talking to Aethalides and while he couldn't hear what was going on, mostly down to the ringing in his ears and trying to collect himself, he could tell from her facial expression that it wasn't good.

Hell, just looking at *everyone's* facial expressions he could tell it wasn't good, Meania looked downright terrified, huddling closer to him and it helped to ground Jason a little bit. He needed to keep that kid safe, gods be damned.

"Well," Aethalides said as he turned back to the others, pulling out a packet of cigarettes, seeming to think better of it and instead going for his hip flask. "That happened."

"How in trouble are we...?" Icarus asked.

"Pick a number between one and ten," Aethalides said, with a dull expression. "Then times it by one hundred and it *still* wouldn't be the right amount..."

"Oh gods..." Icarus whispered, putting his head in his hands. "I don't want to die!... again..."

"No workarounds?" Xbalanque asked and Aethalides shook his head.

He took a drink of his flask and wiped his mouth with the back of his hands. "Look, I'm not going to lie... it's not going to be good. At all. But... I might be able to stall them. It was my orders and decisions that got us into this mess..." Aethalides tapped an uneven tune on the side of his flask, looking at the ground in thought. "I won't begrudge you leaving and finding somewhere to hide, at least before the gods get here."

No one moved. Not a single person made a move to leave,

even Icarus who seemed absolutely terrified. Well, all except for Cillian and… was that a chihuahua?

"Not staying, Cillian?" Aethalides teased him.

"Like hell! I don't want to end up cursed like all of you," the elf gestured to them. "Even if you did save me. I don't owe you anything!"

"No loyalty among thieves huh? Still, I think the Archives and the Portside raiders worked well together," he flashed him a grin. "What you say we make it a regular thing?"

Cillian scowled at him. "Over my dead body, Aethalides," he growled out before quickly making his leave.

Aethalides turned back to the rest of them, looked them all over and then rolled his eyes with a laugh. "Gods, how'd I get stuck with a sappy lot of loyalists like you, huh? And *you?*" He turned to Medea, pointing at her, his expression stunned. "You're not going to make a break for it?"

Medea shrugged and smiled. "I don't know, maybe I just like the idea of eternally torturing Jason."

"Huh!?" Jason cried out alarmed and she waved him off.

"Not you, darling, another Jason."

"Oh. Thank god…" he rubbed at his forehead, taking a breath and desperately trying to calm himself down. At least enough to focus on everything around him.

Suddenly out of nowhere a bright burst of light appeared in front of them, nearly blinding him and when it faded there stood a man with a glow haloing him and glowing purple eyes. Winged sandals at his feet, dressed in Ancient Greek clothes and cloak wrapped around his person holding a staff that had two snakes coiled around it and wings at the top. A hat rested on waving white hair and he was tanned like he'd been in the sun for days.

Everything about him was pleasant to look at, even his face, though it was marred with worry and concern, was good looking by any standards. He was like Rune in the sense that he was too perfect.

"Aethalides-."

"Dad, I know…" Aethalides sighed, swigging from his flask. "Don't sweat it."

"I…" Aethalides's father blinked and then looked away. "I can't do anything, they won't listen and.."

"Dad, I told you it's fi-."

"No, it is not fine!" The god, because that was the only thing he could be, paced back and forth, running a hand through his hair after taking his hat off. "You are in so much trouble and I can't do anything to protect you from-."

His words were cut off as an even brighter and somehow grander burst of light appeared in front of them. Jason had to cover his eyes and look away when it flashed, exploding like a firework that had sparks falling to the ground once the light was gone.

He had sort of understood the weight of everything, but now it was finally hitting him, when he looked across at gods and goddesses that looked down their noses at them like they were insects. Jason supposed to an immortal being that could literally alter the cosmos, they probably all were.

The gods and goddesses that arrived were clearly from different pantheons, dressed like the royalty of their various cultures. Some he knew thanks to pop culture osmosis, but others he had no idea.

The one who had seemed to be the spokes god for the group was definitely Zeus, there was no mistaking the white beard and Greek clothing with lightning emblems and eagles.

He clasped his hands together and grinned, eyes sparking

442

with lightning for a moment as he looked them over.

"And there they are," he boomed, his voice echoed like thunder, everything about this god was... loud and kind of obnoxious, Jason wasn't going to lie. "Our new oracle and the traitors."

"Lord father-," Aethalides's own father tried to interrupt, even getting between his son and Zeus for a breath moment, until Zeus told him a glowing warning look.

"Hermes, you are already in a lot of trouble... Do you want to be in more...?" Zeus challenged, raising an eyebrow. "You were one of my most trusted of children and then you do this. You know just how to break an old man's heart, son, do you want to smash it even further?"

Hermes, who was Aethalides's father and oh boy, now Jason's head was spinning, backed down, looking awkwardly away. Jason could actually feel sorry for the guy, since Zeus was... well, manipulating him and not even in a subtle way. Judging by Aethalides and even Hermes's expression they both knew it.

"Now, traitors, hand over the oracle to us," Zeus continued. "And maybe we will lessen your punishments... only slightly, of course," he laughed loudly. "You did disobey a direct order from your gods."

"Not *my* gods," Boudicca snarled.

"Or mine," Vali joined in and Xbalanque laughed, raising his hand and giving a little wave.

"Yeah, or mine. By Xibalba, my gods aren't even *alive* any more, can't exactly disobey them."

"Yes," Zeus bit out, looking a little put off. "Be that as it may... you should still know better. Anyway, since your pantheon is dead and the Celtic one..." he turned his attention to a god who looked less than interested in being there. "Are being difficult," the celt looked over and made a rude gesture, causing Zeus to huff and look away. "It's been decided that whichever pantheon is closest geographically will be the one to decide your fault which is… oh, the norse!"

"Oh *goody,*" Vali deadpanned, looking over to Xbalanque with a flat expression. "Welcome to my Hel."

Xbalanque grinned from ear to ear. "Hey, least we're not alone, huh Vali?"

Zeus and his groupies seemed even further put out by the carefree attitude the others were presenting, Hermes looked like he didn't know if he should laugh or scold them like naughty children. There was no denying the very evident grin on his face though.

"Anyway!" Zeus boomed, interrupting any further chatter. "What will be decided now is which pantheon has the oracle. They are in short supply these days… so I believe-."

"The Norse should have them!" A one-eyed god, who was clearly Odin, spoke up, interrupting Zeus mid-sentence.

"Beg ya' pardon?" Zeus blinked and then laughed. "No. No, *you* are not getting them! Why do you need an oracle, you have the Norns!"

"A *hardly* reliable source," Odin growled out, then pointed at Zeus with his spear. "What do you need the oracle for? You have the fates!"

"Oh yes, the fates, such wonderful and reliable sources if you like getting your future read to you in rhyme!"

"And the grey *sisters.* Not to mention your *own* oracles, your own *son* is literally the god of *prophecy!* " Odin then pointed his spear at Hermes. "And *he* can perform rustic divination!"

"Ah, that's just me playing knuckle bones…" Hermes

spluttered, raising up hands in surrender, sending a small glare at Odin. "And by the gods do not bring me into this-."

"Yes, don't bring my children into this or I'll bring your *wife* into this!" Zeus cried out, pointing his finger at Odin. "We all know Frigg can see the future! She knows the fate of every man, woman and God!"

Odin gaped. "Frigg doesn't tell me anything!"

"Well, I can't help you with your marriage problems, Odin and I doubt an oracle is going to help-."

Odin laughed loudly, interrupting him again. "Oh, that is rich coming from you, god of *one-night* stands!"

"If I may," the Egyptian god who was with them, with a head of a hawk or something, stepped forward. Decorated head to toe in gold and riches, their mouth never moved; it was like he was speaking in their minds. "Egypt would have use of an oracle and can we also refrain from bringing petty squabbles into this. It doesn't help."

"Oh, I'm sorry, is Thoth's book of knowledge not enough info for you?" Zeus snapped.

"We have only just gone over the fact that Greece has a lot of prophetic beings, including two of your children."

"Horus, buddy, I'm *begging* you, stop bringing me into it," Hermes pleaded.

"Apologies, Hermes," Horus bowed his head to him and then shrugged. "But we can't deny that it's true."

"Oh, you know what, what the hell, I'll throw in," the Celtic god spoke up, haphazardly throwing his hand in the air. "The Celts should have the ora-."

There was a resounding no from all of the others. With Odin throwing in the fact that the Celtic gods would often have prophetic dreams every other week.

Jason slowly leaned over to Xbalanque. "Is it always like this…?"

"Trust me, *this* is nothing…"

"All right, if the Celts can't have the oracle, then how's this for a crazy concept, huh?" The Celtic god crossed his arms, tapping his foot impatiently on the floor. "We hand the oracle over to the Mesopotamian pantheon. Ya' know… the pantheon they're *literally* part of!"

"Good gods no! Why would we do that?" Zeus cried out.

The celt sighed, pinching the bridge of his nose and turning away from the arguing. "Yeah, how stupid of me, why would we do that…?"

"I don't know why you're all fighting over Meania," Xbalanque said idly. "They're young, they don't know how to use their powers."

The gods paused in their bickering and looked over at them, then looked to Meania who shuffled closer to Jason at the looks. He instinctively put his arm out in front of Meania to protect them, not that there was much he could do against the gods if they decided to do anything.

"Are you… saying that they can't… call up prophecies themselves?"

"Yep."

There was a beat of silence and then Zeus burst out laughing.

"Well, why didn't you just say so!" He cried and walked to Hermes, slapping him good naturedly on the back. "You had us worried their son! We thought you found an oracle with *actual* use!"

Hermes blinked. "Uhhhh… Sorry, father… I'm trying to catch up, what-?"

"What's the point in having an oracle who can't call up

things at a drop of a hat!" Zeus laughed. "Never mind, eh? And here I was looking forward to punishing some mortals, it has been an age!"

"It's mildly concerning how much you enjoy punishing mortals, Zeus," Horus mumbled.

The Celtic god threw his hands up. "Well, if that's all I'm going. Bye."

And just like that he was gone, with the rest of the gods following, leaving just the archives and Hermes left.

Hermes threw his arms out, staring at where they had been standing. "Unbelievable!" He cried out. "All of that… that hassle and stress for absolutely nothing!"

Jason was surprised everything happened so quickly and easily, looking at the others they looked just as surprised. Aethalides was gulping down whatever was in his flask, turning to his father with a look of worry.

"Dad, what the hades?" He cried out. "Are we safe then? Meania's safe?"

Hermes waved him off. "Eh, let's be honest, this issue's just been put on *pause*. They'll wait for when Meania can call up prophecies at a whim, then this mess will come back again," he sighed, resting his hands on his hips a moment. "Better hope I can convince the original council to come together before then… but that's *future* Hermes's problem. *Current* Hermes just wants to sit down at club Bacchus and have a very… very long drink."

"So…" Icarus spoke up awkwardly. "We're… okay to go home?"

The god nodded. "Yes. Yes, you can go off home."

Aethalides relaxed, slipping the flask away and muttering something about wondering if Arachne had done with the cleaning.

Jason found himself following the group through the streets after Hermes left, it was that he was in daze then fully in control of his actions. Besides, he had questions and the only place he was going to get answers was if he stayed.

Aethalides randomly asked Jason and Meania what they wanted to drink, then was on his phone texting, all the while Jason was staring at the buildings and various different kinds of people that were now wandering the streets. Opening up their stores, getting ready for work or leaving for school, it was... just like his world and at the same time not in the slightest.

Eventually, they made it to a huge building that had a garden at the front, which was fenced off. A beautiful gate at the front, the building itself looked like an Ancient Greek temple, with beautiful marble columns and steps. Though the door had been busted hin at the front, it seemed all of the debris had been cleaned away and straightened out. Places and things that had obviously been knocked over and damaged were now back in what he guessed were their original places.

Jason looked around the main entrance in wonder, eyes wide and staring, Meania was doing very much the same thing.

"Arachne's preparing the drinks now," Aethalides said, then grinned at the two newcomers, beckoning them to a huge set of double golden doors. "So, detective, Meania, if you'd like to come this way..."

He shoved the double doors open, revealing a large circular room filled with books and bookcases, various other pieces of art and furniture, and a beautiful ceiling. A large desk was in the middle, chairs around it and a chalkboard and marker board were mixed amongst the various pieces of wooden furniture. Notes and documents were spread out across the table, strings were placed on a crock board like in an old-fashioned detective novel.

Just on the other side of the table sat a man… who looked like part spider, part human, dressed in African tribal garb. A grin stretched across his face as he saw them.

"A story with a happy ending!" He declared. "Or perhaps… a to be continued…?"

As if on cue, Meania's eyes glowed a bright gold and their mouth started to move, almost of its own accord.

"Buried deep underground, what was lost will be found, the days of barking are upon us, and a new friend will be among us. On leather wings darkness shall fall and a crown of eyes will behold all!" The kid then gasped, falling back a little and their eyes stopped glowing. "That… that was a big one…" Meania whispered. "I've never… had one quite like that before.."

"Well, there's a first time for everything," Anansi grinned.

"An issue for another day," Medea said, crossing her arms. "I am not running around on another pointless adventure any time soon."

Aethalides waved her off, climbing onto the table and flashing a grin at Jason and Meania. "Don't worry about it kid! Prophecies are always a big load of confusing cloak-and-dagger nonsense. Whatever happens, we got this! So, without further ado, Detective, Meania," he extended his arms out, gesturing to the room around them. "Welcome to the Archives!"